SHADOWS IN SCARLET

BOOKS BY LILLIAN STEWART CARL

Sabazel
The Winter King
Shadow Dancers
Wings of Power
Ashes to Ashes
Dust to Dust
Garden of Thorns
Along the Rim of Time: Stories
Memory and Desire

SHADOWS IN SCARLET

LILLIAN STEWART CARL

WILDSIDE PRESS

SHADOWS IN SCARLET

Wildside Press
www.wildsidepress.com

For Alan Stewart Carl
and his bride, Jennefer Sutton, M.D.
We haven't lost a son, we've gained a doctor

CHAPTER ONE

By late afternoon the Virginia landscape was drenched with heat. Amanda wanted to rip off her stays, hoops, petticoats, and gown and run naked across the lawns to the river. But the tourists' ticket of admission to Melrose Hall didn't include a strip show.

She opened the front door of the house and curtsied. "My thanks, sirs and mesdames, for your kind attentions. Please do us the honor of visiting the gift shop upon your departure."

Her flock of visitors, smelling of sunscreen and sweat, piled into the glare. A little boy pointed his plastic flintlock at her. "Stick 'em up!"

"Pray tell me, sir," Amanda replied with her brightest smile and a flick of her fan, "which items you would have me paste, and where I should cause them to be affixed."

Some of the tourists laughed. Others looked slightly bewildered.

Still smiling, Amanda turned the sign reading HALL OPEN around to HALL CLOSED. PLEASE COME AGAIN. She slammed the door, locked it, scooped the cap from her head, and announced, "Hey! Twenty-first century! I'm back!" to the paneled walls of the entrance hall.

Her voice echoed and died. A tread of the staircase creaked. A stack of leaflets slumped over the edge of the Chippendale sideboard and pattered to the floor. The sweaty roots of her hair made her scalp feel cold. Shrugging away her chill, she told herself that they knew how to build houses in the eighteenth century. Thick brick walls and wooden doors kept out not only heat but noise.

Amanda stuffed her cap and her fan into her pockets and stooped painfully to pick up the fallen leaflets. On their covers the words MELROSE HALL, GATEWAY TO THE PAST topped a trio of period portraits: Page Armstrong, the planter-patriot who built the house in 1751. Sally, his daughter, the belle of Tidewater Virginia. James Grant, a British officer, dazzling in scarlet coat and tartan kilt.

Inside the leaflet were early prints of Melrose and a sketch of the battle of Greensprings Farm, fought on a similar July day at a nearby river crossing. Amanda felt sorry for the British soldiers in their high collars and stiff coats, trying to conduct a proper battle in spite of the heat and opponents who hid in the underbrush like homicidal squirrels.

"Whew," said a voice behind her. "I feel like a steamed dumpling."

Amanda spun around. One of her fellow interpreters was walking down the staircase. "Carrie! It was so quiet I thought everyone was gone!"

"Not quite," Carrie replied. "I found two strays. Young sir and miss?"

A teenaged couple emerged from the shadows of the upper hall and shyly descended the stairs. Amanda had to look twice to figure out which of the scrawny, long-haired, T-shirted figures was the boy and which the girl. Inspiring, she thought, what maturity did for the male body. Not that she'd encountered any inspiring men recently. She stacked the leaflets back on the sideboard. Carrie unlocked and opened the door.

"Sorry," said the girl. "I wanted to hang out in Sally's room for a minute. I mean, she was cool, so pretty and everything."

"Not necessarily," Amanda explained, abandoning her role as character in favor of teacher. "Portrait painters in Sally's day spent the winters painting generic bodies and the summers going around from plantation to plantation adding faces. She may have had smallpox scars, or Page a lumpy red nose, or Grant knobby knees and jug ears."

The boy looked out from beneath his hair like a small animal from the underbrush, warily. He urged the girl toward the bright light of the outside world. But she hung back, her lipsticked mouth a stubborn line. "It says in that leaflet Sally and Captain Grant fell in love, but he was killed at Greensprings Farm, like, a tragedy, you know."

"So they were automatically drop-dead gorgeous?" returned Amanda.

"I'm afraid," Carrie, mother-of-teens, said gently, "the story about Grant is probably just that, a story. Like the one about Sally turning down Thomas Jefferson's proposal. We know from Jefferson's diaries that he hardly knew her. The 71st Highlanders were billeted at Melrose for ten days or so, yes. But Sally might not have been here then. We know from the regimental rolls Grant was here, but that doesn't mean he had the time of day for Sally. He probably spent his off hours polishing his shoe buckles or powdering his wig."

"But Grant ran up this staircase," the girl countered, "yelling at his troops, 'The Yankees are coming! The Yankees are coming!' and slicing the banister with his sword."

"If he liked Sally so much, why the vandalism?" Amanda asked. "And there might have been some other officers upstairs, but the troops would have been outside. Probably downwind." She ran her hand along the silky wood of the banister. Her fingertips detected several grooves, rounded by years of varnish. "Dr. Hewitt, the archaeologist, thinks these scars date from the Civil War. Or even later, when that Armstrong cousin sold the paneling, the balusters, the glass, and finally the entire place."

The girl shrugged away the lecture in historical method. Taking the boy's arm, she paraded him out the door as though imagining them in long gown and knee breeches respectively.

"Thank you for coming!" Amanda shook her head. She liked a good romantic tragedy just fine. She liked a good they-lived-happily-ever-after romance even better. But at the end of the day a story was just a story.

Carrie locked the door. "You know, I'm really rather glad she didn't believe us. So few young people have any sense of romance these days."

"All *my* romantic illusions have been thoroughly trashed," Amanda told her.

"That's a shame. By the time you get to be my age you could use a few."

Laughing, Amanda turned toward the staircase. "You going home now?"

"Yes. The boys have baseball games, thankfully on neighboring fields. Jack has to work late so I get to be parent-designate. See you Friday. Let's hope it's a bit cooler then."

"Why do you want to work here two days a week when you could spend all five in the nice air-conditioned stacks at the library?"

"I'd be missing half the fun of working in Colonial Williamsburg if I didn't get to dress up now and then. At least I get to play a servant, and don't have to wear stays."

"Thank you, that's just what I needed right now."

Carrie grinned. "Let me know if there's anything you want from town."

"I sure will. Thanks. Wish the guys home runs from me."

"Cheerio." Carrie disappeared into the kitchen wing of the house.

Melrose was only a few miles from Williamsburg, and Amanda's car was parked in a tool shed behind the house. Carrie, though, had taken her under her wing last May, right after Amanda's ascent into graduate school, when she'd interviewed for the internship at the newly restored mansion. Of course, getting the internship meant she was now not only a character interpreter but the official caretaker, and had better go close the lined drapes in Sally's bedroom before the fabric of the bed hangings faded.

The original of Sally's portrait hung at the head of the stairs, picked out from the shadows by a ray of sunlight. In the glare Amanda could see the ridges of paint swirling one into the other. This painting was a custom job. Sally really had been attractive. She'd had large blue eyes, blond curls, a soft, rounded chin that could have been either demure or stubborn, and a minuscule waist that implied frequent sinking spells. After marrying one of the Mason boys, whose father had signed the Declaration of Independence, she'd produced a pack of children and lived to a ripe old age. Maybe she got her jollies remembering an affair with an enemy officer, maybe not. Whatever, Amanda had a hard time seeing a tragic heroine in that banal face.

She didn't see herself in that face, either. Her eyes were brown, not blue. Her wavy brown hair was cut so short she had to conceal its ends beneath the period cap. Her chin, far from being soft, was cut as distinctly as her cheekbones. At five-nine she was probably taller than Sally, and, if the portrait was accurate, not as buxom. Although the cone-shaped bodice of an eighteenth-century dress acted like a primitive Wonder Bra, which is why Sally—and Amanda—wore a scarf called a fichu tucked into its low neckline.

Chin forward, Amanda turned into Sally's bedroom and creaked across the floorboards to the window. Beside it stood a small table holding a bit of embroidery, a thimble, and the original of Captain Grant's portrait, a miniature of his face and red-coated torso. According to the picture, at least, he'd definitely had the chiseled features of a romantic hero. A white wig set off ironic dark eyes that seemed to know what people were saying about him behind his back. Amanda wondered where the picture had come from. It certainly could've inspired a few fantasies.

She squinted out of the window into the sun. At the end of the garden an archaeological team plugged away at the remains of the summer-house, or gazebo, or pavilion, depending on what period of history you were considering. Just below the window strolled several plainly-dressed men and women, playing only a few of the slaves who'd watered Virginia's prosperity with their blood, sweat, and tears.

Behind them came Carrie, Wayne Chancellor at her side. He'd already taken off his coat and waistcoat and was making hangman's noose gestures with his knotted neck cloth. Wayne was as hearty and as heavy as his character Page Armstrong—like a Keebler elf on steroids—although at twenty-four he was only a year older than his "daughter" Amanda. For somebody who'd never made it out of adolescence socially, she thought, he played pompous middle age to a tee. But then, his family had once owned Melrose. Blue blood will tell.

She knocked on the window. The departing figures looked up, smiled and waved. Wayne sketched a low bow. His gray wig slipped over his forehead. He peered upward from beneath its rim like a nearsighted sheep and blew kisses toward the window.

In your dreams. Amanda pulled the curtains shut and turned around. Her eyes still adjusted to the light, she tripped, lurched forward, caught her foot in the hem of her dress, and fell to her hands and knees. The table thunked to the carpet beside her, spilling its contents. "Way to go, Grace!" she exclaimed.

She sensed a vibration in the floorboards, an echo of her fall, or of the tourist buses revving up and pulling out the main gate, or maybe even distant thunder.

Using the bedpost as support, Amanda hauled herself to her feet. She set the table upright and checked it for damage. Nothing, thank goodness. The embroidery, thimble, and miniature had landed safely on the rug. She arranged them on the table top, then turned to smooth down the edge of the carpet. It was already flat, its fringes lined up like little soldiers. She must have tripped over her own feet.

That was it. Time to change back into civilian clothes.

Her apartment at the end of the service wing of the house was a module of real time, complete with television, microwave, CD changer, computer, and Melrose's resident pet. The electronics were silent when Amanda opened the door, but the pet leaped down from the seat of the most comfortable chair and meowed. Like his namesake, the Marquis de Lafayette, he expected to be obeyed.

"Yes, Master, yes, Master," Amanda told him, and went into the kitchen. The whir of the can opener sent the gray and black tabby into ecstasies of affection. Entangled in both skirts and cat, Amanda got a reeking mound of meat by-products into a bowl and on the floor. Dumping her now that she'd served her purpose, Lafayette went to work on the food.

In the bedroom Amanda shed her costume, struggling with persnickety laces and hooks. If she'd learned nothing else from this job, she'd learned why eighteenth-century aristocrats had body servants. And yet in her own clothing, a loose T-shirt, shorts, and sandals, she felt oddly awkward, her gestures broader, her stride longer, her voice louder. She seemed to occupy more space. Weird, when the period dress contained so much more fabric.

She finished morphing by drinking a glass of iced tea, plain, no sugar. Leaving Lafayette grooming his already sleek fur, Amanda picked up her clipboard and walked outside to begin her evening tour of inspection.

The sun hung just at the tops of the trees, casting stripes of shadow across the grass. At the foot of the lawn shimmered the James River, its far bank lost in a moist haze. Clouds massed on the horizon. Crows called from the parking lot, probably fighting over some pizza crusts.

Amanda made an about face and gazed narrowly at the house. Not one rust-red chimney sagged out of plumb, not one white stone facing was dirty. The two and a half story main section, flanked by the one-story service wings, was a model of Georgian grace. Three years ago it had been a mess, a clumsy 1850s portico pasted onto the facade, brick-work cracked, woodwork scarred or missing. That was when the Chancellors had the wisdom—and the tax incentives—to donate it to the Colonial Williamsburg Foundation.

Amanda picked up a couple of candy wrappers, stowed them in her pocket, and headed around the end of the kitchen wing of the house. The sun slipped behind the trees and a cool breath of air, scented with rain, teased her cheeks.

Across a gravel drive lay the kitchen garden, herbs and vegetables arranged in tidy rows. Beyond it the formal gardens were still under reconstruction. The brick-walled terraces close to the house had been replanted with roses and other flowers, but the ones beyond the boxwood allee were still overgrown, waiting for the touch of the landscape archaeologist and the banker both.

There was a puddle in the path, Amanda noted. Better check the drainage system. And. . . . She craned her neck over the boxwood. The archaeologists were standing around like onlookers at an accident. Maybe somebody had been bitten by a snake. She crunched off down the path toward them.

The summerhouse had once been surrounded by an artificial wilderness, trees and shrubbery carefully planted to look "natural." Now it was natural with an attitude. The archaeologists had waded into the tangle of blackberry bushes with machetes, and only reached for their shovels a week ago. Underbrush and a few small trees hemmed in the site. Leaves of everything up to and including poison ivy tossed in fitful gusts of wind. Insects hummed.

Bill Hewitt looked like a praying mantis kneeling by the trench cut into the pale dirt. The hairs of his moustache trembled as he scraped delicately away with a spoon. A couple of his gofers stood by, holding trowels, brushes, and plastic artifact bags. The rest of the crew, volunteer students, was so quiet Amanda could hear them breathing.

She edged her way through the dirty and sunburned backs, for once failing to appreciate those that were male. "What is it?"

Hewitt glanced up. "Ah, Miss Witham. You're just in time. Take a look. Very interesting."

He drew back. From the mottled dirt at the bottom of trench emerged a regular series of brown ridges. *Roots,* Amanda thought, and then, *No. Bones. Human bones.*

Another chill trickled down her spine as she leaned forward over the grave.

CHAPTER TWO

Amanda realized she was looking at a rib cage, an upthrust shoulder at one end and a similarly upward-curved pelvic bone at the other. The rest of the skeleton was still buried. It looked like the body had been rolled into an unevenly dug hole, head and feet flopping into the deeper ends. Someone sure hadn't had any respect for the dead. . . .

Well, at least that someone had buried him. Her. If not, the bones would've been disturbed by scavenging animals. What a way to go. Amanda straightened and waved away a gnat that was trying to fly up her nose.

". . . drainage here," Hewitt was saying. "Dry soil. Preserved the bones. And hopefully clothing or personal effects to date them by."

"Would you like me to call the police?" Amanda asked. "Or are the bones old enough to be out of their jurisdiction?"

"We'll notify them, of course. But these bones are very old. It's an archaeological matter, not a judicial one. Other than the usual legalities of digging up human remains."

"There were gangsters running rum on Chesapeake Bay back in the thirties," someone said. "Maybe this is a revenuer who got rubbed out."

"We'll check the records."

"The Chancellors moved here in the twenties," said Amanda. "The summerhouse was already a ruin by then."

"Ditto."

"The bones might belong to a slave," suggested someone else.

"The slave cemetery was over there." Hewitt waved toward the row of outbuildings beyond the kitchen garden. "The Africans made sure their friends and relatives had proper burials. They almost always added broken pots and such as grave decorations."

"Could it be an Indian from before the European settlements?" asked one of the students. "Or some early settler who died in the Indian attack of—whenever. . . ."

"1622," said Hewitt.

"And the Armstrongs just happened to plunk their summerhouse down right beside him?" replied one of Hewitt's assistants. "No, I bet this body dates from after 1751, when Melrose was built."

"This type of landscape gardening," Amanda offered, "the formal terraces and little recreational buildings, was really trendy in the 1770's."

Hewitt stood up, rubbing particles of dirt from his hands. "We'll cover this up with a sheet of plastic tonight. Get back out here bright and early tomorrow. Get the entire body uncovered. It'll have to be moved, with the reconstruction of the summerhouse and everything. Identification, that's the tricky part, legally and otherwise. Might have to call in the Smithsonian."

"What if," one of the students asked, "the rest of the body isn't in there? What if it was dismembered or something?"

"We're scientists. Leave the sensationalism for the tabloids." Hewitt's black eyes shot the girl a withering glance. She withered. "Let's get the plastic spread out and staked down. Move."

Amanda wondered how she should enter this on her daily summary—under "associated features?" But it was Hewitt's responsibility to make a formal report. She only had to note the body's existence. As an artifact, not a person. With a grimace of sympathy for the unknown deceased she worked her way back through the group of students and headed toward the house.

The sun set, leaving a thin, greenish twilight. Clouds rose halfway up the western sky. A glowing quarter moon, half a disc, hung high overhead. Each of Melrose's windows gleamed faintly, as though interested in the scene in the garden.

The poor guy, if it was a guy, had probably been stuffed into his makeshift grave late at night. Amanda thought of Scarlett O'Hara shooting the Yankee soldier and burying him in her back yard. No telling how many real-life bodies were lying in odd corners of the Virginia countryside. There'd been enough battles over the years to produce an army of skeletons.

Amanda locked the outer door behind her and turned on the exterior floodlights. She thought of Robert Frost's poem, where the skeleton of the murdered man stands outside the door, chalky fingers scratching chalky skull. . . . "That's what I get for cramming English," she said to Lafayette, who was waiting by the cat flap in the apartment door. He tilted his head to the side. If he'd had eyebrows, he would've arched them.

She turned to the next page on her clipboard and made her tour of the interior, Lafayette by her side like a general at inspection. Parlor, dining room, drawing room, library, bedrooms—the period furnishings were all accounted for, the attic and cellar doors were locked, the dehumidifiers were working. She really was hearing thunder now, a mutter rising and falling beneath the thump of her own feet.

She shut the door to her apartment and set the alarm system. As she turned toward the kitchen the phone rang. "Melrose Hall, Amanda Witham."

"Amanda!" exclaimed Wayne's deep voice. "I just heard about the body!"

"That was fast."

"Bill Hewitt's having dinner with Mother and me tonight—you know, about the grant for the landscaping—but he called to say they'd found a body behind the summerhouse and he'd be late. Did you see it? Is it really gross, like on *X-Files?*"

"No way," Amanda replied, and added to herself, *thanks, the literary references were enough.* "It's nothing but bones."

"Are you scared? You want me to come out there and keep you company?"

Like she didn't know what he meant by that? "You're living a couple of blocks from Bruton Parish Church and its cemetery," she told him. "Are you scared?"

"Those are legitimate bodies. Buried will full rites and all that."

"So?"

"So the ones that aren't buried properly get kind of restless. . . ."

"Thanks for thinking of me, Wayne. But everything's cool."

"Well, if you're sure . . . Coming, Mother! I'll see my little girl tomorrow, then, okay, Sally?"

"Good night, Wayne." Making a face, Amanda hung up the phone.

The body in the back yard would be a great excuse to ask a guy over, if she knew any guys more appealing than Wayne. Not that Wayne was repulsive. He was a big, lovable, clumsy puppy who could use a semester at obedience school. His family's wealth made him one of Virginia's most eligible bachelors, but it wasn't his immaturity that was going to keep him one. It was his mother.

A shame the summerhouse was gone long before Cynthia parked her broom at Melrose. The thought of her sipping tea, pinkie extended, a few paces from a positively indecent dead body would've made Amanda grin with glee if she wasn't also thinking of that body as a living, feeling human being who'd probably met a gruesome end.

She opened the windows in her kitchen, living room, and bedroom, and switched on the ceiling fans. She wasn't allowed an air conditioner—its bulge would ruin the look of the house. But the approaching storm sent a cool if damp and musty breeze before it, stirring the turgid air. Lafayette arranged himself on the sill of the living room window, his tail draped artistically over the computer on the desk below.

Amanda popped a frozen lasagna dinner into the microwave and threw together a salad. Tonight she'd definitely get some work done. That was the reason for this job, after all, over and beyond its basic appeal. She was getting an apartment, spending money, and good experience for her resume while she wrote her thesis on the socionomic aspect of historical artifacts. She liked these long, quiet, solitary evenings. She enjoyed being on her own. Really.

Thunder grumbled closer. A few raindrops plopped onto the roof. The breeze fluttered Lafayette's fur. Amanda watched the local news while she ate, and was cleaning up when Lafayette woke suddenly from his doze and looked out the window, nose twitching, ears pricked.

A rabbit? Amanda asked herself. A deer? The kitchen garden attracted all sorts of wildlife. . . .

Every hair on Lafayette's body shot upright. He leaped from the windowsill, scattered the papers on the desk, and dived beneath the couch leaving only his bottle brush of a tail exposed.

The nape of Amanda's neck prickled. She turned off the TV and the lights and looked out each window in turn. Beyond the floodlit halo surrounding the house the night was pitch black. She might as well have been standing on a stage trying to check out the audience. From the bedroom she could see only a smooth sweep of lawn, silent and empty. From the kitchen window she caught an impression of tree limbs tossing in the wind. The living room window overlooked the gravel drive, the kitchen garden, and the first terrace. Raindrops made blotches on the brick. The breeze was growing cooler by the moment.

Maybe someone was out there. One of Hewitt's students, playing a prank on her. Or someone with more sinister motives. The furnishings of the house included some choice artifacts. If anyone tried to get inside, though, the alarms would raise the dead. . . .

The alarms would call the police, Amanda corrected. She closed the thick wooden slats of the venetian blinds and turned the lights back on. Then she punched the number of the other two caretakers, an elderly couple who lived in a small house where the driveway met the main road, a good quarter of a mile from the Hall itself.

"No," Mrs. Benedetto answered Amanda's question. "We haven't opened the gates for a living soul. Someone could have climbed the fence, though."

"You think?" Amanda could hear every word of the sitcom on the Benedetto's television. A brass band could have marched up the drive and they wouldn't have noticed.

"Would you like us to call the security service, dear?"

"No—no problem. Sorry to have bothered you."

Rain pattered down outside, sounding like gravel slipping and sliding beneath stumbling feet. Lightning flashed. Amanda peered around the edge of the window blind, waiting for the next bolt. There! In the sudden brilliance she could see every tree, every brick, starkly defined all the way to the eaves of the forest. Nothing and no one was outside.

Amanda blinked away the after-image of garden terraces and boxwood allee. Wearing stays, the eighteenth-century corset, all day had cut off the blood flow to her brain. Was she ever out of it. With an aggravated snort, she put on a classical CD and sat down at the desk. No computer tonight, not with the approaching storm. She'd work on her outline.

Okay. Candles, for example, had both technomic and socionomic uses—for light, yes, but also for status, like at a dinner party, or for marking an occasion, like on a birthday cake. Then there were clothes, which both covered the body and indicated class. Like the aristocratic Sally with her corsets and her pokey little hooks and buttons, sending a very clear signal that if she had to work at all, she worked with her mind, not her hands. And that was the continental divide of Virginia society.

The problem was that it was the silk-stocking crowd who inventoried their belongings, and bought pattern books, and wrote letters gossiping about fashion, leading the unwary researcher into assumptions about the culture as a whole. . . .

The door that led into the rest of the house rattled in its frame and the cat flap shivered. Amanda stared at it. Air pressure from the storm. No one could have opened an outside door into the Hall. Even someone with a key would have set off the alarms. And she could see the alarm panel from where she sat, green lights steady, all systems go.

She turned back to her notebook, wondering if Abigail Adams in her stays could even remotely be considered the Gloria Steinem of her time period—or Mary Shelley, writing *Frankenstein* buttoned up to the chin. . . .

The room disappeared in a blast of white light that was gone as quickly as it had appeared. The music stopped in mid-phrase. Amanda sat goggling blindly into total darkness as thunder exploded in her head. *Shit!* Lightning had taken out a nearby transformer. A good thing she hadn't turned on the computer. A good thing she had a flashlight. Swallowing her heart, she rose from her chair and groped across the room.

The flashlight was in the kitchen cabinet. She flicked it on and waved the circle of light around the room. Lafayette had subtracted his tail and was completely hidden. Raindrops poured over the roof, slowed, and stopped. A cold wind sent the blinds knocking against the window frames.

The phone still worked. She called in the power outage, then considered her options. If someone was snooping around the house, they now had an engraved invitation to come inside. The doors were locked, yes, but it would be easy enough to break a window. Her presence wouldn't stop a thief from taking the silver tea service in the dining room, or a vandal from trashing the crystal wineglasses in the library, but she was supposed to be keeping an eye on the place even so.

Amanda opened the door of her apartment and listened. A few stray plunks were raindrops outside. The wind was a sigh in the distance. The house was so utterly silent her ears rang, like she was listening to a seashell, compartment after compartment filled with dank air. . . .

No. Wait. From somewhere in the house came a faint clatter. Something had fallen over. Something had been knocked over. *Great.*

She glanced back at the sofa. A pair of disgruntled golden eyes caught the light. "Thank you for your support," she whispered. The cat's eyes vanished.

No way she was going to call for backup until she'd scoped out the situation. Tucking the telephone into the pocket of her shorts, she tiptoed into the hallway. She took a step, stopped, and listened. Nothing. No silver clashing, no glass breaking. She took a few more steps and arrived at the door leading from the service wing into the rest of the house. Several of the doors in the Hall squeaked. She couldn't remember if this was one of them.

Turning off the flashlight and holding her breath, she eased the door open. It went quietly. On the other side was the passage that led between the library and the parlor. The darkness was so thick Amanda felt as though she could have scooped it up in handfuls. Feeling her way, she inched toward the entrance hall. Was that a scraping sound? She couldn't tell whether it came from above her head or in front of her.

The doors into the parlor and library were shut, just as she'd left them. She listened at each one. Nothing.

With a tiny bump that sounded loud as an explosion she walked into the door leading into the entrance hall. She laid her ear against the wood. Silence. No wind, no rain, no falling objects, just the all-encompassing silence of the grave.

Get a grip! Amanda ordered herself, and set her hand on the doorknob.

Then she heard the breathing. Slow, slightly uneven breaths, like those of somebody old or sick. Or somebody trying to be very, very quiet.

Amanda waited a moment, willing herself to breathe. Most of her friends had jobs in nice bright office buildings. But no, she had to shut herself up in a dark old house with someone—something. . . .

So look already, and then go for 911. Slowly, carefully, she turned the knob and opened the door a fraction of an inch. Cold air flooded through the opening, raising gooseflesh on her body. From her vantage point she could see almost the entire entrance hall. If anyone was there he was standing in the dark.

But no, it wasn't dark. The windows on either side of the front door were rectangles of very pale, very faint luminescence. The clouds must be lifting outside. And yet that wasn't the light that gleamed on the paneling and picked out the reds and golds of the Turkey carpet. A fragile glow radiated from the foot of the staircase, the one spot Amanda couldn't see. *What the. . . ?*

She lifted the flashlight—it was the size of a policeman's nightstick, and almost as heavy—but didn't turn it on. Pushing the door open, she stepped into the cold. She picked up one foot and put it down. She picked up the other and put it down. The balusters made vertical lines against the cloud of silvery light. Not a flashlight, not a candle. . . .

Amanda balanced on the balls of her feet, ready to run, ready to swing her makeshift weapon. She closed her eyes a moment, then opened them again.

The glow darkened and solidified. It was the size of a human being. It was shaped like a human being, head, body, legs. And yet Amanda could still see the edges of the steps indistinctly through its—through his—form. A warm sigh dissipated the chill in the room, and she smelled whiskey.

Good God. She stepped back, flat-footed, and lowered the flashlight.

He sat on the fourth step from the bottom, his legs with their checkered stockings splayed, his green and blue kilt draped over his knees. His coat shone scarlet and his waistcoat white, as though lit from within. Across his lap he held an empty scabbard.

It had to be a trick. A projection, special effects—Stephen Spielberg had dropped by to test out some equipment. . . . The electricity's off, Amanda reminded herself.

The soldier looked up from the scabbard, and his eyes met hers.

This guy has had a bad day.

His eyes were a smoky blue-gray, his knotted brows dark, his expression that of a kid facing an algebra test. Reddish-brown hair fell over his forehead. His face was translucent, carved by light against darkness. Amanda recognized that face. She'd seen it over and over again, in paint and print. Captain James Grant, late—very late—of His Majesty's 71st Highlanders.

This guy has had a bad couple of centuries.

Maybe if she turned the flashlight on him he'd vanish. But she could see him just fine, more than fine. . . . Again she closed her eyes. She counted to five, watching the pixels of static behind her lids. When she opened them he was still there. And he was still looking at her.

His lips moved. He croaked. Frowning, he grimaced and tried again. His voice was a wisp of velvet. "Have you seen my sword, then, lass?"

Her voice sounded like a crow's. "Ah—no, I haven't. Sorry."

"Taken by the enemy, I'll be bound. Scoundrels. Not fit to deal with a gentleman."

Like she was going to argue with him?

Slowly his brows smoothed. His eyes started at the top of Amanda's head, worked their way down to her toes, and moved up again. One corner of his mouth turned upward. "I do beg your pardon, Madame. I seem to have interrupted you at your toilet. If you would care to complete your dress. . . ."

"No problem. Er. . . ." Her interpreter's training kicked in. "I don't believe we've been introduced."

He tried to stand and sank back again. "I find myself begging your indulgence again, Madame. I am James Grant of Dundreggan, at your service."

"Amanda Witham of Chicago. At yours, I guess." *This isn't happening. I am not standing here making conversation with a ghost.*

"And this is Melrose Hall, is it not, in His Majesty's colony of Virginia?"

"It's Melrose, yeah. Yes."

"In faith, the battle must have been particularly fierce, I am—fatigued."

No kidding.

His lashes fell over his eyes. With a groan he slumped back over the empty scabbard. The pale glow around him faded, draining the colors in his uniform.

Amanda took a step toward him. Light flooded in the front windows and the alarm system began to whoop. Her entire body convulsed.

No one was there. The hall was lit only by the shine of the floodlights outside. The staircase rose blankly toward the second floor. Amanda galloped back down the corridors to her apartment, slamming doors behind her.

All the lights were on in her living room and kitchen. She threw herself at the control panel and killed the deafening screech of the alarm. The sudden silence made her ears ring.

No, that was the phone ringing. First the Benedettos, then the police. No, no, Amanda explained, lightning struck a transformer, and when the power came back on it started the alarm, no, everything's all right, thank you anyway.

She hung up the telephone. Her legs wobbled and her head spun. She staggered to the couch and plopped down.

She hadn't seen him. She'd imagined him. He'd been a trick of the light. Of the darkness. . . . It hadn't happened. It couldn't have happened.

Lafayette oozed out from beneath the couch and looked accusingly up at her. She looked right back at him. "He's the body in the garden, isn't he? You heard him coming, from the summerhouse back to the staircase he remembered."

The cat didn't blink.

"But what the hell is James Grant, of all people, doing in a hole in the ground in Melrose's garden?"

The cat stretched and yawned.

"I did see him, didn't I? I haven't lost it. I'm not nuts. I saw him." Amanda lay back against the throw pillow, staring upward at the ceiling. She saw a scarlet coat, an empty scabbard, and a fall of reddish-brown hair above a puzzled face. She heard a cultured baritone saying, *I do beg your pardon. . . .*

He'd been there. She'd seen him. And no way did he have knobby knees and jug ears.

Amanda looked down at Lafayette. "Like you'd make a believable witness? Yeah, right."

He sat down and started to wash his face, committing himself to nothing.

CHAPTER THREE

The morning was far from cool. The showers of the night before had simply added to the Amazonian atmosphere. By the time Amanda checked out every room of the mansion she was thoroughly hot and bothered.

Not one door was open. Not one window was cracked. Of all the things in the house, only two had been moved: the miniature of James Grant was lying on the floor of Sally's bedroom and her portrait at the top of the stairs was hanging off-center. Which was relevant and all that, Amanda told herself as she put both pictures back where they belonged, but didn't explain anything.

Nothing else was out of place. Melrose Hall was locked up as tightly this morning as it had been when Amanda settled down to her dinner last night. No one could have gotten into the house and played a trick on her with video projectors or tape recorders. Even if there'd been a secret passage—and there wasn't, the place had been worked over during renovation—there was still the slight problem of producing special effects without electricity.

Great. Amanda poured herself into the straightjacket of stays, garters, hoops, petticoats, dress. She had to make an effort to focus her eyes. When she'd finally gotten to sleep last night she'd dreamed of staircases snarled with blackberry and scarlet coats blotched with mud.

She was trying to fluff up the hair that wasn't tucked beneath her cap when the back doorbell buzzed. Leaving Lafayette snoozing in a tangle of sheets, none the worse for *his* night, she turned off the alarm and answered the door.

Wayne's beefy face was already glistening with sweat, even though he hadn't put on his coat and his wig yet. Beside him his mother was her usual cool and classy self. Her pouf of blond hair softened the sharpness of her features. Her size-six summer dress was color-coordinated with her hose and pumps. "Good morning, Amanda," she said in her beautifully moderated voice. "I hear you had some excitement last night."

Cynthia always made Amanda feel like her knuckles were dragging the ground. "Not really. Just a quick power outage because of the storm."

"I'll bet you were scared," said Wayne hopefully.

"Just a little startled," she lied.

A uniformed policeman appeared around the corner of the house. "Nothing unusual out here, Mrs. Chancellor. May I look around inside, Miss?"

"Sure," said Amanda. "But I already. . . ."

"Please come in, Officer," said Cynthia. Amanda found herself plastered against the wall of the corridor as Mrs. Chancellor and her entourage swept by. With a shrug she closed the door and followed.

Upstairs, downstairs, in Sally's chamber the procession went. "Everything's fine," Cynthia announced at last, from her observation post on the stair landing. "Put on your wig, Wayne, it's almost opening time."

Wayne smoothed the woolly wig over his dark curls. The policeman sneaked a look at his watch. Amanda stood with her hand on the newel post, eyeing the treads of the staircase.

He'd been sitting right there, in the face of common sense. She hadn't imagined him. She hadn't hallucinated him. The closest she'd come to anything alcoholic was the scent of whiskey on his breath. And he had been breathing. That heartbreaking groan. . . . She wondered if he knew he was dead. She wondered how her brain was able to deal with the matter of daily life and the anti-matter of James Grant without exploding.

No, she wasn't going to tell anyone what—who—she'd seen last night. They'd think she was a liar, nuts, or both. Just the kind of person Colonial Williamsburg wanted caretaking an important property.

Cynthia's heels clicked down the steps. "I'll check in with Bill on my way out. Helen Medina will be by sometime today to put together a news release. There's not much we can say until Bill has some more information about the body, but I'll see if I can hurry him along."

"Excuse me?" Amanda asked. "News release?"

"The body in the back garden. Our visitors will be thrilled."

Amanda saw little plastic skeletons for sale in the Gift Shoppe. "Ah, yeah, sure."

"It was nice seeing you again, Amanda." Cynthia extended her hand, probably, Amanda thought, expecting her to kneel and kiss her wedding ring.

Amanda spread her skirts in a low curtsey. "I have the honor to remain, Madame, your most humble and obedient servant."

"You've learned your lines so well," murmured Cynthia, radiating graciousness. "Come along, Officer, let's go view the body. I've always found forensics procedures fascinating, haven't you?" She swept out of the door, leaving behind her a whiff of expensive fragrance. The policeman followed.

Wayne stood awkwardly by the sideboard. "Bye, Mother. . . ." The door shut. He turned to Amanda. "You were being sarcastic, weren't you?"

"Moi?" she replied with a grin.

Laughing, Wayne advanced toward her, arms outstretched. "How about a morning kiss from my little girl?"

"So that our guests may discover us in an unseemly moment? Fie, Papa, fie." She slipped out the door, turned the sign around to Hall Open, and assumed her pose on the stone steps.

Wayne took a magisterial stance beside Amanda, but his voice was uncertain. "Not that I really think of you as a daughter, you know."

Here we go again. "I've noticed."

"I mean—have you thought any more about that movie? The new Brad Pitt flick is opening this weekend. . . ."

She'd thought about a movie. Theatres were air-conditioned, for one thing. And Melrose didn't have either cable or a VCR. But Wayne was not relationship material. "I'd enjoy taking in a movie," she told him, "as long as it wasn't a date. Just friends, know what I mean?"

"Yeah, I get it." His face fell. He probably heard that one a lot.

Amanda scanned the landscape. No visitors were strolling up the gravel paths or across the glistening green of the grass. A couple of gardeners planted marigolds by the ticket office. A boat glided down the river. Birds sang. The sun shone pitilessly in a blue sky.

"I didn't have too many friends when I was growing up," Wayne said. "Melrose is kind of isolated, at least when you're an only child like I was. Like I am."

Amanda had never thought of her younger brother and sister as valuable socializing agents before. "When did you move into town?"

"When I got my driver's license. Mother wanted me to be closer to the high school so I wouldn't have to drive so much. And since my father had just passed away she wanted to be closer to her friends."

"The place was getting to be a maintenance problem, wasn't it?"

"It was getting pretty shabby. Which bothered Mother a lot more than it did me. I'd build forts with wood from the old stable and dig dungeons in the cellar and do chemical experiments with blackberries and paint flakes and stuff. I never blew anything up, though." He shook his head sadly.

Amanda smiled. "I grew up in a brand new split-level. Our cellar was partly a rec room and partly my dad's workshop. Melrose's cellar must have been really spooky before it was cleaned out."

"Oh yeah. I used to scare the heck out of myself down there, imagining that old furnace was some kind of monster."

"I would have imagined bodies buried beneath the floor. All these old houses need at least one good ghost story."

"We're falling down on the job, aren't we? You'd think at least one self-respecting spook would be hanging around here, but no."

"You never heard mysterious footsteps or had cold spots in the hallway when you were a kid?"

"People ask me that all the time. But my father grew up here, you know, and his father, and neither of them ever saw more than a death-watch beetle or two. Maybe we can make up a good story about that body behind the summerhouse. If it wouldn't scare you, that is," added Wayne, "with you having to stay out here alone and everything."

This is where she'd come in. Amanda glanced toward the driveway. Good—the cavalry was coming. A group of tourists advanced toward the house, escorted by Roy Davis, an interpreter playing one of the footmen. "... my wife was sold to another plantation," he was saying. "I know I'll never see her again. It wasn't as hard on Master Page when his wife died, I reckon."

"Heads up," Amanda muttered to Wayne. He extended his elbow. She placed one hand on his forearm and with the other opened her fan.

"Welcome to Melrose Hall. My name is Page Armstrong." Wayne's expansive gesture almost threw Amanda down the steps. "Allow me to present my daughter, Sally."

Amanda recovered herself with a curtsey. "Please come inside."

Roy bent in an anachronistic but understandably sardonic bow. With embarrassed looks, unsure whether to play along with the game, the sightseers walked into the house. Amanda shot Roy's departing back a rueful smile. The interpretation program was, after all, a fantasy that only worked because everyone ignored its paradoxes. If she and Wayne and the others brought history to life, why couldn't the ghost of James Grant bring life to history. . . . *Yeah, right.*

Wayne dragged Amanda across the threshold with him. "I designed Melrose myself. The classical symmetry of the house represents the ultimate human faculty, that of Reason. As my friend Thomas Jefferson said so meaningly the other day. . . ."

Amanda fixed Sally's sweet, biddable smile on her face. Another normal day at Melrose had begun. Depending on your definition of normal.

As more and more sightseers arrived, Amanda and Wayne separated and conducted different groups. By now she had her role down pat, and recited it by rote. Fortunately none of the tourists asked any questions more difficult than, "What kind of underwear you got on there, lady?" Only a few inquired about the bones. Amanda directed them to the gardens.

At last she was once more turning the sign around and locking the door. After the glare of the sun the entrance hall seemed as dark as Wayne's imaginary dungeon. She felt like something growing on a dungeon wall. She was surprised she didn't leave a slime trail on her way to the kitchen.

"See you tomorrow," she called to the other interpreters. They jostled each other out the door. Wayne, his face the color of a ripe tomato, waved at her and ran for it.

Amanda raced down the corridor to her apartment, pulling off her clothes on the way. Lafayette, at his post outside the cat flap, rated only a quick, "How can you look so cool with all that fur?" Before the last tourist bus had belched out of the parking lot Amanda was in her shower. A shower on a hot day was as good as sex.

Sometimes even better, she thought with a grimace. The twenty-first century had left the subtleties of drawing room flirtation and seduction far behind. Now it was cut to the chase and change the channel. . . . As if those eighteenth-century subtleties had extended to the bedroom. It had simply taken longer to get there then, that was all.

Amanda toweled off, stepped into a T-shirt and shorts, and fed the cat. Clipboard in hand, she set out on her tour of the house.

A whisk of the carpet sweeper took care of some dusty footprints. The shell earrings attributed to Pocahontas were disarranged in their case—a shake set them right. The tail of Amanda's T-shirt polished a smudge from the pier glass in the spare bedroom. For one ghastly moment she thought a silver hairbrush from Sally's dresser was missing, but she found it on the table by the window, reflecting a blaze of sunlight next to the dull shapes of the embroidery, thimble, and miniature. *Kids!* No matter how she watched, the small hand was always quicker than the eye.

With the curtains closed the room glowed amber, as though lit by candlelight. Amanda picked up the portrait of Captain Grant. Yes, it was definitely the same face she'd seen last night, even though his eyes had apparently been blue, not brown as depicted here. His expression in the portrait was much more confident than it was in life. . . . *In death.*

She turned the miniature over. The frame was an ornate metal one of the period, but its backing was a modern piece of acid-free cardboard. Cautiously, with the tips of her fingernails, she pulled out the tiny pins holding the portrait and its backing in place.

The picture was painted on a thin piece of wood. On its back several words were written in lushly curved eighteenth-century handwriting: James Grant. Dundreggan. 1780. And he died in 1781, Amanda thought.

Millions of young men died in wars—her grandfather's brother had become a statistic on Omaha Beach. Her mind couldn't take in millions. It could take in one.

Of course it was Wayne who'd hit the target. James Grant's ghost was restless. Because of his body's slapdash burial, Amanda wondered, or because the burial had been exposed? And why had the burial been so slapdash to begin with? She toyed with scenarios of James staggering wounded from Greensprings Farm, back to Sally's arms. . . . No. The Armstrongs wouldn't have had any reason to hide his body. They'd have turned it over to his regiment, like the nice honorable aristocrats they were.

She put the picture and frame back together and returned it to the table. Clipboard in hand, she stood at the head of the stairs and listened. The house was silent. Faintly from outside came the sound of birds singing. *Get over it,* she told herself, and clomped down the steps. Seeing a ghost had been a hell of an experience, but she wasn't going to include it on her resume.

Amanda went out the back door and inspected the lawns, the drive, the kitchen garden. Everything was in order, including Lafayette stretched sphinx-like in her living room window. She headed down the boxwood allee toward the summerhouse and the bobbing heads of the archaeological crew.

How long before Hewitt identified the body as Grant's? If he ever did. It would depend on what associated artifacts he dug from the grave. If Grant had been stripped of his uniform no one would ever know who he was. That wasn't right, Amanda thought. James Grant deserved the dignity of his name. But making herself look like a total idiot wouldn't help him.

Several dirt-daubed students carrying tools and water jugs passed her on their way to the parking lot. "How'd it go today?" she asked one.

"Got almost everything up," he replied. "Kept having to stop and deal with kibitzers, though."

"I don't think we've seen even the first wave of kibitzers yet," Amanda told him.

He shrugged. "There won't be anything to see other than the footprint of the summerhouse, not past tomorrow anyway. Not unless we turn up another body."

"Please don't," Amanda said under her breath. That was all she needed, phantom regiments trooping up and down the stairs at night.

Judging by the tangy scent of bug repellent which hung over the excavation, every insect in Virginia had come for lunch and now strummed and throbbed irritably in the underbrush. On the trampled weeds were arranged various trays and boxes piled with brown-stained lumps. Bill Hewitt stood thigh-deep in the trench, holding up a trowel for Helen Medina's video camera.

"Great," the press officer said. She pulled a red bandanna from one of the many pockets of her vest and mopped at her glasses. Her bun of gray-streaked hair, held together by a pencil and a swizzle stick, sagged a little lower on her neck. "Now do something with the bones, Bill."

Hewitt clambered from the hole and knelt down by one of the boxes. Amanda inched forward. She expected to see a more or less articulated skeleton, like an anatomical chart, but what lay in the tray was a pile of brown pick-up sticks. Hewitt lifted the skull in one hand and its jawbone in the other. Fitting them together, he held them up for the camera. "What we have here," he said, "is the skull and the detached mandible of a man probably between twenty and thirty-five."

No reason the empty eye sockets should retain an image of the blue-grey eyes and the personality that had looked out from them. But Amanda had expected to feel some tingle of fear or even disgust at the bones, and all she felt was sorrow, that mortality was so dull.

Hewitt put the skull down and picked up a long bone. "This is the femur," he said. "By measuring its length we'll be able to tell approximately how tall the man was. By studying the growth at the ends of this bone and others, we'll have a better idea of his age."

"Bill," protested Helen, "this is deadly. No pun intended. Can't you jazz it up?"

"I'm not a movie star," Hewitt said.

"Well no, you're not, are you? Okay, let me get a few more general shots and we'll find some talent to do a voice-over. What's in these boxes?"

Hewitt acknowledged Amanda's presence with a nod and bent over one of the trays. "Bits and pieces of fabric, leather, and metal. Lots of metal. He might have been a military officer. Revolutionary War, maybe.

Or Civil War. There's an epaulette." His forefinger indicated a dirt-encrusted doodad that could have been anything from a tea strainer to a dead hedgehog. Amanda shook her head. Hard to believe those lumps were the silver buckles and braid in Grant's portrait.

"Doesn't look like much," said Helen.

"When the conservation people get done it'll be photogenic," Hewitt promised. "This object still in the ground is interesting. I think it's a scabbard."

An uneven muddy ridge barely emerged from the soil. Amanda felt a tickle between her shoulder blades. She'd seen that scabbard already. Then it had been cleaned and polished and held in strong hands. Now it was tarnished and crushed by the weight of dirt and time. . . .

The tickle between her shoulder blades was a bug. She contorted herself until she could slap at it.

"Just a scabbard?" Helen asked. "No sword?"

"Not yet. We'll give the hole another going-over tomorrow. Sift out trouser-buttons. Shreds of fabric. The small bones of the hands and feet. If the sword's there it's buried deep."

Don't hold your breath for those trouser buttons, Amanda thought. And she doubted that the sword was in the grave, since Captain Grant was wandering eternity without it.

"Hmmmm." Helen looked narrowly at the lengthening shadows and reached for her camera case. "Let me know when you get everything tidied up. I need some personal details, bringing history to life and so on."

Amanda turned a laugh into a cough. "When can I visit the lab?" she asked. "I'd like to know what you find out about the body."

"Next Monday?" Hewitt suggested. He wiped his hand across his domed forehead, adding one more smear of dirt.

"I'll be there. Thanks." She scratched her back. "So what happens to the bones if you can't identify him?"

"They'll be re-interred. With his comrades, if we can at least establish which war he was in and which side he was on. Assuming it makes a difference after all this time."

"Someone was waiting for him to come home," said Helen.

Thank you, Amanda told her silently.

"I didn't mean," Hewitt began, and then shrugged. "I'll keep you posted, Miss Witham, Miss Medina."

"Ms.," Helen corrected with a grin.

"Amanda's fine," said Amanda, even though she hated to discourage Hewitt's courtly manners. "I'll check back with you tomorrow."

The last bedraggled student carried off the last dirty box. Amanda and Helen strolled away through the dusk, leaving Hewitt to cover the excavation site with sheets of plastic. "You want to come in for a glass of tea?" Amanda asked.

"Thanks, but I promised Lady C. I'd drop in this evening and sketch out ideas for a video about the body."

"Isn't Cynthia jumping the gun? No one knows anything yet." Mentally Amanda crossed her fingers behind her back.

"Yes," said Helen, "but she serves a damn good brand of bourbon."

Laughing, Amanda waved Helen off to the parking lot and went back inside the house. Dehumidifiers on. Floodlights on. Alarms set.

She flopped down on the couch, pitched the clipboard onto the chair opposite, and scratched her back against the throw pillows. It'd be nice to have a guy around, she thought, if only to reach the places she couldn't reach.

Twilight lingered outside, making Lafayette a silhouette against the pale square of the window, but her apartment was dark.

I'm not alone at night, she thought. It didn't seem to bother the cat that he couldn't go out after dark because of the alarms. He was so smugly certain he owned the house he had to be a reincarnation of Page Armstrong himself. His black and silver stripes and white breast even made him look formally dressed. Amanda wondered how old he was. Wayne said he'd appeared as the renovations were getting underway and kept coming back, no matter how many times the Benedettos tried to take him in. Not that that was a problem, the tourists loved him and he made a good little buddy. . . .

Lafayette sat up, his ears cocked forward, his eyes reflecting the last few rays of light. Amanda, too, sat up.

Lafayette's ears flipped back. His teeth flashed sharp and white as he hissed. In one fluid movement he was off the windowsill, across the desk, and under the couch.

Now what? Amanda got up and peered out the window. Nothing moved within the floodlit perimeter of the house. . . . Wait a minute. The cat hadn't been looking out the window but through the room and at the door.

Oh for the love of. . . ! Without turning on the lights, Amanda tiptoed across the room, put her hand on the doorknob, and flung open the door.

Nothing. The corridor was dark and empty and—cold. Very cold. But Grant had appeared last night—she'd gotten the message, already . . . A soft warm breeze dissipated the cold, caressing Amanda's face and raising gooseflesh on the back of her neck. The scent of whiskey filled the air around her. A man's questioning laugh echoed in the corridor. Then warmth, scent, and laugh were gone.

Amanda backed away and shut the door behind her. She turned on the lights, wincing at their glare. So he intended not just a cameo but a continuing role? Was that it?

Great. She was now caretaking a haunted house. Which was one protocol that sure as hell wasn't written up in her textbooks.

CHAPTER FOUR

Amanda peeled off her dress, petticoats, and the fashionable torture device of the stays. Thank goodness she had a different outfit for every day of the week, and full use of Colonial Williamsburg's laundry services. She'd read how the reek of Queen Elizabeth I's elegant velvet gowns would have dropped a moose at ten paces. Personal hygiene had made some progress over the centuries, even if advertisers wanted to take the "personal" out of it.

Thursday had gone well. She'd been preoccupied—go figure—but the tourists had come and gone in an orderly manner, Wayne had been thoroughly professional, and temperatures had been a bit cooler. Lafayette had earned cute points playing with Roy and a dangling piece of paper. No telling how many family vacation albums immortalized the likable tabby.

Once more in T-shirt and shorts, Amanda made her inspection of the house. From Sally's room she saw Bill Hewitt's crew packing up and heading home. "They must have found everything there was to find," she said to the miniature portrait by the window. "I'll go ask about your sword."

The painted features gazed silently up, not at her but past her. Making a face at herself in the mirror—*talking to his picture, right*—she hurried down the stairs and intercepted Hewitt on the first terrace. "What else did you find?"

"Buttons. Finger bones. Swatches of fabric."

"So the grave is empty now? You never found a sword to go with the scabbard?"

"Yes, the grave is empty," said Hewitt. "No, there was no sword. I'll send the paid workers out here tomorrow to continue tracing the footprint of the summerhouse. The students I'll keep with me in the lab. This is a textbook case. Monday about one o'clock?"

"That's cool. Thanks." Amanda stood bopping the clipboard against her thigh while the excavators' cars pulled out of the parking lot. Silence fell over the sun-saturated lawns and roofs. The opening at the end of the allee that had once framed the summerhouse now framed nothing but leaves trembling in the wind and shadows stretching across the grass. Even if she walked down there she wouldn't see anything except a hole in the ground. James Grant deserved better than a hole in the ground. Not that everyone didn't come to one—or its equivalent—in the end, but the traditional rituals added some dignity to the process.

She dawdled at her circuit of the house, picking up the odd piece of litter, propping up a top-heavy zinnia in the kitchen garden, watching a boat cut a furrow in the shining surface of the river. The sun sank. The dusk thickened, softening the precise face of the Hall.

At last Amanda went inside, pushed buttons, and flicked switches. She stared into her freezer at the boxed meals. No reason she couldn't go into town and buy herself a Big Mac, but she was oddly reluctant to leave the house. And it was too far out for pizza delivery.

She pulled out a Chinese dinner, microwaved it, and ate it in front of the television. Nothing was on but reruns of reruns. She turned the television off.

Her ears were tuned so finely to the sounds of the house that Lafayette's slurps as he groomed himself sounded like a lion dismembering a zebra. But beyond the hums of the refrigerator and the fans she heard nothing.

Her computer stared blankly at her. Yes, she had to work to do. Just one more quick inspection tour would do.

She walked through the house, thinking that even while the light fixtures were carefully shaded, the rooms that had been designed for candle and lantern-light seemed harshly lit by electric bulbs. In the entrance hall she stood with her hand on the switch but didn't turn on the lights. The glow from the dining room was more than enough to show her the staircase.

It ran upward into night, empty. The warm, still air pressed against her damp skin. The only presence was her own.

Like that Zen tree in the forest, did a ghost exist only if someone alive was there to see it and hear it? Amanda had seen and heard it. Him. Unlike Wayne, who'd been scared by his own imagination, she hadn't imagined the man on the stairs. If she needed any proof, Dundreggan was written on the back of the miniature. She'd never heard of the place until he'd named it.

She wasn't scared. Amused, sort of. Intrigued, like any red-blooded woman would be by an attractive man. Resentful, even—that man was putting her in an awkward position. If she wasn't careful she'd have to decide between the truth and ridicule or a lie and her conscience. . . .

The truth, Obi-Wan Kenobi said in *Return of the Jedi,* depended on your point of view.

Amanda turned herself around and walked back through the house, plunging each room into darkness behind her. In her apartment Lafayette was asleep on his favorite chair, half turned on his back, thoroughly at peace. Must be nice, she thought as she sat down and booted up her computer.

Carrie Schaffer arrived at the Hall Friday morning with new scripts for the interpreters, which she handed out at a council of war in the main kitchen. "Helen's news release hit the papers last night," she explained. "There's nothing like a dead body, no matter how old, to bring in the sightseers. Can't I turn my back on you for a minute, Amanda, without you digging up some new attraction?"

"I didn't dig him up," Amanda replied. "Bill Hewitt dug him up."

"Showing people the gravesite and answering questions means stepping out of character," protested Roy.

Wayne nodded. "The Armstrongs didn't know there was a dead body at the foot of the garden, did they?"

Did they? Amanda asked herself. Page the host would never sneak up behind a guest and crack his skull with a fireplace poker or slip a letter opener between his ribs. Whether Page the patriot—and the father—might have gone right ahead and offed an enemy was another matter.

"Do the best you can," Carrie said. "We're skating a fine line between realism and parody here anyway."

"Just as long as we get points for artistic interpretation," said Amanda. Everyone laughed except Wayne, who looked faintly puzzled.

One of the women playing the part of a house servant glanced out the window. "Here comes a gaggle of little girls. Maybe I should say a giggle of little girls."

"Battle stations," called Wayne, in his best bass voice.

Funny, Amanda thought as she turned toward the door, when he was around his mother Wayne's voice rose a full octave.

The girls were waiting on the doorstep. "Welcome to Melrose Hall," Wayne began, and Amanda made her first curtsey of the day.

By the time she reached her last curtsey it was not so much the tourists' questions about the skeleton as her own cautious answers that were rubbing a blister on her patience. Aware of her own irritability, she was extra nice to Wayne when he complimented her on her dress, the same one she'd worn every Friday. "Thanks. Your mother did a good job picking out fabrics and designs, didn't she?"

"She's an expert on eighteenth century stuff—furniture, clothing, you know. Some of my earliest memories are of being dragged around to estate sales and flea markets. She found a lot of period pieces for the Hall." Wayne opened the door to the kitchen and ushered Amanda through.

Carrie was sitting at the table filling in a report. "We had more visitors than usual today," she announced. "Just wait until tomorrow. It's going to be a zoo."

Wayne took off his wig, loosened his neck cloth, and mopped his face. "How about dinner at the nice, cool Trellis, ladies? My treat."

He knew Carrie would have to go home to her family. Amanda didn't have the energy for another "just friends" speech. She abandoned her brief vision of wineglasses slippery with condensation, meat and vegetables which had never touched microwaveable plastic, and dessert, any dessert, as long as it was chocolate. "Thanks, Wayne. But I really need to work on my thesis."

"Oh. Well, okay. See you tomorrow."

Carrie waited until the noise of his footsteps on the gravel walk outside had faded and died before she said, "He has a heck of a crush on you."

"You think?" Amanda retorted, and added more seriously, "Every relationship I've ever had has been safe. Nice. Shades of beige. Just once I'd like to attract a guy with some zing, some style."

"Jack wasn't exactly Mr. Sophisticate when I married him, but he got better."

"Don't even think about matchmaking." Amanda flopped down in a chair and squeaked as the fake whalebone of the stays gave her a vicious poke. Aristocratic women didn't flop, did they?

"Good God, no," Carrie returned. "We girls get to make our own matches and our own mistakes these days. If Sally met handsome Captain Grant now she'd run away with him and have a quick glorious fling. And end up in a council house on the wrong side of the Britrail tracks, mobbed by kids who ask for biscuits instead of cookies, running up a transatlantic phone bill begging Page to send her a plane ticket home."

Amanda's whoop of laughter was reduced to a wheeze. "And you were the one talking about the importance of romantic illusions!"

"Illusions in the sense of ideals, not delusions."

There were delusions, Amanda told herself, and then there were delusions. "Where did that miniature of Grant come from?"

"Cynthia bought it at a London auction house several years ago. She's been on the art and antiques circuit for years, so the dealer knew it was something she'd want and contacted her in plenty of time for the sale. Earning himself a tidy sum in the process, no doubt."

"And before that?"

"Someplace in Britain. In Scotland, I guess, since Grant was in a Highland regiment. He had to come from somewhere, didn't he?"

Other than the fourth dimension, Amanda thought. "It says Dundreggan on the back of the picture. . . ."

Carrie's brows rose.

"I knocked it over the other day," Amanda explained. "It's all right, I put it back together."

"Watch it, young lady," Carrie told her with mock severity. "Never heard of Dundreggan, sorry. I can look it up, if you like, when I get back to the library next week."

"I'll see what I can find on the Net. Clan Grant, that sort of thing."

"The other day you'd hardly admit James Grant existed."

"Yeah, well. . . . I thought I'd include Melrose's cast of characters in my thesis. Hang the artifacts on the family tree."

"Human beings wandering among the jargon in an academic paper?"

Amanda grinned. "All this time you thought I was a meek little scholar and I turn out to be a radical anarchist."

"There's plenty about Page and Sally at the library," Carrie went on. "About all the Armstrongs, for that matter, if you're wanting to get that close and personal. But Grant. . . . Hmmm. The histories on this side of the Atlantic are written from the American point of view, naturally, but maybe I can order his military records from the UK. An army bureaucracy grinds slowly, but it grinds exceedingly fine."

"There're regimental museums all over the UK, aren't there? And everybody's got a web site these days." Amanda saw menus and links unfurling like battle flags before her eyes.

Carrie stood and stretched. "Why don't you ask Cynthia where the miniature came from? Art dealers aren't always as picky as they should be about provenience, but Lady C. would never buy something that wasn't authentic."

"Thanks a lot, Carrie. You're a big help."

"No problem. Can't have you wandering the groves of academe all by yourself, you might get mugged by a footnote."

"Isn't that the truth." Careers were made and broken on the strength of your sources. The problem was, Amanda had a source she couldn't footnote at all.

"I'd better run," Carrie went on. "Every now and then I have to maintain the illusion I'm a responsible housewife and mother. See you tomorrow."

"Take care." Amanda hauled herself to her feet, saw Carrie out into the amber-rich sunlight of early evening, and locked the door after her.

She stood for a few moments listening. The house was silent, like the chattering groups of tourists had taken sound away with them. The moist air echoed hollowly in her ears. Not a breath stirred.

Smooth move. If Hewitt managed to identify James Grant's body, she was going to owe Carrie some kind of explanation for her premature interest in him. And yet she couldn't bring herself to wait for proof that might never come. *What a coincidence,* she rehearsed, *that I should just be asking about the man. . . .*

Don't worry about something that hasn't happened yet, she told herself. She went into the library and searched the shelves for an atlas. The only one she found dated from the seventies. Wayne's name was pencilled on the flyleaf in the painstaking hand of a child who's just learned to write cursive. Dundreggan wasn't listed in the index. She turned to the map of Great Britain and stared blankly at it, but no mental light bulbs went on.

She replaced the book and headed back to her apartment for her evening ritual of cat food, T-shirt, inspection tour, and a quick meal. Nothing was changed from the night before, unless it was Lafayette's pose on the windowsill, left-to-right instead of right-to-left.

She considered going to see the Brad Pitt movie—there was style for you—but since she'd told Wayne she had to work honor dictated she sit down and work. Using Melrose's inhabitants as examples did fit what she was doing. She could start out with Page building the house in the best model of the Age of Reason, and then contrast those ideals with the meager possessions of the servants and slaves below stairs. . . .

She booted up and checked her e-mail. Two engaged college friends were asking for advice on wedding dresses. Speaking of the socionomic significance of clothing—like you're really going to be able to wear that bridesmaid's dress again. . . . *Always a bridesmaid?* Amanda asked herself, and answered, better to be the bridesmaid than to connect with the wrong guy.

Lafayette raised his head and looked out into the deepening twilight. Footsteps crunched along the gravel path. "Amanda?" called a woman's voice. "It's Lucy Benedetto, dear."

"Come around to the door," Amanda called back. "I'll let you in."

Lafayette laid his head down again, not one hair ruffled. The steps wended their way around the end of the wing. Amanda turned off the security system and opened the back door.

The elderly woman materialized from the gloom outside the halo of lights. "I made too much pie for our supper tonight. Vernon and I thought you might like to have some." She held out a pie plate, carefully wrapped in a clean dishtowel.

The odor of cinnamon wafted upward. Gingerly Amanda took the warm plate. Its weight implied an entire pie. "That's really nice of you. Thanks. Come on in. . . ."

"Oh no, no, I need to get back, it's almost time for the Pavarotti concert on PBS. We just—well, we just wanted you know we're right up the way if you need us. A nice young girl like you being all alone here and everything."

"Thank you," Amanda told her. "But I'm doing just fine. Really. No problem."

"Oh. I see. It's all right, then. Well, good night." Lucy retreated into the darkness.

"Good night. And thanks a lot for thinking about me." The woman was gone.

Okay. . . . Amanda took the pie into the house. It was apple, she discovered. She cut herself a monster piece and closed her eyes while its butter and spice melted on her tongue.

So what was that all about? she asked herself, suspecting that the pie was only an excuse for Lucy to act protective. Maybe she'd seen some horror story on a talk show about young women living alone or something.

Wayne, the Benedettos—everyone wanted to protect her. They meant well. They didn't mean to patronize her. She didn't have to get into anyone's face with the "I am woman hear me roar" routine. Why, she'd even seen a ghost and handled the situation just fine.

A soft brush against Amanda's leg made her jump. It was Lafayette, demanding to know what she was eating. *Fine,* she told herself. *Yeah, right.* She offered the cat a bit of apple. He sniffed. With an indignant snort of tuna-scented breath he stalked away.

Amanda took her plate to the desk, sat down, and inserted a Pearl Jam CD into the changer. Then she sent a search engine into cyberspace. In for a penny, in for a pound, she thought. Knowledge is power. She was groping for yet another rationalization when a long list of "Highland Regiment" sites scrolled down the screen in front of her.

Saturday and Sunday were Melrose Hall's busiest days. Amanda didn't have time to eye the staircase. Wayne didn't have time for any of his eager-puppy numbers. Carrie didn't have time to discuss miniatures and morals. Amanda curtsied, and spoke her lines, and was glad to notice she was getting less jumpy about her supernatural experience the further it receded beyond her event horizon.

By the time she fell into bed Sunday night she was just about ready to conclude the house wasn't haunted after all. Maybe she had imagined that quick, bright laugh Wednesday evening. She sure hadn't heard the least bump in the night since then.

Amanda pushed the sheet down so that the breeze from the ceiling fan blew on her T-shirted chest. James Grant's appearance had been a momentary novelty of time and reason, she told herself. Someday, way in the future, she'd have a good anecdote for historic preservation conferences: *You know, I never believed in ghosts until. . . .*

Funny, how disappointed she was.

CHAPTER FIVE

After a couple of weeks without air conditioning, walking into the cool interior of the Rockefeller Library raised gooseflesh on Amanda's arms and shoulders. Virginians in the eighteenth century hadn't suffered as badly from the heat as their modern-day descendants, she decided. They'd expected to sweat. It was knowing you didn't have to that caused some sort of temperature dissonance.

Carrie was barricaded behind stacks of books, papers, magazines, and catalogs. Other publications crept ameba-like out from the main pile on the desk, across the floor, over a chair, and up the shelves. Family photos traced the progress of Carrie's sons from infancy to Little League. A scrawny pot of ivy sat on the windowsill next to a plaque reading, A TIDY DESK IS THE SIGN OF AN EMPTY MIND.

"Hi!" Amanda said.

Carrie looked up, over the top of her glasses. "Even if I didn't work at Melrose three days a week I still wouldn't get all this cleared away. It generates itself. Spores."

"Hello? It's me!" Amanda raised her hands defensively.

"Sorry. I'm on a guilt trip." Carrie picked her way from behind the desk and hoisted a book the size of a small tabletop from where it leaned against the wall. "Old Ordnance Survey maps of Scotland. One mile to the inch. I found Dundreggan."

Amanda helped Carrie get the book balanced and opened atop the desk. "I'm way out ahead of you—I found it on the Internet last night.

Not that a computer grid is nearly as cool as an old map." She inhaled the book's heady odor of paper and mildew. "I'm with Captain Picard on *Star Trek,* even with all the electronic stuff he likes to sit down with a book."

"There it is," said Carrie, pointing to the left-hand page. "Dundreggan House. Not a town but a building."

"They're calling it a castle now, but then, it has to be over two hundred years old if Grant lived there." Amanda's eye left the square marked Dundreggan House and moved over its surroundings. Not all the names on the double-page spread were weird: to the right of mouthfuls like Invermoriston and F"URW Garamond SC"Drumnadrochit the length of Loch Ness lay like a thick serpent diagonally across the map.

From beneath the book of maps Carrie pulled out a smaller book titled *Chronicles of the Highland Clans.* "How about this? Seats of Clan Grant: Castle Grant. Kinveachy. Dundreggan, foundations laid circa 1282. In possession of the Grants since the fifteenth century. Current owner Alexander, Lord Dundreggan." She flipped to the copyright page. "As of 1981, at least."

"Sweet," Amanda told her. "I didn't get that far. I spent most of my time with the 71st Highlanders. But I figured Captain Grant would have a pedigree. Officers were automatically aristocrats."

"They had to be. They had to buy their commissions. So what did you find out?"

"According to the roll of the 71st Regiment of Foot, aka Fraser's Highlanders, there were two officers named Grant, Captain James of Dundreggan and Lieutenant Archibald of Drumullie."

"Maybe you should say 'leftenant', British-style."

"I know you studied there, show-off. I'd sure like to go there sometime." Reluctantly Amanda closed the book of maps. "I e-mailed the Public Records office in London for both men's military records and gave them your fax number. If you don't mind. Here you are behind on your own work, you shouldn't have to help me with mine."

"It's not as though you were looking up the Maharajah of Bangalore, is it?" Carrie retorted. "Captain Grant—both Grants, I guess—had something to do with the history of Williamsburg. I can probably get an article for the magazine from this."

You think? Together Amanda and Carrie replaced the book in the corner. "You are coming to lunch with me, aren't you? All I had for breakfast was cold apple pie—I overslept, and the cleaning service ran me out."

"Lunch is not only part of the deal, I'm coming to the lab with you at one. Speaking of magazine articles, Bill Hewitt's planning one about the Melrose skeleton. He's cleaned the insignia and wants me to look them up."

"All right!" Amanda leaned over to pick up her purse. *What a coincidence I'd get interested in the guy just when his body appears. . . .* "I'll go dig around in the stacks."

"Come drag me away at eleven-thirty." Carrie surveyed her desk, hands on hips, like a lunchroom monitor walking in on a food fight.

Amanda settled down with a copy of Thomas Mason's account books. Sally's son may have had his qualities, but legible handwriting was not one of them. She had to force herself to focus on the issues: Architecture as a design for living. Form follows function. How many structures had been "restored" to something that in no way served their original purposes?

It may look good, but could your toddler fall off it, over it, or down it. . . . It isn't necessarily the evil that men do which lives after them, it's their stuff. And the good is often hidden with their bones, Amanda concluded, with the feeling that wasn't the exact quote.

After a while she found herself sketching a man in a kilt and high-collared coat on the margin of her paper. Okay, okay, so James Grant's ghost was a lot more interesting than Thomas Mason's possessions. Go figure. She glanced at her watch and pushed back her chair.

Carrie was typing furiously at her computer keyboard. Amanda padded into the office, found a plastic cup in the trash, and filled it at the water fountain in the hall. Carrie didn't look up until she poured the water on the ivy. "It's no use, it's just going to die. I don't buy plants, I rent them. Somewhere out there are dozens of little leafy things wearing haloes and playing harps."

"Is there a heaven for plants?" Amanda asked with a smile.

"Jack maintains there's a heaven for small appliances." Carrie saved her files, took off her glasses, and pulled her purse out of a drawer.

"If you follow that reasoning far enough," said Amanda, "the food we eat must be translated to a great restaurant in the sky. I am the resurrection and the sandwich."

"Just find me a piece of chocolate cake," Carrie returned, "and I'll give it the last rites."

They were still laughing when they settled down in a restaurant in Merchant's Square, just outside the Historic Area. The visitors in their halter tops and shorts seemed more wilted by the heat than the interpreters in their long skirts and waistcoats. *Mind over matter,* Amanda thought. She had to remind herself to speak modern English to the waitress. Every time she was surrounded by tourists her speech automatically thickened into two-hundred year-old cadences, rich in courtesies and subordinate clauses.

"I wonder if Cornwallis and his troops would recognize Williamsburg today," she mused over her salad and iced tea.

"If not, Mr. Rockefeller and the Foundation have wasted their money," answered Carrie.

"And what did the lads from the Highlands make of the colonies? The officers probably thought Virginia was Outer Boondock."

"But the troops may have gone back to their villages warbling how everything's up to date in Williamsburg."

"Those who went back," said Amanda, wondering again why the body of an officer, a patrician, a gentleman, as he would have been labeled in those days, had been dumped like a potted plant.

The waitress whisked away their plates and deposited slabs of chocolate cake. Amanda and Carrie genuflected, murmuring the usual litany over the size of the servings, the calorie content of the ingredients, and the negative effects of both. Then they dug in.

The taste still lingered in the back of Amanda's mouth when she and Carrie arrived at the nondescript, fifties-functional style building housing the archaeology labs. One of Hewitt's assistants ushered them into the long, narrow room of the bone lab. The incandescent glow of the afternoon leaked in around the window-blinds, only partially warming the chill purplish glow of the fluorescent light fixtures.

The walls that weren't lined by tall shelves stacked with carefully labeled cardboard boxes were lined by low cabinets filled with similarly labeled drawers. Every horizontal surface was covered with books, papers, boxes, microscopes and other tools of technological necromancy, and a Noah's Ark of animal bones.

The only human bones—*his* bones—were laid out on a table in the center of the room, from the skull with its jaw properly placed down to the feet with their tiny bones in ordered rows, more tidily than they'd lain in their grave. Beneath them stretched a sheet of white paper. They were so clean only a few grains of dust dotted various pencilled remarks.

Amanda shook her head. The skeleton was nothing more than an exhibit in a museum, less personal than an old pair of slippers. James Grant had a lot more character in the flesh, no matter how insubstantial.

Bill Hewitt stood over the table holding a pair of calipers. A magnifying glass protruded from his shirt pocket. His hunched shoulders and out thrust head gave him the air of a vulture considering its prey. "Miss Witham," he said. "Carrie."

"Hello, Dr. Hewitt," returned Amanda. "Please, it's Amanda."

"How's it going, Bill?" Carrie asked.

"Not bad. Let me run down the checklist with you. First. Are the remains human? Yes. Any idiot can see that. Second. Do they represent a single individual or the commingled remains of several?"

Carrie and Amanda chorused, "A single individual."

"Absolutely." Hewitt set the calipers down by the skull, where their metallic gleam emphasized the dullness of the pitted brown bone. "When did death occur? The bones are dry, cracked, and stained. Cartilage, flesh, and hair are absent. The accompanying artifacts are well decomposed. With the datable evidence of the clothing and the site of the grave I'd say our individual died about two hundred years ago."

"Revolutionary-era, then," said Carrie.

"Sex?" Hewitt went on. "Look at the brow ridges and the shape of the pelvis. A mature male, obviously."

"Obviously," Amanda said.

"Age?" Hewitt's forefinger indicated the skull, the pelvis, the long bones of the legs. ". . . symphyseal pits, iliac crest, femoral trochanter, saggital sutures," he said, leaving Amanda far behind, and at last concluded, "Probably in his twenties."

"Nothing so far," Carrie said, "to keep us from identifying him as a soldier in the Yorktown Campaign."

Hewitt's forefinger counseled patience. "The shape of his skull indicates European ancestry. The length of his longer bones indicated a height of about five foot eleven. Not heavily muscled, but not thin. Teeth in good condition. Right-handed. No significant anatomical anomalies. No signs of old diseases or injuries. No characteristics that are out of the ordinary. A fine male specimen of his time period."

"No diseases, no injuries, not heavily muscled. Probably from the upper classes," suggested Carrie. "We know from the epaulette he was an officer."

"Sounds good," Amanda said, trying to hold up her side of the discussion without offering any opinions that could all too easily turn into facts.

"Cause of death," stated Hewitt. "A bullet in the chest."

Amanda flinched. *Ow.*

The archaeologist held up a small plastic bag containing a lump of lead. "The bullet was with his ribs in the grave. It must have been lodged in his chest when he was buried. You can see the nick on the breastbone. The entrance wound."

"Shot through the heart," Amanda said.

"Probably."

"Died instantly."

Hewitt shrugged. "It's likely."

"At least he didn't linger long enough to suffer," said Carrie. "In those days if your wound didn't kill you and the doctors didn't kill you, the infection almost certainly would."

"Manner of death," Hewitt went on. "Homicide."

"Homicide?" repeated Amanda. "Oh, because he was shot by someone. Well, there was a war going on. The battle of Greensprings Farm was just up the road from Melrose."

"I can't tell whether the bullet is from a musket, a rifle, or a pistol," said Hewitt. "But yes, it's probable he was killed in battle. Carrie, take a look at these. . . ." He turned toward the smaller table.

Amanda stared into the eye sockets of the skull. Shot through the heart. Killed instantly. He probably never knew what hit him. That quick a switch from life to death would sure leave you disoriented—in more ways than forgetting which dialect to speak to a waitress. *Have you seen my sword?* he'd asked. Maybe the last thing he'd done in life was draw it and—well, lead a charge. Inspire his troops. Something appropriately macho.

The eye sockets were empty. Nobody home. Amanda did an about-face and joined the others beside a counter spread with flattened swatches of decayed cloth, something that looked like a moth eaten fur muff, and a tidy display of metal bits, some partially-cleaned and gleaming dully, some still tarnished into charcoal. Again Amanda thought how a man's stuff outlived him.

". . . red jacket with embroidered buttonholes, and wool material in a tartan pattern," the archaeologist was saying. With a dental pick he lifted a scrap of cloth. The pattern was mottled and dark but discernible—green and blue squares overlaid with a red stripe. "He was not only British but a Highlander."

"The 71st Regiment of Foot," said Carrie, with half a glance at Amanda. "They were at Williamsburg in July of 1781. Some of them were billeted at Melrose."

"And this particular officer left his calling card." Hewitt pointed to several small discs.

Carrie groped in her purse for her glasses. "Pewter buttons, each with an incised '71.' Most obliging of the man. And that's—a buckle?"

"From a shoulder belt, I'd say."

Carrie and Amanda bumped heads over the buckle. It was crisply cast, a thistle and a crown over a disk engraved with another '71.' Along the bottom bar of the buckle ran the words, *NEMO ME IMPUNE LACESSIT.* "The motto on the arms of Scotland," said Carrie. "'No one pushes me around and gets away with it,' more or less."

"Or, informally, 'Wha daur meddle wi' me.'" Amanda hadn't been digging around in Scottish history for nothing, although she probably didn't have the accent right. She pointed to the letters carved along the top bar of the buckle. "And that?"

"Quicquid aut facere aut pati," read Hewitt. "The regimental motto."

"Something about everyone either performing or suffering," Carrie translated with a frown of uncertainty. "Between 'do or die' and 'all for one and one for all,' I guess. I'll look it up. Oddly enough, Amanda was already researching the 71st Highlanders."

Amanda opened her mouth and shut it again—nothing she could say was going to bail her out now. The lackluster sheen of the metal fittings was no way like the subtle shine that had illuminated James Grant's ghost, but it was bright enough.

"And this." Hewitt lifted a long cardboard box from the end of the cabinet and opened it. Inside, on a bed of cotton wool, lay the scabbard. It gleamed a dull gray, its surface pocked with corrosion, its length bent into an obtuse angle. "Thirty-five inches long. Steel, not leather, fortunately, or it wouldn't be in this good a shape. It was excellent quality in its day. Presumably the sword was, too, but we didn't find that. It could have been lost or looted in the battle."

"A wealthy man, to carry such a weapon. . . ." Again Carrie glanced at Amanda, and murmured, "Naw."

The faint chemical smell of the lab was mingling uneasily with the chocolate in the back of Amanda's throat. She remembered to breathe through her nose before she started hyperventilating.

"There's a badge," said Hewitt. He pointed to the open end of the scabbard. A bronze ellipse was fixed just below the rim, its surface raised in a design.

Amanda leaned closer. "It looks like a pyramid with grass growing out of it. Are those words curving over the top, or smoke?"

"Oh boy." Carrie took off her glasses and pinched the bridge of her nose. "Oh boy. It can't be . . ." She put her glasses back on, plucked the magnifying glass from Hewitt's pocket, and peered intently at the badge.

Amanda braced herself. *Incoming.*

"I looked that up this morning," said Carrie, slightly strangled. "It's the crest of clan Grant. A burning mountain—Craigellachie, in Strathspey. The words say 'Stand Fast.' Bill, these bones might belong to James Grant."

"Not *the* James Grant," Hewitt said warily.

"Yes, the British officer from Melrose Hall. In the miniature portrait reproduced on the front of the brochure. The one Sally Armstrong had a crush on. The one who ran up the stairs with his sword. . . . Wait a minute. Amanda said there were two Grants in the 71st. This might be the other one. Since they didn't have rank insignia then, I don't know."

Amanda realized she was biting her lip. She released it.

"How about this?" Hewitt produced one more cotton-filled box. "A snuffbox. It was in his sporran. That fur pouch there. Probably badger."

On the cotton rested a small brass box, its lid a bas-relief of a battlemented building. In the harsh light of the lab Amanda could see every incised stone. Beneath the—the castle—a word was etched in flowing script: *DUNDREGGAN.*

Nothing to do now, she informed herself, but take the bullet. A metaphorical bullet. But this was what she wanted, to give the man his name back again. It was what he wanted, wasn't it?

Carrie turned, her eyes bulging. "It is him! James Grant of Dundreggan! Jesus, what a coincidence!"

"James Grant." Hewitt nodded, slowly, as though rolling his individual brain cells into their proper holes.

Amanda deflated, sagging backward against the table that held the bones. They stirred behind her, making quick dry rustles on the paper. Cold fingers touched her neck—the draft from the air conditioning duct above her head. Somewhere a door slammed. She repeated, "What a coincidence." Bless Carrie for saying the words first.

"It's circumstantial evidence, but that's what archaeology is," said Hewitt. "Odder things have happened. We turned up what might have been Thomas Jefferson's toothbrush several years ago. The context was right. The content was right. Why not?"

"The triumph of curiosity over chance?" Amanda suggested.

Shaking her head, Carrie handed Hewitt his magnifying glass. He turned it thoughtfully in his hand. "Why were you already researching James Grant, Amanda?"

"Carrie and I were talking about romantic illusions, about the story of James and Sally. Then I knocked over the miniature portrait. It was like he threw himself at me." She grimaced. That sounded so lame.

But Carrie was chuckling. "Can't resist a handsome face, huh?"

Amanda grabbed the bait. "Or a man in a uniform. Clothing as an indicator of class, that sort of thing. And with the oral tradition at Melrose—I mean, stories are artifacts, too."

"True enough," Hewitt said with a nod.

Maybe not quite true enough, Amanda thought, but she quit while she was if not ahead, at least not behind.

"But why was he buried in the garden?" asked Carrie. "The record, what record we have, indicates he died in the battle at Greensprings Farm. He could have been wounded, I guess, and returned to Melrose."

"Killed instantly," Hewitt reminded her. "Maybe he was ambushed by local partisans just before or after the battle. They buried him secretly so his compatriots wouldn't come looking for revenge."

"And the other British assumed he was killed in battle," offered Amanda. "Seems kind of sloppy to lose an officer like that, though. A peasant, maybe, cannon fodder, but an officer?"

"A wealthy man," Carrie added. "Good family connections, no doubt, to secure his commission. Proud enough of his name and his ancestral estates to carry mementos of both around with him. Not the man you'd expect to end up in an obscure, unmarked grave."

"We'll probably never know the truth." Hewitt lifted his magnifying glass and turned from the badges back to the bones. He peered so intently at them Amanda expected them to disintegrate before his eyes. "If we could find living relatives we might be able to do a DNA test, confirm his identity. Then let them decide what to do with the bones. Carrie, will you ask for Grant's military records from England, please? Time to move from the forensic evidence to the historiography."

"Amanda already has, Bill. I'll let you know the minute they come in."

"Good, good. Very efficient."

"Thank you," Amanda told him, although efficiency had nothing to do with it.

Carrie put her glasses back into her purse. "This has been absolutely fascinating, Bill, but I have to get back to the library."

"Thank you, Dr. Hewitt," Amanda said. "It's all just too cool for words."

He waved vaguely in their direction. The women showed themselves the door.

Carrie burbled about Grant and Melrose, probability and congruence, as they walked across to the library. Amanda didn't have the chance to respond with more than the odd monosyllable, which suited her just fine.

"Thanks," Carrie said outside the door. "That was the best lunch break I've had in years. I'll write up another new spiel for the tourists—properly larded with 'it is believed' and 'the evidence points to', of course—and bring it with me tomorrow. I hope London answers your query soon. I can't wait for the next chapter in the Grant saga."

"There may never be another chapter," Amanda pointed out, as much to herself as to Carrie.

"Curiosity over chance, remember?" Waving, Carrie hurried into the building.

Amanda unlocked her car, waited a minute while the heat dissipated, and then drove away on automatic pilot, only a tenth of her mind noticing such petty details as traffic lights.

The rest of her mind rocked and rolled. *All right!* Hewitt had named James Grant's bones sooner than she'd dared hope, thanks partly to the tips she herself had given Carrie. But she'd gone way overboard worrying about her supernatural source.

Why shouldn't she already be on the trail? She was a grad student in one of the historical disciplines, wasn't she? If Williamsburg archaeologists could find Jefferson's toothbrush in a place he was known to have lived, in a stratum dated to the time he'd lived there, then nothing was all that weird about finding Grant's bones under similar conditions. So they hadn't been looking for the toothbrush or for the bones. That only legitimized the discovery.

Still Amanda felt like she'd just gotten away with something underhanded. . . . Yeah right. Like Hewitt, or Cynthia, or even Carrie would believe the truth. It was Wayne who'd believe her, and that sure wouldn't help.

What was really coincidence was that she was the person—the woman—loitering outside the gates of purgatory when they opened far enough for James Grant to slip through. She hadn't asked for him. While she was interested in his time period, her only interest in psychic woo-woo was the occasional New Age album.

It was like he threw himself at me. And she hadn't exactly thrown him back. So what if she was susceptible to a handsome face—or at least to the image of one? She had hormones. She had intellectual curiosity, too. Helping James reclaim his name and his rank—repaying a two hundred-year-old insult—had started her on a great research project. All was well that ended—well, no, she had to get her thesis and its foot-notes together. Maybe she could come up with a good reason why James Grant was buried in Sally Armstrong's back yard.

Amanda turned into a supermarket parking lot and stopped. Her budget would stretch as far as a basket of blackberries. Native blackber-ries, in memory of the long-vanished flesh of James Grant. *Rest in peace.*

CHAPTER SIX

Amanda woke up Tuesday morning with the taste of fermented blackberries on her tongue. She gulped down cereal and coffee, then brushed and rinsed. The sting of mint cleaned not only her mouth but the lingering images of her dreams, of rushing anxiously from room to room trying to save the furnishings from battles which raged through the entrance hall and up the staircase.

She left Lafayette perched regally on the windowsill and strolled through the house, opening the drapes and relishing the last few moments of peace before the invasion began. The cleaning crew had left wooden surfaces gleaming and fabrics crisp and fresh. The odor of potpourri almost masked that of mothballs. From Page's window Amanda surveyed the manicured green lawns with their golden filigree of marigolds. The shadow of the house stretched away from Sally's window, reaching nearly to the site of the summerhouse. The archaeological team trooped across the garden carrying the tools of their trade, shovels, trowels, and ice chests. Wayne and Roy advanced from the gate. A distant cloud bank hinted that the clear morning sunshine might be only the calm before a storm.

Turning, Amanda brushed against the table. The miniature portrait plopped onto its face. She picked it up. No, she couldn't glue it to the tabletop.

She'd never again be able to think of James's handsome face without also thinking of the empty eye sockets of his skull. . . . Now that was getting way too sentimental.

Downstairs, Carrie handed out new fact sheets. Taking up his position on the steps, Wayne informed Amanda he was a Page right out of history, get it, get it? The stays protected her ribs from his nudging elbow. She bared her teeth in a laugh and threw herself gratefully on the first school group to appear around the corner.

Just after noon Cynthia Chancellor and her perfectly coordinated apparel arrived in the front hall. She set a Bloomingdale's shopping bag next to the sideboard and announced, "Well, Amanda, I hear you've been a very clever girl. Imagine guessing the identity of the bones before Bill Hewitt, even!"

"That isn't exactly what . . ." Amanda began.

Carrie peered through the parlor door. "Oh, good afternoon, Madame. May I be of assistance to you?"

"Oh no, no, I beat the others out here is all. I get so eager about these things. Melrose is becoming one of the premier historical attractions of the area, no doubt about it."

"What others?" Amanda asked.

"Bill and. . . . Why, here's Lucy and Vernon now. Come in, come in."

The Benedettos stepped into the house looking like serfs entering the castle, not sure whether they're going to be pelted with coins or with dung. "Hello, Mrs. Chancellor," Vernon said, adjusting his tie. "You wanted to see us?"

"I wanted you to be here as part of the little ceremony I've arranged," Cynthia said, "since you do so much for us here at Melrose Hall."

What ceremony? Amanda asked herself. Oh shit, she'd missed something on the schedule.

A group of tourists surged from the parlor into the entrance hall, Carrie at point. "It has been our pleasure to welcome you to Melrose Hall. Please do us the very great honor of stopping by the gift shop as you return to your carriages."

"Where's the dead body?" a teenager asked.

"Deceased persons remain in their homes for only a day or so, until the funeral rites can be performed," Carrie answered. "The bones of the poor wretch consigned to a most unsuitable grave in the garden are now in Williamsburg Town. I could tell you somewhat of . . ."

The boy interrupted, "You mean there's nothing to see?"

"I very much regret," Carrie began, to be interrupted again, this time by Cynthia.

"We'll be setting up a small display here in the entrance hall in just a few minutes, if you'd like to wait. Outside."

Oh. Thanks for telling me. But Amanda had to hand it to Cynthia, the woman eased the tourists out the door and down the steps with the skill of a carnival barker. And the place was starting to resemble a carnival, as another tour group streamed out of the library.

"If you would do us the very great . . ." Wayne was saying, and stopped in mid-phrase when he saw his mother.

"In just a few moments we'll be setting up a small display about the British officer buried in the garden," she told the sightseers. "If you'd like to wait outside."

The tourists exited. Bill Hewitt, Helen Medina, and several gofers carrying cardboard cartons, light standards, and display panels entered. "Here you are!" trilled Cynthia. "Wayne, run upstairs and bring down the miniature portrait of Captain Grant. Amanda, bring some wineglasses from the dining room—on the silver tray, the one I picked up in the Portobello Road in London. Carrie, help Helen with her lights."

Amanda raised an eyebrow at Carrie as she hurried past. Carrie quirked both of hers. The Benedettos retired to a corner. Cynthia shut the front door, closing out the circle of sunburned faces on the top step.

When Amanda returned with eight crystal glasses, the most she could fit safely on the tray, the exhibit was almost ready. One side of the hall was flooded with light so bright it drained the rich brown of the paneling into ash. In the glare stood the display flats, below the carved and scrolled wooden arch that bisected the hallway at the foot of the staircase. Laminated maps and sketches filled most of the panels—Amanda recognized them as standard-issue Yorktown Campaign illustrations. Wars looked much tidier, she thought, before the invention of photography.

Several small photos showed James Grant's bones both as they emerged in clumps from the ground and lay at parade rest in the lab. Her face carefully neutral, Amanda dodged Helen, who was snapping picture after picture of the assembly process, and set the glasses down on the sideboard.

Hewitt fixed a long Lucite box to the middle of the right-hand panel. Inside was the scabbard, mounted on thin prongs that made it look like it was floating in mid-air. One of Hewitt's assistants hung a smaller container on the opposing flat. Amanda craned forward. This box held four bits of brown bone, three no larger than pencil stubs and one considerably smaller. Finger or toe bones, she thought, and a molar. Hewitt was keeping the other ones in the lab until . . . Until when?

Until either he ran down some relatives or Cynthia could orchestrate a funeral, all the national news organizations suitably represented, of course.

"Bill and I decided," the woman was saying, "that it wouldn't be in good taste to display an obviously human bone, like a femur or, especially, the skull."

"Everyone having seen loose teeth," Carrie returned, without pointing out that displaying human remains was as much a matter of law as of taste. Scientists weren't nearly as cavalier with bodies as they used to be.

"Absolutely. So we chose these little, rather anonymous pieces of bone, and the scabbard, and . . ." Cynthia indicated a third Lucite box, ". . . the silver buckle, a button, and the snuffbox. A shame we don't have the sword. The scabbard is very nice, but it's got that bend in it, and even with the badge it's just not as dramatic as a sword would be, is it?"

Helen shook her head. "Inconsiderate of Captain Grant, not to leave his sword."

But he did leave it, thought Amanda. At least, it wasn't with his ghost.

Hewitt stepped back while one assistant tacked information cards beneath each box and illustration and another fixed a long, narrow lamp to the top of each panel. Vernon Benedetto mopped his balding head with a handkerchief. Wayne thumped down the stairs with the miniature, which he offered to Hewitt.

Cynthia beckoned. Wayne changed trajectory and gave the portrait to her. She held it up before her eyes, in the classic Hamlet-and-skull pose, and sighed. "Such a handsome young man. Cut down in his prime. Of course he was the enemy, we have to remember that, but Sally must have seen something in him, some sympathy for the Cause, perhaps. The Scots had been rebels themselves not long before. Here you go, Bill. Between the bones and the scabbard, I think."

Deadpan, Hewitt accepted the portrait and placed it in the last Lucite box. He hung it on the flat, turned on the lamps, and adjusted their shades so that they illuminated the displays without glaring into the eyes of the viewer. His minions gathered up their cardboard cartons and retreated into the faraway—and no doubt cooler—back regions of the house, passing Roy and a couple of other interpreters in the shadows of the hallway.

Helen turned on her video camera. Cynthia fluffed up her hair with her fingertips and posed herself beside the exhibit, hands folded, one foot turned out. She smiled like she was about to start turning letters on *Wheel of Fortune.* "It was only last week that we discovered a human skeleton in the gardens behind Melrose Hall. Thanks to the efforts of our staff, the bones have already been identified as those of Captain James Grant, the dashing hero of one of the best-loved legends of Melrose . . ."

"Luck," muttered Hewitt. "The archaeologist's best friend. Dumb luck."

Smart luck, Amanda amended silently.

Wayne sidled closer. "Mother's amazing, isn't she? To have such energy at her age."

Cynthia was maybe a whopping fifty-five. As for her energy, she'd probably wither and die if isolated from the adulation of mere mortals. Lucy, peering from behind her husband's bulk, caught Amanda's eye and winked. Amanda stared. Lucy nodded and smiled, eyebrows working, as though the two of them shared some secret. *What is going on with her?* Amanda asked herself.

". . . thank you for your support of Melrose Hall and Colonial Williamsburg," Cynthia concluded.

Of course "the staff" wasn't meant to actually appear on camera any more than the furnace stokers mingled with the first-class passengers. Funny how Amanda was thinking of furnaces. With the lights and crush of bodies, the already warm hall was sweltering. She tried fanning herself, but the fan was only coquettish ornament, and barely stirred the air. The silk of her gown stuck to her skin with each shallow breath. She sent a silent thank-you to the pharmaceutical industry for antiperspirants and deodorant soap.

"Are you all right?" whispered Carrie.

"Hyperventilating, as usual," Amanda wheezed.

"Hang in there."

Sweat trickled from beneath Wayne's wig. Vernon's head was as shiny as the polished banister. Helen's hair straggled out of its bun and down her neck. "Over to the side," she directed. "Point to the scabbard. Now to the portrait. Look thoughtful. Thoughtful, not spaced-out."

Cynthia took Helen's direction with a resigned air, and waited while Helen changed back to her still camera.

"Okay, Bill, this is your baby, into the picture—Cynthia, squeeze to the side—don't worry, you'll still be in the frame." Carrie turned a laugh into a cough.

By the time Helen finally switched off the lights even the impeccable Cynthia was drooping. But her production number wasn't over yet. "Where did you put those glasses, Amanda?" she called. "Oh, I see, on the sideboard. Eight—just right."

Not counting the dark faces in the recesses of the hallway, Amanda thought, and looked around. But Roy and the others were gone.

Cynthia reached into her shopping bag and pulled out a bottle of Glenlivet. "We should make a small toast to Captain Grant. Since clan Grant country is in Strathspey, where Scotch whiskey comes from, how else to toast him but with Glenlivet?"

"Outside of the fact Dundreggan isn't in Strathspey but further west," murmured Carrie.

"And there's perfectly good whiskey made elsewhere in Scotland," Vernon added under his breath.

"You know what she means," whispered Wayne. No one stepped on Cynthia's lines.

She poured a splash of amber liquid into each glass and made sure each person had one. Amanda held the cool crystal to her nose and inhaled. The peat-smoky tang of the whiskey reminded her so strongly of James Grant's presence on the staircase it was all she could do to keep from looking over her shoulder.

Cynthia lifted her glass. "To Captain James Grant, of the 71st Highlanders. May all victors be as charitable to the defeated as our sainted founding fathers."

Wayne pinged his glass against Amanda's. She drank. The whiskey seared her tongue and sent a dry steam into her sinuses. It was sacrilege to drink whiskey this way. She imagined a cool, rainy evening, a flickering fire, a man's scented breath in her ear—the right man, of course, not the same old been there done that. . . . What she really wanted right now was a vat of iced tea, a couple of gallons to drink, the rest to swim in.

With a chorus of coughs and throat-clearings everyone swallowed his or her drink. Helen smacked her lips appreciatively and glanced at Cynthia, but the bottle was already back in the bag.

The glasses clinked onto the tray. Carrie trotted toward the kitchen. Helen stowed her cameras away and disassembled her lights. Hewitt bellowed for his assistants. Cynthia opened the front door and invited the crowd—which had dwindled considerably, Amanda saw—in to see the new display. "Wayne, dear, explain all of this. Remember to stay in character."

Wayne tugged futilely at the neck cloth swathing his neck and began, "I have just received the intelligence that the bones of a British officer were found buried in my garden. Who could have committed such an impiety I cannot say. Even now, in the midst of war. . . ."

Amanda smiled. A shame he couldn't play Page all the time. Playing an adult he became one.

The Benedettos stood next to the sideboard with Cynthia. All three faces turned toward Amanda. Cynthia's blue eyes checked her out like she'd check out an item in an antique sale. Amanda looked down to see if the fichu was still tucked modestly into the plunging neckline of her dress. It was, even though its dampness made it clingy.

If Cynthia had had a sense of humor, Amanda would suspect she was setting her up for a practical joke. But no. The woman, in her own inimitable way, was just recognizing Amanda's good work. *Wasn't she?*

Smiling indulgently, Lucy edged Vernon crabwise through the crowd of visitors and escaped. Amanda cast an envious glance after them—clouds had doused the sunshine, and the trees were bowing in a breeze—and went up to Cynthia. "Mrs. Chancellor, that miniature of James Grant."

Tilting her head to the side, Cynthia bathed Amanda in a cordial smile. "Lovely, isn't it? A remarkable find, if I do say so myself."

"Where did it come from?"

"I bought it in London."

"From who in London? Whom," Amanda corrected quickly.

"How kind of you to be concerned about its authenticity. You're quite right, we mustn't put anything on display that isn't genuine. But not to worry. I took tea at the Savoy with Lady Norah Grant, who put the miniature on the market. Her husband, Lord Dundreggan, passed away several years ago, and these ancient families, you know, sometimes they're a little short. . . ?" She left the phrase hanging tactfully in the air.

"So the miniature was still in the Grant family? And there's a Grant family for it to be in? Sweet."

"It certainly is. Lady Norah was selling some other very fine pieces as well. Inappropriate for Melrose, sadly—all I could take off her hands was the miniature. She was so—I shouldn't say grateful, should I? Very gracious about it all."

Amanda visualized a delicate white-haired old lady sipping tea from a bone china cup. She'd worn faded finery to the meeting, linen or silk, perhaps, out of fashion but made elegant by her refinement. So what if she had to sell up to the colonials, she'd show them what manners were.

Cynthia took half a step closer to Amanda and dropped her voice. "Lady Norah is an odd person. A bit eccentric. In the fine old tradition of the British aristocracy, of course." Her pearly fingertips made a fluttering gesture.

"No kidding." Amanda couldn't imagine what combination of traits Cynthia would call both gracious and eccentric. Maybe Lady Norah drank her tea from its saucer or ate the paper doily beneath the cucumber sandwiches. Whatever—in Cynthia's eyes, her title would forgive her anything short of a capital crime.

But if James had living relatives, it was up to them to decide what to do with his bones. Amanda asked, "Mrs. Chancellor, have you talked to Dr. Hewitt about burying the bones yet? Dr. Noel-Hume reburied the skeleton of the woman he found at Martin's Hundred, who was killed in the Indian raid of 1622, but then, since he was never sure who she was there were no relatives . . ."

"I was there, it was a lovely Anglican funeral with the rain coming down like tears." Cynthia cut herself off in mid-sigh. "I have to run, dear. Important meeting. I'm simply frazzled sometimes from all the responsibilities, but, well, matters have to be attended to. I'm glad to make whatever contribution I can." She gathered up her bag and patted Amanda's forearm, leaving damp prints on her skin and a breath of floral scent in her nostrils. "Stay as sweet as you are."

"My greatest ambition, Madame," Amanda replied with her deepest curtsey. She watched Cynthia cut through the tourists and disappear down the steps, then gathered up the dirty glasses and fled toward the back of the house. With a jangle of crystal and a swish of silk she burst into the kitchen, set down the tray, and seized the glass of iced tea Carrie held out to her.

"Don't drink it . . ." Carrie began.

Amanda gulped. Pain stabbed her frontal lobe. "Damn," she said, and collapsed into a chair.

". . . too fast." Carrie's mouth crumpled in a wry smile. "Sorry."

Amanda ran her condensation-wet hand over her face as the pain ebbed. "I know I'm fresh out of college, on my own for the first time, but do I really look that much like a little lost lamb?"

"What?" Carrie asked.

"Everyone's trying to protect me and take care of me."

"You poor thing, to have people liking you."

"That's not what I mean. It's that Cynthia makes me feel like she's got her knife and fork and the mint jelly ready. And Wayne—I mean, I know that being protective is his way of showing he wants me and making himself feel stronger—he's got self-esteem issues and everything. . . ." She shook her head. "If I were Wayne I'd have moved to Timbuktu years ago, to get away from Cynthia."

"But you're not Wayne. And Cynthia isn't your mother."

Shuddering, Amanda sipped at her tea. It went down without fighting back. "Actually it was my mom who gave me my thesis topic. Sort of."

"Is she into antiques, too?"

"No way. What she's into is supporting her kids. She and my dad would take me to historic houses until their eyes bugged out, just because I wanted to go. In one of Frank Lloyd Wright's mansions in Oak Park she commented on how small the kitchen was compared to the rest of the house—obviously Wright never cooked his own meals."

"Ah," said Carrie. "She's a pioneer in gender studies."

"Well, yeah, she's a junior high home economics teacher, and was saying for years that guys ought to take her class, too." Amanda drained the glass and hauled herself to her feet. "That is a good display Cynthia brought in. She knows her business. She's just so, so . . ."

"Yeah, she is. But don't get on her enemy's list. She drove a reference librarian to tears last year."

"Let me guess. She doesn't shout, she uses cold contempt."

"A stiletto instead of a bludgeon," Carrie agreed.

"I'll try to stay on her friend's list, then. I sure do need a good reference from her. Maybe if I get an insulin injection every now and then." Amanda gave Carrie a curtsey—a courtesy—and went back to the front of the house. She was still hot, but at least she could start looking forward to closing time.

At the front door she picked up the next group of tourists. As Roy had pointed out, it was hard to field questions about James without stepping out of character. She took a cue from Wayne and pretended to be Sally, horrified and heart-broken at the macabre discovery at the foot of the garden. Which brought Amanda back around to wondering just which sainted founding father had shown so much charity to the defeated he'd dumped his body into a hole in the ground like garbage.

By closing time Amanda felt as though she'd been sautéed in oil. She stood waving on the front steps while the last visitors disappeared around the corner. The clouds were dense now, blue-gray with rain, and the wind, if humid, was at least cooler than no wind at all. She turned the sign around, locked the door, and looked toward the display. Its Lucite and brass and gilt shone in the lamplight, making the rest of the entrance hall seem doubly gloomy. The morsels of bone did not shine.

She contemplated the mottled steel length of the scabbard. It had been smoother and shinier in James's insubstantial hands. Which wasn't surprising. He'd been holding, she supposed, a memory of the scabbard as it had been. Just as his clothes, and his body, for that matter, were memories.

Maybe the physical remains of something, alive or inert, had to continue to exist before its ghost could also exist. Maybe you could take it with you. The ancient pharaohs might have had it right. If it was buried with you its ghost—its shade—stayed with yours all the way into—what? An afterlife? Or simply a repetition of patterns set while alive? No. James had looked right at her. He'd talked to her. He hadn't been some kind of holographic echo talking to a long-gone Sally Armstrong. He'd been confused.

Well, that made two of them. But the issue was academic now. Amanda turned off the lamps over the display and shrouded the artifacts in shadow. Either thunder or her stomach was rumbling as she walked the darkened corridors back to the kitchen.

Wayne sat in a chair, his neck cloth and wig lumped on the table beside him, his curls matted against his head. Lafayette squatted on his lap, more like a lion guarding his prey than a pet being cuddled. "Carrie said to tell you she'd see us on Friday, unless we need something before then."

"If we get overwhelmed," Amanda told him, "we can send an SOS."

"SOS," repeated Wayne. "Save our souls. Have you ever wondered where our souls go after we die?"

"Everyone wonders that. That's why we have religion, to name a destination and give you a ticket to get there."

"What about James Grant? He never got his ticket, did he?"

"No funeral, you mean? No. I bet your mother will organize something, with or without the modern-day Grants. A Presbyterian minister, I guess, since he was Scottish. And there're British graves at Yorktown, aren't there?"

"I think so, yeah." Wayne frowned. "But what about in the meantime? You have to stay out here with him, all alone and everything. If you'd like to move into town, Amanda, I'm sure Mother would pay for a hotel room. Or there's our own guest house in the back yard."

"Thank you, Wayne, but I'm the caretaker. I have to stay here."

"Then I could come out here. I could leave the car up the road and walk in, if you don't want the Benedettos to know. It's okay, I'd sleep upstairs, just so I could, like, be in the house and keep an eye on you."

She couldn't say, "I'd rather be alone with a dead body than with you." She groped for something else. The truth, that the ghost had already come and gone? A cliche, that she could take care of herself? She settled for a firm, "No."

Wayne's frown turned petulant. "You're just like Mother, aren't you? You don't need anybody. You're tough. One tough cookie."

Maybe he meant that as a compliment. Maybe he didn't. "It's starting to rain," Amanda told him. "That silk waistcoat will be ruined if it gets wet."

He looked down at his ample waist, partly concealed by the cat. "Oh. Yes. Well, if I'm not wanted here. . . ."

"I didn't say that, Wayne." She could add some sop about what a good job he was doing playing Page, but there was no need to patronize the man. "Good night. See you tomorrow."

Amanda managed to separate Wayne from Lafayette and maneuver him, his bits of costume, and his umbrella out the door. She watched through the window as the huddled figure became a dark smear in the rain and then vanished.

Sheets of water poured from the sky, drummed on the roof, and ran from the eaves in gurgling waterfalls. Creating her own waterfall in the sink, Amanda washed the eight wineglasses. She chimed them pensively together as she dried them, relieved to at last be alone.

Yeah, right. Like she wasn't flirting with denial. It wasn't so much that she needed someone, it was that she'd like to have someone. She simply wasn't accepting applications from any Tom, Dick, Harry, or Wayne.

The rain slowed, and the thunder faded grumbling into the distance. Amanda returned the wineglasses to the cabinet in the dining room. A decanter sat on the table. She put it back on the sideboard and propped the silver tray behind it. Next door, in the library, a quill pen dribbled black ink across the blotter on the desk. She replaced the pen in its inkwell. The blot was an artistic curlicue, like a word in eighteenth century handwriting, so she left it. She'd have to pay closer attention to the visitors, she told herself. Someone was going to pocket something, and Colonial Williamsburg would take its cost out of her already slender paycheck.

She plodded up the stairs and inspected the bedrooms. Everything was accounted for. From Sally's window she could see a gleam of western sky. Sally's portrait at the head of the stairs glowed faintly in the thin light, so that her expression seemed less demure than distracted.

Lafayette sat at the foot of the stairs, whiskers twitching, as if to say, "Hurry up! Don't you know it's past my dinner time!"

"Well, excuse me!" Amanda gathered the furry creature into her arms and draped him over her shoulder. Without a glance at the display she walked back to her apartment. Lafayette tolerated his ride with good grace, using the opportunity to flick his ears at the darkened corners and sniff the air made stale and musty by the heat.

Once the cat had been fed and was washing his face, Amanda threw herself into the shower. Thank goodness people didn't have to clean themselves with their tongues. Not that a few mutual licks and nibbles between lovers weren't all to the good, but the clean needed to come first. . . . Boy, did she have it bad tonight, she thought with a grin.

When she went outside in her usual T-shirt and shorts she was exhilarated to discover that the wind was fresh and cool. She took off her shoes, waded barefoot through the wet grass, and splashed in the puddles until it was too dark to see more than the shape of the house. Her feet were wonderfully cold, if covered with grass and mud. She rinsed them off at the faucet outside the door, went back inside, and locked up behind her.

It took her only moments to fling all the windows in her apartment wide. Lafayette took up residence on the sill in the bedroom, his nose pressed against the screen, while Amanda baked herself a frozen pizza and followed it with another piece of apple pie.

After all the human voices of the day, the rain and the thunder, even the chime of crystal, hearing no noise but that of leaves and wind left Amanda's ears ringing. Her own footsteps seemed so loud she found herself tiptoeing. She tried the television and turned it off. She sat down at her computer, checked her e-mail, and got up without tackling the thesis. She hung up today's gown and fussed over the ruffles on tomorrow's. With the breaking of the heat wave she should have been relaxed, and yet the air itself seemed to hum. Some kind of atmospheric front, she told herself. The living room was actually getting chilly.

Amanda went through her music collection and inserted a CD of

James Galway playing Debussy's "Reverie." The melody was high, sweet, and clear, like wine. It tightened the hairs on the back of her neck. She strolled into her bedroom without bothering to turn on the light. Lafayette was a statue on the windowsill, his unblinking gaze typically inscrutable. The draft from the open window was downright cold.

All right! She pulled her flannel nightgown from a dresser drawer. There was no reason she couldn't sit around in her pajamas, she wasn't putting on a fashion show.

Just as she took off her T-shirt and shorts, Lafayette leaped down from the windowsill. Every hair on his body bristled. He hissed. Amanda glared at him. Some critic, he wasn't even her own species!

The cat dived beneath the bed and crouched there, grumbling and muttering like a tea kettle almost at the boil. She pulled off her underwear and tugged the nightgown over her head. The flute music vibrated in the air. With an almost audible pop the chill dissipated. A shape moved in the mirror hanging above the dresser.

Amanda spun around. Her jaw dropped. Her heart splatted against her rib cage.

James Grant stood in the bedroom doorway. He was illuminated perfectly clearly by the light in the living room, light that not only outlined his body but glowed through it. His scabbard dangled empty at his side. His kilt rippled and his hair fluttered in the humid breeze from the window. His scarlet coat gleamed. He was smiling.

I saw his reflection in the mirror. . . So he was a ghost, not a vampire.

He was a man. And he'd been standing there, enjoying the view, while she changed her clothes.

That smile was devastating, charming, sophisticated, mischievous. "My apologies, Miss Witham," he said. "I should have acquainted you with my presence, but your beauty rendered me mute. A veritable Aphrodite you were, stepping from your garments as though sharing your comeliness with the gods of Olympus."

What a line, Amanda thought. She closed her mouth. Little pieces of her heart pattered in her throat, her wrists, her stomach.

James walked toward her. His blue-gray eyes were lamps lit with tiny sparks. He extended his hand. "May I play Ares to your Aphrodite?"

This is not happening. . . . Yes, it was. Amanda lifted her hand. He clasped it tightly, his fingers firm and strong—no, he wasn't touching her, he had no body to touch her with, her hand was enclosed by a warm pressure, a cool tingle, no more substantial than air and yet of incredible substance.

He bent. His incorporeal lips touched her living skin. Hot and cold chills surged up her arm. Her stomach melted. Her eyes crossed. She heard her voice make the shaky gasp that had always before acknowledged a considerably more intimate gesture.

He was gone. Amanda was standing in the center of her bedroom, her hand extended into whiskey-scented thin air. From the living room came the delicate melody of "Reverie." But James had been no reverie. Amanda could still feel his kiss on her only too solid flesh.

CHAPTER SEVEN

The face that looked back at Amanda from her bathroom mirror was hollow-eyed. She dusted her cheeks with blusher, hoping to make herself look more like blooming Sally Armstrong and less like wilting Amanda Witham.

She might have dozed for a minute or two last night. One of those minutes was the one Lafayette had chosen to jump onto her bed. She'd jerked awake and cussed him out. The cat had given her one of his patented "what's your problem?" glances and settled down for a long summer's nap.

He wouldn't make any better a witness this time out, Amanda told herself. But Lafayette had seen James Grant just as much as she had, even though the cat was hardly as thrilled about the encounter.

Not that she normally got her jollies by performing strip teases for casual bystanders. It's just that James wasn't casual, wasn't a bystander, and sure as hell wasn't the same old been there done that.

Yeah, and he wasn't alive, either.

She smoothed the bedspread around Lafayette's sleeping body and went about her business, turning on, turning off, unlocking, opening up. She saved the lights over the display in the entrance hall for last, and spent a few minutes contemplating the painting and the scraps of bone. Her questions of yesterday were no longer academic. Wayne and his childlike love of the spooky had come closer to answers than she had. With the return of James's bones to the house, James himself had come back.

Although his ghostly presence seemed only partially connected to his physical one. Otherwise he'd still be at the lab with the majority of his bones. Whether he'd been at the lab, Amanda couldn't say and didn't know how to ask. The bottom line was that James was imprinted on Melrose Hall, where he'd spent his last days, and to Melrose Hall he'd returned.

Maybe her presence *was* attracting his. If the legends were true, his image of Melrose included that of a young woman. But he didn't think Amanda was Sally. He'd remembered her name from their first meeting, and called her by it at their second—"My apologies, Miss Witham."

So much for conventional horror movie wisdom. This ghost wasn't horrible. He was charming, if thoroughly unnerving. So much for assuming any original source had to be inaccessible and/or deadly dull. No pun intended.

She offered the portrait a wry smile. She'd be feeling eyes on the back of her neck from now on, even if James never appeared again. But she hoped he would. Unlike Alice, she was ready, willing, and eager to believe this one impossible thing.

Amanda walked out onto the front steps and surveyed the lawns, the trees, the river, the sunlight. Already the day was sultry, promising another blast furnace afternoon. She visualized last winter in Chicago, ice floes piled against the shores of the lake. She visualized ditto at Cornell, snowdrifts up to the windowsills. Still she was hot.

Here came Wayne. He sure wasn't your stereotypical rich kid, she thought. When it came to his job, he was dependable as they came.

Wayne stopped at the foot of the steps and made a courtly bow. "Good morning, Miss Witham."

It sounded stilted when he said it. Amanda curtsied. "Good morning, Mister Chancellor. I trust your evening passed pleasantly?"

"I fear it did not. I would have preferred your company to that of the television." He shrugged away the antique language. "I'm sorry if I offended you yesterday. I didn't mean to imply that you're scared or anything out here. It just came out that way."

"I wasn't offended. Anyone would be a bit nervous alone in a big old house. Well, not all alone. The cat's here."

Wayne nodded earnestly.

"It's just that I have work to do," Amanda went on. "And after sharing an apartment with three other women my last two years of college, it's a treat to have all this room to myself."

From the entrance hall came a familiar slithering, pattering sound. Amanda ducked back inside and blinked the sunlight out of her eyes. Yes, the leaflets lay fanned across several feet of carpet, Sally's, Page's, and James's shiny faces repeated again and again. But Amanda had checked the leaflets only moments before. They'd been neatly stacked at the foot of a blue-and-white Chinese vase nowhere near the edge of the sideboard. A breeze might have messed them up, but it would have taken a gale to spread them so far across the floor. And not the least breath of air stirred through the open door.

"Rats," she said mildly and noncommittally as Wayne loomed beside her.

"They must have been right on the edge." He knelt down, his large hands gathering and stacking the leaflets before she could ease herself to her knees to help. "Here you go. Let's put them next to the vase." Voices and footsteps approached the steps outside. "Oops. Off we go, Sally. Ready?" Wayne turned back to the door.

Amanda looked from the sideboard to James's portrait and back again. Maybe last week the leaflets had fallen all by themselves. Maybe yesterday the decanter and the pen had been moved by tourists. And there'd been a hairbrush misplaced, too—she couldn't remember when.

The morning after she'd first seen James she'd found both his picture and Sally's out of place. Today the leaflets had been tossed across the floor. When James kissed her hand last night she'd sensed—well, call it a force field. James could move objects. Whether he was aware of what he was doing when he wasn't visible, or was just a formless impulse like a poltergeist, she couldn't say. Whatever. James had once again, however unwittingly, put her in an awkward situation. Just like a man.

Outside, Wayne was saying loudly, "Welcome to Melrose Hall. I am Page Armstrong. My daughter, Sally, will be joining us . . ."

Amanda stepped out into the sunlight. She delivered her lines and with Wayne led the first tour of the day into the house.

She was showing the second tour out the door when she spotted Cynthia bustling along the gravel walk, immaculately turned out in skirt and blazer. Behind her came a group of similarly suited men and women. Helen Medina brought up the rear, in her shapeless khaki looking like a chicken pecking along behind a party of penguins.

Wayne, leading a fresh group of sightseers into the house, said to Amanda from the corner of his mouth, "Donors and other VIPs. Mother may have no official standing with CW, but she works hard."

Promoting the program and herself equally. Amanda stood aside with a curtsey as Cynthia started up the steps. "Good morning, welcome to Melrose Hall."

"Good morning, Amanda," Cynthia returned, bestowing her brightest smile. She turned to her entourage. "This is one of our character interpreters, playing Sally Armstrong. Isn't she just the sweetest thing?"

Everyone nodded and smiled, except for Helen, who pointed her forefinger at her mouth, stuck out her tongue, and crossed her eyes. Amanda winked in agreement and intercepted the next clump of tourists.

As she led them through the hall and up the stairs she heard a few words of Cynthia's lecture, ". . . up the staircase with his sword—touching love affair with Sally brought to an untimely end—Hewitt—museum quality reconstruction . . ."

Amanda herded her group through the bedrooms, down the back stairs, and through the rooms on the first floor, returning at last to the entrance hall. The collection of dignitaries was just moving into the library, Helen's flashbulbs popping at their heels.

". . . genetic fingerprinting," Cynthia was saying, "like obtaining a blood sample from Prince Phillip in order to identify the remains of the Czar and his family. Or from the people claiming to be descended from Thomas Jefferson and Sally Hemings!" She tut-tutted. "Of course we're almost certain who our body was, but it makes a nice exercise for the students—oh yes, the family is still extant, I'm a close friend of Lady Norah Grant—I called her Tuesday night—very gracious, very interested, as you can imagine, in her late husband's ancestor—and her ancestor, too, she tells me—her son the Honorable Malcolm will send a blood sample—aristocrats, you know—I'm sending them the excavation reports, it seems only courteous."

Yes! Amanda said to herself. Hewitt had muttered something about DNA sampling on Monday. So they were going for it. The Grants must be wondering what all the fuss was about. But no, James had been, if not Malcolm Grant's multiple-great grandfather, at least his multiple-great uncle. The modern family understood that James deserved his identity.

Amanda circled her sightseers in front of the display in the hall. "How shocking to discover the poor wretch buried in the garden. He was a young man, we believe, a soldier who made the ultimate sacrifice. But such are the fortunes of war. As the great historian Herodotus wrote, 'In peace, children inter their parents; war violates the order of nature and causes parents to inter their children.'"

Some of the tourists looked thoughtful. Others didn't react. Amanda suspected she was making Sally more of an intellectual than she'd really been, but what the heck, as a widower's only child, Sally could well have been allowed the run of Page's library. No one knew much about Sally, after all. Thomas Mason's papers were about himself and his property, not his mother. The first suggestion of any relationship between Sally and James Grant occurred in a breathless 1847 letter from one of Thomas's daughters, several years after Sally's death.

In her capacity as Sally's clone, Amanda saw those sightseers out, picked up some more, and dispensed her lines again. She made an effort to keep her voice from becoming monotonous, varying her spiel from group to group, but even so she came close to falling asleep on her feet before the afternoon was over. Fortunately the last couple of tours included several visitors with intelligent questions, so that by the time closing time arrived she was still conscious.

She locked the door and leaned against it. Its wood was cool against her sweaty skin. She thought at first a faint hum in the air was the silence in her ears, then identified it as coming from the lights above the display. She plodded across the hall and turned them off. James's thumbnail-sized face disappeared into shadow.

"We're leaving now," Roy called from the back hallway. "See you tomorrow."

"Bye," Amanda returned.

The slam of the kitchen door echoed through the house. She walked toward it, waiting for Wayne to pounce from a dark corner. But she reached the back door just in time to see him disappear with the others into the parking lot. She could feel sorry for him, she thought, and a little guilty about rejecting him. But pity and guilt did not make a relationship.

She bolted the kitchen door and trudged back to her apartment. Lafayette wasn't there.

Amanda gathered up her shorts and T-shirt and took them into the bathroom with her, making sure the door was shut before she took off her dress. Big deal—James probably had X-ray vision. If he couldn't walk through locked doors, he could sure materialize inside locked rooms.

Her vocabulary was stretched too thin, she thought as she climbed into the shower. How to define a ghost? All the ghost stories that had come down through eons of human history and literature were variations on a theme, not a set of cut-and-dried rules. The theme being that of a restless spirit who didn't realize it was dead, or had left some kind of unfinished business, or needed something from the living.

She soaped, rinsed, and exposed as much of her body to the spray as she could without gymnastic training. When she stepped out onto the bathmat she felt delightfully cool.

Cool, not cold? Amanda looked warily around, but already the brief chill was dissipating. Just the effect of the water. Nothing supernatural. It was still daylight, and he'd never appeared until after dark. He was flexible, though. He'd first materialized in the part of the house most associated with him and little changed from his own time, then in the part most changed.

If there were rules, she'd have to figure them out for herself. Assuming she got any more data. James might have done what he came to do, or gotten what he came to get, and departed at last.... No. Putting a name to his bones hadn't been enough. Wayne must be right again. Ironically, James's spirit demanded a proper funeral even while it proved itself too vital for the grave.

Amanda dressed, took her clipboard, and checked out the house. With the exception of a gum wrapper on Sally's bedroom floor, all was in order. As it was outside. She strolled down to the site of the summerhouse and checked out the excavation. The area of pared-away vegetation extended further. Several trenches revealed a line of postholes. With much of the underbrush removed the area no longer seemed oppressive, just forlorn. Amanda wondered what it had looked like in James and Sally's day. Had there been a British picket stationed at the little building? Or had it made a nice little secret rendezvous for certain young lovers? "Lovers" in the eighteenth century sense, of course. Surely Sally wouldn't have. . . . *Naw.*

Amanda walked slowly back through the lengthening shadows. The evening was humid and silent. A slight odor of decay hung on the still air. Even the birds seemed to be dozing in the heat. By the time she went back inside the house she was imagining herself the last human being on Earth.

The evening news revealed that there were plenty of other people on Earth, many of them busily making trouble for the rest. That hadn't changed in two—or six, or eight—hundred years. "Get a life," she said to one public figure who tonight was almost foaming at the mouth, and turned the television off. When the cat flap swung open she jumped. Lafayette strolled into the kitchen with a pointed glance at the can opener.

Outside the apartment night thickened. Fed once again, Lafayette settled down in his chair. Amanda turned on the light in the kitchen and the one on her desk. She forced herself to sit down at the computer, but after she'd checked her e-mail found herself seeing not what was on the screen but what was reflected in it. Maybe if she put on some music. Would Smashing Pumpkins or Radiohead scare him away?

A chill tightened her nape and shoulders, as though ice slid down her spine. She bolted to her feet just in time to see James Grant appear literally out of thin air.

Lafayette bristled, his claws snagging the cushion. The drones of the computer and the fans were an undercurrent to the drum roll of Amanda's pulse. She closed her eyes and opened them again. James was still there, blinking dazedly as though suddenly awakened from sleep.

His eyes focussed on the cat. He scowled, taking an abrupt step forward. Lafayette hissed and dived for the door. The cat flap banged back and forth, slowed, then stopped.

James turned toward Amanda, one hand on the scabbard, the other extended. His scowl disappeared so quickly Amanda wondered if she'd seen it, consumed by the brilliance of his smile. "Good evening, Miss Witham. It seems as though the wee beast does not care for me."

"No accounting for tastes." She'd look ludicrous curtseying in shorts, so she nodded. "Good evening, Captain Grant."

He cocked his brows. His hand remained extended, palm up, fingers inviting. She stepped forward and placed her hand in his. Electricity tingled in her skin. This time instead of bending over her hand he raised it to his lips, so that she felt not only the kiss but the full impact of those smoky blue-gray eyes. Her face grew so warm she knew she'd flushed scarlet—*way to go*—even though her fingers were cool and dry. The room was no longer cold, but tropical.

She reclaimed her hand. James's lips, still parted, went lopsided. His brows tightened. He looked around him with the part cautious, part suspicious air of the children Amanda lectured on chamber pots and feather beds.

She looked at him—a military historian or re-enactor would give his eyeteeth for this close a look at an authentic uniform.

James seemed less indefinite now, in manner and physical appearance both. His body only hinted at translucence. She couldn't see the lamp beside the computer through it, let alone any of the furniture. His clean-cut face was defined as clearly as the intricacies of his clothing. The white ruffles at his throat and wrist shivered as though to a pulse. Buttons, fittings, and epaulette gleamed against his scarlet jacket and its white facings. His waistcoat, revealed by the turned-back skirts of the jacket, was also white. His sporran, the equivalent of a pants pocket, was sleek fur and dangling tassels.

He wasn't, unfortunately, wearing the old-fashioned great kilt, several yards of wool pleated and belted around the waist with the rest billowing artistically upward and pinned at the shoulder. While the belted plaid was the classic Highland garment—in the Scottish climate wearing a blanket was a good idea—by the time James joined the army the powers-that-be had recognized that in battle it was a burden. No longer was it feasible for the soldiers to throw off the plaid and run into combat in their shirts the way the old Highlanders had done.

So James was wearing the small kilt, the lower half of the belted plaid, somewhat fewer yards of blue-green Government tartan pleated and pinned around his waist. While it wasn't the modern kilt, it was definitely a step in its evolution.

That the entire outfit with its heavy, multi-layered fabrics was hopelessly impractical for Virginia's climate, Amanda told herself, didn't detract one bit from its splendor.

Despite the detail, however, James wasn't quite there. Something was odd about his appearance, something was *weird,* in the truest sense of the word. . . . That was it. In light of the lamp, every object in the room cast dark shadows. But the pleats of James's kilt, the deep lapels of his coat, the scabbard against his side cast no shadows at all. He stood on the rag rug with Amanda's shadow lapping his feet, but he himself didn't have one. It was like his body, his clothing—his image—were lit from within by a memory of light.

James looked around. With an effort Amanda didn't duck.

"This place is Melrose Hall?" he asked.

"Yes. The servant's quarters, more or less."

"You are no maidservant."

"No. I'm kind of an actress."

"Indeed? Have you performed the plays of Mr. Sheridan? When I was last in London his work had earned such plaudits I was obliged to attend School for Scandal three times."

"Not that kind of actress." She shrugged aside the cognitive dissonance of talking to someone who'd seen Sheridan in the original. "I'm like a teacher, acting out lessons."

He eyed her clothing. "You astonish me. But then, much of what I've seen in the colonies I've found astonishing."

"How so?"

"The American militiamen will not fight a proper battle. We charge at them and they run away like dogs. We've captured some who have no uniforms, but are garbed in buckskin, like red savages."

"Shocking," said Amanda.

"Williamsburg Town," he went on, "might be considered a pleasant village in England, but for the misery of the summer heat, of course."

"Tell me about it."

"But I am, Miss Witham." He stepped closer. "Charlestown, now, is well-favored enough. However, the customs of the country are exceedingly strange. Colonel Lindsay of Balcarres—our commanding officer, a gentleman of fine family and good connections—himself remarked upon the Negro slaves waiting upon table in homes almost as fine as any in Europe."

"Most of us think that's pretty strange, too," Amanda returned dryly. Lindsay of Balcarres, Charleston—she already knew those names from her research. But she wasn't about to cut him off in mid-flow. "You've been to Charleston?"

"I regret to say that many good men died at the hands of the rebels in South Carolina, although not so many as died of the sweating sickness."

Malaria. "Are all your men from Scotland?"

"A goodly number are Gaelic speakers from the Highlands, a superstitious lot, but fierce fighters and docile in camp, ever mindful that a good report be made of them to their relatives. Many more will die here in Virginia, I'll warrant, before we crush this rebellion."

"Do you think you'll win?" Amanda asked with a quickly suppressed grin.

"If I were obliged to give the orders, and not Lord Cornwallis, I should march our troops onto our ships and return home before another dawn rises in the east. If these poor fools of colonists allow themselves to be misled by the lies of France and Spain, and are bold enough to rebel against His Majesty's government, then I say let them go, and be damned to them. . . ." James grimaced and bowed. "I beg your pardon, Miss Witham, I know not where your sympathies lie. With the master of the house, I daresay."

Amanda didn't ask him whether his own relatives had donned the white cockade of Bonnie Prince Charlie and rebelled against His Majesty's government not long before he was born. "Page Armstrong's loyalty to—er—the Continental Congress is well-known."

"Indeed," James said graciously, with another bow. "I should now present myself to Earl Balcarres, I suppose, but I do not, I cannot . . ." He sent a long, dubious look at the computer by the window, shook his head, set his jaw, and turned away.

Here was a man deep in denial. He knew where he was, but his surroundings weren't quite right. Amanda's clothing alone must have thrown him for a heck of a loop. But his pride kept him from betraying his confusion, just as honor made him treat her like a lady even though her clothes sure didn't make her look like one.

What should she do? Ask him whether he knew he himself had died in Virginia? Whether he remembered the blow to his chest that had been a shot through his heart? Tell him that two hundred years had passed him by? But as much as she was—figuratively—dying to know why he'd been buried in the Melrose gardens, asking a ghost about his death had to be the ultimate in bad manners.

James peered into the dim interior of the bedroom. His left hand continued to rest on the top of the scabbard, his fingers cupping the oval with the family crest. His right hand smoothed the fall of hair from his forehead into the auburn ponytail that curled down his neck. The soldiers of his time had greased their hair, hosting colonies of fleas and lice. Amanda wasn't sure whether the gentry had been any tidier, but James's hair, oddly lit as it was, seemed quite clean. She was glad he wasn't wearing the precious white wig of his portrait.

His accent was barely recognizable as British—it was a lot flatter than the rounded tones of today's BBC announcer. And Amanda heard no trace in his voice of the burred Rs and glottal stops of the Scottish dialect. But Robert Burns—James's contemporary—had raised a few brows by writing in everyday Scots. Aristocrats like James spoke "proper" English.

"Your soldiers are Gaelic-speakers," she said. "You can speak Gaelic, then?"

"Yes, I have the Gaelic. A curious tongue." He turned back toward Amanda. "Have you seen my sword, Miss Witham?"

Back to that. "No, I haven't. Maybe it was stolen. Maybe it was broken."

"Fine Stirling steel it is, a weapon I'd be loath to lose. Why, when I applied it to Melrose's banister it cut deeply into the wood but took no damage itself." Again he smiled. "My most humble apologies for that, Miss Witham. I was impetuous, even rash, but circumstances demanded action."

The legend was true, then. So much for historical cynicism. She could just see him charging up the stairs, rousing his fellows to do battle, like a character in a PBS costume drama. Except for him it was real.

There was one question she had to ask. "Did you meet Sally Armstrong when you were—ah—here before?"

"Miss Armstrong," he said, eyes glinting. "So fair a nymph to spring from the loins of the old Roman, her father. She set her cap at me, she did, but my dolt of a cousin, Archibald, offended her by his forwardness. It was late yesterday evening the Armstrongs left Melrose, to stop with relatives until His Majesty's troops move onward." His gleam dulled into uncertainty. He was probably trying to form a definition of "yesterday."

That settled that, thought Amanda. Sally really had been attracted to James, Page or no Page. But then, any woman who wasn't seriously hormone-impaired would be attracted to him. "Archibald Grant is your cousin?" she asked.

James didn't answer. He slumped, as though the weight of vulnerability and doubt had gotten too heavy. The odd flat illumination of his face made him look younger than his twenty-odd years. Considerably younger than his two hundred years. He said slowly and thickly, "May I wait upon you again, Miss Witham?"

"Yeah, sure," she returned, and caught herself. "Yes, if you please."

"Most excellent." He reached toward her. But his eyes went empty, like a man lapsing into unconsciousness, and he disappeared. Not even the scent of whiskey lingered in the air.

Amanda fell back against the edge of the desk and held on with both hands. *I'm never going to get used to that.*

She was going to have to get used to James's sudden appearances and departures. She'd asked him back, hadn't she? Using the excuse of research was all well and good, but it wasn't the historical details that made her knees weak and sent her corpuscles into somersaults.

That was what did make relationships, she thought. An intellectual, emotional, physical connection. . . . What sort of future she'd find in romancing a ghost she couldn't begin to guess.

CHAPTER EIGHT

She made quite a picture, Amanda told herself, standing there in her colonial-era gown with a phone pressed to her ear. But since she had a window of only half an hour between the time Carrie arrived at the library and Melrose Hall opened for business, she'd dressed before making her call.

"Carrie Shaffer," said the slightly out of breath voice in her ear.

"Hi, it's Amanda. You must have just walked in the door. Sorry."

"Don't apologize—the sprint for the phone got my blood pumping. What can I do for you?"

"Tell me if those records have come in from London, yet."

"No, what I got was a note saying the personnel files of the Scottish Regiments are at the Scottish United Services Museum in Edinburgh."

"Go figure," said Amanda with a groan.

"I'll fax them this morning. What else have you found out about the 71st Highlanders?"

Between James' narration of what to him were current events and her late-night net surfing, Amanda was on top of it. "Fraser's Highlanders. Raised in 1775 by Simon Fraser, Lord Lovat. His father was the Simon Fraser, Lord Lovat, who holds the dubious distinction of having been the last peer of the realm to be beheaded. On Tower Hill, yet."

"One of Bonnie Prince Charlie's cohorts during the Jacobite Rebellion?" Carrie asked.

"That, plus he was a real scoundrel. In his eighties when it all caught up with him. Anyway, his son went around Scotland raising regiments trying to get back in the good graces of King George. The wee, wee German lairdie." Amanda sang the refrain of the derisive Jacobite song. "The first Fraser's Highlanders fought in the French and Indian War in the 1760's. Our 71st Regiment is the second. They landed in South Carolina in 1779 and were darn near wiped out by malaria. Commander was one Colonel Alexander Lindsay, Lord Balcarres."

"Yeah, Martin, be right there," Carrie said. "Sorry, Amanda, I've got a council of war. Overdue book policies. The sweet rolls and coffee are more tempting than the actual meeting, you understand, but I need to go."

"No, I'm sorry," Amanda told her with a laugh. "Enough is enough already. Just one more thing. When you fax Edinburgh, see if they know what happened to James Grant's sword."

"That's a pretty long shot, but I'll ask. Oh, and Cynthia was in here last night checking out a couple of prints. I suspect she and they will be appearing on your doorstep any minute now."

"Much as I'd like to go raise the drawbridge, I guess I'd be better off lowering it. Thanks, Carrie. See you tomorrow." Amanda turned off the phone and replaced it on its cradle.

Funny, she'd never been all that interested in military history before. But then, it'd never been so up close and personal before. She'd tossed and turned all night, remembering James's smooth baritone voice, the bewilderment and pride mingled in his face, the blue-gray eyes opening onto another world. Lafayette, disgruntled, had spent the night on the living room chair and departed through the cat flap as soon as he'd had his breakfast.

Amanda started her morning round by pausing in front of the portrait of Page in the library. "The old Roman," James had said. A good description. Page's granite jaw could have buttressed the Coliseum. No surprise James was intimidated. Even though—or especially since—it had been Sally who had thrown herself at him.

But, Amanda thought as she turned on the lights over the entrance hall display, James himself had given Page an alibi. Both Armstrongs left Melrose "yesterday evening"—in other words, on the evening before the day James died. Unless Page had sneaked back to erase a blot on his daughter's reputation.

James had said something, though, about his dolt of a cousin offending Sally. So why wasn't Archibald in Page's gun sights? For a moment Amanda considered James heroically taking a bullet for his cousin. But no. While the enraged-father-as-murderer scenario explained why James had been buried in the garden, it made assumptions about Page Armstrong Amanda simply couldn't justify.

She unlocked the front door and walked out into the sunlight just as Wayne arrived at the foot of the steps. "Greetings!" he called. "Look what Mother got from the library, since the miniature of Grant is only from the waist up." He indicated two framed prints beneath his arm.

They found space for the pictures at one side of the display flats. "Cool," Amanda said, and added to herself, an engraving, no matter how prettily hand-colored, wasn't nearly as cool as the genuine article.

"That one's an officer with the Black Watch," said Wayne. "Not the right regiment, but the right time period. The other one's from the right regiment, but from twenty years later, during the Napoleonic wars. At least he gets to wear pants."

The soldier's tartan trousers looked to Amanda like something her father would have worn in the sixties, except they weren't bell-bottoms. "Kilts are really sexy," she retorted.

Wayne guffawed and made a limp-wristed gesture.

Amanda shot a pointed glance at his knee breeches and silk stockings.

"Look at those hats," Wayne went on, oblivious. "Whoa."

Both soldiers wore Kilmarnock bonnets, blue woolen cylinders banded by red, green and white checks and adorned with feathers. Maybe it was just as well that while James had died with his shoes and socks on, he'd crossed into another dimension without his hat. "Fashion doesn't take any prisoners, does it?" Amanda said. "But the Highland soldiers were outstanding fighters, no matter how they dressed."

"I'd like to see them tackle an Abrams tank."

"Yeah, right." Amanda turned toward the door.

Wayne pulled her back again, clasped her shoulders, and bent his face close to hers. "We need to talk, Amanda. Before the others get here."

"What else can I possibly say to you, Wayne?" She tried to shrug him off but his hands stayed firm, if very gentle. It was like confronting a giant teddy bear.

"We're friends, right?" he asked.

"Most of the time."

"But, you know, that's a good place to start a relationship, between friends."

Amanda shook her head. Years of wheedling Cynthia for favors made Wayne incapable of taking "no" for an answer. "That's not where our friendship is heading. I'm sorry, but there it is."

"I love you," he said with a earnest sigh. The odor of Crest Mint Gel bathed her face.

"No you . . ." No matter how annoyed she was, she had no right denying the man his feelings. Although she could fudge her own a bit. "Listen, Wayne, I'm not looking for Mr. Right just now. Okay? I need to get my master's degree, and find a good job—it's not like I'm in computer science, you know, my brother's barely a senior and already has a position lined up."

His hands kneaded her shoulders. His face sagged.

"Besides," she went on, pulling against his grasp, "I'm not so sure that Mr. Right, or Miss Right, isn't a lot more likely to sneak up on you when you're not looking. Now will you please let me go?"

He released her so abruptly she lurched back into the display flat. The Lucite box with the bone fragments slid onto her shoulder and she grabbed it with both hands. James's portrait fell onto its face. Wayne leaped forward to seize one of the prints. A long breathless moment later, the wire holding the second one broke with a ping and it crashed to the floor.

In spite of her stays Amanda was on the print before Wayne could reach it. It wasn't broken. Had she knocked it over or was James making his presence known again?

She replaced the box with the bones, opened the one with the miniature and set it upright, propped the print against the leg of the display, and scowled. "Good one, Wayne!"

"I'm sorry," he moaned. "That was beyond stupid. You're not going to sue me for sexual harassment, are you?"

And lose my job? Amanda retorted silently. But he was already crushed. She didn't need to rub it in. Reversing her scowl into a stiff smile she said, "Come on. Get a grip. Everything's cool."

A movement in the back hallway was Lafayette, padding purposefully toward the front door. Amanda swished across the hallway—it was very satisfying having long skirts to swish—and opened the door for him. She followed him down the steps, intending to go all the way to front gate and shanghai a group of Cub Scouts if necessary, but already several people were advancing along the gravel walk. "We're in business," she said over her shoulder, and switched her mental facilities into antique-speak.

To his credit, Wayne pulled himself together and played Page in his usual accomplished way. In fact, he'd obviously been doing his own research. Again and again during the day he stopped his tour groups by the display and regaled them with stories of the Highland regiments.

"After the rebellion of 1745, the English encouraged the creation of Highland regiments in order to employ the Highlanders in a manner advantageous to England. 'And no great mischief if they fall', as General Wolfe has pointed out. Prime Minister William Pitt has authorized the recruitment of men even from the disaffected clans, because 'not many of them will return.'"

By the end of the day Amanda was wading in. "By raising regiments, the Scottish gentry assimilates with the dominant English culture. For the ambitious landowner, the army is a way to social advancement and often a way to reclaim land confiscated during the late unpleasantness."

"What about the peasants?" someone asked.

"Some tenant families are blackmailed by their landlords into putting their sons into scarlet coats," replied Wayne. "Even so, more than one soldier returns home to find his family gone and his cottage destroyed. Some of the misrepresentations made to the recruits are leading to demands for honorable treatment and even mutiny."

"Those settlers who came here from Scotland," Amanda went on, "have found their loyalties tested during the present hostilities. Some fight for the King, while others have gone to the British colonies in Canada."

"And, if the truth be told, there are voices in Parliament which support the rights of the American colonies," concluded Wayne.

A tourist with a bristling gray moustache inspected the prints. "Have you ever thought that the armies with the fanciest uniforms are almost always the ones that lose? The Nazis during WWII, for example. Oh, excuse me," he added with a smile, "I suppose you haven't heard of that one."

Amanda and Wayne shared a calculatedly puzzled glance. "But I follow your reasoning, sir," Amanda said. "It is evidence of complacency and pride to bring the same uniforms to Virginia's or to India's heat that served so well in Britain's chill. Or, many years ago, for Roman officials to build open villas in that same British chill, as though sheer force of will can dominate a climate."

The sightseers laughed. Wayne bowed them out the door into the blast of heat and sunshine. "Many thanks for your company. If you would do us the honor to visit the gift shop."

Amanda glanced at the miniature portrait. If Cynthia had the bright idea of hiring an interpreter to play James this summer, he'd need an outfit with an air-conditioner, like an astronaut.

Wayne shut the door. "I'll run upstairs and make sure everything's okay. You can do the downstairs."

"Thanks." That was Amanda's job, but if he was trying to make up, she wasn't going to argue. She strolled through the library and replaced a couple of books that were lying open on the desk. The ink blot still curled across the blotter, with the addition of a tic-tac-toe game and a couple of four-letter words in childish printing. She tore that sheet off and threw it away.

In the back hall she ran into Roy. "How's it going?"

"Some of the tourists have really good questions," he answered. "You'd swear others just fell off the turnip truck. One guy asked me . . ."

A sharp cry echoed through the house, followed by a series of muffled thuds. Something substantial was falling down the stairs—maybe that something substantial which had just gone up the stairs. Amanda grabbed her skirts and ran, but Roy beat her to the scene.

Wayne lay crumpled at the bottom of the staircase. Strewn behind him, marking his path down the steps, were his wig, one of his silver-buckled shoes, and his pocket watch. His face was ashen.

Roy knelt beside him and cradled his head. "Are you all right?"

By easing herself down the newel post Amanda was able to kneel, too. "Wayne?"

Wayne's eyelids fluttered and his mouth twitched. "Fear not, fair lady, 'tis but a flesh wound."

"Wayne!" Amanda patted him down, but found only a scraped knee that was bleeding through his hose. Good thing he was so well padded. "Move your fingers and toes. Now your arms and legs, yeah, like that. I don't think anything's broken. Unless you cracked a rib—does it hurt to take a breath?"

"I hurt all over," Wayne groaned. "But no, the ribs are okay."

"Man, you're going to have bruises on top of your bruises," Roy told him. "Come on, let's see if you can stand up."

Roy was much more help to Wayne than Amanda was. She had to concentrate on getting herself to her feet. But once there she took Wayne's other arm. He swayed gently between her and Roy, taking inventory. "My ankle," he said at last, and tried to put his weight on his unshod foot. "Yow! No go, folks. It may not be broken but it's sure as hell sprained."

"Maybe we should call an ambulance," Amanda suggested.

"Oh no, no," protested Wayne. "No way. Just help me to my car, I don't drive with my left foot anyway."

"All right," Roy said reluctantly, "but I'm coming with you. You have to get to a doctor."

"I'm okay," Wayne insisted.

His color was better, Amanda noted. She walked up the stairs to collect his watch, shoe, and wig, and gave all three to Roy. "I'll come with you."

"No, no, no," said Wayne. "I'm just fine. You have to lock up the house."

"All right. But I'm going to call and check on you."

"No need, I'm fine—ouch!" Wayne took a step, then another. By leaning heavily on Roy he made it out the door, down the steps, and into the sun.

Amanda draped Wayne's other arm over her shoulder. The three of them hobbled down the gravel walk in an awkward five-legged gait. "What happened?" she asked. "Did somebody leave a candy wrapper on the stairs?"

"I—er—I don't know," Wayne replied. "I just fell over my feet, I guess. You know how clumsy I am."

There was something behind his words, an edge Amanda couldn't quite classify. He *was* clumsy, she thought, although more socially than physically. She'd heard that Princess Diana had thrown herself down the stairs to get her husband's sympathy. But even Wayne wasn't that neurotic, to risk breaking his neck just to make Amanda feel sorry for him.

What if he'd arranged the wig, the shoe, and the watch, then jumped from the bottom tread and thrashed around to make noise? But he wasn't asking her to come home with him and soothe his brow.

She grimaced. It wasn't light work hauling Wayne down the slipping and sliding gravel of the walk. He wasn't faking his ankle, that was for sure, any more than he was faking the scrape on his knee. Even if the fall had started out as a stunt, he really was hurt.

At last they had Wayne at his car. Roy offered to drive. Wayne wouldn't hear of it. Rolling his eyes, Roy climbed into the passenger seat. "I'll call the Benedettos and let them know my car's still out here," he told Amanda. "I'll catch a ride with Carrie tomorrow."

"I'll bring you myself." Wayne offered Amanda a jaunty grin missing only Indiana Jones's old hat. The engine roared and the car pulled out, scattering gravel.

Amanda was too short of breath to call good-bye. She stood panting, her lungs filled with the odors of auto exhaust, Wayne's after shave, and sweat. Her shadow stretched out before her, pointing to the gardens. *Gardens,* she thought.

Tomorrow the garden club was holding its monthly luncheon in the dining room, one of the many perks Cynthia had retained when she donated Melrose to CW. Thank goodness Carrie would be here. She doubted Wayne would be. She saw him mummified in adhesive tape and painted with iodine, laid out on a Williamsburg Collection reproduction settee, Cynthia feeding him chicken soup from a demitasse spoon. Maybe, she thought, he was trying to get attention not from her but from his mother.

If they gave out Oscars for most irritating person, today Wayne would've won hands down. But he had so many redeeming features, reaming him out wouldn't be one bit satisfying. Which was even more irritating.

Amanda stalked back into the house feeling like a lathered horse. She spent a long time doing aquatic aerobics in the shower. Then she fed Lafayette, who had of course finished his rounds and was ready for dinner well before she'd even thought about hers. By the time she'd gone through the grounds and around the house it was almost dark.

Turning on all the lights in the upstairs and downstairs halls, she checked out the top of the staircase. She found no kinks in the carpet, no lost pencils, nothing to have made Wayne fall. Sally's painted eyes looked impassively down from her portrait, offering no help.

All right, Amanda told herself, so there was nothing here for Wayne to have tripped over. That didn't mean her crazy theory was right. His fall had been an accident. It was surprising more accidents didn't happen, with the interpreters running around in unfamiliar clothing. He'd snagged his shoe buckle against his opposite ankle or something. Just because he was playing the situation for all it was worth didn't mean he was guilty of . . .

Whoa. Amanda stopped dead on the fourth step from the bottom. What if Wayne had seen James? Just a glint of scarlet in the shadows, maybe, enough to startle him and make him miss the first step? That would explain the edge in his voice—he wasn't sure he'd seen anything at all, let alone a ghostly figure. Better to be called a klutz than nuts. But it'd been full daylight, which made that scenario, too, unlikely.

She made a mental note to ask Wayne. It'd be sort of comforting to know someone else had seen James, however briefly.

Back in her apartment Amanda gathered sandwich fixings from the refrigerator and tucked the telephone between her shoulder and cheek. "Hello, Mrs. Chancellor? This is Amanda Witham at Melrose. I was just checking to see how Wayne is doing."

"Why, how nice of you to call," replied Cynthia's candied voice. "He's resting comfortably, thank you. A bit of a sprained ankle, some bruises, nothing too bad. The doctor suggested he stay home tomorrow." Wayne's voice bellowed in the background, then was muffled as Cynthia either closed a door or pressed a pillow over his face. "Can you and Carrie handle the visitors all alone? Of course, you'll have the 'servants', and the caterers for the luncheon, and I'll be there with the garden club, if there's anything I can do to help. I'll try to have Wayne back out there on Saturday, he'll be limping, but we'll just have to pretend Page has gout or something. Thank you again for calling, you're so sweet to think of us. Good night."

"Good ni . . ." The line was already dead. Amanda set the phone down on the cabinet, wondering how Cynthia had learned to speak entire paragraphs without breathing.

Tonight the cozy apartment was too small and too warm. Amanda wrapped her sandwich in a napkin, turned off the floodlights, and stepped out into the night. She sat down on a bench beside the front walk. The trees, the lawn, the river were sketched in shades of gray beneath a lucid Prussian blue sky. Between bites of sandwich she watched a glow on the eastern horizon swell into the rising moon. Just past the full, it made a bronze oval like the badge on James's scabbard. In the pale light the shadows of the trees darkened to inky black. *Is this romantic or what?* Amanda asked herself. She might as well be at the multiplex wallowing in some vivid fantasy.

A cold breeze lifted her hair, but not one leaf rustled. Gooseflesh rose on her skin. She spun around. Speaking of fantasy. . . .

James was seated comfortably next to her, one arm and hand resting on his lap, the other crooked over the back of the bench. He glowed faintly in the darkness, shadowless. "Good evening, Miss Witham."

"Erk . . ." She gulped down a mouthful of ham and cheese. "Good evening, Captain Grant."

"Please, continue with your repast. I—I have already supped." James's eyes fell and he frowned, as though trying to remember something. Like the menu of a meal eaten two hundred years ago.

Amanda nibbled at the crust of the bread. But she didn't want the sandwich any more, not when she had such a feast for her senses.

James seemed every bit as concrete as he'd been the night before. The planes and angles of his profile were cut flawlessly against the moonlit night. His lashes concealed his downcast eyes. His hand on the tartan fabric was lean and strong, the nails neatly pared. The topic of eighteenth-century fingernails wasn't on Amanda's agenda, but she suspected James's should have been dirty.

Was it his wealth that had kept him and his uniform spiffy after two years' slogging around the southern colonies? Or was she seeing him not as he had actually looked at his time of death, but how he imagined himself to look? If he were generating his own image, though, he'd have his sword. And the scabbard at his side was still empty.

Maybe this was how she wanted him to look, attractive not only physically but conceptually, the ultimate mysterious stranger.

He raised his head and smiled at her. The bread turned to dust in her mouth. Her analysis burned to ash in the light of his eyes.

This guy is good. Really good. And he knew it. She put the rest of the sandwich down on the low wall behind the bench. Having him watch her eat was like having him watch her change clothes, rushing things a bit for a—what? Second date?

He tilted his head to the side like a bird contemplating a worm. "Your color is high, Miss Witham. I trust you are not succumbing to the sickness of these warm climates, that which is caused by the putrefaction of vegetable matter and the unhealthy night air. Perhaps we should retire inside."

"No problem," she said. "Very few people around here get mal—the sweating sickness—any more."

"Indeed? How fortunate."

"I—er. . . ." Well, this wasn't a date, was it? Weather, a celebrity scandal, the latest movie—those topics weren't going to cut it. But James, like most people, liked to talk about himself. If she got him going on what to him was contemporary color, she could use the details to punch up her thesis. As long as she remembered all the suitable academic qualifiers. James was definitely a source she'd have to keep secret. Not Deep Throat, but Deep Kilt. "Tell me more about London. I've never been there."

"Ah, London. New squares and new streets rise up every day in such a prodigy of buildings that nothing in the world can equal it except old Rome in Trajan's time, perhaps. But Rome today is sadly decayed, as are its monuments, and London has been built afresh since the great fire of the last century. Mr. Wren's churches are famous for their handsome steeples, and the mighty dome of St. Paul's rises over all, the equal of St. Peter's without a doubt."

"You've been to Rome, too?"

"Certainly. A gentleman must have a proper education, mustn't he?"

"I imagine you've been properly educated," Amanda said dryly.

James grinned, taking her meaning. His hand slipped away from his lap and took hers. Funny how someone who hadn't the least concept of electricity could send electric sparks through her body. Doubly funny, that though she wasn't really touching him, she could feel him the way she could feel a breeze on her cheek or water trickling down her back.

"It seems she hangs upon the cheek of night," James murmured, "Like a rich jewel in an Ethiop's ear; Beauty too rich for use, for earth too dear."

Those lines from *Romeo and Juliet* weren't nearly as moldy an oldie in 1781, Amanda told herself. In James's slightly ironic voice the phone book would seem profound. She cleared her throat. "What about 'My love is like a red, red rose'?"

His eyebrow quirked. "A colonial verse?"

"Robert Burns."

The other brow rose.

"You've been spending too much time in London and not enough in Edinburgh."

"Edinburgh," he said. "The tenements crowded together above the dark depths of the loch and the castle frowning over all like a specter of ancient and weary Time. And yet I am told there are plans afoot to build a fine new city in the best model of London."

"Some Scot you are, singing the praises of London."

"And why not, Madame, when such interchanges make a beneficial mixture of manners and render our union more complete? Scotland's union with England, that is to say." His amendment only emphasized the double meaning of his earlier words. His thumb caressed the hills and valleys of her knuckles, considering the possibility of other, more private, hills and valleys.

Amanda was caught between amusement and lust. *I can't really touch him,* she reminded herself. Then why was the flirting of his thumb across her knuckles so exciting?

Amanda raised her free hand and set it against James's chest, on the silver buckle of the shoulder belt. The buckle she'd seen tarnished and dirty, and which now lay in the box in the entrance hall, still stained with age. Beneath her fingertips it gleamed like myth—Laurian silver or Tolkien's mithril—there, she could sling around literary references just as well as he could.

She sensed pressure, and coolness, and the faintest, most distant vibration, as though a heart beat in the chest beneath the belt and the scarlet coat. But it was only an illusion of a heartbeat, wasn't it?

She dropped her left hand, retrieved her right, and stood up. The man wasn't real—yes he was, he was a real ghost—he was as real as she wanted him to be and as he wanted himself to be. This place was real. This time was real. Why couldn't her fantasy be real, too?

The moonlight shimmered on the river and spangled every leaf and branch as though the Virginia landscape, too, wore silver fittings. A footstep crunched on the gravel walk. He was standing behind her. Every follicle on the back of her neck tightened to the quick cool stirring of—his breath, he had breath, or a memory of breath.

"Amanda?" James asked. "If I may presume to address you so familiarly."

"Yes," she replied.

"Be not melancholy. The war will soon end. All will be well, in one way or the other."

"Yes." She turned around. No surprise James was close behind her. She found herself nose to chin with him. The ruffle at his throat and the kilt at his knee were subtle tickles against her chin and her thigh. His arms closed around her, leaving her hands spread on the fragile resonance that was his scarlet coat and his chest beneath. *Go for it.* Wreathed in the smoky sweet aroma of whiskey, she opened her lips for his and shuddered in delight at his kiss.

It was a teasing hint of a kiss, a delicate merging of lips and tongues, more a tension in her skin and a melting warmth in her stomach. And yet his body was undeniable beneath her hands and mouth, leaning insistently into hers, *there.* She'd never felt anything like it before. She wasn't just turned on, she was flying high.

After several long and gratifying minutes Amanda came up for air. She hung onto James until her knees stopped bending backwards, like a giraffe's, and then looked into his eyes.

At a distance of only a few inches they were no less vivid, crinkled with pleasure. Pleasure, not triumph. Sally Armstrong would have slapped his face for an embrace and a kiss a lot less invasive than that one. She would have had the vapors for days worrying it would tarnish her reputation. To Amanda the kiss was only the overture and the curtain going up. *On what?*

James spoke first. "If I have offended your delicate nature, Amanda, I apologize. But your beauty overwhelms me."

If she responded with a crass twenty-first century retort, would he vanish? She didn't want to find out. She didn't know what she wanted. She didn't know what he wanted, for that matter—he had his name back, didn't he?

As a man of his time, he might want an evening's recreation from her. As a man out of his time, he might want comfort from a living woman. Or he might be repeating the pattern imprinted on him before his death—Melrose and a woman. "What do you want, James?" she asked.

He blinked. Uncertainty moved like a wave up and down his face. His eyes looked somewhere beyond Amanda, beyond the moon and the night. "I want my sword," he said.

Duh. She should've figured that one out for herself. And just how symbolic was his sword anyway, especially now? But James Grant had, thank goodness, lived long before Freudian theory. "What if I find your sword for you?"

"Then, then. . . ."

She'd done it now. His body thinned, so that she could see the dimly lit windows of her apartment through his chest. Even though she could see her hands and arms embracing him, she could no longer feel him.

As long as he ignored his circumstances, she thought, as long as he pretended he knew where he was and what he was doing there, he could maintain the illusion of life. "James."

His face firmed. His eyes focussed on Amanda's, gleaming hard as gemstones. "If I had my sword I could go home with honor, home to Dundreggan, honor intact—with my sword I could avenge . . ."

He was gone, but his voice lingered in a cry of rage and pain. Even after it, too, faded, Amanda stood stock still in the middle of the path.

Avenge what? His death? But why should he have to return home to do that? The American hand that fired the fatal bullet had long ago turned into American dust.

"Go home with honor," he'd said. Maybe he'd left Scotland under some sort of cloud. Maybe his service here in the colonies was intended to buy him back his honor, the honor a man of his era and his class would think more important than life itself.

A man of his era. Amanda looked up at the indifferent face of the moon. It wasn't fair. Why should the one man she could never have be more compelling than any other man she'd ever met?

CHAPTER NINE

"Robert Burns," read the entry in the encyclopedia, "began writing poetry in 1783." No wonder James had never heard of him, Amanda told herself. "Ae fond kiss and then we sever, Ae fareweel, and then forever." Burns had his depressingly realistic moments.

She shut the book, put it back on the shelf, and closed the doors of the cabinet. Her reflection wavered in the glass, a twenty-first-century woman wearing eighteenth-century fashion and dabbling in eighteenth-century romance.

Back then a kiss would've been filled with mystery and magic. Now nothing about the entire spectrum of physical love was at all mysterious, let alone magical. Of course, if the mystery was gone, so was the shame. You lose some, you win some.

Amanda's former roommates might have settled for casual encounters on back seats and park benches, but she never had. She'd planned her relationships carefully, trying to create magic and mystery. Her former lovers—all two of them—were nice, well-meaning guys, and the relationships had been rewarding enough within their contexts.

So here she was in a very old context that was plenty new to her. Amanda left the library, went into the main kitchen, and unlocked the back door. The morning was hazy but fresh, like James's eyes. And just about as warm.

He was a man of his time, not hers, she reminded herself. The glow of the Age of Enlightenment hadn't necessarily illuminated the shadowy corners of the bedroom. By eighteenth-century standards James was being very bold with her. Partly from the soldier's eternal imperative—now or never—but also because of Amanda's seemingly unconventional dress and manners. Last night's kiss alone put her beyond the pale. Now he'd expect her to put up or shut up.

"Good morning!" Two white-coated figures stood before her, one male and one female, carrying covered trays and grinning from ear to ear.

Amanda grinned back. "Oh! Oh, hi! Sorry, I didn't see you come around the corner."

"You were a million miles away," said the woman.

"About two hundred years away, actually," Amanda replied. "You're from the caterer, aren't you? Come on in, make yourself at home." She stepped back from the door so they could get inside, and hovered while they went back and forth to their truck.

Soon Carrie and Roy arrived, too. Roy stayed in the kitchen to brief the other interpreters on today's line—that Page had been unexpectedly called away to a meeting of the House of Burgesses.

Carrie and Amanda fixed a placard to the OPEN sign by the front door: WE REGRET THAT THE DINING ROOM OF MELROSE HALL WILL BE CLOSED FROM NOON TO TWO P.M. TODAY. "Hope no one will be too disappointed," said Amanda as they took their positions at the top of the steps.

"Maybe Cynthia will let us leave the door cracked, so the peasants can catch a glimpse of their betters at feeding time."

Amanda laughed. "Heard anything from Wayne?"

"Not directly. Cynthia says he's making a speedy recovery, and will be back at work tomorrow. What happened, anyway?"

"He tripped over his own feet," Amanda replied cautiously. "I thought at first he'd done it on purpose, to make me feel sorry for him, but he really is hurt."

"Poor Wayne. He's like Frankenstein's monster, put together from Cynthia's leftovers."

"Will he ever be struck by lightning and transformed into a man?"

"Not if he runs to Mommy every time a storm comes up." Carrie shook her head. "If we don't get a fax from Edinburgh today about our mysterious Captain Grant we'll have to wait until next week."

"Rats. I could try and find an e-mail address for the Grants themselves, I guess. Or just ask Lady C. for their phone number."

"You've really gotten hooked on the guy, haven't you?"

"He's a little more exciting than anyone in real time," Amanda told her, right up front.

"Hard to make out with a miniature portrait and some bones, though," teased Carrie.

Amanda managed an inscrutable smile. The first customers of the day came walking up the path and she and Carrie dropped into their roles.

One group came and went, and two, and three. By late morning the dining room was resplendent with white linen and bone china, and delectable smells were wafting from the kitchen. The interpreters used every excuse to drop by and sample the rejects—an overdone roll, a too pale strawberry, a radish rose that looked more like a dandelion. Even the archaeological students were attracted from the depths of the garden, their muddy feet smudging the back steps while the caterers handed goodies out the door. Lafayette padded tirelessly around legs and between tables and chairs, pouncing on any scrap as it hit the floor.

Cynthia and the florist arrived just before noon. Lady C. stood over the woman while she set out the centerpiece, a lush but tasteful arrangement of roses, carnations, lilies, and baby's breath. The florist escaped down the walk past the incoming pastel dresses of the garden club.

Amanda and Carrie curtsied and directed the dozen or so women inside. A few lingered by the display in the entrance hall, commenting on the truth of the famous Melrose legend, but still the dining room doors shut promptly at noon. The clink of silver against china and various feminine twitters began to filter into the hallway. "Cynthia runs a tight ship," Amanda commented.

"She gets things done, no doubt about it," returned Carrie. "Roy's been grazing in the kitchen long enough. Let's put him on the front door and see if there's some extra salmon mousse."

There was, as Lafayette's satisfied smirk confirmed. The courses came and went, soapsuds bubbled in the sink, and one last bite of peach melba dissolved on Amanda's tongue. "Delicious," she told the caterers. "Thank you for letting us have some of the leftovers."

"If I wrap up the rest," the man replied, "you think those kids digging in the garden will eat them?"

"They won't even wash their hands first," Carrie assured him.

Back in the front hall Roy was ushering another tour group outside. The dining room door opened and Amanda glanced around at it. "Amanda, dear," said Cynthia. "Bring in that picture of James Grant, would you please?"

Amanda took the miniature out of its box and into the dining room. She expected Cynthia to be seated at the head of the table, but no, she occupied a modest spot midway down its side, opposite the door. Amanda set the portrait down between Cynthia's coffee cup and the centerpiece. When she turned to slip out again, Cynthia's manicured talon seized her wrist and pulled her back. "This is Amanda Witham, who plays Sally Armstrong for us. She's the sweetest thing, so pretty and polite."

Amanda shaped her mouth into a demure smile, and said to herself, *if you only knew.* "May I be of assistance, Madame?"

"Yes, dear, you may. We've had quite the daring idea for our entertainment today—well, to be fair, it was Julia's perfectly brilliant suggestion." A bird-like woman in frilly pink—Cynthia's stooge, Amanda guessed—nodded weakly. "Betsy, you'll give your little talk on tax reform next time, won't you?" A large woman in a lilac tent attempted a smile. "We need for you to close the blinds, Amanda, and light that candle on the end of the sideboard. I think you'd better turn off the fans, too. We're going to have a seance."

Amanda opened her mouth, found it empty except for a couple of words that wouldn't lie gently on Cynthia's shell-like ears, and closed it again. She shuttered the windows, turned off the box fans in the corners, took a book of matches from the sideboard and with a whiff of sulfur lit the candle.

"Bring it here," Cynthia directed.

Amanda set the candlestick next to the miniature. James's painted features gazed from their frame with the same ironic self-awareness she found so stimulating in the—existing—man.

"Now turn off the lights," ordered Cynthia. "But stay there by the door, please, so you can turn them back on."

Amanda flicked the switch, plunging the room into dusk. Lines of white light edged the shutters. The candle gleamed a steady yellow. Without the breeze from the fans the room grew warm and close, the odors of food, roses, and bath powders thickening the air. Voices rose and fell in the entrance hall, then with multiple footsteps receded upstairs.

"Now let's all place our hands on the tabletop and close our eyes," said Cynthia. Dutifully everyone splayed her fingers on the table and ducked her head. Amanda stood watching. Did anyone really believe she could summon James's ghost? Surely Cynthia didn't. She was merely playing games with the household legend and its archaeological sequel.

"Oh dear," Cynthia said with a little laugh, "I'm not quite sure how to begin. I mean, it's daylight and everything. Well. Let's try calling him." She raised her voice. "Captain James Grant, are you here? Give us a sign if you're here. Your physical form has been here a long time, Captain Grant. Let us know if your spirit is here as well."

Silence. Sweat gathered along Amanda's hairline. She strained her eyes through the shadows. On the one hand she wanted James to suddenly appear, preferably standing on the table, and scare the crap out of Cynthia. On the other hand she wanted Cynthia to blow it big time. James didn't come and go on anyone's whim. He had a mind of his own.

A cool draft tickled her face and then was gone. Air movement around the door?

"You remember Melrose Hall." Cynthia's voice was losing inflection, becoming hypnotic. "You spent almost two weeks here, Captain Grant. Do you remember sharing tender moments with Sally? Do you remember cutting at the banisters—you were a naughty boy, weren't you, Captain Grant?"

Amanda blinked. The room darkened as the candle no longer burned yellow but a deep orange red.

"Captain James Grant, are you here? Give us a sign."

Upstairs a door slammed. Everyone around the table jumped, and one or two eyes glinted before shutting again.

"Eyes closed, ladies," Cynthia said. "Hands on the table."

Another draft brushed Amanda's warm cheeks, cooling them. *It's going to hit the fan now,* she thought. They shouldn't have called him. Whatever formless consciousness he was between appearances was as mischievous as a poltergeist.

Cynthia leaned forward, pursed her lips, and blew. The candle went out, its trail of smoke a ghostly gray shape wavering upward. Several women squeaked. The dense, scented air was congealing in Amanda's lungs. Her eyes, adjusted to the dark, detected Cynthia's slow and subtle movements.

Her right hand went into the pocket of her dress, then, holding something that glinted in the feeble reflection of daylight, snaked forward. "Captain Grant," she crooned. "James Grant, give us a sign that you're here." Her voice concealed the snips of the nail scissors. Three decapitated roses fell to the tablecloth. Slowly Cynthia returned her hand to her pocket and closed her eyes. "Captain Grant?"

The nerve! Amanda thought with an incredulous grin. Other people played games. Cynthia orchestrated Olympic events.

The candle flared with light again. The candlestick rose from the table, one inch, two, and tilted to the side. Amanda's grin changed into a grimace. One candle might not burn the house down, but James's presence didn't need to be playing with fire, any time, anyhow. *James? Hello?*

Maybe his force field responded to her emotion. Maybe he got bored playing around. The candlestick settled back down. The leaves and flowers of the centerpiece bowed as though to a stroking hand and then straightened again.

The room was dark and silent and hot. Amanda tried to breathe. But Cynthia hadn't noticed the candle move. If her eyes had been open just then, Amanda would have seen them shining like a cat's.

"Turn on the lights, please, Amanda." Cynthia's voice was calm and composed. "Well, my goodness."

In the sudden rush of light the three red roses and their scattered petals looked like bloodstains on the white tablecloth. Their color mimicked that of James's painted coat. Several of the women seemed frightened, others skeptical, but none of them were shrugging it all away. Cynthia rose from her chair. "I'll be having a few words with the florist. If the flowers had been fresh-cut they'd have survived the heat without any problem."

"But what if it was the ghost?" someone asked. "The candle went out and lit itself again, didn't it?"

"A draft, no doubt—I'm afraid nothing happened that can't be explained rationally—but it was fun, wasn't it? Something to tell your neighbors about." Cynthia picked up the miniature and gave it to Amanda. "Put this back, please. It's almost two o'clock, we have to get the room cleaned up and opened again. . . ." The party was over. The ladies of the garden club went murmuring, heads close together, across the hall and out the front door.

Amanda paused in the dining room doorway to see Cynthia sweep the table with a long, speculative look. A slight smile played across her pink lips. She tucked her purse beneath her arm with the air of a soldier shouldering his rifle. Turning, she met Amanda's eyes. Not the least trace of embarrassment crossed her expression. She closed one mauve eyelid, set her forefinger against her nose, and sailed out the door.

Yeah, right. Amanda put the miniature back into its box and returned to the dining room. The candlestick was still on the table. She replaced it on the sideboard, next to the three others in the set. The candle's stark white didn't match the creamy shade of the others. *Aha!* Cynthia had smuggled in a candle that wouldn't stay extinguished—Amanda had once put a set of smaller ones on her father's birthday cake. Yes, there was the original candle, tucked into a drawer of the sideboard. She pried the trick candle from its holder and put the real one back.

Here came the caterers, invading the room with plastic bins and brooms. Amanda scooted into the entrance hall. How soon, she wondered, before the garden ladies told everyone in Tidewater Virginia about the mysterious happenings at Melrose and another rush of tourists descended upon the place? Clever of Cynthia, to pretend nothing strange had happened. Too obvious a ghost wouldn't be nearly as believable.

But then, had Cynthia played the trick, or had it been played on her? She'd gone to the trouble to create a ghost when there really was one. Amanda was almost sorry James hadn't gone ahead and set the tablecloth on fire, except she wouldn't have wanted any of the other women to have heart attacks. She doubted if the devil himself could penetrate Cynthia's brass shell.

Amanda dumped the prank candle in the trash just as Carrie looked in the kitchen door. "A seance?" she stage-whispered. "Who does she think she's kidding?"

"No one," Amanda replied. "She's merely casting rumor upon the public waters, hoping it'll return in the form of more admissions."

"Why do I want so badly to throw a cream pie in her face?" Carrie disappeared toward the front door.

Grinning, Amanda followed and greeted the next group of tourists. But her humor wore thin as the afternoon dragged on. Should she tell Carrie how Cynthia faked the seance? Carrie would get a kick out of the truth. But if Amanda started talking about James as a ghost, rather than as a historical figure, she might give herself away. Tomorrow, she decided, after everything had settled a bit. It wasn't as though Cynthia's cunning was hurting anything—it was all in the cause of historical preservation—and it wasn't entirely dishonest, although Lady C. meant it to be.... Since when, Amanda asked herself, did the end justify the means? Cynthia got her jollies from manipulating people. She deserved Carrie's cream pie in the face.

Between the day's heat and its moral questions, by quitting time Amanda felt as wrung out as one of the caterer's dish rags. She handed the last of the food to the departing students, waved good-bye to Carrie and Roy, and checked over the kitchen. Everything was ship-shape, as usual for anything under Cynthia's control.

Amanda washed and changed and roamed around outside. The summerhouse excavation was looking very tidy, the foundations completely exposed and marked with little tags. She hoped his students had brought Dr. Hewitt some of the luncheon goodies.

Japanese beetles were eating the roses in the top terrace. Amanda noted the fact on her clipboard. And the kitchen garden needed weeding. She pulled out a tuft or two of green herself, before it occurred to her that she might be murdering some kind of antique onion or spinach.

She went back inside and inspected the house. Not one object was out of place. The desk blotter was pristine. In the entrance hall the portrait, the bones, the silver buckle and fittings, were anonymous shapes in the shadows. James must have tired himself out waving the candle around. Amanda couldn't even imagine how much energy it took to levitate an object, let alone materialize.

She was back in her apartment before she realized she hadn't seen Lafayette. She tried running the can opener. Nothing. Surely he hadn't eaten so much in the main kitchen he wouldn't at least see what she had to offer.

In the gathering darkness she walked through the house again, opening closet doors and dresser drawers. Lafayette looked up from his nest on a stack of towels in a kitchen cupboard and meowed.

"What are you doing in there?" she asked him. "Had to check out an open door? Sleeping off the salmon, I'll bet. You might have been in there all night. Come on."

Lafayette stretched and yawned, making it clear that he was only cooperating out of generosity and good breeding. He followed her back to her apartment and accepted a few morsels of food.

Amanda stood holding the cat kibble and wondering whether James's invisible alter ego had either lured Lafayette into the cupboard or shut the doors once he was already inside. The conscious James wasn't exactly a cat-lover, but then, in his time period few people were. . . .

Assuming James had shut Lafayette in the cabinet was like assuming Wayne had thrown himself down the staircase, Amanda told herself firmly, and put her momentary misgiving away with the box of cat food.

CHAPTER TEN

Amanda shifted tubs and bags haphazardly around the interior of the refrigerator, telling herself she should eat a serving of crow for letting Cynthia to make an accomplice out of her. But she was fresh out of crow. She was reaching for a package of cheese when the phone rang.

"Melrose Hall. Amanda Witham."

"It's me, Carrie. Guess what?"

"The fax came in?"

"Sure did, about eleven o'clock this morning. Martin left a message on my machine, so I ran up here to the library and picked it up. I'll meet you at the McDonald's in fifteen minutes—that way I can pick up some burgers for the guys."

"You're on," Amanda said. She grabbed her purse and car keys and let herself out of the house. Cynthia's dainty little garden party edibles, while delicious at the time, hadn't stayed with her. Nothing like a scholarly quest to work up an appetite. Or intriguing sexual prospects, for that matter.

The bright colors and slick lines of the McDonald's contrasted nicely with Melrose's antique graces. Amanda bought herself a Big Mac and a Coke and found Carrie at a booth in the corner, sucking reflectively on a milkshake. A brown envelope lay on the table in front of her.

"Gimme, gimme," Amanda said, sliding onto the opposite bench. She reached for the envelope but Carrie slapped her hands away.

"All in due order, Miss Witham. First of all..." Putting on her glasses,

Carrie took out a page of paper overflowing with eighteenth-century script. Two lines were highlighted with a yellow marker. ". . . the statistics: Captain James Grant of Dundreggan, Inverness-shire. Born Dundreggan, March 1754. Died Virginia, July 1781."

Amanda thought, *he is—was—twenty-seven.*

Carrie pulled two more papers from the envelope. "This page is a letter from Colonel Alexander Lindsay, Earl of Balcarres, to James's parents. Dated July 7, 1781, the day after the battle at Greensprings Farm. The other page is a transcription."

Even from her upside-down viewpoint Amanda could see that the second page was typewritten. "That must have been done a long time ago, judging by the typeface, but anything's better than plowing through eighteenth-century handwriting. What does it say?"

"I'll spare you the formal syntax, but what it boils down to is that James died a noble death leading his troops. No more details given, but a bullet through the heart doesn't leave much room for details."

"Tell me about it," Amanda said, and remembered how James had answered when she used that expression on him.

"Balcarres goes on to tender his respects to James's uncle, who we've met before—Simon Fraser, Lord Lovat, who raised the 71st. James might have been a grandson of old Lord Lovat of Tower Hill fame."

"A little nepotism at work here?"

"Standard procedure. And he had a fiancée, Lady Isabel Seaton."

"Fiancée?" repeated Amanda. "He left not one but two girls behind him?"

"All that about Sally might be just a story," Carrie pointed out. "As you said yourself, in real life they might never even have met."

"Yeah." Amanda made a face—she'd almost let the cat out of the bag. Casually she dredged the pickles from her burger.

"Balcarres says he's sending James's sword home to Isabel via his aide-de-camp, one Archibald Grant. Remember him?"

"Yes, I do." Cousin Archibald the dolt. Amanda visualized some pimply youth with buckteeth and a hee-haw of a laugh, and so little finesse at romance he made Wayne look like James Bond.

"Balcarres finishes with the usual 'I have the very great honor to remain, etc., etc.' What's interesting is that there's a note at the bottom of the transcription, in the same typeface: Quote, 'James Grant was the younger of two sons.'"

Amanda peered at the uneven lines of type. "He couldn't inherit, so he went into the army. More standard procedure."

"Yeah, but listen to this. 'James's elder brother pre-deceased him, but the letter informing James of this did not reach him before his own death.'" Carrie shook her head. "He was the laird of the castle and didn't know it—there's irony for you."

One that he might not appreciate, Amanda thought. She bit, chewed, and swallowed. "So who did the property go to? Does it say?"

"'Dundreggan House devolved upon Archibald Grant, James's cousin, who also served in the 71st. (See letter) He returned from the American wars in 1781 and married Lady Isabel Seaton in 1782.'"

"Cousin Archibald sure didn't waste any time, did he?" Amanda said with a snort. "So he not only inherited Dundreggan but Isabel. Most women back then being more or less property themselves, if you'll excuse the editorial comment."

"I doubt if Isabel was either rich or crazy enough to do her own thing. She was lucky if anyone bothered to ask her opinion of either engagement. Anyway, the note ends by saying, 'James Grant's sword is on display at Dundreggan House.'"

Go figure, Amanda told herself. Where else would it be? Like most puzzles, the answer was obvious once you knew it. "It was there when that note was written," she cautioned. "Is it dated?"

"No. It might be as old as the eighteen-nineties or whenever it was they invented typewriters, but it's signed in a good twentieth-century scrawl. Malcolm, I guess. Malcolm Grant."

"Cynthia said something about Norah's son The Honorable Malcolm giving a blood sample for the DNA tests. Might be him. The whole family must be ancient." Amanda imagined withered, white-haired codgers sitting around a Gothic fireplace, knitting needles and antique typewriter clacking away. "I bet they were doing genealogical research. My grandmother's into that, she has us traced all the way back to Suffolk in England."

Amanda pulled the pages toward her. But they were only copies, modern ink on modern paper. It was the words that mattered, voices gossiping over time's back fence. She slipped the papers into the envelope and gave them back to Carrie.

With a last mighty slurp Carrie finished her milk shake. "I don't know how long this letter and the transcription have been in the museum in Edinburgh. Years, possibly. Decades." She glanced at her watch and took off her glasses. "I need to go. The family deserves some kind of food, even if it isn't home made. See you tomorrow."

"Sure. Thanks a lot for calling me tonight."

Amanda ate the rest of her burger without really tasting it. So there it was. The sword. As objects of desire went, it was higher on James's list than Amanda herself was. And it was back home, just where it should have been, just where he wanted to go. *To go home with honor.* Maybe Isabel, in the classical tradition of the time, had told him either to return with his shield or upon it—either after honorable battle or dead. But he hadn't returned at all.

Amanda threw away her trash, went out into the night, and turned her car back toward Melrose. The garish lights of the twenty-first century faded behind her. She imagined herself driving back into the past. A group of red-coated soldiers would appear from the trees at the side of the road, startled by her headlights the way James always seemed startled by consciousness.

And why hadn't Balcarres sent the scabbard back with the sword? Maybe the two had been separated in battle. The Brits had found the sword on the field, but James's body, with the scabbard still at his side, had been picked up and buried by passing farmers or slaves. She could see someone burying a body where it had fallen if it hadn't been found right away. After a couple of days in July anyone, no matter how handsome, would be ghastlier than Stephen King's worst nightmare.

James had to have died with his colleagues. Otherwise, how did Balcarres know he was dead the day after the battle? But if he had died at Greensprings Farm, why was he buried at Melrose?

Maybe the Colonel hadn't returned the scabbard because it had that kink in it, and the sword wouldn't fit it any more, so they went ahead and buried it with James's body. At Melrose. She kept returning to Melrose.

Literally. In past the gatehouse she went, and parked her car in the shed. The floodlights defined the walls and windows of Melrose Hall almost without shadow, she noticed, just as James's body was defined by the lights of time and space and desire.

Once inside her apartment Amanda checked the alarm systems, petted Lafayette, and eyed her computer. Yeah, she was getting a lot done. Nothing like a man to thoroughly distract a woman from her work. Even though this man could help her with her work. She had to ask the right questions—she needed to take notes. Although she was hardly going to take notes in the middle of a clinch.

The room went cold, like a freezer door swinging open. Lafayette growled, deep in his throat, and fluffed up his fur. Amanda turned slowly around. James Grant stood in the bedroom door, scowling at the cat.

Lafayette arched and hissed and made tracks for the door. The flap slapped back and forth. Paws scrambled down the corridor into silence. The chill ebbed from Amanda's skin, leaving her glowing with warmth.

James raised his eyes to her. His frown softened into a rueful laugh. "I hold horses and dogs in the highest esteem. I find the hunt, the dogs baying after the fox, the horses streaming over the hedgerows and across the fields in the greatest similitude of a cavalry charge, to be vastly amusing. But cats—cats are sly creatures, and I fear I have little love for them."

"He's just scared of you," Amanda said, and added to herself, *I bet you're more than a little scared of him, too.* James wasn't so far removed from the days when cats were thought to be witch's familiars. And it was only in the last few decades that fox hunting had become politically incorrect.

He was looking at her, and cats and horses weren't what was on his mind.

She scrambled for words. "Thank you for not frightening anyone at the garden club lunch today."

"I beg your pardon?"

"The women in the dining room today, who were calling your name. Thank you for putting the candlestick back down again. It's not a good idea to play with fire—though of course you know that."

He stared at her as though she wasn't speaking English.

"You didn't hear anyone calling your name today?"

"No, I did not. I'm very sorry, Miss Witham, Amanda, if I could have been of assistance to you and yet failed to be so."

"Where do you go when you're not with m . . ." She stopped abruptly.

Too late. His puzzled expression crumpled into outright confusion. "Why, nowhere, but to sleep and to dream—in faith, this night has lasted a prodigious length of time, until the light of day seems but a dream itself." He grimaced fiercely, shrugging not just his shoulders but his entire body, rejecting her question, his answer, and the implications of both.

That hadn't been a fair question, she told herself. And yet she'd confirmed her hunch that he was truly aware only when he was focussed in physical form. Flattering, to think he was only conscious when he was with her, and that the moving objects were nothing but left over scraps of energy. Of potency, she thought. Of virility.

James stepped toward her, hands outstretched, palms up. "Are you frightened of me?"

"Oh no, not at all." She raised her hands and placed them in his grasp.

"Aren't you the saucy one? Perhaps you should be frightened of me, Amanda." He pulled her into his arms and kissed her.

She was ready for him. She fingered his coat and his belt, pressing herself against his body as insistently he pressed against her, hanging on his mouth and tongue—*oh yeah.* She could sense him in every fiber, every nerve ending. Maybe it was all a delicate equation of matter and energy, of relativity in defiance of time and death. She didn't care. For someone with no physicality he was sure physical.

Would he be able to take off his clothes or were they permanently part of his image—if rumor was correct he wasn't wearing anything under his kilt anyway. . . . *Whoa.* She pulled away to catch her breath. She'd never raced from the starting gate to the finish line this fast, but then, she'd never been afraid a guy would disappear in the backstretch, either.

He followed so eagerly they did a quick dance step across the floor and kissed again. His hands were beneath her T-shirt, like butterflies on her ribs, climbing upward. *Oh yeah.* She wondered whether he could deal with hooks and eyes and zippers. But he was awfully good at this. He'd probably known all about the lacings of petticoats and stays. As a bachelor, an officer, and a gentleman he'd had every chance to get it on with. . . .

Whoa, she thought again, and stiffened. If James thought he was still alive, then he thought he was engaged to Isabel. His engagement was the reason he'd resisted Sally's advances. But if Isabel was marriage material, listed in the "respectable" category of womanhood and therefore strictly unavailable, then all-too-available Amanda was most definitely not respectable.

Like she hadn't already known that? But now it was in her face. And now she knew she didn't want to play the whore for James any more than she did for any man. Even with him, there had to be more to it than academic curiosity and biomechanics.

"Hey, slow down, things are going too fast here." She pushed him away and stood wheezing, as hot and humid as the breeze that rattled the venetian blinds.

James was kind of pink in the face himself. He drew himself up, standing to attention, and fixed Amanda with a gaze that was remarkably tolerant, considering. "I beg your pardon, I am too impetuous. But your beauty. . . ."

"I get the message," she said.

He frowned. "What can I say to you, Sweeting, to reassure you?"

Sweeting? That was a good one. Smiling wryly, she took another step away from him before her own senses sucked her back into his arms. Once you start necking, she thought, you stop talking, as though a relationship could have only one dimension at a time. Dealing with James's weird dimension was difficult enough without throwing out all the other ones.

"I think," she said, "I may know where your sword is."

"Indeed?"

"Earl Balcarres sent it back to Dundreggan."

"He sent it—why should he do that?"

"You were injured," Amanda said carefully. "He sent your sword to Lady Isabel Seaton, as a memento."

"Fearing I would die." The pink drained from his face. "Isabel. Yes, I remember Isabel. A lightsome lass, with a smile much as yours, Amanda; a smile that opened the gillyflowers like the rays of Phoebus himself. It has been long indeed since I last saw Isabel." James's image wavered on the air like the smoke from Cynthia's extinguished candle.

Amanda winced. Once again she'd forced him to look out of himself, away from the moment. She'd hurt him. She wasn't sure whether she'd done it to learn about him or to make sexual points against him.

"Isabel, and the garden at Dundreggan—it seems naught but a pleasant dream. I remember much better the evil dream of Charlestown and sickness and death. And death." James's form solidified again, but he was stili pale. His brow was furrowed and his lips tight. "Amanda, I am fair embrangled, all is strange around me, I know not where I am—Melrose—Virginia—and yet. . . ." He reached toward her.

Damn it all anyway, Amanda thought. It was just human instinct to reassure yourself by hanging onto someone else. And it wasn't like he was aroused any more—she'd taken care of that as surely as if she'd thrown cold water on him.

She hugged him and laid her cheek against his shoulder. It was like holding the wind. She ached for him, for the poor lost soul, neither living nor dead. No matter what he might have thought of her when he was alive, now he was dead. Now he was vulnerable and he needed her. Their relationship—whatever it was—was unique.

With a whiskey-soft sigh, James wrapped Amanda close to his chest. "Death," he said, so quietly she could hardly hear him. "The thought of death confounds me. I think of death and I think of Archibald, my cousin, all the deadly sins wrapped in the figure of a man."

"The seven deadly sins? Like sloth and lust?"

"Lust, greed, envy—so is Archibald, a serpent in my bosom. I saw him and Isabel laughing together in the garden—in the garden where we had plighted our troth. When they saw me they stopped laughing and turned away, shamefaced. I donned the scarlet coat that night, and the next day I departed my homeland. But Archibald came later, after Charlestown, bearing letters from Isabel, letters that were proper enough, and yet—and yet were cold."

A shiver slipped like an ice cube down Amanda's back.

James was becoming thinner and thinner. She wasn't holding him any more. She groped through the air.

His voice was distant but still crisp and clear. "Archibald is holding a pistol, a cocked pistol, and the muzzle of the pistol points at me. He smiles a smile that has in it no humor, no affection, nothing but malice. A flash of light—I am blinded and struck all aback—oh God, what is this, what does this mean? No!"

An invisible movement. A rush in the air. A drinking glass sitting on the kitchen counter leaped against the wall and shattered.

"James!" Amanda called. But he was gone, leaving nothing behind but the tang of whiskey in her nose and mouth and the moist glow deep in her abdomen.

"James?" She sank to the floor next to the shards of glass as though kneeling over a sprawled body. But that body had been thrust abruptly from life into death two hundred years ago.

Warily she collected the broken bits of glass. They chimed like a tolling bell. So now she knew. As Hewitt said, James had died by homicide. And what a tidy little murder it had been, done in the midst of battle. James had been betrayed by his own cousin and, by extension, his fiancée. No wonder his shade couldn't rest.

If he wanted comfort, Amanda thought, she was his, semantics be damned. If he wanted revenge, even after all this time, then she'd help him get it. Maybe she was playing with fire herself. . . . No. Fire was dangerous, true, but it also meant warmth and light. "James?"

He was gone.

CHAPTER ELEVEN

Amanda opened the front door, admitting a burst of sunshine. Lafayette whisked by her skirts and paced off along the top of a brick wall, his tail straight up in the air like an exclamation point. He'd never come back to the apartment last night. Neither had James. Amanda felt bad about the cat, but not as bad as she felt about the man.

Way to go, she told herself. According to one theory, as soon as a ghost realized it was no longer alive, it would disappear. She could only hope that James's desire either for her or for revenge was stronger than a minor detail such as death.

Now she understood why he was trapped between this life and the next, alone and lost. It must be precious little comfort to him that Archibald hadn't shot him in the back. James's personal honor and that of the Grant family had been violated.

Amanda turned back into the entrance hall. She found a cloth in the sideboard, started polishing the fingerprints from the Lucite boxes in James's display, and considered the evidence against Cousin Archibald.

Means. Even if Archibald hadn't been carrying a pistol since he left Scotland, he'd have found any number of firearms in the British camp. Had poor James tried to fend him off with his sword? Even the primitive pistol of the day would have the advantage of a sword—especially a pistol in the hand of a trusted relative.

Motive. What if Archibald, as Balcarres's aide-de-camp, had intercepted the letter telling James about his brother's death? He'd realize he was the heir. Although wanting Isabel might have been motive enough to get rid of James. That was one way to make her fall into his arms, to comfort her on her loss. Or he and Isabel may have already had some agreement—her letters were cold. . . . Amanda shook her head. She was veering into speculation.

What wasn't speculation was Archibald's opportunity. In the midst of battle, with men shouting, horses galloping, cannons firing, all Archibald had to do was point and shoot. The murder would've taken a minute. Less.

And then that rat Archibald returned James's sword to Balcarres—*here sir, just as I plucked it from his lifeless hand*—and finagled himself a discharge. He'd probably cried crocodile tears over the devastated folks at home. Who really must have been devastated, Amanda thought. James's parents lost two sons in less than a year. And Isabel, whether she'd been unfaithful to James or not, must've felt something when James's sword returned from the wars in Archibald's hand. No telling what sort of line Archibald had used on her to turn her away from James.

All right! Amanda congratulated herself and sent silent thanks to Carrie and old Malcolm Grant. It all worked, it all fit together, except for the one thing that had baffled everyone, from herself to Hewitt, all along. Why was James buried at Melrose?

There. The boxes were clean. Amanda blew a kiss toward the one that held James's portrait, made a face at herself, and put away the polishing cloth. She stepped out the door onto the porch.

The river was a sheet of glare in the morning sun, a boat on its surface almost invisible. The lawn shone emerald green. Amanda could actually smell the heat, a combination of warm grass and stone and a distant whiff of fish. July in Virginia was bright, no doubt about it.

Bright daylight. James had seen the flash of Archibald's pistol. Even if the battle had been fought on a cloudy day, the flashes of the guns would've been invisible. James had been killed at night.

Amanda brought her fist down on the railing. That was it! Archibald had ambushed James in the garden the night before the battle and bundled his body into a makeshift grave. As Balcarres's aide Archibald would have known the battle was coming—the British had provoked it.

All he had to do was act innocent until the regiment was mopping up afterwards, say that James had been killed in action, and trot out the sword.

The scabbard must have been bent when James fell on it. He'd died with his sword in his hand, otherwise it would have been bent, too. . . . Well, it might be bent, Amanda didn't know. It was enough that Archibald had taken the sword and left the scabbard. James never said he'd run up the stairs, slashing at the banisters, the morning of Greensprings Farm. It was much more likely the soldiers had moved out the night before. Who would notice the odd pistol shot in the dark when a camp was breaking for battle?

With the British troops falling back on Yorktown Balcarres wouldn't have had time to ask questions or view the body, even if he'd doubted Archibald's word. And why should he? It showed what respect the Colonel had had for James's family, if not for the man himself, that he'd taken the time to write—or at least dictate—the letter.

Maybe, in one final excruciating irony, he'd dictated the letter to Archibald.

Amanda pirouetted up and down the steps feeling like a *Jeopardy* grand champion. Not only did her theory fit all the facts, it could pretty much be extrapolated from the physical and written evidence. She could tell Carrie about it without giving away anything she'd learned from James personally.

She stopped, winded. And what James wanted, personally, was revenge. Although Archibald Grant was beyond the reach of any earthly jury. Surely, in the afterlife, he'd been turned away from the Pearly Gates and appropriately judged—vengeance being His, sayeth the Lord. But that wasn't enough for James. Even at this late date he could achieve something symbolic by revealing the truth. And that was where Amanda came in.

A bus rumbled into the parking lot, accompanied by the slamming of car doors. Quickly she settled her cap, opened her fan, and stood ready.

Wayne came hobbling along the path, leaning on an elegant walking stick, nursed along by Carrie. "Good morning!" he shouted to Amanda. "I'm back!"

"How are you feeling?" Amanda called.

"Fine, just fine, no prob . . ." He slipped on the gravel and grabbed Carrie's arm.

Between them the two women managed to get him up the steps. "You go and sit in the library," Carrie told him. "We'll send people in to you."

"Are you sure you can manage?" he asked.

"We'll try."

Amanda had Carrie all to herself for two minutes. "What we need to do," she told her, "is get hold of Lady Norah and The Honorable Malcolm and ask for more information. I tried looking them up on the Internet, but you can imagine how many Grants there are in Scotland."

"You searched for the word 'Dundreggan', of course."

"Yeah, and I came up with a company called Preservation Imaging, Ltd. The address is Dundreggan by Glenmoriston, which is the right place. But, you know, Cynthia's never said the Grants are still living there. If Lord Dundreggan died and Lady Norah had to sell off some heirlooms, why not the ancestral lands as well? It happens all the time, what with taxes and death duties and everything. There're clan chiefs living in apartments in Poughkeepsie."

"So let's just ask Cynthia for the number," Carrie said, and added with a laugh, "If it wasn't for you and your crazy crush, I wouldn't have done half this much research by now. In fact, I really should put you down as a co-author on that article. Okay?"

Visions of publication danced in Amanda's head. "Thanks!"

"Cynthia's coming out here this afternoon, by the way."

"Not another seance. Please."

"All she said was something about adding to the display."

Amanda glanced over her shoulder. The Lucite boxes gleamed in the light from the open door. Was that bit of silver moving? No, it was Carrie's reflection as she stepped out the door to greet the first group of sightseers.

"When we get a chance," Amanda whispered, "I'll tell you a theory about why James was buried here."

"Great!" Carrie turned to the tourists. "Welcome to Melrose Hall."

Amanda assumed Sally's personality and went to work. By noon she'd had several interesting conversations with well-informed visitors, not counting the teenaged boy who eyed her bosom and asked, "Doesn't it hurt to be all squished up like that?"

"That, young sir, is a concern appropriate only to myself and my maidservant," she responded tartly, and shut the door behind him.

She took a sandwich and some iced tea to Wayne. The dark paneling of the library seemed to absorb some of the sunlight flooding in the window, and the room was relatively cool. "Every time I step outside," she said, "I feel like I'm going to run into Dante and Virgil."

Wayne looked at her.

"The *Inferno.* You know, the tourist's guide to hell."

"Oh," he said. "That."

Amanda put the tray down on the desk, telling herself that James would have gotten the reference.

"You didn't take Mother's game with the seance seriously, did you?" Wayne asked.

"Was it a game?"

"Sure. She told me all about it. I'm sorry I wasn't here to see it. Damned ankle."

There was her opening. "Wayne," she asked, "when you fell down the stairs, did you see anything—a shadow or something—that startled you?"

"No, I didn't see a thing. Why?"

"Just trying to figure out why you fell." He wasn't lying. He was only a good actor when he played Page.

Wayne was still looking at her. Odd, how different his gaze felt from James's, even though the subtexts were so similar. "You don't have to lie to me, Amanda. I can take the truth."

"Excuse me?"

"You're going with somebody on the sly, aren't you? He comes out here after work, which is why you won't let me stay."

Amanda pretended to inspect a musty copy of *Clarissa Harlow.* Wayne was hitting too close to the mark with that one.

"You can tell me," he persisted. "I can take it."

Maybe she should just make up someone, she thought wearily. Or name the guy she'd broken up with last winter. It'd be easier on Wayne's ego. But she'd said all along she didn't want him, and that was the honest truth. As distinct from the slightly dishonest truth about James. "No, Wayne, there's no one else. We're just not right for each other. You think we could move on past this, please?"

"Sure. Okay." He picked up the sandwich and took a huge bite from it, chewing with sharp, peevish movements of his jaw.

Amanda retreated from the room and grabbed a sandwich for herself in the kitchen. Wayne was tenacious, she had to give him credit for that. Where had he gotten it into his head someone was visiting her after hours?

It was almost closing time when Cynthia appeared like a delicate cloud on Melrose's horizon. She was wearing a flowered chiffon skirt and a peasant vest that made her look cool in both senses of the word—her idea of weekend clothing, no doubt. The woman probably wouldn't be caught dead in a T-shirt and shorts.

"Hello, Amanda dear. And Carrie, how nice to see you again. How's Wayne holding up?"

"He's fine," answered Carrie. "We've been sending people in to him in the library."

"He does a really good job as Page," Amanda added.

"How sweet of you to say so." Cynthia patted her arm.

Amanda's smile stiffened. James's "Sweeting" was endearing, not irritating. Amazing the difference made by a little sex appeal. "To what do we owe the honor of your visit, Madame?"

"How charming!" Cynthia cooed. "Actually I'm first on the scene, as usual. My work is just too fascinating."

"Who else is coming?" Carrie asked.

"The Benedettos, Helen Medina, Bill Hewitt's crew—he's over at Jamestown today—we had to hurry the lab along, but you'll be very impressed." She wafted across the entrance hall and inspected the display. "Don't these prints add to the exhibit, though?"

Amanda elbowed Carrie and waggled her eyebrows in Cynthia's direction.

"Mrs. Chancellor," Carrie said, "as you know, I've been researching James Grant for the journal article. Yesterday I got some very interesting information from Edinburgh. His sword was sent back to Dundreggan."

"Oh it was?" Cynthia turned back around. "How thrilling!"

"It wasn't for sale with the portrait?" asked Amanda.

"No, it wasn't. I'm sure the broker would have told me. It could have been sold years ago, I suppose. Or it might still be a treasured family heirloom. A memento of a brave and tragic ancestor, who went off to—well, he was defending *his* country, wasn't he?"

"We're planning to contact Lady Norah and ask her some questions," Carrie persevered. "If you could . . ."

"Why, I was planning to call her tonight. I'd be happy to ask about the sword for you."

Carrie forced a smile. "That's very helpful, but we were wondering if the Grants are still living at . . ."

"I'll tell you all about it on Monday," Cynthia rolled on. "I'm putting together a little luncheon for the people involved in the Grant project, and I expect both of you to come. My home, twelve noon sharp."

Resistance is futile, Amanda intoned to herself, and said, "Thank you. I'll be there."

A shame the major character in this comedy of manners and errors wouldn't. She still wished James had jumped out at Cynthia during the seance. Several yards of tartan wool would make a great muffler.

Shreds of wool had survived longer than his flesh. *Go home to Dundreggan,* he'd said.

She tried planting another seed in Cynthia's fertile brain. "Mrs. Chancellor, we were talking the other day about a funeral for Captain Grant—what if there's an old family cemetery at Dundreggan, maybe you could ask Lady Norah if. . . ."

Wayne hobbled through the library door. "Hello, Mother."

Cynthia spun toward him. "Wayne, darling, you mustn't walk on that ankle." She pulled a chair from against the wall and seated him in it.

"Really, Mother, it's a lot better. Oh, hello, Mrs. Benedetto."

Lucy crept into the entrance hall. "Hello Carrie, Amanda, how are you? Wayne. Mrs. Chancellor."

Cynthia swept down on the elderly woman. "Why Lucy, where's Vernon?"

"Well, er, ah, he just couldn't. . . ." Lucy flushed. She opened her handbag and looked desperately around inside, as though her husband was hiding there. "He's not feeling well. Sorry, Mrs. Chancellor."

Carrie and Amanda shared an amused glance. Good for Vernon, not to answer Cynthia's summons if he didn't want to.

Roy conducted the last tour of the day through the hall and out the door. His voice faded into the distance. "If you would do us the very great honor of visiting the gift . . ." Not bad, Amanda thought. Just keep on going into the parking lot and away home.

Two of Hewitt's assistants trudged up the steps. "Here it is, Mrs. Chancellor." They started opening boxes and bundles and setting up lights.

"Wonderful! I can hardly wait!" Cynthia stepped between Lucy and Amanda. She dropped her voice, but her whisper could penetrate steel. "Lucy, have I set your mind at rest about those footsteps?"

"The ones going up the drive at night." Lucy nodded soberly. "I hope I wasn't telling tales out of school."

Behind Amanda Wayne emitted an aggrieved sigh. Carrie, on Amanda's other side, looked around curiously.

Amanda thought, *footsteps?* Was that why Lucy brought the apple pie and checked to make sure she was all right, because the Benedettos had heard footsteps? Sure, they could have belonged to a prowler. But between paranoia and the paranormal, Amanda chose a dazed and disoriented James, whose newly awakened perceptions had been drawn toward Melrose Hall. Not that she was going to announce, *Oh that's all right everyone, it was only a ghost.*

"I so appreciate your telling me," Cynthia went on. "The mother's always the last to know." She turned to Amanda and gave her a delicate little half-hug. "I'm so pleased, dear."

Whoa, deja vu! Cynthia and Lucy were looking at her the same way they had the day the display was set up, like tigers eyeing a goat. Suddenly Amanda remembered Lucy's embarrassment the night of the pie. The older woman must have decided the footsteps belonged to a guy sneaking in to see Amanda after hours. Trying to make points, she'd mentioned her suspicions to Cynthia. And to Wayne—everyone knew he had a major crush on . . .

Amanda backed off, only to collide with the banister and the edge of staircase. *No way! I have not been getting it on with Wayne after hours!*

The faces in front of her swelled and deflated like balloons, Cynthia smug, Lucy indulgent, Carrie dumbfounded, Wayne puzzled. Had Cynthia even bothered to ask him about it, for God's sake? But even if he denied everything she'd just think he was being coy—she never listened to anyone, especially him. *Shit,* Amanda thought.

"I've embarrassed her, I'm so sorry, Amanda sweetheart." Cynthia made soothing gestures. "Yes, yes, I know, you and Wayne were intending to keep it a secret—like naughty children, weren't we—but that's all right, I know how to be discreet. Mum's the word, right, Lucy? No announcements yet."

Lucy nodded eagerly, no doubt delighted to be treated, however briefly, as an equal. Cynthia turned to give Wayne a hug, too. His face emerged from her vest flushed with gratification. He looked like a kid taking down his Christmas stocking and discovering Santa had come through after all.

Shit, Amanda repeated. But, *I'm not all hot and bothered over Wayne but over a man who's been dead two hundred years* wasn't going to cut it. "Mrs. Chancellor," she attempted, "I'm afraid there's been a misunderstanding, I'm not . . ."

Helen Medina burst in the door, juggling pieces of camera equipment. "Got it all set up? Super. Cynthia, I'm sure you want to do the honors."

Cynthia, diverted onto another scent, bustled across the entrance hall. Hewitt's assistants had erected a tall display stand beside the panels of the exhibit. Whatever stood on top of it, something about the size of a large vase, was draped with a cloth. Helen turned on the lights and focussed them on the stand.

Amanda sidled away from both the staircase and Wayne's chair, trying to stop hyperventilating. No wonder Sally looked so bland in her portrait. If she splurged on an emotion she'd have suffocated herself.

"Ready?" Cynthia asked Helen.

Helen gave her a thumbs-up. "Have at it."

To the accompanying whir of Helen's video camera, Cynthia posed, smiled, and lifted the cloth from the display. She revealed James's head. Everyone oohed and ahed. The few drops of blood that remained in Amanda's face drained into her feet, leaving her cheeks prickling cold.

"Normally," Cynthia told the camera, "we would do a skull reconstruction with computer graphics. But a 3-D display can be enjoyed by so many more people. Our labs made a cast of Captain Grant's skull, and measured skin depths and muscle connections. . . ."

Her words faded out and in like the whine of a siren. Amanda scrabbled after her wits. The lab technicians had really strutted their stuff with this one. They had the patrician lines of James's face down beautifully—the high forehead, the straight nose, the chiseled lips, the square jaw. The skin was painted in lifelike tones. The glass eyes glinted too dark a blue, but the techies had only the portrait to go on. And the white wig made him look like a fop. Which, in spite of the wig and even the snuffbox, he most emphatically was not.

James wasn't a dummy, staring blankly ahead without intelligence, or emotion, or character. *He was real.*

The entrance hall strobed. Her stomach lurched. She was going to faint. She was going to throw up. She was going make a spectacle of herself right here in front of God, Cynthia, and the Colonial Williamsburg Foundation.

Amanda spun, stumbled down the hall to her apartment, and collapsed on the couch just as the black dots spinning through her vision coalesced into darkness.

CHAPTER TWELVE

Within seconds her head cleared and Amanda was damning her stays and Cynthia equally. *Smooth one.* She'd covered herself in glory that time.

Carrie hurried in the door, sat down beside her, and peered into her face. "That particular shade of green skin doesn't go with a red dress. Are you all right? Or just hyperventilating after that dirty trick Cynthia played on you?"

For a moment Amanda thought she was talking about Cynthia suddenly unveiling James's mortal face. But Carrie didn't know about James. "You know Cynthia," Amanda muttered, sitting up straighter. "She doesn't leap to conclusions, she makes them up out of whole cloth."

"All that about footsteps, you mean?"

"Lucy Benedetto heard footsteps coming this way, I don't know when, last week sometime. So she figured Wayne was sneaking in to see me after hours—he hasn't been too obvious or anything. And she's so anxious to make points with Cynthia she told her. . . . No, I'm not mad at Lucy. She means well. So does Cynthia, for that matter, deciding I'll make her a dandy daughter-in-law, signed, sealed, and delivered on a silver tray. I've got to stop playing Sally, everyone thinks I'm just so sweet and biddable." An acid taste rose in her throat and she swallowed. "Now I've got to either browbeat Wayne into telling the truth or tackle Cynthia myself."

"You don't think Wayne put Cynthia up to it?"

"He seemed just as shocked as I was, if no way as horrified."

"She had me going there for a minute," Carrie said. "So did you. You looked as though you'd seen a ghost."

Something soft but intense exploded inside Amanda's head. The truth about Wayne. The truth about James's death. The truth about James, period. All the truths had to come out, or none of them would be valid. Like a house of cards, each reality leaned against another. "I have seen a ghost."

"What?"

"I think the Benedettos really did hear footsteps. It's kind of comforting that they did. It means I'm not crazy."

"What?"

"Cynthia didn't have to stage a seance," Amanda explained. "Captain Grant's ghost really is here. Lucy heard his footsteps coming up to the house. He's focussed on the house. He died here. That's why he's buried here."

Carrie looked around the room, probably expecting to see white-coated guys with butterfly nets hiding in the bedroom. When she spoke her voice was very gentle. "Amanda, I understand why you're hooked on Grant—it's a compelling story. That skull reconstruction gave me the willies, too. There probably are things going bump in the night here at Melrose, tree limbs and the cat and the house settling. You're here by yourself, of course you're hearing things. But a ghost? Come on."

"I'm not making him up. I'm not imagining him."

"Well no, it's not necessarily your imagination. There's something called autosuggestion, kind of self-hypnosis, like when you're sitting up late reading a horror novel and you just know a monster's hiding beneath the bed. Except you're not seeing a monster, you're seeing this exciting man."

Amanda saw James sitting on the staircase, his scabbard across his knees, his eyes hurt and bewildered. "It's not like that. I have seen him. I've talked to him. I've touched him. I knew it was him before you and Hewitt identified him. He said he was from Dundreggan before I saw the name on the picture."

"I know sexual frustration's been used as an excuse for everything from witches to global warming," Carrie came back, "and I don't mean to imply . . ."

". . . that I'm Exhibit A?" Amanda grabbed Carrie's forearms and fixed her with what she had the awful feeling was a maniacal gaze. "I'm not saying that's not in there. But there's more to it than that."

Carrie met Amanda's eyes evenly but doubtfully.

"You don't believe me, do you?"

"I believe you believe you saw something."

I knew this would happen. But she couldn't go back now. Amanda released Carrie, hauled herself to her feet, and walked over to the open door. Voices echoed down the hall, Helen playing straight woman to Cynthia. Amanda hoped Wayne's ankle would keep him in the entrance hall.

"I know I sound like I've lost it," she said. "But James is real. He's handsome, he's intelligent, he's charming, and in that uniform he buckles a hell of a swash. He actually lived in the eighteenth century—he's given me insights into the speech and the culture I'd never get out of a book!"

Carrie was watching her, not blinking.

"He's different. Even without his sword he's got an edge to him that's, that's—glamorous. You know, the old Scots word meaning enchanting, casting a spell over, not *Entertainment Tonight* glamorous. . . ." She sat back down. "Really. I swear on Thomas Mason's diaries."

"You can actually talk to him?"

"Yes, I can."

"Have you—er—touched him?"

"Oh yeah. When he's solid enough to touch."

"And you're the one who claims to have no romantic illusions."

"This is no illusion, even if it is romantic as hell."

"Are you sure it's no illusion? I mean, okay, so you see him and everything, but even with living, breathing guys you see what you want to see."

"I know," Amanda said with a groan. "I know. Be careful what you ask for and all of that."

Carrie shook her head. "I'm sorry, Amanda. I thought my kids had thrown me every possible curve, but you really take the cake with this one. If you'll excuse the mangled metaphor."

"Mangled metaphors are my stock in trade." At least Carrie was listening to her. Amanda indulged in a rueful laugh of her own. "This is totally absurd. I know that. But it's true."

"Okay, okay, I don't disbelieve you. Is that good enough?"

"That's a start. Thanks."

"You said you had a theory about why he was buried in the garden?"

"It's more than a theory." Amanda launched into the true history of Isabel, Archibald, and James, a tragedy in two acts, concluding, "So it was murder, pure and simple."

Carrie mulled it all over. "The other officers must have noticed James wasn't at his assigned post before the battle."

"So each one thought he was some place else. There hasn't been a battle in history where everybody was right where he was supposed to be."

"Archibald did become the heir," admitted Carrie. "He did go home and marry Isabel, and James really was buried here at Melrose even though the record says he died at Greensprings Farm. But as for Archibald being the guilty party, once you eliminate James's—er, testimony—it's all circumstantial evidence. At a distance of two hundred years, yet. You'll never be able to bring Archibald to trial, let alone prove him guilty."

"Maybe it's just as well the Scots have that ambiguous verdict of 'Not Proven,'" Amanda said. "No, the only way James is going to get any satisfaction at this late date is by my revealing the truth."

"That's what he wants?"

She could hear James's smooth voice in the back of her mind. "He wants revenge. He wants his sword. He wants to go home. I can help with the first, and we may have located the sword, but getting him home? It's up to the relatives, the Grants, to say what they want done with him. No reason they won't just tell Hewitt to bury him at Yorktown. I've tried hinting to Cynthia about old family cemeteries and such, maybe she'd pay for shipping him back to Scotland—making the arrangements would give her an excuse to mingle some more with the aristocracy, after all—but she'd love having a big re-creation military funeral here, too."

"The question," said Carrie, "is whether you're willing to let him go."

Bullseye. Amanda eyed her own hands, folded so tightly on her lap the knuckles glinted white, her bones shining beneath her skin. She was going to have to let him go. Whether as a ghost or as a soldier on the prowl, James was not even remotely a prospect for long-term commitment. "I may not get the chance to do anything. Last night I suggested to him that he was dead. That upset him. He may already be gone for good. Which doesn't mean I can't tell his story."

"No, it doesn't. We need to see if there're any more family records, to back the story up. To give you the excuse to tell it—for the sake of the article, of course."

"The article. Absolutely."

"Cynthia seems to be trying to stake the Grants out as her own personal territory," Carrie went on with a smile, "but we can make an end run around her. If you're brave enough."

"I sure am. After today. After the way she faked that seance yesterday and then made me her accessory after the fact."

"How she'd do it?"

"She smuggled in some nail scissors and cut off the flowers while everyone's eyes were closed, and she brought in her own candle, one of those that won't stay out."

"She's a force of nature, isn't she?" Carrie asked in admiration and resentment mingled. "But you are an accessory. If you spill the beans, she'll just laugh and say it was all a joke, and then give you a bad reference."

"She may do that anyway, after all this with Wayne."

"You stick to your guns with Wayne. If you don't want him, you don't have to have him. This is the twenty-first century."

"Sometimes it is," said Amanda. "Cynthia thinks I'm a sweet little eighteenth-century sap, and James thinks I'm a saucy little eighteenth-century baggage."

Even as Carrie laughed she raised a cautionary finger. "I don't know what's going on here . . ."

"Something weird," Amanda assured her.

"So keep your wits about you, okay?"

"I'll try. But it's kind of like trying to swim upstream. The current can get a little strong."

"Then climb out onto the bank and walk."

"Yes, ma'am," Amanda said, without the least sarcasm.

Cynthia's voice drifted down the hall, making concluding remarks. Amanda made a face. "What's really funny is that when Cynthia had her eyes closed after her flower and candle routine, James lifted the candlestick right in front of her and she never saw it."

"I wish I'd been there." Carrie glanced toward the door. Cynthia's brisk footsteps were approaching, punctuated by Wayne's uneven ones. "Speak of the devil."

Amanda groaned. "I'm going to go hide, if you don't mind covering for me."

"Go on. I'll tell them you're indisposed."

"Don't tell them I almost tossed my cookies, Cynthia will think I'm pregnant and start hiring florists and caterers. God, can you imagine what it would be like having sex with Wayne? Cynthia might just as well be standing there at the foot of the bed giving directions—put it there, dear, in and out, that's right—if she ever bothered to notice the process herself, that is. I'm not so sure she didn't find Wayne under a cabbage leaf."

Suffused with laughter, Carrie shooed Amanda into the bedroom. Where she shut the door and stood listening as Carrie turned at bay. "Yes, she's just fine. Her stays are pretty tight, you know. The heat and—and everything. She's taking a shower before she checks over the house. It's past closing time."

Amanda couldn't hear Cynthia's words, just the sound of her voice in duet with Wayne's.

"Wayne," said Carrie, her own voice retreating, "let me walk out to the parking lot with you. You're certainly brave to come to work with that sprained ankle."

Moments later a door slammed. Giving thanks for a friend like Carrie, Amanda crept out and listened. The house was silent. She felt like she hadn't breathed all day. She stripped off her clothes, dumped them on the bed, and stood breathing deeply. If James wanted to materialize and ogle her again, more power to him. She couldn't blame the moth for being attracted to the flame.

She showered, dressed in blessed loose cotton, and found her clipboard. By the time she'd done the gardens and returned to the house her batteries were running low.

It'd been a relief to tell Carrie about James, yes. But she'd have to deal with Wayne and the bogus engagement tomorrow, and the dreaded Cynthia Monday. And while the very thought of James not only tickled her curiosity but her erogenous zones, she might never be able to deal with him again.

And if he did come back? Well, she told herself, *carpe diem* and all that.

In the entrance hall Amanda looked at the reconstruction. It was hideously empty, a shell inside a husk, a mockery of a human face. James had been alive. Then, between one second and the next, a bullet had stopped his heart and he was—if not dead, then reduced to his minimum. *I want my sword.* Amanda touched the box containing the scabbard as though she could touch the evocative bend in its length. No matter what she did for him—no matter what she did with him—he'd never live again.

She turned off the lights, went upstairs, and stood in front of Sally's portrait. The Armstrongs hadn't had to leave that night. The British had moved out the next day. "But Daddy had to protect you, didn't he?" Amanda said aloud. "Not from James or even Archibald. From yourself. Do I ever know the feeling."

Sally's painted features remained static. Shrugging, Amanda went downstairs and scooted Wayne's chair back against the wall. There was one of Helen's cameras on the floor. She'd probably given it to Wayne to hold. No surprise he'd forgotten to give it back. But Helen would probably be at Cynthia's lunch and admiration society Monday. *The Grant project.*

Not one item in the house had been moved. Good. Amanda would give James a broken glass—he had little left besides passion, both good and bad—but she hoped his unstable temper wouldn't trash some priceless artifact. Carrie might humor her ghostly fancies, but no one else would.

Amanda fed both Lafayette and herself. Two microwaved burritos and the evening news, though, were a poor substitute for what she really wanted. She could see herself and James cuddled up in several yards of tartan wool, exchanging post-coital nuzzlings and tidbits of eighteenth-century history.

Might as well set the scene. She put on a CD of *Greatest Hits of 1777,* which James would think was contemporary music. *He* wouldn't make appalling puns on the title of Bach's "Air on a G String." She'd tell him the musicians were in the next room. Not that he'd care—people of his class weren't inhibited by the presence of servants.

Lafayette went for his evening sortie. Amanda sat down at her computer and sent an e-mail query to Preservation Imaging, Ltd, "Do you have a phone number for Lady Norah Grant?" Then she pulled up her thesis, rearranged the paragraphs and tried different words from the thesaurus. The phone didn't ring. Thank goodness Wayne had the decency to lie low. She'd feel better about him if just once he'd stand up to his mother. But then, she was hardly standing up to Cynthia herself.

The CD stopped. In the ensuing silence Lafayette's return through the cat flap sounded like the report of a pistol. Amanda broke the record for the sitting high jump. But the cat calmly made himself at home on the chair. According to the feline early warning system, then, James was nowhere in the vicinity.

At last Amanda went to bed. She turned the blanket back and sprawled on the sheet, trying to resolve James's scarlet coat and blue-green kilt from the darkness. But the shadows remained shadows. James didn't come.

CHAPTER THIRTEEN

Amanda awoke suddenly from an uneasy sleep. A brushing sensation, like teasing fingertips, traced the inside of her leg from ankle to thigh. "James?"

He wasn't there. Neither was the cat. She peered groggily at the thin light of dawn edging the window blinds. The breeze from the windows and the fan was chilly and she sat up, groping for the sheets. They were compressed into a semicircle by her side. The mattress sagged, as though someone was sitting on the edge of the bed. "James?" She reached out.

The mattress rose back into place. The covers loosened. If his disembodied presence had been there, if she hadn't sensed some lingering figment of a dream, he was gone now.

Amanda dredged herself from the bed and dressed in the day's designated straightjacket. Lafayette was waiting for her in the kitchen, his nose wrinkled suspiciously. She let him sniff her hand, passed inspection, and fed him his breakfast. She was just heading toward the computer when she heard the back door buzzer.

Wayne's solid shape was silhouetted in the window. So much for checking her e-mail. Amanda turned off the alarms and opened the door. "Good morning, Wayne."

"Hi, Amanda. I thought I should get here a little early, just to—to. . . ." His hands wrung the shape from his wig, as though trying to squeeze out words. "Are you feeling better?"

"I'm fine. Come on in." Amanda went around unlocking doors, opening windows, turning on lights, while Wayne limped at her heels. "How's your ankle?"

"Almost well. Mother wanted me to bring the cane again—it was her grandfather's, he was a bank president." He took a deep breath and started over. "Mrs. Benedetto heard footsteps at night. But you told me there wasn't anyone else. So who made the steps?"

"Maybe a peeping tom," Amanda replied. "I hope he got an eyeful. It wasn't anyone I invited, that's for sure." Which was only the truth up to a point—she hadn't invited James originally, but she sure was now.

Wayne frowned, then smoothed his face into a grimace that he apparently meant to be a smile. "I'm sorry about my mom. I know she comes on pretty strong, but she means well."

"By practically announcing our engagement? Without bothering to ask if we even liked each other?"

"I love you, Amanda."

She turned on the lights above the display. No, it wasn't the plasticine lips of the reconstruction that had said those words. She glanced around. Wayne's eyes bulged with sincerity. His wig was starting to look like road kill.

"I know how you feel," she said. "But love has to be a two-way street, doesn't it? And you're going the wrong way down a one-way . . ." She almost said "dead end," but a one-way dead end was where James was stalled. "I'm sorry. Although I don't see why I should keep apologizing because my feelings aren't what you want them to be."

"My feelings aren't what you want, either," he said truculently.

"No kidding." Amanda tried again. "If I'd realized your mother was off on the wrong track about—about us, I could have set the record straight. But it never occurred to me that anyone could possibly think . . ." *Don't kick the man when he's down.* "Either you tell her the truth or I will. This is beyond embarrassing."

"Well it's damned embarrassing for me, too."

The Chinese vase on the sideboard behind Wayne's back rose into the air and headed straight for his head. Amanda stared. James *was* back. But what did he think he was doing with that vase—protecting her from poor feckless Wayne? *James!* The vase circled back, making a perfect landing.

Wayne turned around to see what Amanda was looking at. "What is it? A mouse?"

"Ah—I'm not sure."

"Lafayette needs to get his rear in gear. Why else do we bother to feed him?"

Amanda didn't answer that. She skimmed around Wayne and opened the front door. For once she wasn't greeted by a blast of sun. The morning was cloudy, still, and damp. Wayne stepped out onto the porch beside her, cramming his wig onto his head. She tried to smooth it into shape, so at least he didn't look like a possum was nesting on his scalp.

"Amanda?"

"Yes, Wayne?"

"Just friends?"

"Just friends," she told him. "Take it or leave it."

He started back into the house. "My ankle hurts. I'll go sit in the library like I did yesterday. Can you. . . ?"

"Sure. No problem."

He limped away, favoring his left foot. Amanda looked toward the front gate and was glad to see Carrie hurrying along the walk.

"How's it going?" she called.

"Same as usual," replied Amanda. "Hot weather, stubborn Wayne."

Carrie glanced into the house. "And your other admirer?"

"I haven't *seen* him since Friday, but he's around. I wish . . . Hey, Helen left one of her cameras here yesterday. If I actually got a picture of him, would you believe me?"

"A photo isn't exactly proof—there're double exposures and other kinds of trick photography, but . . ." Carrie shook her head. "Who's being stubborn? Sure, if you get a reasonable picture I'll suspend disbelief."

"It's a deal." Amanda nodded firmly, even as she told herself a photo of crushed bedclothes or a vase floating in mid-air wasn't going to do it. And what was she going to tell James? "Hold still, I'm going to take your picture?" Assuming, of course, he ever re-appeared with enough physical form to photograph. With enough physical form for anything else, for that matter.

"Here they come," said Carrie, and waved a greeting to a troupe of children liberated from Sunday school for a historical trek.

The day passed from normality to tedium. Wayne sat in the library and received homage from the sightseers, leaving Carrie, Amanda, Roy, and the other interpreters to navigate the stairs. Amanda kept a sharp eye out, but saw no more levitating crockery. Clouds covered the sun, a sudden flurry of raindrops drummed on the roof, the clouds cleared and the sun came out. The air was so thick Amanda felt she could cut it with a knife. And not just because of the weather.

At closing time Carrie reminded her of Cynthia's lunch tomorrow. "Excuse me," she amended. "Little luncheon."

"A command performance," said Amanda. "I'll be there."

She locked the front door and, steeling herself, went into the library. No one was there. From the kitchen window she saw Wayne and Roy halfway to the parking lot, Roy slowing his stride to Wayne's uneven pace. The archaeological students joined the procession and silence fell over Melrose.

A piece of paper lay on the kitchen table, Amanda's name at the top. It wasn't in graceful eighteenth-century script but twentieth-first-century scribble. "Don't forget Mother's lunch tomorrow. I promise to behave myself. I can't make any promises for her, but I'll see if I can get her to back off. Love, Anthony Wayne Chancellor."

Crumpling the paper, Amanda pitched it toward the garbage can. Just "I'll see if I can get her to back off," not, "I'll tell her the truth." But then, the truth was pretty subjective right now.

Amanda showered and changed, then made her inspection tour. She fed Lafayette and petted him for a few moments, telling him, "Never mind what Wayne said. You're an important interpreter yourself." The cat offered her a supercilious smirk and proceeded to wash his face.

She finally got to her e-mail, only to find that her query to Preservation Imaging had bounced back with a "we're out of the office for the weekend" message. Tomorrow, then.

Amanda scanned her collection of frozen dinners and instead finished off the pie. She set Helen's camera to low light—the last thing she needed to do was shoot the flash at James. Besides, while he might be reflected in a mirror he might not necessarily show up on film.

The room went suddenly cold. Lafayette, forgetting his dignity, scrambled out the flap. Amanda spun around. When James materialized in the bedroom door she was looking right at him—one moment he wasn't there, the next he was. Her mind hiccuped, even now rejecting the evidence of her eyes. But her senses high-dived into acceptance, sending a flush to her cheeks and leaving her stomach hollow.

James's face was puzzled, almost resentful, as though he, too, didn't quite believe he was there. He gazed up at the fan and the ceiling light, then looked into the darkened bedroom. Amanda lifted the camera, snapped the shutter, wound the film, snapped and wound again.

James turned toward her. She whisked the camera behind her back, and from there eased it onto the desk. But he refused to notice it, just as he refused to notice the computer or the microwave or even the light bulbs. He would lose masculine points, Amanda told herself, admitting he didn't know something. Her father and her brother would rather drive for miles the wrong way than ask directions.

"Amanda," James said, but his puzzlement didn't quite relax into a smile.

"I was afraid you wouldn't come back," she blurted.

"I would not leave you, Sweeting. Your temper is most amiable, and your manner of the greatest civility. Your beauty leaves me giddy. I hold you in the very highest esteem. . . ." His voice died away. Maybe he couldn't remember his lines.

But James wasn't putting any moves on her now. His eyes were uncertain, not quite focussed. His body, looking solid enough when it first appeared, now wavered against the doorway. He half-turned into the bedroom, as though he was reluctant to let Amanda see his face.

He couldn't have picked a better way to draw her closer. She stepped toward him. "James? What's wrong?" Like she didn't know. A broken glass, a flying vase—he must be up to his neck in more frustration than she'd ever felt.

"I very much fear that nothing is right," he said. "This is Melrose Hall, is it not?"

"Yes."

"But not the Melrose Hall I know. Sally and her father are gone. My regiment is gone, and I alone remain. I am undone."

Amanda tried to touch his shoulder, but her uplifted hand met thin air.

"My head is filled by the scent of roses. I know by that most delectable scent I am near the summerhouse, but it is night and my eyes are shrouded by darkness. Archibald is waiting for me, I know, waiting cloaked in shadow like some evil creature of the underworld sent by Hades himself to summon me to that river from which no traveler returns."

"You did return," she said gently.

"So it seems. If the past is but a dream, then this—this present is nightmare, confounding my senses." He thinned almost to nothingness, then solidified. His eyes fixed on Amanda's face like a beacon at the end of a long, dark tunnel. "You, my sweet, serve as Eurydice to my Orpheus, serve as Demeter searching for her lost daughter, braving hell itself to bring me again to—to what?"

"Your home?" she prompted. "Your sword? Revenge?"

He glanced down at the empty scabbard, stroking it with his fingertips. The gesture reminded Amanda of the sensation that had waked her up this morning. "My sword is at Dundreggan, you say?"

"Well, it was. I'll find out for you."

"And if you find it to be there, at Dundreggan, across the seas from this—this beknighted land, how can you bring it to me, or better still, me to it, so that I may . . . No, I cannot rest, not until I have my revenge upon the serpent in my bosom, my cousin Archibald."

"Maybe I can get you home to Scotland," Amanda said carefully, trying not to introduce such concepts as boxes and bones. "Or maybe I could get your sword shipped over here for temporary display. For what that's worth. As for Archibald, he's been—gone for a long time. You're not going to get any personal satisfaction from him, although you can go right ahead and imagine him roasting in hell."

"So then." James had faded out as she talked. Now she could see the doorframe through his body.

Amanda raised both hands, trying to pull him back. "But I can publish the truth about Archibald and the summerhouse at night and—and everything—so that the world will know what really happened. Would that help?"

The scarlet coat, the multi-colored kilt, the shine of silver materialized beneath Amanda's hands. This time she could feel an itch in each palm and a tickle on her fingers, which became actual pressure as James leaned toward her. His eyes glowed hotly. "If you could publish the story of his perfidy, so that my name is remembered and remarked upon by all those of quality in the Island of Britain, why then, Madame, you would have my deepest gratitude."

"Do you want me to say anything about Isabel?"

"Isabel turned against me, there's a stab to my heart, a mortal wound if ever there was one. This facile temper of the beauteous sex. . . ." Briefly his face contorted and his teeth glinted between his lips in a spasm of pain and anger. His left hand tightened on the scabbard, his right made a fist and punched at the doorframe but made only a dull thunk.

"Or we can let that go," Amanda told him hastily. She knew for certain what rewards Archibald had earned from his shot in the dark, but it might be better if James only suspected. There was no proof Isabel and Archibald had been an item before James's death. "I'm sorry about Isabel."

Beneath her hands his body was opaque, almost firm. "It was a warm evening when I went to the summerhouse among the sweet scent of roses, to think upon Isabel's latest letter. As if with intent to console me, Sally came to me there. The American lasses have learned to be bold, I think, though not, of course, so bold as the London . . ." He shook his head. "I beg your pardon, Amanda."

"No need," she said dryly.

He might be smelling roses, but all she could smell was whiskey, its scent alone rising to her head as surely as a stiff drink. Her fingertips sketched the lapels of his coat, the button loops, the leather belt, and moved around his waist to the long coat tails.

"Sally—Miss Armstrong—is indeed a lovely lass, though not so much so as Isabel. I left her behind in a garden, she was promised to me in a garden—I return to the garden, it seems, but so do we all, searching for that first pleasure of mankind within the sacred portals of Eden."

"Before or after the original sin?" Amanda asked.

He grinned. Fabric stirred as he embraced her. It was an elusive embrace, but perceptible. No surprise, she told herself, he was the most focussed and the most centered when he was coming on to her, pursuing the familiar pattern of pursuit and conquest, beyond reason but also beyond doubt. Many a man bolstered his ego on the body of a woman while his id, his subconscious, ran riot with candlesticks and drinking glasses.

James, blissfully ignorant of psychoanalysis, was still grinning. "You are bold enough yourself, Madame, to bandy words with me."

"I'm an American lass, too, you know."

"You ask no apology for the liberties I have taken with your person?"

"No. I'd like for you to take more."

"Indeed," he said, his gaze moving up and down her body. "If I cannot return to my home, then I shall find a home in you. If I cannot recover my sword, then I shall employ a similar weapon, and you will be its sheath."

Amanda tried not to laugh in his face. But he wasn't putting her on. The pun fell naturally from his lips—as an educated man he knew the Latin word for "sheath" was "vagina." And, under the circumstances, she forgave him the unsavory male custom of referring to his penis as a weapon.

A spark leaped between their mouths. She pressed against him. . . . The telephone rang. Amanda found herself posed, arms outstretched, lips parted, touching nothing. "Shit!" she exclaimed, and snatched up the phone—if it was Wayne she was going to burn his ears off. "Hello!"

Several squeals and hums prefaced a recorded voice. "Hello. Have you ever considered the benefits to your loved ones of life insurance?"

She slammed the phone down. She hadn't wanted to be saved by the bell, thank you very much. "James? Come back, James. It was only a noise. . . ."

Nothing.

Amanda threw herself onto the couch and wrapped her arms tightly around her ribcage. She summoned James's image, the smoky eyes, the entrancing smile, the elegant language so typical of his time but so utterly ridiculous today. And the pain, the pain with its edge of anger, beneath his charm.

Either he had one thing wrong, Amanda thought, or he rejected the female role even symbolically. It was Orpheus who had gone to hell to save Eurydice. And he had failed.

CHAPTER FOURTEEN

It was the unaccustomed air conditioning that made the back of her neck crawl, Amanda told herself as she entered stately Chancellor manor. Not Cynthia's smiling face. But still she wished she'd worn a crucifix.

Cynthia whisked her into a living room that looked like an advertisement for a furniture gallery. "How are you this morning, Amanda dear? Well, I suppose I should say this afternoon, it's straight up noon. I'd expect you to arrive right on the dot. Would you like a small glass of sherry? Not that I indulge at lunchtime every day, you understand, but today is special."

"No, thank you. Some iced tea would be nice."

"Of course. I'll get it for you. Sit down." Cynthia's color was high and her flowing skirts snapped as she walked. She disappeared through a swinging door, providing a glimpse of a gleaming country-style kitchen and the two caterers who had fed the garden club on Friday.

Mouth-watering odors wafted to Amanda's nostrils. Inhaling deeply, she perched on the edge of a Queen Anne chair, yanked her skirt down to her knees—odd, how short it seemed—and tried to fluff up her hair. There was something to be said for wearing a cap every day, especially in this humidity.

Wayne lumbered into the room, spruced up in a suit and tie, his limp noticeably absent. "Oh, hi."

"Did you tell her?" Amanda asked.

"Well, not exactly—she's been getting lunch ready, you know, setting the table and stuff."

"What do you mean, not exactly?"

Cynthia spurted back through the swinging door and presented Amanda with a tall glass of iced tea. A green sprig of mint protruded from the top, tickling her nose when she took a sip.

"Mint from my own garden." Cynthia sat down on a settee upholstered in period flame stitch. Several strings of beads interspersed with tiny agate fetishes hung over the neckline of her blouse, and the matching earrings ricocheted off her cheeks as she talked. "Now, Amanda, I must apologize for embarrassing you Saturday."

"Erk," Amanda replied through the shrubbery.

"Apparently Wayne was intending to keep things very low-profile, undercover as it were."

Amanda gagged. Wayne's face went puce.

But Cynthia sailed obliviously past the double meaning. "So the least I can do is pretend there's nothing going on. All right? Just our secret?"

"Mrs. Chanceller," Amanda began, "there's been a . . ."

The doorbell chimed. Cynthia bounced up, necklace clattering, and went to answer it. Amanda glared at Wayne, who studied the Meissen figurines on the mantelpiece.

"Come in, come in," trilled Cynthia from the entrance hall. "Only a few minutes late. And here's Bill coming up the walk."

Carrie and Helen hustled into the living room like foxes before a pack of hunting dogs. "Hello, Amanda, hello, Wayne," said Carrie. "Why is it the phone always rings just at the wrong time?"

"Atlantic Bell's wicked sense of humor," Amanda replied.

"Where's the food?" asked Helen. "I have to get out to the Shirley plantation this afternoon."

Amanda pulled the camera from her handbag. "Helen, you left this at Melrose on Saturday."

"Oh, thanks." Helen shook the camera, as though scolding it for wandering off.

Carrie sat down on the settee, quirking an eyebrow at Amanda.

Amanda told Helen, "I made a couple of pictures myself. Photos of my living room. I hope you don't mind."

"Of course not. Five more exposures on the roll. When I finish it up I'll make a couple of prints for you, okay?"

"Thanks." And what if Helen saw James's ghost? Amanda asked herself. Well, she'd come up with something. Maybe even the truth.

Cynthia ushered Bill Hewitt into the room. He greeted everyone with a distracted nod. His tie was askew and an ink stain edged the bottom of his shirt pocket. He'd probably left three-fourths of his brain back in the lab.

"Sherry?" the lady of the manor asked. "Iced tea? Soft drinks? Bourbon, Helen? Well, we'll just pretend the sun is over the yardarm, won't we? Wayne, take care of the drinks."

He plodded off to the wet bar. Cynthia posed before the fireplace. "Isn't this nice? I'm so pleased you could come today to discuss the plans I have for Melrose Hall. How's the summerhouse coming, Bill?"

"Foundations are traced," he replied. "Carrie found some prints of summerhouses of the period. We're working on plans now. Then we'll estimate the cost of labor and materials."

"Just let me know how much you need," Cynthia told him. "The summerhouse could be the starting point for a nature trail, couldn't it? An extension of the garden tour. Paths through the woods and down to the river."

"Pedal boats?" suggested Helen with an impish gleam.

"You're way out ahead of me, Helen. Yes, boat rides on the river, although I think pedal boats would be a bit small, don't you?"

Wayne doled out the drinks. Amanda tucked her feet beneath her chair so she wouldn't "accidentally" trip him up.

"Children's classes," said Cynthia. "We tend to focus on Sally's love affair with Captain Grant, but she was also a little girl at Melrose."

"We deal with quite a few children at Melrose as it is," Carrie put in.

"We can make the barn into a theatre, and every hour or so show the film Helen and I have been working on. 'Melrose, A Window into History.' And, since we're lucky enough to have all this new information about Captain Grant turn up—and Captain Grant himself, for that matter—we're going to make a separate film about him. He was never the faceless enemy, not as far as Sally was concerned."

Helen raised her glass in acknowledgement. Amanda rattled her ice cubes and thought of James's handsome face.

"I have a designer working on Melrose's own web site, linked into the main CW site," Cynthia went on. "It'll highlight not only the house and gardens but antique and art shows. Rare book sales. Craft shows, as long as everything's good quality. None of that plastic ticky-tacky you see along the highway."

Wayne chimed in, "And you were thinking of a coffee shop in the back of the gift shop."

"A tea shop would be more appropriate, wouldn't it?" Cynthia said. "Tea and scones and butter cookies, that sort of thing."

"Cucumber sandwiches," offered Amanda, deadpan.

"Exactly! And for the piece de resistance, I can't imagine anything that would draw more tourists than a bed and breakfast right in Melrose Hall."

After a moment's silence Helen essayed, "You expect the guests to use chamber pots and bathe in front of the fire?"

"Don't be silly, Helen. We can convert the sewing room at the end of the second floor hallway into a lovely bathroom. It's right above the kitchen, half the plumbing's already there."

"Breakfast?" asked Hewitt.

"The caretaker can get up early and serve a nice little breakfast in the dining room. Fruit, croissants, coffee or tea."

Thanks, Amanda thought. *I needed that.*

"What if Melrose really is haunted?" Carrie asked. "What if the ghost of Captain Grant scares people away in the middle of the night?"

"You've always had such a delicious sense of humor, Carrie," said Cynthia. "We'll go into the dining room now."

Amanda jostled Carrie in the doorway. "Couldn't resist that crack, could you?"

"I'm not going to let her live down that seance."

The dining room was as graciously appointed as the living room. The cherry table and sideboard were polished into mirrors. Gleaming silverware lay on starched linen place mats. The centerpiece was smaller than the one for the garden club but just as lush.

Amanda found herself seated at Cynthia's right hand, with Wayne at the opposite end of the table. She counted six kinds of lettuce on her plate. The dressing was a delectable raspberry vinaigrette.

"Tell them about the Grant project," Wayne urged as the caterer served rolls.

"I was getting to that, dear," Cynthia told him. "First of all, Captain Grant's sword is indeed at Dundreggan, in a display case in the great hall."

"All right!" Amanda exclaimed. "So the Grants still live there?"

"Why, yes. I hate to think what the place looks like, with their financial difficulties and so forth—I believe they're even running a business there—but I know only too well how hard it is to give up a fine old family estate. I let Melrose go for the good of the community, of course."

"Of course," said Carrie.

Cynthia nibbled a lettuce leaf with her front teeth, like a rabbit. "The results of the DNA tests are in, aren't they, Bill?"

"The lab in Baltimore used the newer PCR test," Hewitt replied, crumbs flying from his moustache. "Less precise, but quicker. And we told them we needed quicker."

"The results are hardly going to solve a murder," said Cynthia.

Carrie and Amanda glanced at each other across the table.

"The PCR uses shorter segments of DNA," Hewitt went on. "Effective even if the samples are degraded. Which ours were. Couldn't be helped."

"And?" Helen prodded.

"Malcolm Grant sent a family tree along with the blood sample—he's descended from James Grant's grandparents on both sides of his family. And sure enough, the results show a match between the bones' DNA and his."

"Nice blue blood," muttered Carrie. "Interbred. Probably not a chin in the lot."

"So with the documentary evidence Carrie found for us," Cynthia concluded, "we have a positive ID!"

Helen, Carrie, and Wayne made appreciative noises, Amanda chiming in a moment late. The caterer replaced her empty salad plate with a plate of asparagus rolled in thin-sliced ham and smothered in Hollandaise sauce.

"Mother didn't talk to Lady Norah," said Wayne. "She wasn't in. The son answered the phone."

"The Honorable Malcolm Grant," Cynthia explained. "Very polite, just as charmingly eccentric as his mother. He must be one of those wonderful British military types, don't you think? Very upright, moustache trained just so, habit of command and all that."

So he wasn't old and doddering, Amanda told herself. No reason he should be. Middle-aged, like John Cleese. She set down her fork. "Why do you call the Grants eccentric?"

Cynthia turned to her as though she were Oliver Twist asking for more food. Wayne seemed faintly shocked. "Oh, well, ah—people of their class, you know, you expect certain—well, a certain style. Lady Norah's clothing—the honorable Malcolm's accent—at first I thought it was a servant answering the phone." She patted her lips with her napkin, closing the subject.

So The Honorable Malcolm didn't sound like an actor on Masterpiece Theatre. Nor John Cleese. Amanda saw a fierce Highlander like Wallace's friend in *Braveheart*, just this side of a noble savage, with flowing red locks and a claymore clutched in massive hands.

"Bill," said Cynthia, and Hewitt looked up. "You'll be finished with Captain Grant's bones tomorrow morning."

He swallowed. "I could be. Casts, measurements, samples, photos. It's just a matter of . . ."

"Good. Then you can have them packed up and out to Melrose tomorrow afternoon." She cut herself a piece of ham but didn't put it in her mouth. Her utensils rang against the plate as she set them down. "It's just so exciting I can't contain myself! I have these brainstorms, you see, all the time—new publicity angles, new programs. It's a gift." She surveyed her audience through her lashes, expecting applause, maybe.

Every face around the table turned toward her. Even Wayne was clueless, Amanda noted with a sideways glance, not that that was anything unusual. She was starting to feel nervous, the same way she felt when she saw a police car in her rear view mirror.

"A new publicity angle?" asked Helen.

"Re-patriating Captain Grant's bones. Mr. Malcolm Grant sounded very interested when I put the idea to him. Dundreggan does have a family cemetery, he said, with graves dating back to the seventeenth century. A small private ceremony to lay Captain Grant to rest would make a lovely closing for our film. Why, we might want to do an entire book about Captain Grant—I'll write the introduction, of course. Maybe a TV special, an episode of *Nova* or *The New Explorers* on PBS."

A spear of asparagus wedged in Amanda's tonsils. She sputtered and took a gulp of her tea. *I want to go home,* James had said.

"Yes, Amanda, you clever girl, it was your idea! Just wait until you hear the rest." Cynthia opened her arms like Pavarotti going for the high note. "You and Wayne are going to be Williamsburg's emissaries to Dundreggan!"

Amanda gaped. She was hallucinating. Cynthia just said. . . . She snapped her teeth together before she drooled Hollandaise down her blouse and shot a look at Wayne. His flabbergasted expression had to be genuine. If he were acting, he wouldn't let the end of his tie trail onto his plate.

"You do have a passport, don't you, Amanda?" Cynthia asked. "Wayne, darling, your tie."

The other faces at the table were blurs, and offered no help. Amanda turned back to Cynthia. "Passport," she croaked. "Yeah, I got one a couple of years ago just in case. . . . What do you mean Wayne and I are going to be emissaries?"

"Well it's obvious, isn't it? You and Wayne will leave Richmond Wednesday afternoon, change planes in Newark, arrive in Glasgow Thursday morning, and take another short flight on to Inverness. Mr. Grant very kindly said he'd either meet you himself or find someone to do so. I'm calling him this afternoon with your flight num . . ."

"You've already made reservations?" *I've lost it,* Amanda thought. *I just interrupted Cynthia.*

Cynthia laughed, her necklace jangling, and patted Amanda's arm. "Don't worry, dear, I'm paying all your expenses. Just one more donation to Colonial Williamsburg, right? We'll get some other interpreters to fill in at Melrose while you and Wayne are gone, including someone to stay the nights. I always worry about you out there alone, a woman and everything."

And what? Amanda wanted to ask.

"Helen, give Wayne and Amanda some cameras, please."

"Sure," said Helen.

"Carrie, you'll need to brief them on what you need for your article. And I think it's only fair you list Amanda as co-author."

Across the table Carrie muttered, "Boy, that never occurred to me."

"Bill, the bones. I thought at first we might leave a few of those finger bones on display, but no, that doesn't seem right, does it?"

"Can't usher the man through the Pearly Gates without all of his body parts." Hewitt sounded as though he was starting to enjoy the comedy. It was a comedy, wasn't it? Any minute now Cynthia would shout, "April Fool!"

Amanda looked down at her plate. The ham and asparagus were gone, replaced by a cup of chocolate mousse frilled with whipped cream. A hand holding a pot of coffee hovered in her peripheral vision. "Ah, no thank you." The last thing she needed right now was caffeine.

She was going to Scotland. She was taking James home. Free. No, not free, saddled with Wayne. Talk about every silver lining having a cloud.

Scotland! All right!

"Will a week be long enough?" Cynthia asked, glancing conspiratorially from Amanda to Wayne and back again.

Wayne was smiling his village idiot's smile, his eyes glazed, a morsel of whipped cream stuck to his upper lip. *Anticipating a honeymoon?* Amanda asked him silently. But she wasn't going to enable either of the Chancellors to spoil her mousse. She dipped her spoon and licked sweet chocolate.

"We'll keep the scabbard," Cynthia went on. "Perhaps Lady Norah will send us the sword for display. We could have a nice little ceremony re-uniting the two. Maybe a re-creation of the battle of Greensprings Farm for the film."

I want my sword. Did it matter whether James was near the scabbard—the real, physical, scabbard—as long as he was near the sword? Probably not. Not as long as the truth came out. *I want revenge.* Amanda sucked down the last of the mousse, licked her lips, and envisioned the garrets at Dundreggan crammed with family diaries, letters, signed confessions—anything to back up the murder charges. Which Cynthia could then trumpet from the rooftops as loudly as her heart desired. *Yes!*

"Is everyone finished?" Cynthia pushed back her chair, rose, and led the way into the living room trailing clouds of glory.

"Thanks for the chow," Helen said, "but I have to run. Amanda, Wayne, I'll come out to Melrose tomorrow for a photography lesson, okay?"

"I'll be ready," Wayne said, rubbing his hands together. With her fingertip Cynthia wiped the cream from his lip. Together they turned to Amanda and smiled, teeth gleaming.

"Mrs. Chancellor, we need to get one thing clear," she began. She stepped onto the deep-pile carpet of the living room and turned her heel. Carrie grabbed her arm. "Thanks."

"Bones," said Hewitt. "Thank you, Cynthia—storage box—customs declaration. Bones. Bye."

Cynthia opened the door. "Sorry you can't stay longer. But we'll get together soon and discuss our plans. How about a television series on historical houses and the people who lived there? I could introduce each episode. I have contacts at WETA in Washington, you know."

Hewitt shoved Helen out of the way and ran out the door. Carrie, still grasping Amanda's arm, scooped both their purses from the floor and headed for open air, murmuring, "Thank you so much for the wonderful lunch, Amanda and I need to put our heads together for that article, so much research to do, what a wonderful opportunity this is."

"I always wanted to go to the UK," added Amanda. "I really appreciate your generosity, even though there's something you need to know. . . ."

"She'll love Scotland," Carrie concluded. "Lunch was wonderful. See you tomorrow, Wayne."

They were outside. The door shut behind them. The moist sunshine seared Amanda's cheeks and drew thick beads of sweat from her forehead. She tasted chocolate in the back of her throat, cloying sweet, like Cynthia. That buzz she was hearing was probably cicadas in the shrubbery, not her brain on overload. "Scotland. Wednesday. What'll I wear?"

"I'll lend you a couple of sweaters."

"My hair's a mess."

"Go down to Beauty World and ask for Maryann. She'll give you a quick trim, fix you right up."

The sun glinted off the windshield of her car and Amanda winced. "Geez, talk about a Catch-22 situation. Good thing you hauled me out of there before I spilled the beans about the engagement. If Cynthia knew the truth she wouldn't be sending me to Scotland with Wayne, would she? Or would she?"

Carrie rolled her eyes. "Here we were plotting an end run around her and she makes an end run around us. By giving you just what you want, the Grant family archives."

"Like I'm going to give her what she wants? No way am I taking on Wayne. I mean, now he's got his mother pimping for him."

"It's not his idea. And Cynthia just thinks she's being a cool contemporary mom. If the sexual connotations ever even occurred to her, she banished them to the woodshed."

"If Wayne wasn't such a doormat I wouldn't be getting a cool trip," Amanda said, shaking her head. "But it's because he's a doormat I want to strangle him and feed him to the Loch Ness monster. Geez."

"Just don't do him in until you've brought me all the information you can find, including annotated copies and complete documentation. Okay?"

It was a toss-up between four-letter words and a laugh. Amanda chose the laugh. She groped in her purse for her car keys. "Okay. I resign myself to the whims of fate. Where's the beauty shop?"

Carrie gave her directions. "See you tomorrow. Assuming you'll be all right out at Melrose tonight."

"I'd rather deal with James than Wayne any day. I guess he'll be happy to hear he's going home."

"Uh-huh," Carrie said cautiously.

"I did get his picture. I think. I'm not sure just why it's important to me that I have a picture of him. To prove it to you, I guess."

"No, to prove it to yourself," Carrie told her. "Say hi to the gals at the beauty shop."

Amanda unlocked her car and climbed in, wondering whether one or the other of the Chancellors was watching her from the house and gloating. The truth wouldn't make any difference to Cynthia, she decided. Lady C. moved in mysterious ways, her wonders to perform.

A quick shampoo and trim did settle her down—women had hairdressers, men had bartenders—and she spent her grocery money on a twill skirt and a waterproof jacket. She checked with her bank and made sure her credit card would work in British ATM machines, just so Wayne couldn't pick up all the tabs.

Amanda returned to Melrose late in the afternoon, changed her clothes, and called her parents in Chicago. "Guess what? Mrs. Chancellor is sending me to Scotland to take the bones back—sure, I'll send you photos—yeah, I have my passport, it makes a good ID." She didn't tell them about Wayne, just that a fellow interpreter was going along. She certainly couldn't tell them about James. *I've fallen for a ghost—yeah, he's a bit old for me, but it's just a Highland fling anyway. . .*

She returned from her tour of the house and grounds to find Lafayette dozing on her new skirt. She lured him away by spiking his usual dinner with a bit of leftover lunchmeat.

While she brushed the cat fur from the twill she made a mental checklist. Suitcase. For a week, just one. A carry-on. How big would the box of bones be? She'd need money for porters. And she had to organize her notes. Going away and leaving her thesis in a drunk and disorderly condition was like going out without clean underwear.

In the gathering darkness Amanda threw together what perishables she had in her refrigerator and ate them, not that she really tasted a thing. Then she checked her e-mail. There was a note from Preservation Imaging with Dundreggan's phone number, signed, *Malcolm Grant*. Too late now, she'd be on his doorstep in a couple of days. Not that Cynthia had bothered mentioning her name, it seemed, as Grant hadn't picked up on it. Either that or he was a total snob. He wasn't into self-promotion, though—she still didn't know just what Preservation Imaging, Ltd, did, although it sounded intriguing.

Amanda was e-mailing her friends with the scoop when the phone rang. "Melrose Hall."

"Hi," said Wayne's voice. "It's me."

"Wayne, what am I going to do with you?"

"I've got it all figured out. When we get back from the trip we'll tell Mother we discovered we just couldn't get along with each other and so we're breaking up."

"That 'I Love Lucy' routine is so old it's got whiskers on it."

"It'll work, really."

"Nothing's working like I expected it to. It's worth a try, I guess. But Wayne. . . ."

"Yes?"

"Oh, nothing. I need to go. I have to get myself organized."

"It'll be a cool trip, we'll have a good time, you'll see."

"Good night. See you tomorrow." Amanda hung up. She was getting more and more cranky with Wayne. She hated herself for it, and she hated him for making her do it. But he'd backed her into a corner. He was probably just stalling her with his "we're breaking up" plot. He intended to come back engaged for real. . . . She was not going to let poor testosterone-impaired Wayne ruin her trip.

This was sweet. A busman's holiday, a chance to do some significant research, a chance to get out of the heat, a chance to help James. To help him rest. To help him leave her forever.

This time Lafayette didn't yowl and scratch. Deeply offended, he marched briskly away and banged through the flap. Amanda felt the sudden chill gratefully—what was a bit of chill outside her body when the inside was flushed with warmth?

A moment later she was skimming the floor into James's arms. If he'd been solid she'd have knocked him backward. As it was, he caught her in a deliciously airy embrace, tartan swirling. His kisses were cool, moist, headier than whiskey. She allowed herself a lengthy greeting before trying to speak.

"James."

His lips and tongue caressed her neck, sending shivers down her back. His hair felt like spider webs against her ear.

"James, I have to tell you something."

His right hand dived beneath her T-shirt and cradled her left breast, thumb teasing the hard peak of the nipple. *Oh yeah.* No wonder the man had risen from the dead. That much testosterone would launch a Saturn rocket.

"James!" she squeaked breathlessly. "Wait a minute!"

He looked up, eyes dancing. "Yes, Sweeting? What would you say?"

"I have good news. I'm going to be able to take you home after all."

"Home."

"Scotland. Dundreggan. Just like you wanted."

"Ah." He frowned, and she could no longer feel his hand. "How kind of you, to undertake such a perilous journey on my behalf, but I fear I don't quite . . ."

Understand? No, he was much too proud to admit he didn't understand. "Your sword is at Dundreggan. You'll be there with it. And after I help write the article about you, everyone will know how Archibald—what Archibald did to you. You'll be able to rest."

"Ah." His hands fell away, letting her T-shirt fall. "My bones, you mean to say. You will return my bones to Dundreggan."

"Yeah, that's about the size of it."

"'Good friend, for Jesus' sake forbear to dig the dust enclosed here,'" James quoted. "'Curst be he who moves my bones.' Not that my bones are similar to those of Master Shakespeare, and they have already been disturbed, have they not, or I would not be . . ."

A ghost, Amanda finished for him. She'd done it again, hadn't she? She kept stepping in it with James like Wayne kept stepping in it with her.

"Melrose is more vivid in my mind than Dundreggan," James sighed. "Yet I am called to the land of my birth as Odysseus was called to Ithaca. But his Penelope was faithful and my Isabel was not."

"Don't worry about Isabel. That's history, you'll excuse my saying so." Amanda put her hands on his shoulders, or at least set her hands in the air next to the image of his shoulders, but he had faded so far she had nothing to touch. Maybe she shouldn't have told him, should simply have packed him up and carried him away. But no, that wasn't fair. If he woke up in Scotland he'd be more disoriented than ever. He deserved to know what was happening to him.

If he woke up. Once his physical remains left Melrose, the last place to activate his consciousness, he'd probably be gone for good. Once his physical remains were buried in Scottish soil he'd definitely be gone for good, because he'd have gotten what he wanted.

James's eyes shone like a cold northern sea lit by the last rays of the setting sun. *"An ciaradh m'fheasgair mo bheath air claoidh,"* he murmured, *"mo rosg air dunadh's 'a bhas gun chli.* It is a song the soldiers sing. 'When day is over and life is done, my eyes closed, my strength gone.' My strength gone. . . ."

He vanished from the circle of her arms. Amanda dropped her hands to her sides. "James, your strength isn't gone. Not when you're with me." She waited. Nothing. "James, we don't have much more time!" Nothing.

She punched the back of the couch with her fists. A cloud of dust rose into the air, hardly less substantial than James himself.

He might soon be at rest, but she wasn't so sure about herself.

CHAPTER FIFTEEN

Amanda stood in her usual pose in the entrance hall, but her mind was focussed on the night before. James didn't seem to have much control over his appearances and disappearances. He wasn't teasing her. . . . *Yeah, right.* Most men would love to vanish at heavy emotional moments.

A tourist group traipsed down the stairs, Wayne at their heels. "Have you seen Captain Grant's ghost?" a girl asked him.

"Stories of ghosts and spirits," he replied with a grave nod of his bewigged head, "are grounded on no other bottom than the fears and fancies and weak brains of men. Belief in ghosts is a sign of ignorance and gross superstition, fitting only for the vulgar classes."

Nope, Amanda thought. James wouldn't have believed in ghosts either.

"There was an article in the newspaper about that lady having a seance out here," the girl persisted, "and flowerpots crashing and stuff like that."

Wayne had the good grace to look embarrassed. "I'm very much afraid, miss, that no flowerpots were broken. I believe the lady was simply entertaining her friends. Thank you for your visit to my home. Please do us the very great honor of stopping by the gift shop." The sightseers stepped out the door and were swallowed by the afternoon sun.

Wayne pulled out a handkerchief, mopped his face, and said to Amanda, "My understudy's doing great. How's yours?"

"Vicky's a real trouper, picked up the lines instantly. And she looks more like Sally than I do—shorter and rounder in the face."

"Not as pretty as you are," Wayne said gallantly.

"Thanks." Another group of tourists arrived in the doorway and Amanda went to greet them. So far no one had taken the tour twice, and been confused by two different sets of Armstrongs.

When Amanda led this group back down the stairs she found one of Hewitt's students taking the four morsels of bone from the Lucite box. On the floor beside him sat a light wooden crate lined with stiff foam. In cutout shapes in the foam nestled James's skeleton.

The tourists gawked and pointed. The student explained what he was doing. Amanda hung back against the banister, her eyes moving from the portrait to the reconstruction to the mound of the skull peeking from the box. All three were empty illustrations of James, not the real man. The real man was a pattern in light and time. He couldn't be contained in or defined by wood, or foam, or bone.

The man she knew wasn't the same man he'd been in life, Amanda told herself. Her James was a tragic figure, with the appetites of the flesh but not its support. His touch was charmingly delicate because he wasn't up to anything stronger. His manner was appealingly vulnerable because his self-esteem had decayed with his body. If she'd met him as a living man, either in his era or outside it, she wouldn't have smiled at his boldness or sympathized with his temper. But she wasn't meeting him as a living man, was she?

The tourists were gone. "Here it is," the student said. "Hell of a long way to go for a funeral."

"Better late than never," Amanda replied vaguely.

The student unrolled a layer of foam over the bones and put the wooden lid loosely atop the box. "We've put some silica gel in there, but still, with this humidity, Dr. Hewitt said to leave the lid ajar until the last minute. Can you screw it down right before you leave?"

"No problem." Amanda took the screwdriver and set it on the sideboard. "Thanks."

She stood for a long moment after the student left, considering the crate. The oblong box. The coffin. It had handles at either end and a tidy little plastic pouch for the necessary papers. The word Fragile was stamped on every side. *You're going home, James.*

The screwdriver rolled clattering across the sideboard and pinged against the Chinese vase. Pleasure, Amanda wondered, or frustration? For a man so fair, James sure could play the brooding Byronic hero.

She hitched up her bodice and welcomed the next band of visitors.

At closing time Amanda shooed Wayne out the door with the others and headed back to her apartment pulling off her cap and loosening her gown. She didn't have to dress tomorrow, just hang around backstage ready to lend a hand if anyone needed her. Wayne was picking her up at two. In a limousine. Was she ever going to enjoy living on the right side of the tracks for a change.

Lafayette sat on the couch, guarding Helen's camera bag. The photographer hadn't tried to teach Wayne and Amanda the subtleties of filters and f-stops. She'd said, "Point there, punch here, wind this. And for God's sakes don't forget to take off the lens caps." She'd left box after box of film, figuring that if the travelers took lots of pictures some of them had to turn out.

Amanda stowed the film, zipped the bag shut, and patted Lafayette. She made her rounds of the house and the garden and turned off the lights in the entrance hall display, but not before taking one last look at the snuffbox with its relief of Dundreggan. She'd be there herself day after tomorrow. Her nerve endings tingled with anticipation.

The box of bones still sat beside the sideboard. No sense in leaving it there. All the other luggage would go out the back. Not that she thought of James as luggage. Tucking her clipboard beneath her arm and the screwdriver in her pocket, she lifted the wooden box and carried it back to her living room. It was surprisingly light. But then, there wasn't much inside.

Night fell. Dinnertime came and went. Amanda sewed on a button, pressed a blouse, and packed. No James. She made back-up copies of her thesis. No James. She sent off a couple of e-mails and surfed the Web. Funny how studying up on the Scottish ferry schedules didn't produce any Scots.

Lafayette seemed kind of restless, she thought hopefully, sniffing at the packing crate by the door, leaping on and off the windowsills. But the air was turgid, not cool. "James," she said aloud, "it's our last chance."

Nothing.

Lafayette hopped onto the bed and proceeded to lick himself down. Amanda pulled out a needlepoint project that she'd intended for her mother two Christmases ago. She stitched away and channel-surfed at the same time. Letterman's and Leno's jokes weren't particularly funny, especially those dealing with the harder edges of romance. An affair with a ghost might eliminate some of the hazards of intimacy, but only the physical ones.... She stabbed her finger so deeply she drew blood.

The night was hot and silent. Lafayette dozed. Amanda turned off the television and the lights and went to bed, where she twitched so restlessly the cat got up and left.

So much for the best-laid plans of man—and woman—to get laid, she thought with an apology to Burns. She'd try one more thing. "James," she said aloud, "James, when you're with me you're strong again."

The reflection of the outside floodlights filled the bedroom with a pale glow. An icy breath of air made her sit slowly upright. Her skin prickled. The hairs on her head rose. Her T-shirt billowed in the draft and then stilled as the cold ebbed.

James stood beside the bed, neither lighted nor shadowed, a shape and a gleam of scarlet. "Hush, Sweeting, would you wake the neighboring houses?"

All she had to do was appeal to his ego. *Duh.* "There aren't any neighboring houses."

He grinned, eyes twinkling, and unbuckled his shoulder belt.

Yes! Amanda's heart leaped, sending blood blazing into more than her face. She reached for him. In a smooth pirouette he evaded her. Fine, she was up for a strip show.

His shoulder belt and scabbard clanked, and the buttons on his coat flashed and jingled. His waistcoat and neck cloth fell silently, like white ghosts. James dropped his sporran onto the shoulder belt. A quick two-step and he was rid of his shoes and hose. Holding Amanda's eyes with his own, he unbuckled the belt that clasped his kilt around his waist and tossed the length of wool onto her feet. The phantom fabric tickled her toes.

His white shirt, its hem at mid-thigh, seemed no paler than his skin. Than his ephemeral flesh. But it sure looked like real flesh now. She was in meltdown. She peeled off her T-shirt and opened her arms. "James, I love you, I want you."

"Why speak of love, when its demonstration is so greatly to be desired?"

Yes!

His weight, heavier than she'd expected, pressed her back against the pillow. His body was solid beneath the cloth of the shirt and his lips eager against hers. His breath was scented with whiskey, sharp and smoky. His tail of hair spun through her fingers.

In one deft movement he scooped the shirt away and she lay naked against his naked chest. Against her fiery skin his seemed cool and dry. "My own," he whispered. "My sweet." His hands stroked her body, insistent, no longer either subtle or delicate.

She caressed his shoulders, his chest, his flanks—nothing metaphysical about him now, he was there, was he ever there, skin taut over muscle and bone, substantial bones, not the empty mocking shells that lay in the box in the next room. She pulled his head down to her breast, guiding his mouth—"There, yes."

And again he was pressing her into the pillow. They were wrestling, she realized, each trying to out-maneuver the other. So let him get on top, no problem. . . . He was between her thighs, hard against the damp heat of her flesh. Okay, okay, the foreplay had started the night he'd kissed her hand—a quickie was fine if it was intense enough and if she got any more intense she was going to explode—which was the general idea, although the process of getting there was half the battle—not that this was a battle, not really.

She grasped the firm double mound of his buttocks and wrapped herself around him, remembering his joke about sword and sheath. . . . In one thrust he was inside her to the hilt.

She gasped—good thing she'd been turned on for days, well lubricated by her own fantasies. The sensation rolled like an ocean wave through her body and broke over her fingers and toes and the crown of her head. He existed. He was real. She planted one heel against the bed and the other against his calf and hurried to catch up. *Oh yeah oh yeah.*

The bed was creaking. Her own voice was making funny little sub-vocal squeaks and sighs. He was a swordsman all right, he didn't need Stirling steel to make his point—his face above hers was a bas-relief against the darkness, half turned aside, eyes closed, teeth gritted, concentrated into life—the barriers of time and death thinned, broke, and disappeared.

His hand knotted in her hair, pulling her head back so sharply her scalp stung. "Ow!" She tried to twist away, but not to lose either the rhythm or the crest of the sensation.

His body pinned hers and pulled away and pinned it again and hung there, shuddering. Her muscles spasmed in reply—*yes!* The flash point was like a pistol shot in the dark, sudden, bright, and then gone.

Amanda exhaled shakily into the air above James's head. So that was it. For something she'd wanted so badly it'd sure gone by fast. Time dilation, maybe. But what a ride. *Yes.*

James sprawled on top of her, weighing no more than a heavy blanket, his fingers splayed against her scalp and his cheek tickling hers. "Amanda," he whispered. "My sweet, my own, you have made me strong again."

"Seems the least I could do," she croaked. It wasn't like she hadn't gotten anything out of the deal. In a minute or two, once she had some saliva back in her mouth, she'd ask him about his life and times—what did he really think of the Jacobite cause, how many servants did they have at Dundreggan, who had he met in the salons of Edinburgh. And after awhile she'd teach him a few things about leisurely lovemaking.

He raised his head. She could see the fan blades rotating through his features. "You are mine, Amanda. Mine. . . ." And on a sigh of words and whiskey he vanished.

She hadn't even had time to deflect his words with a joke about possession being nine-tenths of the law. "James?"

No reply.

Her arms flopped down to the bed, empty. So, she asked herself, did you ever think even for one minute he was going to turn out to be a sensitive new age guy?

For a long time she lay wallowing in sweat and sentiment, every perception of the last—five minutes?—looping round and round in her mind. She'd actually told him she'd loved him, hadn't she? Well, there were worse words for a man to hear on his deathbed.

Her scalp ached and she rubbed at it. No, he hadn't pulled out a handful of hair. As rough sex went that tug was fairly minor, she supposed. It hadn't spoiled the excitement of the moment. Not that she'd allow it to happen again, given the chance. . . .

There wouldn't be any more chances. James had gotten what he wanted. At least, of all the things he wanted sex had been the easiest for her to provide. She still had to get him home, back to his sword, and tell his story. Revealing the truth was the only justice, the only revenge, he was ever going to get. She owed him that much for aiding and abetting her fantasy. "I promise," she said into the darkness.

He was gone.

Her skin was getting clammy. She sat up and turned on the bedside lamp. No need to do much mopping up—she might just as well have had a particularly vivid erotic dream.

She groped among the covers pleated at the foot of the bed, then over the edge onto the rag rug beneath. She didn't find so much as a button. Even now she had no physical evidence James was anything more than a figment of her imagination.

Imaginary or otherwise, she told herself, he really was history now. Compelling, fascinating history, but history nonetheless. He was a footnote, not part of the main text of her life. Maybe it was time for her to be brutally honest and admit that that was just as well.

Putting her T-shirt back on, Amanda turned off the light and collapsed back onto the pillow. She was so wrung out she should've dropped off like a rock. But no. Her body was wrung out. Her mind was wound tight. She dozed and woke and dozed again, and at last simply forced herself to stay in the bed until her alarm rang and Lafayette looked in the bedroom door, his whiskers at full disgruntled droop.

Groaning, she stood up, showered, dressed, and fed the cat. Her own toast and coffee cleared away a few cobwebs. She finished packing. On her way out the door she leaned over and stroked the packing case. *Good-bye, James. Thanks for the adventure.*

Even though she wasn't officially working, still the morning seemed to go by on fast forward. The further away Amanda got from her coffee the more dazed she became, ambushed by both sleep and memory, until it was a surprise to look out Sally's window and see a long white limousine drive up to the back of the house. She glanced at her watch. It was five minutes to two.

She hurried down the stairs and handed over the clipboard of office. "It's not as though I won't be back next week. And Roy and the others know all the ropes."

"A lot of trouble can come up in a week," said Jeff, who was playing both Page and temporary caretaker.

Vicky, Sally's stand-in, elbowed his ribs reprovingly. "We'll keep an eye on things, don't worry."

"And I'll keep an eye on them," said Roy from the front door.

"I tried to shove my own stuff out of the way," Amanda told Jeff, "but move things around as you want. I really appreciate . . ."

Two tour groups arrived simultaneously at the front door while a third descended the stairs. A couple of children running for the outside door knocked into the display. Vicky seized the reproduction head before it rolled. Amanda's exit was anything but graceful.

She hurried into her apartment, pitched a couple of last-minute items into her suitcase, stuffed a paperback into her purse, and patted Lafayette's sleek fur. "Be a good little guy while I'm gone."

He opened an eye and flicked an ear—*like I appreciate being patronized any more than you do?*

"Amanda!" Wayne, the fly in the ointment, yelled from outside the bedroom window.

"Come give me a hand already!" she yelled back.

The lid of James's crate was still ajar. She set the screws in their holes and twisted them in tightly. Wayne bustled in the door. "Here's your plane ticket, unless you want me to keep it for you."

"Thank you." She slipped the ticket into her purse.

"Is that the body? 'There is some corner of a foreign field that is forever Scotland'?"

Whoa, a literary reference. "That's the point, isn't it? We're taking him back to his own field."

Wayne hoisted the crate. "Come on. The driver's waiting."

Amanda put the screwdriver in her suitcase, slammed the lid, and locked the locks. "How did I get into this?" she said with a laugh.

"It wasn't my idea," Wayne told her.

"Yeah, I know," she said in the same tone. "It was your mother's."

"That's the problem, isn't it?" Wayne was dead serious. "My mother."

"Well, yeah. Not that it matters now."

"I tried to tell her what you wanted me to tell her, but I just couldn't get it out."

"So you didn't want to acknowledge the truth yourself."

"No, not . . ." Wayne put the crate down again.

"And she wouldn't listen anyway. I know, I know, she's a control freak. Let's go."

"Hey, you're getting a really nice trip out of this. You could show a little appreciation."

That attitude was all she needed. "I'm grateful. What I'm not, is for sale."

"You hate me because of my mother."

"I don't hate either one of you. Geez, Wayne. . . . Listen, I'm tired, you're tense, let's not get into it, not now."

"You think I'm a spoiled little rich kid, don't you? Come on, admit it." He hunched his shoulders and stuffed his hands into his pockets. His lower lip started to protrude. "You think I'm a Mama's boy."

"Well, sometimes you damn well act like it," Amanda heard herself say. "You sure you don't have a stamp on your butt saying, 'Property of Cynthia Chancellor'?"

He stared at her.

Take a wild shot and hit the bulls-eye. Shit. "Wayne. . . ."

"Fine. Forget it. Forget everything." He pulled his plane ticket out of his pocket, wadded it up, stuffed it back in. He turned on his heel and stamped off down the hallway. The door slammed. An engine started up.

Amanda ran to the window. The limo glided up the drive and disappeared into the parking lot, headed for the main road. *The turkey!*

She banged her head against the window frame. It was her own fault. All this time and she had to tell him off now. The trip, her promise to James, her job, it was all running like water through her fingers. . . . No. Sometimes James had been no more substantial than water, and yet she'd stiffened him up very nicely. Which was one reason she was so damnably spaced out now.

The trip was still valid on its own terms, if not on Wayne's. She picked up the telephone. "Carrie, it's me. I'm sorry, but I need you to drop everything and get out here to Melrose."

"What?"

"Wayne just trashed his plane ticket and drove off in a snit. Well, in a limo. I need you to drive me to the airport."

"You're going without him?"

"Hell, yes. I'm out of here."

"Then so am I. Be right there."

"Thanks, Carrie, I owe you."

Roy tapped lightly on the open door. "Ah—the limousine just drove away."

"Wayne decided not to go," Amanda told him. "Help me get this stuff out to the parking lot, please."

"Sure." Roy hauled the wooden crate while Amanda, her purse and carry-on bag slung like James's belt diagonally across her chest, dragged her suitcase with one hand and clutched the camera bag with the other. "Does this mean Lady C. will be on the warpath?" Roy asked.

"Hey, I'm following orders like a good little soldier. I doubt if Wayne has enough guts to repeat to her what I said to him." No need to go into details. "She's going to be after his scalp, not mine."

"Wayne who?" said Roy, setting the crate down on the curb. "Never heard of him."

If Carrie didn't break the speed limit getting out to Melrose, she at least stretched it a bit. Amanda threw her things and the crate into the car and they zoomed off. All the way into Richmond she gabbled incoherently about Wayne and Cynthia, until at last Carrie said, "I imagine Cynthia will be plenty upset with Wayne. Even if he does tell her what you said, she'll see it as his problem, not hers. You just take it easy and enjoy your trip."

"Take it easy? Cool, calm, and collected *moi?*"

"Bon voyage." Carrie stopped the car in front of the terminal. Before she had time to think about what she was doing Amanda had rented a luggage cart for James's crate and the camera bag and was standing in the check-in line, forcing herself not to look over her shoulder.

When she finally made it to the counter she checked the crate through to Inverness, Scotland, explaining, "Archaeological artifacts. Bones, that sort of thing."

Expressionlessly, the agent clicked at her keyboard and applied labels. Amanda's suitcase and the box disappeared into the bowels of the airport. *Two plane changes. This is no time to lose my luggage, folks....*

"Here you go," said the agent, "First Class all the way."

"Excuse me?"

"Next time," she said, "why don't you use the First Class check-in, the lines are shorter."

"Oh. Yeah. Thanks." Hoping she didn't look as dazed as she felt, Amanda turned away. Why did Cynthia have to be so damned generous and efficient and everything—she made it impossible to get past irritation into outright loathing. First Class. *All right!*

Half an hour until boarding. Amanda told herself she had no reason to act like The Fugitive. If she was lucky, Wayne would spend enough time sulking before going home she could make a clean getaway. If not, if Wayne and/or Cynthia showed up in the next few minutes, she'd just have to go with the original plan, that was all.

The last thing she wanted was to go with the original plan. She lurked in a gift shop, checking out the lurid covers of paperback novels, T-shirts, and Souvenir of Virginia bric-a-brac.

Halfway to the next Ice Age her flight was announced. Flashing her boarding pass, Amanda cut into the front of the line and almost ran down the jetway into the plastic-flavored air of the 737. Her seat was next to a window. Wayne's empty aisle seat made a good privacy fence.

She watched her fellow passengers struggle past, carrying so much junk they looked like refugees from a war zone. Bumps and thumps resounded beneath her feet. The luggage was coming on board, suitcases, golf clubs, cardboard boxes. A wooden crate.

The flight attendant offered Amanda some orange juice. First she sipped, then, realizing how thirsty she was, she gulped. The seat was good. The juice was good. Life was good, all because of a man who was dead.

The engines began to drone. The plane vibrated, moving away from the gate. She watched the terminal building diminish, and the landscape spin, and finally the jet poised itself like a cat ready to leap and sped down the runway into the air.

They couldn't catch her now. She was away free.

She'd thrown caution to the winds twice in the last twenty-four hours. Funny how exhilarating it was not to be cautious. Funny what a relief it was to know recklessness was behind her. You can only dodge a bullet so many times, she thought. Even the swashbuckling James had learned that.

Telling herself she didn't have to be any more cynical than was absolutely necessary, Amanda settled back and let herself drift into memory, physical and otherwise.

CHAPTER SIXTEEN

Amanda's purse, carry-on, and the camera bag had been heavy enough in Richmond. By the time she'd lugged them through mile-long concourses in Newark and Glasgow—the latter at what seemed like two a.m. but which turned out to be seven—they'd shape-shifted into bags of bricks. Good old Wayne, always there when you didn't need him, never there when you did.

But now she was sitting in yet another window seat, staring out at a hypnotic scene of blue sky above and billows of gray and white cloud below. She might as well be flying over the Sahara. . . . No. The plane was descending. The clouds parted, revealing a glittering blue sea and hills so green and cool her heart leaped with joy. Scotland. It had taken comedy and tragedy both to bring her here, but here she was at last.

James had spent weeks, maybe even months, making the same trip. And she'd done it in a matter of hours. Of course the price for speed was jet lag. Amanda yawned and collected her stuff.

Inverness Dalcross read the sign on the terminal. *Ceud Mille Failte.* Inside the waiting crowd was a blur of sweaters and ruddy cheeks. There, a hand was holding up a piece of cardboard reading Williamsburg. Thank goodness for a native guide.

The hand belonged to a slightly built man of somewhere between forty and sixty. His head was a classic egg shape, silver hair angling across a broad brow, narrow chin disappearing into the houndstooth scarf tucked into his coat collar. His pale eyes searched the crowd with a benevolent curiosity that made Amanda smile. Malcolm Grant. Just about what she'd expected, once she'd pared away all the flights of fancy. "Hello," she said. "I'm Amanda Witham from Williamsburg."

He tucked the sign under his arm and shook Amanda's hand. His hand was fragile, more suited to a pen than to either sword or plowshare. "How do you do, Miss Witham. I believe there's to be a gentleman as well?"

"Mr. Chancellor decided not to come. I'm alone. You haven't gotten a call from him or his mother or anyone?"

"Oh no, no one's rung me, sorry."

Amanda wondered just what was going on back at stately Chancellor manor. Then she decided she didn't care. "I have a suitcase and the crate with the—er—remains."

"Well then, we'd best be off to the luggage carousel." Mr. Grant took her camera bag and tried to take her carry-on as well, but she hung onto that—the cameras alone made him sag visibly.

He led the way down a corridor, asking about her flight and whether she'd visited Britain before—all the usual courtesies. His accent was only mildly Scottish, the odd burred R and compressed vowel clinging to standard Oxbridge English. He'd probably spent years studying south of the border. Why Cynthia had made that snide remark about his accent Amanda couldn't fathom.

The wooden crate and the suitcase were there, much to Amanda's relief. She waved off Mr. Grant's help and wrestled them onto yet another luggage cart. He insisted on pushing. The cool, damp outside air was like a splash of fresh water on Amanda's face.

It took some maneuvering to get the packing case into the minuscule trunk of Grant's car and to wedge the suitcase into the back seat, but at last he was opening a door and bowing Amanda inside. He expected her to drive? Oh. The steering wheel was on the right. She knew that.

She clambered in, wrapped the seat belt around her chest and waist, and braced herself. Even so, the turn out of the parking lot made her cringe. "Sorry," she said. "I thought that bus was going to run right into us."

"Drive on the other side of road, do you?"

"Afraid so. This takes . . ." The car spun into a traffic circle and

Amanda closed her eyes. When the centrifugal force let up she opened them again. They were back on the straightaway, passing green pastures tufted with black-faced sheep. "This takes a bit of getting used to."

"I should imagine so."

"I'm looking forward to meeting your mother," Amanda went on. "Cynthia—Mrs. Chancellor—had tea with her in London."

"I beg your pardon?" The pale eyes flicked confusedly in her direction.

"Lady Norah. Or was Cynthia just making that up?"

"Oh my goodness!" He threw his head back, laughing so heartily the scarf slipped away from his throat and revealed a clerical collar. "I'm so sorry, Miss Witham, I never introduced myself, did I? I'm Lindley Duncan, rector of St. Columba's C. of E. church in Invermoriston."

"Oh," said Amanda. If yesterday she'd been moving on fast forward, today she was thinking in slow motion.

"That's Church of England in Scotland. We're not all Presbyterians in these parts. The Dundreggan Grants especially, being made of stubborn stuff. The family motto isn't 'Stand Fast' for nothing."

"'Stand Fast.' Yes, that's on the badge on the scabbard."

"Malcolm couldn't collect you, there's a spot of bother in the glen. And Norah's expecting the stonemasons. I'm terribly sorry to have misled you."

"You didn't mislead me, I just had it in my mind that Malcolm was . . ." Her tongue was thick. She tried again. "We got a copy of some historical notes from the museum in Edinburgh that looked like they'd been written a long time ago, and they were signed 'Malcolm Grant.'"

The reverend Mr. Duncan smiled and nodded. "That would have been Malcolm, Alex's father. Alexander Lord Dundreggan, that is, who passed away several years ago. Malcolm was quite the genealogist. Gassed in the Great War, never quite the ticket after that, unfortunately, and so turned to sorting the family archives."

"The Grants have a history of military service?"

"Every generation has a son in the military. Now it's Archie. Archibald, as he's known on Sunday."

That's right, it was the earlier Archibald who'd generated the Grants, not James. Amanda shook her head, trying to jump-start her brain—but not too hard, in case she suddenly woke up in her bed in Melrose Hall. Another Archibald Grant. She imagined a distinguished Ministry of Defense type who would have had his rat namesake shot on sight.

They entered the city of Inverness, passing a high-rise brick parking lot, a turreted Victorian train station, and tiny stone shops that had probably been hastily shuttered for the battle of Culloden, eight years before James's birth. When Duncan stopped at a traffic light Amanda swiveled, goggle-eyed.

A McDonalds, its plate glass window painted with yellow arches, was inserted into a hundred-year old facade. Several shops were draped with tartan fabrics and T-shirts reading, "I'm a Wee Monster from Loch Ness." In the middle of the intersection stood a medieval stone market cross. The pedestrians looked like pedestrians anywhere—at least, somewhere cooler than Virginia. Old women wore frumpy headscarves and raincoats. Young men wore jeans, windbreakers, and a variety of bizarre haircuts.

Amanda grinned. Here, time was relative. With its emphasis on one correct historical period, Williamsburg was starting to look bland.

The light changed. The car moved on, across a river, down a road lined with buildings, and past a tall green mound circled with gravestones. "Tomnahurich," Duncan explained. "The ancient meeting-place of the Frasers, now a cemetery."

James would recognize that, Amanda thought. "Is that where—James Grant's bones, that is . . ."

"No, we've arranged a burial service at Dundreggan chapel."

"That's really nice."

"Seems only right the young man should come home after all this time."

Home with honor, Amanda repeated to herself. And suddenly, for the first time, she wondered what the Grants would think of the story of murder and betrayal she'd promised to tell.

If the older Malcolm had found documentation detailing how James had really died, then the present generation already knew the truth. There was no reason they should take it personally. Some families might think a cattle rustler or a bank robber hanging from the family tree was exciting.

But what if the older Malcolm hadn't found the truth? Without documentation, Amanda could only offer the story as a theory. And who was she, anyway, to appear out of nowhere spouting bizarre theories that turned two hundred years of family history upside down? It wasn't their fault who their ancestor was.

During Cornwallis's surrender at Yorktown, she thought, the British bands had played "The World Turned Upside Down."

The car rumbled over a bridge crossing a canal and accelerated into the countryside. Sunshine broke through the clouds just as a body of water opened to the left. The water gleamed the blue-gray of James's eyes. "Loch Ness?" Amanda asked, remembering the map in Carrie's office.

"That it is."

"Have you ever seen the monster?"

"No," Duncan said with a chuckle, "I haven't seen the monster. It hardly matters, though, whether it's there or not. By now the story's taken on a life of its own. A lot of local people are making a good living from the legend, and it's bringing pleasure to tourists and scientists the world over. As you might say about my profession, faith makes facts unnecessary."

Amanda glanced over at him. "The human mind is hard-wired with the need for myth?"

"Hard-wired?"

"Like read-only memory in a computer . . . Never mind. I think you're right. Whether the story is true or not doesn't make it any less legitimate." Where that put James's story she wasn't sure.

The loch grew wider and its banks higher. White houses perched on the slopes, bright against the green. The wake of a passing boat was a long V of foam against water whose darkness hinted at its depth.

"I hope I'm not making any trouble for Lady Norah," Amanda said. "I've never even talked to her myself."

"Don't worry yourself. Norah's related to the Grants and the Frasers herself. She and Malcolm are quite interested in Grant family history. The return of a prodigal son makes a fine footnote."

"A prodigal son?"

"James Charles Edward Grant," returned Duncan, with a nod toward the trunk of the car. "I would imagine he found his names to be a bit of a liability among his English friends."

"I never knew his middle names," said Amanda. Had he been named for James, the Old Pretender, as well as James's charming but feckless son Bonnie Prince Charlie? "Was James's mother a daughter of old Lord Lovat?"

"A granddaughter, actually, but the old scoundrel's blood ran true in James. Quite the black sheep, he was. Good job young Lord Lovat had his regiment to hand, to give the lad a worthwhile occupation."

A black sheep? Amanda repeated silently. *James, not Archibald?* Not that she'd ever doubted James's, well, high spirits. He didn't smell like whiskey because he'd been a teetotaler. He wasn't a smooth seducer because he'd been celibate. And his friends and relatives wouldn't exactly have appreciated his short fuse. So he'd been human. But he'd served his time in purgatory. Purgatory having its moments, she thought with a tingle in more than the roots of her hair.

Curving away from the loch, the road entered the village of Drumnadrochit. Tourist buses lined up outside a group of buildings labeled THE OFFICIAL LOCH NESS MONSTER EXHIBITION. Amanda could almost hear the camera shutters clicking as Duncan slowed to make a right angle turn around a war memorial.

The road returned to the side of the loch above the tumbled red ruins of Urquhart Castle. A piper paced the parking lot, the wail of his bagpipes echoing across the water. Amanda shrugged—it was no hokier than Wayne in his curled wig and knee breeches.

Here the road was hacked into a slope so steep that in places netting covered the bare rock face, keeping the boulders from falling onto the pavement. On the opposite side lay the loch. Amanda squinted between the tree trunks as they flashed by, not really expecting to see Nessie extend a flipper and wave.

A huge black-winged creature dropped over the side of the embankment, hung in the air for half a heartbeat, then with a roar vanished up the loch. Amanda's jaw dropped. No, it couldn't have been a pterodactyl.

"A Harrier jet," Duncan said with a smile. "The pilots race up and down the water like things demented. I saw one tear up the loch at

Glenfinnan once, almost took the top off the monument. Archie's a Harrier pilot, in the Falklands now. I believe he's the officer responsible for ordering the beer and the Mars Bars."

Archibald was a . . . Amanda tried rubbing her eye sockets. Duncan was talking about the existing Archibald.

The minister saw her gesture. "We're almost there. It's getting on for noon. Norah said she'd ask Irene—the woman who does for her—to prepare one of her lovely salmon salads."

"That sounds great," Amanda replied, not sure she'd be able to tell a salmon from a shoe. It might be almost noon here, but her internal clock was firmly convinced it was past five, quitting time, and her body was duly quitting. She yawned, almost splitting open her face.

When she opened her eyes again the car was passing through Invermoriston, a village of white-painted houses. Duncan turned up a narrow road that led away from the loch, alongside a river burbling among huge boulders. A couple of miles further on Amanda's sand-rimmed eyes snapped open at the roadside sign, DUNDREGGAN CASTLE. *Almost there. Almost home.*

The car nosed onto a one-lane road which climbed upward among rocky pastures and Scots pines standing like lonely sentinels. "The Victorians romanticized the old houses," Duncan replied. "They tarted Dundreggan up a bit, but not enough to spoil it, fortunately. And they started calling it a castle. But, as you can tell by the name—'the fort of the dragon'—it was indeed fortified, many years and many modifications ago. Malcolm and Norah are working on a restoration program. I'm sure they'll have quite a few questions about your work in Williamsburg."

"Anything I can do to earn my keep." On a spur of land overlooking the river valley crouched a small stone building, the Celtic cross before its door directing the eye heavenward.

"We'll be having the burial services there on Saturday," Duncan told Amanda. And, taking pity on her, added, "Today being Thursday."

"Oh. Thanks." Amanda watched the chapel until it disappeared behind a green slope. When she faced forward again it was to see a stony embankment sprouting gray towers, chimneys, and walls. "Oh!"

The car dived into an avenue lined with trees whose rushing

shadows flickered bright and dark, bright and dark, making Amanda dizzy. One more turn, through an ancient stone gateway festooned with ivy and lichen, and there was Dundreggan, House or Castle, surrounded by gardens just as Amanda had imagined it. Except she'd pictured a structure along the lines of Windsor Castle. What she saw was a building little more than twice the size of Melrose, although considerably less symmetrical.

It looked like Dundreggan had been accumulated rather than built. A central keep was flanked with wings, towers, and ells, by the size and shape of their windows dating from several different eras. The only common element was the slate roof, gleaming the deep gray-black of a thundercloud behind its crow-stepped gables. A white and blue Scottish flag fluttered from the topmost tower. The castle perched comfortably atop its hill, its irregularly spaced windows like bright eyes gazing over the countryside. Amanda thought of a dowager duchess, left behind by time and fashion but regretting nothing, and was enchanted.

A black and white border collie loped toward the car. Two workmen looked up from a perimeter wall where they were substituting fresh blocks of silvery stone for weathered and discolored ones. Above and beyond the wall spread the sky, its crisp blue blending with the tender blue shades of distant mountains.

Against the castle wall stood a gorgeous herbaceous border, flowers in every color of the rainbow rising from drifts of shining leaves. A woman in shapeless coveralls and green calf-high boots stood up, tossed down a trowel, and wiped her hands on her hips. The gardener? Amanda asked herself. Or, with any luck, Lady Norah herself?

Duncan parked the car next to the mason's panel van. He got out and rubbed the collie's ears, murmuring, "Aren't you a good boy, then?" The dog sat down politely, his tail scattering gravel.

Amanda opened her door and stood. She was so limp the wind almost swept her off her feet. Her cotton skirt and jacket fluttered wildly. She took an enormous breath of the chilly air and its tang of—peat smoke? she wondered. Or was the air itself flavored with single malt? She felt halfway to plastered without having drunk a drop.

The coveralled woman strode across a lawn that would have made a golf course's groundskeeper cry. Her face was strong, square, and pink-cheeked from the wind and from her work, not cosmetics. "So, Lindley, you seem to have misplaced one of your flock."

"Mr. Chancellor decided not to come. This is Amanda Witham."

"How do you do," said the woman. She extended her hand, saw how dirty it was, and snatched it back with a grin. "I'm Norah Grant."

Norah wasn't one bit older than Cynthia, Amanda estimated, although she was taller, almost as tall as Amanda herself. "Amanda Witham. Thanks for taking me in—I feel like I was forced on you."

"Not a bit of it," replied Norah. "You're not what I expected. Mrs. Chancellor was chattering on about this sweet little child, her son's fiancée, and I imagined you to be of doll-like proportions and all of sixteen. I don't believe she even mentioned your name. Amanda. Lovely."

"She sees me as a doll," Amanda returned. "Keeps me under control that way. And I'm not her son's fiancée. That's a big, big mistake."

"A proper cock-up?" Norah suggested with another grin.

"Is it ever." Amanda laughed. "And she hinted you were much older, I'm afraid. Genteel decay and everything."

"I wondered when I met her in London if Mrs. Chancellor has a background in the theatre."

"She should." Amanda decided she liked Norah very much.

Duncan had dragged the camera bag and suitcase from the car and was now trying to extract the crate. "Let me," Amanda said, and helped him put it on the ground.

"Is that the skeleton, then?" Norah asked. She picked up the suitcase and threw the camera bag over her shoulder like a sequined evening purse. "Come along, we'll put him in the hall, it's changed a bit since his day, but I daresay that won't make any difference to him."

Yeah, well.... Amanda was beginning to appreciate James's confusion when he found himself in a world not quite his own, even though his was temporal jet lag and hers was spatial.

"I must be going," Duncan said. "Confirmation class."

"Won't you stay to lunch?" asked Norah.

"Much as I hate to miss out on Irene's cooking, no. I'll ring you about the services."

"Righty-ho. Thank you for collecting Miss Witham."

"Amanda, please" said Amanda, and to Duncan, "Thanks a lot. Sorry I'm so spaced—er—disoriented."

"Quite understandable. And you're welcome." Smiling pleasantly, Duncan climbed back into his car and drove away. The masons fumbled a stone block and danced aside, laughing and swearing. Amanda picked up the crate. Funny how it seemed heavier now than it had back at Melrose.

Inside the box something moved. Amanda stopped dead, every sense alert. *James?* But she heard, saw, felt nothing. A piece of bone had probably been jarred loose—baggage handlers took Fragile as a challenge—and had rolled against the wood. But whether his spirit was still out and about didn't matter. When she fulfilled her promise to him that weary spirit could rest at last.

Amanda carried the box toward the house, her steps muffled by the green, green grass of home.

CHAPTER SEVENTEEN

The dog trotted at Norah's heels as she led Amanda beneath an arched gateway—Amanda glanced up to see whether guards were getting the boiling oil ready—and through a huge iron-bound wooden door. Inside, a whitewashed passage floored with stone led to a spiral staircase, its treads hollowed by generations of feet. Amanda inhaled eagerly of the musty odor of age, finer than perfume.

Up the stairs they went, Amanda starting to pant beneath the weight of the box, and into the medieval great hall. The hammer-beamed ceiling was two stories high. Heraldic flags hung above the wainscoting. A fireplace big enough to spit and roast Wayne Chancellor filled one wall. A sideboard groaned beneath pewter goblets, platters, and pitchers. Among all the artifacts—antlers, paintings, a faded tapestry, pikes and axes—Amanda focussed on one.

Inside a display case, on two wooden cradles, lay a sword. A basket-hilted eighteenth-century sword. She set the crate down with a thunk and bent over, so close to the glass her breath misted it.

This was exactly what she expected. Every curlicue of the brass guard was polished bright and smooth. The blade was a length of shining steel. *A sword I'd be loath to lose,* James had said. Little appetite as she had for weaponry, Amanda could see what he meant. This sword was a work of art.

A small plaque on the floor of the case read, James Charles Edward Grant, 1755-1781. Fraser's Highlanders. 71st Regiment of Foot. Died in the service of his country.

Well, Amanda thought, he'd certainly been prepared to die in the service of his country.

"We were most intrigued to hear you'd turned up the man himself after all these years," Norah said.

"Mr. Duncan called him a black sheep." Amanda stood up. The shine of the steel floated ghostlike behind her eyes.

"He was a rogue, right enough, but when he's this far removed that just makes him all the more glamorous."

Glamorous. Oh yeah. "It wasn't his cousin Archibald who was, well, kind of a problem?"

"Archibald? I believe his service in America was the only interesting moment in his long and fearfully dull life. But then, the dull men are the ones who settle down and beget descendants like us."

So the Grants didn't know the truth. *Great.*

"You'll be wanting a wash and brush up and a meal," Norah went on. "We're not waiting lunch for Malcolm. Lindley told you, I suppose, he was called away up the glen. The shepherds were in a bit of a stramach with their program and he went to sort it for them."

"The shepherd's program?" repeated Amanda, imagining some sort of Nativity pageant.

"One of Malcolm's undertakings," Norah explained, "is organizing the estate's business on computer as well as making plans for restoring, renovating, and conserving the house. He does contract work for other properties in the U.K. as well—he has his own company, Preservation Imaging. And in his spare time, what there is of it, he's putting the family history on computer."

That made sense, Amanda thought. But since there was no way Norah could have any children older than thirty, Malcolm must be a flabby computer nerd, Carrie's chinless wonder.

Norah squared the packing crate beneath the display case. "How are the mighty fallen, then, and other appropriate lines. Lindley has the ceremony well in hand, so I'll let him wax the poetry. Let me show you to your room." Norah walked toward the door.

So James was home, Amanda thought. She'd got him as close to his sword as he was going to get—funny, how it was in better shape than the man himself. As for her telling his story, if Malcolm was putting the family history on computer he must have some original sources.

Right now, though, Amanda wouldn't stop to pick up an original source if it fell at her feet. She wanted a bath, fresh clothes, and some food, or she'd slip into a coma. Turning her back on the sword and the crate, she followed Norah from the room.

Still hauling the suitcase and the camera bag, Norah led the way along a couple of corridors, up a short flight of steps, and through a sitting room furnished with easy chairs, a couch, and a TV set.

"Dundreggan is a lot bigger inside than it looks outside," Amanda said. "I'll have to roll string out behind me."

"It's hardly a model of domestic planning," Norah told her. "Every generation's had a hand in, with predictable results. Here you are."

All right! Again, just what she'd—well, maybe not expected. Hoped. The bedroom had a beamed ceiling and a four-poster bed. A sixteenth-century hooded fireplace contained an electric heater. The window was cut in a wall so thick its sill made a cushioned seat.

Norah put the camera bag on a chair by the hall door and opened another door beside the bed. The bathroom plumbing dated to the turn of the century, but there was a modern shower over the claw-footed tub. A vase of flowers stood in the window alcove. "Switch on the towel rail here," Norah said, indicating a set of thick, fluffy towels draped over metal tubing. "For the shower, turn this knob to heat the water."

Amanda tried out the controls, got hot water, and promised to be ready for lunch in an hour.

"Can you find your way? Back down the spiral staircase and turn left until you smell the food."

"I'm in great shape. Thank you, Lady Norah."

"Norah, please. The 'Lady' makes me feel like a pedigree horse or dog." And she disappeared through the door, leaving an elusive scent of green leaves and rose petals behind her.

Amanda tried to catch her breath. The crisp white pillowcases and thick comforter were tempting, but if she lay down she wouldn't get back up until tomorrow morning. Instead she unpacked, took a shower, and discovered why heated towels were such a big deal—the window in the bathroom let in a draft Norah might have said was brisk but which to Amanda was downright cold.

It woke her up, though, and as she dressed in jeans and one of Carrie's sweaters she remembered the chilly draft that had always announced James's arrival. She'd thought that was some kind of ghostly energy conversion. Now she began to wonder if he was merely re-creating the temperature of home. She hoped she wouldn't get the bends from such an abrupt change of climate.

Allowing herself fifteen minutes to find her way through the house, Amanda set out in quest of lunch. She only took one wrong turn, which brought her to a long room fitted out with bookcases. Ancient morocco-bound books stood cheek by jowl with this year's paperbacks. A state of the art computer set-up, complete with laser printer, scanner, and fax, covered the top of a massive Victorian desk. The aroma of leather and paper hinted at scholarly doings. Everything was so totally perfect, Amanda told herself, that something had to go wrong.

Every corridor and alcove was hung with pictures and photographs, most of which glided past Amanda's glazed eyes in a jumble of faces and fabrics. But one set of portraits on a landing of the spiral staircase leaped out at her.

A small painting to one side was identical to the miniature of James at Melrose, except it was full-length. Yep, there he was, coat, kilt, and shoulder belt, frozen forever in youth. What in the miniature was ironic self-awareness looked in this larger and presumably original version like arrogance. So maybe this portrait was accurate. She'd kind of suspected the man hadn't often turned the other cheek.

The portrait must have been commissioned by James's parents when he joined the regiment. It sounded like he'd been packed off to the army to keep him out of trouble. There was a lot she didn't know about him. A lot she'd never know. She'd better be happy that she'd known, and made a difference to, his ghost.

She identified the two large portraits hanging side by side by brass labels on their frames. Archibald was depicted in middle age, his face drawn downward by his dark suit and the gravity of his social position. Amanda glimpsed something of James's sardonic humor in the height of Archibald's forehead and the angle of his brows. But James was formed from light and air. Archibald was molded from clay. He looked every bit as solid, and as stolid, as Norah implied. And why not? As a murderer he hadn't had even fifteen minutes of fame. By the time this portrait was painted he'd rationalized it all away.

How he'd ever won Isabel's affections Amanda couldn't imagine. She stepped to the side to check out the portrait not of James's fickle fiancée, but of Archibald's wife. Isabel, too, was painted in middle age. Her eyes were large and dark, and the fine bones of her chin and cheekbones supported rather than hid behind the added flesh of her matronly years. Unlike Archibald she was smiling, or at least considering a smile, if not necessarily pleased with herself then at least contented with her lot.

Put modern clothes on them all and the story would make a pretty good movie of the week. Amanda went on retracing her steps, and sure enough smelled the aroma of baking bread at the foot of the staircase. She passed a dining room with a medieval barrel-vaulted ceiling, its furnishings an assortment of styles dating from the eighteenth and nineteenth centuries, and stepped into a stone-flagged kitchen whose cupboards and appliances were younger than she was. Herbs grew in pots along a windowsill. A wine rack stood beside a shelf of cookbooks. The dog lounged picturesquely underfoot, accompanied by two cats, one a striped tabby like Lafayette, the other ginger-colored.

Norah stood at the counter cutting vegetables. She now wore chino pants and a turtleneck. An older, shorter, and rounder woman stirred something at the stove. At a refectory table sat a similarly rounded elderly man and the two stone masons, their clothes gray with dust but their hands and faces scrubbed pink. Each man nursed a tall glass of amber-colored liquid Amanda doubted was iced tea.

"Here's the American lass," said one mason, a man about her own age. "And a right bonny one she is, too."

"Hello, lassie," said the other, an older version of the first. Their smiles were open and friendly.

So were everyone else's. Amanda felt like Miss America posing on the runway in Atlantic City.

"Amanda," Norah said, "This is Irene and Calum Finlay. They've lived at Dundreggan longer than I have and are absolutely indispensable. And two John MacRaes, father and son. Our walls would have come tumbling down long since if it weren't for several generations of MacRaes."

"Nice to meet you," said Amanda, aiming for the Miss Congeniality award.

"Sit yourself down," Norah told her.

Amanda took the closest empty place and tried to exchange small talk with Calum and the Johns. But while Norah's accent was only a bit thicker than Duncan's—Amanda suspected a posh girl's school in England—the others spoke such rich brogues she not only had to listen carefully but to stare at their faces, taking in every visual cue. They'd think she was some sort of moron. But no, they were staring back. Her accent was giving them just as much trouble.

"Here you are," said Irene, setting a plate before Amanda. "This'll put roses in your cheeks."

"Thanks," Amanda said, and dug in.

She ate salmon that was so meltingly fresh even her numb tongue could tell it was not shoe leather, served with homemade mayonnaise, tomatoes, cucumbers, and cress. She ate vegetable soup dense enough to float a spoon. She ate crusty warm bread and sweet butter.

In spite of Amanda's good appetite, the MacRaes excused themselves before she finished, as did Calum, and Irene started washing the dishes. Norah lingered politely over a second cup of coffee, her alert blue eyes sweeping the room with satisfaction, and, Amanda felt, gratitude.

Amanda savored the last bites of her gooseberry pie, drank a cup of coffee, and leaned back, satisfied. Funny, how both food and sex left you mellowed out. Something about sensory overload.

Norah's fingernails were short, clean, and bare. Her only make-up was pink lip gloss and a dash of mascara. The wrinkles at the corners of her eyes and mouth were smile-lines. Her chestnut-brown hair, swept back from her face, displayed its silver streaks like a veteran displaying her medals. She wasn't a petite woman, but her posture was regally unaware that hourglass figures were out of fashion.

There was the difference between a real aristocrat and a wannabe like Cynthia, Amanda thought. Norah didn't have anything to prove. If Cynthia thought that was eccentric, then that said more about Cynthia than it did about Norah.

Irene scooped some leftover salmon onto a saucer and set it down in the corner. The cats roused themselves and raced toward it. The dog looked up hopefully, tail patting the floor, until Irene gave him some, too.

"The dog is named Cerberus," Norah said. "We took him in as a charity case. As a sheep dog he's a disgrace to his profession, sits there with a fatuous smile while the sheep run amok. But he's a fine pet."

"Cerberus," Amanda repeated. How appropriate for Dundreggan to have a dog named after the guardian of the gates of hell.

"The cats are good mousers," Norah went on, "although I confess we've made pets of them, too. My son, with his appalling sense of humor, named them 'The Catchers', Margaret and Denis, after the former prime minister and her husband."

Amanda laughed. "Which of your sons has the appalling sense of humor?"

"They both do, but Malcolm's the one at home and so most likely to inflict it upon us."

"Mr. Duncan told me your son Archie is a pilot. It's traditional for the younger one to join the military, isn't it?"

"Oh aye, but we're doing it backwards this century, since the two great wars took everyone. Archie's the elder. He inherited the title when my husband Alex died, but little of Alex's affection for the property, I'm afraid." She frowned slightly, and then her brows shrugged the frown away.

Amanda nodded. Cynthia had, of course, gotten it all right. Being a widow, Norah was "Lady Norah," not "Lady Dundreggan." Malcolm was "the Honorable," not "Lord Dundreggan," therefore he was the younger. "Neither of your sons is married?"

"No, not yet. Malcolm is looking more seriously than Archie, I believe. There's certainly no new Lady Dundreggan in the offing."

"A' titles are little mair than words noo," said Irene from the sink.

"They've never been anything but," Norah said with smile. "Games of power and precedence that would be ludicrous if they weren't so deadly. It's the land that matters, the land and the family."

Amanda nodded agreement.

"I understand," Norah went on, "you're writing a book on James Grant's life and death in America?"

"One of our librarians is writing an article, and I've promised to bring her material. It may balloon into a book."

"Alex's father organized the family papers a good many years ago, before my time. Malcolm and I have a squint at them every now and then, but we've never focussed on any particular period."

"But he's putting it all on computer?"

"Oh aye. He'll be glad to find the appropriate material for you. There's an unpublished autobiography written by James's cousin Archibald, I believe. He inherited Dundreggan on James's death. But you were asking about him earlier."

An autobiography! *Yes!* Amanda considered high-fiving Norah but contained herself. "The museum in Edinburgh sent us a copy of the letter telling James's family of his death. It mentions Archibald."

"The letter written by Lindsay of Balcarres. Malcolm Major must have been right pleased to uncover that one. I believe he donated it to the museum with a few notes attached."

"Yes, he did. The notes were really helpful."

"I hope his notes turn out to be only the tip of the iceberg, then." Norah drained the last drops from her cup and stood. "You're welcome to copy anything you find. We have a small photocopier in the library."

"The government and its paperwork," added Irene.

"Dundreggan is a listed building, which means we have to obtain consent from the bloody great bureaucracy if we want to so much as repair a window." A rueful smile turned up one side of Norah's mouth. "If you'll excuse me, I'd best go deal with some of that paperwork now. If you'd like to explore the library. . . ."

Amanda stood up, folding her napkin. Despite the coffee she was so sleepy Norah's voice advanced and receded like an ocean wave. "Thanks, but I'm still under the influence. Maybe I'll just look around, if that's all right."

"By all means. We don't have any mysterious locked dungeons, although you'll find quite a few lumber rooms filled with things I keep hoping are valuable antiques but which I suspect are rubbish. Dinner is at seven."

"Thank you." Amanda turned to Irene. "Can I help with the dishes?"

"Ah, no, away wi' ye," the woman replied, her mock ferocity making it clear no one invaded her domain except Norah.

Amanda walked back upstairs to her room and perched on the window seat, feeling like Rapunzel in her tower. Below her lay a walled garden teeming with roses of every color. Beyond it stretched the lawn and the driveway and the outer wall where the masons tapped away. Calum stood nearby, smoking a pipe and either offering advice or gossiping. Beyond him spread the awesomely beautiful landscape of stone, sky, and mountain. . . . Amanda's eyes closed. She sat up with a jerk. If she went to sleep now she'd never sleep tonight.

Wow, a night's sleep. Between James and the airplane, she'd forgotten what that was. Jet lag, sex lag—funny, though, how those sweaty and exhilarating minutes already seemed way in the past, like something she'd read about, not actually done. And it wasn't that they'd left her exactly mellow, either. . . . This time her head fell forward. She staggered to her feet.

The afternoon stretched ahead of her like a long road, bedtime only a distant glow on the horizon. One step at a time, she told herself, and opened the camera bag. No way her fuzzy brain would be able to work the video camera. She took the still camera and went back downstairs, glancing again at the three portraits. The eternal triangle.

She was only putting off the day of reckoning, she told herself. Sooner or later she was going to have to meet the James exposed in the family papers. The scoundrel—charming, of course. The rogue—lovable, ditto. Archibald's version would hardly be impartial, but still she was going to have to cut James some slack. Maybe more than some. And yet his ghost wasn't the man he'd been, was it?

Amanda went out the front door and took pictures of the castle, of the view, of the masons at work. Cynthia would want a soundtrack for the film—a piper piping a lament, or a voice singing the Gaelic song James had quoted, assuming Amanda could find it.

A gate in the interior wall led into the rose garden. She was headed in that direction when Irene looked out the door. She uttered a string of diphthongs of which Amanda understood only her own name and the word, "telephone."

Suddenly she was wide awake. What? Cynthia couldn't leave her alone long enough to do her job? It wasn't her fault Wayne had bailed at the last minute.

Irene went into the house and came back carrying a phone. Amanda sat down on a stone bench beside the garden gate, squared her shoulders and pressed the phone to her ear. "Amanda Witham."

"Hi! It's Carrie!"

"Carrie?" *Whew.*

"I hope I figured it right and it's two pm over there and not two am."

"You're right. I just had a delicious lunch with Norah. You wouldn't believe this place. It's absolutely gorgeous. And cool."

"I have no doubt," Carrie said dryly. "Pardon me while I rev up my air conditioner and admire the view of the water cooler."

"I'm already taking pictures," Amanda assured her. "I'm glad it's you. I thought it was the dragon lady. Who was dead wrong about Dundreggan being run down, by the way."

"I haven't heard a cheep from Cynthia or from Wayne, either. And I'm not going to rattle their cage. I'm calling about the robbery."

"Robbery?"

"Someone opened the Lucite box holding James's scabbard and took it."

"James's scabbard?"

"Roy noticed it was gone after you left yesterday afternoon. He swears someone was in the entrance hall the entire time, but they couldn't have covered it every minute."

Amanda frowned. She'd left yesterday afternoon, not last month. "A bunch of people were milling around right before I left. And I asked Roy to carry the bones out to the parking lot, so he wasn't there. Shit."

"The police were all over the place, even stopped a school bus that was leaving. Bill Hewitt came out at closing time, but I guess Cynthia's grapevine broke down, because she didn't. Bill's going to call her this morning. Talk about being caught in your own trap—her publicity stunts may have attracted a dishonest collector."

The cold stone of the seat was anesthetizing Amanda's rear end. "You're doing more than just letting me know, aren't you?"

For a long moment the line echoed hollowly. Then Carrie said, "Well,

I sure haven't told anyone else this, Amanda, and I apologize right up front for the way my mind works, but I couldn't help but wonder. . . ."

"Whether I grabbed the scabbard on my way out?"

"You might have asked yourself whether James would want his sword without its scabbard."

"Yeah, well, I did ask myself that." Amanda re-thought her answer. James touched the scabbard the way he touched her, and for just about the same reason. It, and the sword, and she herself took him back to the time he was strong. The vulnerability she found so attractive he found deeply disturbing.

Carrie couldn't bring herself to ask the obvious. Amanda could. "What about James? He would have had just enough time to move the scabbard from the display in the entrance hall to the packing case before I shut the lid. I'll go look. And if I find it?"

"You'd better start thinking up some good explanations, preferably ones that don't involve supernatural intervention."

"I don't suppose I can just bring the scabbard back with me and stuff it beneath a bush so the cops will think it was there all along." The chill of the stone radiated up her spine, pinching her shoulders. "I'll call you back, Carrie. Thanks."

"Good luck."

Amanda pressed the button on the telephone, wondering whether Carrie meant *good luck, I hope you find it*, or *good luck, I hope you don't?*

Like it mattered now? Either way, it was too late. She got up, rubbed the cramped muscles in her behind, and limped into the house. Not knowing where the telephone belonged, she left it on a chest in the lower hall next to a vase of iris and roses.

She went upstairs again, telling herself that back home people paid good money for stair climbing machines. She got the screwdriver and went back down.

The great hall was silent. Dust motes danced in bars of sunlight that stretched diagonally down from the high windows. The sword glittered. Amanda pulled the crate away from the display case, knelt down on the planks of the floor, and with a squeal of rending wood unscrewed the screws and pried open the lid.

One edge of the layer of foam was wrinkled. She lifted it. The scabbard lay snugged along the side of the box, the oval badge repeating the oval shape of the skull, the words "Stand Fast" a caption to the empty eyes.

She must have heard it knock against the bone when she'd taken the box out of the car. The scabbard had probably been knocking against bone all the way across the Atlantic, but the skull wasn't damaged. The bone was firm and chalky cool to her fingertips. She already knew James was hard-headed. *Stand fast.*

"Well thank you very much!" she said, and gave the crate an impatient push. Who the hell did James think he was? Or, more to the point, who did he think she was, screwing her around like this? And after she'd happily helped him do it literally, too!

She could still hear his voice, like a wisp of velvet, murmuring "You are mine, Amanda." Only now instead of shrugging away those words she cringed. She'd known something was going to go wrong, but it sure didn't have to go wrong this soon. Or to this extent.

Amanda picked up the scabbard and tucked the foam back around the bones. Still kneeling, she held it up to the sword. Oh yes, if there hadn't been a kink in the weathered steel the two would have fit perfectly. Like her body had fit his, briefly, but not so perfectly after all.

"You've seen the sword, then, lassie," said a voice like a wisp of velvet. "Goes wi' yon scabbard, does it?"

Amanda spun around so fast she almost dislocated her neck. Three feet from her eyes stood a pair of athletic shoes and wool socks. Above them extended a well-worn and very nicely shaped pair of blue jeans. Over the jeans hung a fisherman's knit sweater, arms akimbo. Above the sweater a young, handsome face, topped by tousled auburn hair, looked down at her. His eyes were blue-gray. His smile was boyish and sophisticated at once.

She knew those eyes and that smile, knew them intimately, and yet they weren't the same. The bones of this man's face had been beaten from different steel. They'd been tempered two centuries longer. This man's slender hips and broad shoulders were refined by shadows.

Amanda sat down hard on the floor, the scabbard across her lap. She might as well be wearing Sally's stays for all the air that was making it into her chest. "You," she stated, jabbing the air with her forefinger. "You are Malcolm Grant."

One of his eyebrows lifted warily upward, as though her next move would be to hand him a subpoena. "I'd best be ownin' the truth of the matter, then. Aye, I'm Malcolm Grant. And you're the lassie from America. You're no what I expected."

He extended his hand. Amanda watched herself take it. He both shook her hand and pulled her to her feet still clutching the scabbard in her left hand. His palm was warm beneath a superficial coolness and his grip was firm. He smelled of fresh air. His blue-gray eyes were clear, not at all smoky. They shone like searchlights focused on her face.

"No," she said, "you're not what I expected either." She managed to let go of his hand and step back.

The scabbard wrenched itself out of her fingers. She made a grab for it, but it clattered to the floor. The noise was loud and brash, bouncing back from the high ceiling.

It lay at Malcolm's feet. He tilted his head in appraisal. "That's a challenge, is it? You're throwin' doon the scabbard instead o' the gauntlet?"

But all Amanda could do was stare, for once completely out of answers.

CHAPTER EIGHTEEN

Malcolm looked from the scabbard to Amanda's face and grinned.

She blinked, reminded herself to breathe, and rebooted her brain. The first command that came up into her mind was, *don't let either of these guys get to you!*

Yeah, well, it was too late for that, wasn't it? Picking up the scabbard she said as lightly as she could, "I sure don't have much of a future in historic preservation if I throw artifacts around, do I? I shouldn't even be handling this without gloves."

"Let's put it awa', then, like proper historical preservationists." Malcolm lifted the lid of the display case, carefully holding the glass by its wooden frame.

Amanda placed the scabbard in the space between the sword and the plaque with James's name. The dull, pitted metal with its ungainly kink seemed sad next to the burnished elegance of the blade. But then, it had had a lot harder trek to the present day.

No way in hell could she explain to the Grants that the scabbard wasn't supposed be here, that it should still be in its Lucite box in the entrance hall at Melrose. Like she couldn't explain that she hadn't dropped it, it'd thrown itself down. She shot a wary glance at the wooden crate, remembering James's words: *I want revenge.*

"A shame the scabbard's a bit crumpled," said Malcolm, lowering the lid of the case. "Mind you, Calum could straighten it at his wee smiddy, but I reckon it's best to preserve it as it is."

Amanda slipped into academic mode. "The repair work would leave scars. The contrast between the two speaks volumes about time, decay, and conservation."

"And the standard display model for a sword is unsheathed and parallel with its scabbard."

"Yes." So Malcolm was more than a pretty face and a ready tongue, he was preservationally competent. But then, someone—Norah, Duncan—had already said Malcolm was working on conservation plans for Dundreggan. Good for him.

He turned toward the crate. "That's himself, is it? May I?"

Amanda waved her hand—*go for it.*

Kneeling on one knee, Malcolm rolled back the layer of foam. His fingertips traced the jaw hinge and cheekbone. His palm swept back over the arch of the skull as though brushing hair from the face of a child. His hands, Amanda saw, were long and lean, moving with a sensitivity only a man with a lot of self-assurance could afford to show.

Amanda closed her eyes. *This isn't happening, either.*

His smooth baritone murmured, "So you've come hame, then, for auld lang syne. But you never kent the delights o' Burns, did you? Puir beggar, what a shame to die so young and so far awa'."

Yes, it is. And she was going to have to deal with it. Amanda opened her eyes. Malcolm was still kneeling beside the crate, his left forearm braced on his upraised thigh, his right hand resting on the wooden rim. "Cynthia didn't need to strong arm you into giving a blood sample for DNA tests," she said. "The resemblance is amazing."

He looked from the nested bones up to her face. "It is?"

"The miniature," she said quickly. "The miniature portrait Cynthia bought in London. It's copied from that portrait in the stairwell, isn't it?"

"Oh aye, but I never saw much likeness masel'. I dinna suppose we ever see oursel's as others see us, though. Which brings us back to Burns." He tucked the foam around the bones, stood up, and set the lid atop the crate. "Your battles are done, lad. Rest in peace."

That's the idea. "I guess you should tighten the lid. The lab packed him up with silica gel. But then, it doesn't matter whether his bones are preserved or not, not any more."

"We need to let him return to the dust from whence he came, right enough. But we can do better than this packin' case. Lindley has a coffin for him. And Mum's arranged for a proper headstone."

"That's really above and beyond."

"We're his family. He'll have to take us whether he wants us or no."

Which left James between a rock and a hard place, Amanda thought. He couldn't ask for more respect. And yet the people who respected him were descended from. . . . She knew whom they were descended from. She, at least, wasn't going to hold them accountable for that shot in the dark.

Leaving the screwdriver on top of the box, Amanda turned and strolled toward the door. As she'd intended, Malcolm fell into step beside her. Attractive as he was, disillusioned as she starting to be with James, still she felt like the worst sort of hypocrite eyeing the one in front of the other's—remains.

"Just one thing," said Malcolm. "What's your name?"

"Oh! I'm sorry. Amanda Witham. Glad to meet you."

Again they shook hands. "You e-mailed the business address askin' for Mum's phone number," Malcolm went on.

"That was before I knew I'd be coming here. Before Cynthia sent me off like a FedEx package. No wonder your mother was expecting a little kid."

"Cynthia? The snotty woman who rang last Sunday?"

"The what?"

"Mistress Snotty, Mrs. Anthony Chancellor." He imitated Cynthia's too-cool-to-melt-butter drawl and smiled mischievously.

Amanda laughed. "Yeah, you've got her number. What'd she say to you?"

"No so much what she said as hoo she said it. I was thinkin' you were a sweet, simperin' little doll-child, wi' hair ribbons and frilly socks. I reckoned if her son's engaged to you then he's stealin' the cradle blind. And here you are, lackin' two inches of my ain height, chuckin' antique cutlery at me."

"It wasn't exactly cutlery," Amanda told him. "And I am not and never have been engaged to her son. Who isn't here. He decided not to come. Me, I'm not even going with anyone." Maybe she shouldn't have added that last factoid, but Malcolm took it in with a sober nod.

They stepped through the doorway of the great hall onto the landing of the stairs. Sunlight shone through the slits of windows and was reflected off the whitewashed walls, making the staircase a well of light. Just around the bend hung the three portraits. They stopped in front of them.

"May I have a look at your camera?" Malcolm asked.

She'd forgotten the camera draped across her chest. "Sure. It's not mine, though, it's CW's. Colonial Williamsburg's." She handed it over. He squinted through the eyepiece and adjusted the lens. "Please, take pictures," Amanda went on. "I'm supposed to come back with lots of documentation. I even have a video camera upstairs."

"Do you, noo? I helped film the excavations at Whithorn Abbey, I'd be pleased to help."

"That's cool. Thanks."

If Duncan's accent was inflected Oxbridge, and Norah's was hardly any less "proper," Malcolm's accent ran up and saluted the St. Andrews cross of the Scottish flag. No wonder Cynthia hadn't been able to understand him, not on the telephone. Following his words gave Amanda an excuse to look at him. He was like James, and yet he was definitely not like James.

James's painted face stared into eternity, his expression obscured by the gleam of sunlight on the surface of the picture. Malcolm lowered the camera. "Too much light. But I suppose you have ower many photos o' the miniature already."

"On every brochure," Amanda answered. "Cynthia implied that you and your mother were living in genteel poverty, forced to sell off family heirlooms like the miniature."

"Every now and again we sell the odd mathom—to use Tolkien's word—for the ready. A bit o' cheese-parin' never goes amiss, but we're no on the dole."

"Cynthia usually acts like Lady Bountiful. She's not anything official with CW, you understand, but she's a major donor and really does do a lot of good work for them, so they put up with her."

"She's ower the top, Mum said."

"Too much, you mean? Definitely."

"My condolences." Malcolm handed back the camera and pointed to

Archibald's portrait. "My ancestors were a gey respectable lot. Even wi' so many gone for soldiers, we've no had a true wastrel since yon James. Just as weel he dinna inherit, I'm thinkin', although he might have settled had he survived the skirmish in America."

"The grand and glorious Revolution, a skirmish? Heresy, Mr. Grant, heresy!" Amanda returned Malcolm's laugh. Side by side they descended the stairs. "Men of James's time and class were usually into gambling," she essayed.

"Gamblin', wenchin', duelin', drinkin'—the lot. We have a letter to James from his dad, threatening to cut him off if he didna behave himsel'. The same letter suggests a marriage wi' the Seaton lass. Isabel. She was the daughter of some business associate."

Okay, so James had deserved a rap over the knuckles. Maybe even a swift uppercut to the jaw. He hadn't deserved to be murdered. "James and Isabel were engaged when he died," said Amanda. "That's in the Balcarres letter—the Museum in Edinburgh sent us a copy."

"Oh aye. Bit o' a soap, eh? James dies, Archibald gets the girl and the brass. Snotty said you were researchin' a book aboot James."

"An article, actually, about the discovery and identification of his body. An exercise in historical archaeology. But it may turn into a book yet, it's getting more complicated by the minute."

"My grandfather, also Malcolm, was plannin' to write a book aboot the family history. He spent years collectin' and organizin' his sources but never put pen to paper. Or type to paper. I'm thinkin' he hoped to find somethin' glamorous among the begats and the bequeaths. But no joy. Dead respectable, as I said. You've brought us a family skeleton noo, but it's no the sort that rattles awa' in the cupboard."

"I wouldn't be so sure," Amanda returned, and at Malcolm's puzzled look amended, "Sorry, my brains haven't caught up with my body."

They turned down the hallway at the foot of the stairs. Arranged engagement or not, Amanda thought, James really had cared for Isabel. But even in a day and time when many men were allowed full rein and most women wore choke-chains, Isabel might not have been too thrilled about a match with a rogue, no matter how charming. Amanda was surprised James's ghost didn't resemble Marley's in *A Christmas Carol,* except James's would drag a chain of playing cards, wine bottles, and petticoats. And stolen artifacts. The scabbard was his, yeah, but he damn well could have trusted her enough to tell her what he was up to. My own, my ass, she thought.

Malcolm led the way into the kitchen, where he opened the refrigerator. "Would you like a piece?"

"Of what?"

"Bread and jam, or a bittie cheese."

"No thank you, Irene fixed a wonderful lunch for us."

"Whilst muggins here is slavin' awa' tendin' to the farm." Malcolm collected supplies from refrigerator, breadbox, and pantry, and built himself a sandwich. Cerberus materialized from beneath the table, trotting to Malcolm's side like a shark scenting a disturbance in the water. "Oh it's you, is it? Okay, okay, here you are."

Amanda sat down. The dog ate his treat, sniffed around to make sure there wasn't any more, and settled down at her feet. She petted his warm, sleek head while his tail brushed rhythmically across her ankles, deciding that if dogs condescended to purr, this one was purring. "Dundreggan seems to be in great condition. It must be a nightmare trying to fight the damp rot. How often do you have to re-point the masonry?"

"It's like paintin' the Forth Bridge—you're no sooner done than you're startin' in again." Malcolm sat down opposite her and contemplated his multi-layered sandwich, an architectural triumph. "We're barely keepin' ahead o' entropy. The walls shift, the doorframes buckle, the floors sink. One loose slate on the roof and you've a wet plaster ceilin' comin' doon on your heid. The place is held together by the plumbin' pipes and the electric flex installed in 1911." He took a bite, chewed, and concluded, "Last week a stone fell from the dinin' room ceilin' slap into Lindley's soup."

"Way to welcome the clergy!" Amanda said. "What did he say?"

"He was right polite, considering it could've bashed his head, and asked for a cloth to wipe the soup off his shirt. Mum said, a good thing he's no a Calvinist, we can just pour another glass o' wine for an Anglican and he'll soon forgive and forget."

"Telling tales on me, are you?" Norah walked through the door and helped herself to a bite of her son's sandwich. "I see you've made your own introductions."

"It's a do-it-yourself age," Amanda told her.

"Malcolm was hoping to ask you questions about opening the house to the public," Norah went on, pulling herself up a chair.

"Theme park Scotland," Malcolm said. "Tartan dollies. Balmorality."

"An educational center," retorted Norah. Her tone indicated they'd been chewing over this topic for a long time.

"Williamsburg manages to be a class act," Amanda said helpfully.

"But Williamsburg has been restored to one time period," said Norah. "Which time period do we choose? How much restoration should we do?"

"Ye Olde Gothicke Victorian crenellations on the south tower have to go," Malcolm said, "They're no only unsightly, the mortar's rotted through."

"But even the Victorian renovations are a part of the castle's history." Amanda offered. "Williamsburg is one thing. Dundreggan is another. I love the eclecticism, all the different time periods mingled madly together—that's where you're unique. You should capitalize on that."

The similarly blue eyes of the Grants moved from Amanda's face to each other's and back again. "We'll be havin' a lot to talk aboot," Malcolm told her. He popped the last of his sandwich into his mouth and licked his lips.

"Anything I can do to help . . ."

Cerberus leaped up, emitted an interrogative "woof?" and stared toward the door. All three faces turned that way, but no one was there.

"It's only Morag." Norah widened her eyes in mock horror. "Whenever the floors settle and creak or a door goes off balance and closes itself, we say it's Morag. The *genius loci,* I suppose, the guardian spirit of the house. We don't have a real ghost, sad to say."

"Grandad's dad saw a gray shape in the upper hall," Malcolm said, "but he probably had a smudge on his eyeglasses. We're sadly lackin' in permanent bloodstains and walled-up nuns and bumps in the night. Tourists love ghost stories."

"Theme park Scotland," Norah reminded him. He made a face at her.

Cerberus sat down again, still staring at the door. Ambivalently, Amanda thought. She knew how he felt. She remembered how Wayne had said something about Melrose not producing any ghosts for the tourists. That had helped convince her James's ghost was real.

And now she was starting to get the queasy feeling that James's only-too-real ghost had accompanied his bones across the Atlantic.

"I'm sorry to have to ask, but my friend and co-author from Williamsburg called earlier, and I really need to call her back. I'll call collect."

"Rubbish," said Norah. "Phone Virginia all you wish. You're here on business, after all. The telephone's on the kist in the hallway."

"Thank you." Amanda collected the camera and headed out the door.

The phone still sat next to the vase of roses and iris, on top of the carved wooden chest Norah had called a "kist." Amanda took it up the stairs to her room, shut the door, and dug out the phone number. She put the phone to her ear.

It was dead. Too far away from its base. Back down the stairs Amanda went, giving James's portrait an exasperated glance as she passed. She sat on the bottom step and punched in the long strong of numbers. Along with hollow thrummings from the earpiece she heard Malcolm's and Norah's voices in the kitchen, talking and laughing. She'd gotten so used to Cynthia and Wayne's dysfunctional relationship it seemed odd to hear mother and son interacting like equals. Like her own mother and brother didn't get along just fine. . . .

"Carrie Shaffer."

"Hi, Carrie. It's me, calling from the misty isles." From the open front door a block of sunlight reached almost to her feet, etching sharp shadows in the uneven stone floor. "Well, sunny isles right now."

"Did you find the scabbard?"

"What do you think? Yeah, it's in the box with the bones. The Grants think I brought it along intentionally. I guess you might as well tell the police that that's what I did—last minute impulse or something. I'll bring it back next week. My return ticket's for Thursday."

"You shouldn't take the rap for James."

Like I have a choice? Aloud, Amanda said, "Oh, now you're admitting he's real?"

"I didn't say that," Carrie asserted. "I mean—well. . . ."

"I took the scabbard. *Mea culpa.* Don't worry, I'll take lots of photos of it next to the sword, which is where it is right now, and maybe they'll give me time off for good intentions or something."

"I don't see any other way of handling it," Carrie said. "I'll call the police and tell them the news. Maybe I can confuse the issue—oh, look, here's a memo Amanda left for me before she left—sorry, I haven't cleaned off my desk. And that's no lie. How's it going, by the way? What are the Grants like?"

The cats ambled through the door. The ginger one—Denis—rolled onto his back and stretched luxuriously on the sun-warmed pavement while Margaret, the tabby, made a good imitation of a sphinx, right down to the supercilious expression.

"Great people, mother and son both," Amanda answered. "Wayne and Cynthia should take lessons."

"I still haven't heard anything from either one of them, thank goodness."

Amanda made a face. "Listen, Carrie, I'm really sorry to jerk you around."

"Hey, I'm a mother, I do a great marionette impression."

Malcolm came whistling down the hall, stopping abruptly when he saw Amanda sitting on the steps. He smiled. She smiled and scrunched herself against the cool stone of the wall as he bounded upward. "I'd better go, I'm running up the Grants' phone bill."

"Lots of pictures, now. Letters, diaries, old laundry lists. And don't worry about the scabbard."

"Yeah, right." It was James's fault, not Carrie's. "Yes, ma'am. Bye." Amanda turned off the telephone and sat with it in her lap, telling herself that if they were handing out blame, she needed to get in line.

James hadn't realized what he was doing, she rationalized. He'd taken the scabbard during daylight—he hadn't been either in a material state or in his right mind. . . .

Not that Amanda was in her right mind. She was firmly convinced it was the middle of the night. The sunlight pouring the door seemed as weird as the shadowless light on James's body. But while sleep deprivation sure wasn't helping, her big problem was that everything was happening too damned fast. . . .

Footsteps, slow and deliberate, came down the spiral staircase behind her. The stone wall she was leaning against went from cool to icy cold. As one the cats leaped up, turned toward the sound, and bristled.

Well, that answered that question. Amanda scrambled to her feet and walked slowly up the stairwell. *James?*

The footsteps were closer, but still around the bend of the wall.

James?

One of the cats hissed. Both of them shot out the door. Amanda took several more steps, until she could see the landing where James's picture hung.

The footsteps stopped. Nothing and no one was there. The sunlight glanced off the paint-ridges on the surface of the three portraits.

Amanda hurried upward and looked into the great hall. It was empty. The tapestries, the mounted weapons, the fireplace were unchanged. The wooden crate sat mutely before the display case. Behind the glass James's sword and scabbard inscribed parallel lines. The sword was a bright streak of bravado. The scabbard was a tarnished and disfigured *memento mori,* a souvenir less of a fleeting relationship than of death.

James, please, for both our sakes, let it go. . . .

Nothing.

With an exhalation that was a much a snort as a sigh, she walked over to the display case and raised her camera. Only once did she trip over the crate as she jockeyed for position. The photographs would guarantee the immortality of the reunited sword and sheath. That was the only immortality James would ever find.

CHAPTER NINETEEN

By dinnertime Amanda caught herself telling Norah, Malcolm, and the Finlays how Melrose Hall had been built in the seventeenth century. Then she couldn't remember what year her sister was going to graduate from high school. *Hello? Earth to brain?*

She excused herself and went to bed.

The summer evening lingered outside her window, filling the room with a golden glow. Amanda snuggled into the comforter and slid dizzily down the steep slope to unconsciousness. When she awoke it was to darkness so dense she had to touch her eyelids to make sure they were open. Of course she hadn't left any lights on. And she hadn't put her watch with its LED on the bedside table. Not that it mattered, she was just going to go back to sleep. . . .

From the hall outside her door came the sound of footsteps. It wasn't Norah's "Morag," the normal creaks and settlings of an old house. The steps were firm and regular—no, they hesitated, like someone was looking for the right room.

The still air was so cold and damp Amanda was surprised she couldn't see her breath against the darkness. She blinked her burning eyes. There, a dim rectangle was her window and a shape at the foot of the bed was the wardrobe where she'd hung her clothes.

The footsteps started again, and paused just outside her door. The knob rattled impatiently, then began to turn.

James.

With a plink the knob returned to its resting position. The door stayed shut. The window-rectangle brightened. She began to make out the shape of the bathroom door, defined in the fragile light of dawn.

She waited a while, the cold prickling between the individual hairs on her bruised scalp. Then with a long sigh she burrowed further into the warmth of the comforter. Of course James was confused and unfocussed. The abrupt change of scene had left *her* thoroughly out of focus, and she was, most of the time, a conscious human being. But with the funeral tomorrow, he didn't have much time to collect himself.

Not that she really wanted him to collect himself. She'd already said good-bye to him, over and over again. It was time for some closure. . . . Now that was cold. Have sex with the guy and two days later you're rooting for him to disappear. Hadn't their brief affair meant anything?

Sure it had. That was just it. She wanted to lay James safely to rest before he did anything else to make her mad. Before she found out any more about what he'd been like when he was alive. She wanted her memories of him to be like the sword, not the scabbard—brightly polished, not pitted and tarnished. She sure didn't want to regret having done what she'd done.

Amanda drifted into incoherent dreams, and woke at last to a brilliant morning. Choirs of birds caroled outside the window. The room was still cold. Nothing supernatural about that.

She got up, dressed, and only then looked at her watch. It was five-thirty. *Good one.* Between her scrambled internal chronometer and the early dawn this far north, she was awake hours before anyone else.

Arming herself with a notebook and a pen, Amanda tiptoed past the other bedrooms and managed to step on each creaking floorboard. It must have been James in the corridor last night, because beneath his insubstantial feet the floor hadn't creaked once. Not that she'd doubted they were his feet.

She still had one-third of her promise to him to keep. And he, stubborn as he was, had wanted to remind her. To nag her about it, like she couldn't be trusted.

Cerberus met her on the staircase, gladdened by the sight of a human being. He trotted behind her to the library and made himself comfortable in the sunlight flooding through the three tall windows. The carpet where he lay was threadbare, and the easy chairs were somewhat frayed, but all were immaculate. The marble swirls of the eighteenth-century mantlepiece were polished to such gleaming whiteness they looked like a meringue, while the empty grate was an abstraction in Brasso and blacking.

On the wall above the mantel hung a family tree, meticulously calligraphed except for the names of the most recent generation—Archie, Malcolm, several cousins—which were printed in a different hand. Malcolm's father Alexander was a second son himself, Amanda saw. His older brother had died in 1940, probably a casualty of war. Norah had been eighteen years younger than her husband and was now only fifty-two. Archie was twenty-seven and Malcolm twenty-three, her own age. Had she ever been out of it, imagining Norah and Malcolm as doddering old stereotypes.

Higher up the chart were James and his brother, named Donald after their father. Next to the thick branch of Isabel and Archibald's seven children, Donald and James were lonely blighted twigs. But their generation was closer to the bottom of the chart than the top. Amanda's eye moved further upward, tracing the tree back into the mists of time and wishful thinking—Robert the Bruce, Malcolm Canmore, Aidan of Dalriada. *Wow,* she thought. In the vast lake of history Williamsburg was only a wading pool.

She petted Cerberus and moved on to the bookcases, pulling out and replacing books. From a high shelf she took a two hundred-year-old copy of *Tristram Shandy.* The leather covers were mottled, but the pages were clean and dry. She had college textbooks that weren't in this good a condition.

On the flyleaf was inscribed, *JAMES CHARLES EDWARD GRANT, 1775.* Even his handwriting was bold, a flourish of ink that reminded her of the ink spill on the blotter at Melrose. Maybe his swagger was his reaction to a domineering father. Or to being the younger son. Or maybe he was defaulting to the masculine bottom line—be strong or be ridiculed, a fate worse than death. Not that death had slowed him down much. Amanda closed the book, put it back on the shelf, and moved on.

Family photographs crowded each surface. Through the mutations of fashion she could trace the history of Britain, right down to a photo of

Malcolm standing next to a slightly taller, slightly older man wearing a pilot's flight suit.

On the floor beside the desk stood a space heater. Next to the computer keyboard lay a tin whistle. A cross-stitched motto hung above the printer: "These buildings do not belong to us only . . . they are not in any sense our property to do as we like with them. We are only trustees for those that come after us. William Morris." *Right on,* Amanda thought.

Okay, so she'd killed an hour. She stood in the center of the room, arms braced against her hips. There were cupboards beneath each bookshelf, a filing cabinet next to the desk, and what looked like a medieval chest against the far wall. If I were family papers, she asked herself, where would I be?

She opened a cupboard. Ah, letters. She pulled out a ribbon-wrapped bundle. The top envelope was stamped and postmarked Invermoriston, Nov 2, 1970. *Miss Norah Cameron,* read the address, written in a precise male hand, *12 Balfour Place, Fort William . . .* Oops, Amanda thought, hurriedly replacing the bundle. The last thing she needed to do was snoop through her hostess's old love letters.

Cerberus looked up, ears pricked. The library door swung open with a slow squeal and Amanda clambered to her feet. Malcolm stood in the doorway, holding a tray brimming with crockery. This morning his hair was neatly combed above its close-trimmed nape and his jeans were a fresh dark blue. "So you've got stuck in," he said.

Amanda glanced at her feet, wondering what she'd stepped in. "Excuse me?"

"You're hard at it already."

"Afraid not. I don't know where anything is, I'm just poking around."

"And workin' up an appetite, I expect." Malcolm set the tray down on a low table before the fireplace. "It's only tea and toast, but either Mum or Irene will be along presently for the eggs and sausages."

Carrie had warned her about the wretched excess of the British breakfast. But the toast looked great. "Thanks," Amanda said, and sat down beside the tray. "I hope I didn't wake you up."

"Oh no. It's sic a grand mornin' I thought I should be makin' a start masel'. I'll play mother, shall I?"

"Excuse me?" she said again. Either she needed some caffeine or a translator, she wasn't sure which.

"I'll pour the tea," he returned. He sloshed milk into a cup and filled it with tea, making a steaming caramel-colored brew. "Sugar?"

"Damn the calories, full speed ahead." Amanda burned her tongue on her first sip and turned to the toast, arranged neatly in a little rack, cool but crisp. The butter spread smoothly and the marmalade was tart and fresh. She stuffed her face while Malcolm kept her cup filled.

Cerberus sat close by, his adoring eyes watching each bite disappear. Amanda couldn't imagine a less appropriate name for such a cream puff of a dog. He looked like he'd have trouble guarding the pantry, let alone the gates of Hell.

At last she looked up into Malcolm's keen blue gaze. "I really have eaten square meals before. Sorry to be such a pig."

"No a bit of it," Malcolm replied. "You're hungry. No shame in that. I canna thole scrawny women who greet and whinge ower their plates as though appetite were mortal sin."

"And why do they do that?" retorted Amanda. "Because men like scrawny women."

"Ah, no, a woman should have a proper figure." His hands sketched a figure eight, paralleling the movement of his eyes up and down her body. "But it's a wee bit early to be flirtin'," he conceded, with a grin that wasn't at all repentant.

Amanda laughed. Too early in the morning? she wondered. Or too early in the acquaintance? She thought of James's bones downstairs and her laugh became a grimace. *Down, girl.* "You know a lot about James. I guess your grandfather told you about him."

"No, my grandfather died in 1939. In self-defense, I reckon. His generation thought they'd sorted the matter in the first war, but no, that was only the preliminary round."

Amanda nodded encouragingly.

"As for James, I've told you the lot. I'm workin' on a computerized genealogy, but I'm only as far as the sixteenth century and the Grant who was lady-in-waitin' to Mary of Guise. The program's American, like most. It's a right scunner to have a spell checker tellin' me 'honour' has no 'u' and 'defence' is spelled wi' an 's'!"

"The nerve!" Amanda said with a grin.

"But you're wantin' the eighteenth-century ephemera. This way." Malcolm piled his napkin on the tray, dodged around Cerberus, and opened a cupboard behind a settee in the far corner of the room. "There you are. My grandfather organized and labeled everythin'."

"Good for him, to take pity on us ink-stained wretches." Inside the cupboard, on two shelves, were stacked several paper-stuffed file folders. She could tell by the color and texture of the papers, not to mention the style of handwriting, that this collection was the one.

"I canna get past the first chapter o' Archibald's memoirs masel'," Malcolm added. "The man never met a subordinate clause he didna like. And he uses initials instead o' names, pridin' himsel' on his discretion, I'm thinkin', but makin' it a right bugger to decipher."

Amanda remembered Thomas Mason, a dull man with a high opinion of himself, and mentally girded her loins. "It's okay. I'm motivated."

"I'll leave you to it, then. Do you mind if I listen to music while I work?"

"Please tell me you're not into heavy metal."

"I dinna think so, no. Mild-mannered rock 'n reel."

"Rock 'n what?"

He smiled indulgently. "Folk rock. Just the ticket for historians."

"Whatever works," she told him with a shrug, and sat down on the floor beside the cupboard.

Archibald's memoirs were a thick stack of paper in a pleated cardboard folder, neatly labeled in the same typeface as the faxed letter. Amanda pulled a page from the middle and blessed her course in paleography.

The tight, finicky handwriting read, ". . . finding the tenants ever hopeful of improvements, and yet aware of their own responsibilities in the furtherance of agriculture in the glen, Mr. R—and I proceeded toward Cluanie, where we stopped for a meal amidst the glorious scenery of mountain and loch so aptly described by Boswell in his volume of travels with Dr. Johnson. . . ." Archibald seemed blissfully ignorant of the full stop, Amanda thought. She slipped the page back into the stack and leaned the folder against her knee.

A thinner folder was identified as "Collected letters from Isabel Grant, nee Seaton." Letters to James? Amanda set that bundle in her lap, along with the one marked, "Letters from Donald, Lord Dundreggan, to his sons."

Several other folders she set to the side, not recognizing the names or finding the dates out of her range. The last one was labeled, "Miscellaneous." She almost set it aside, too, until she glimpsed a typewritten sheet inside. "Copy of the letter from Alexander Lindsay, Earl of Balcarres, dated July 8, 1781. The letter itself is now in Edinburgh." That might be relevant after all, Amanda told herself, and put the folder on the bottom of her pile. Bless the older Malcolm, she thought. He was making her job a piece of cake, considering.

She piled everything on the settee and went after her notebook. It was right where she'd left it, by the fireplace.

Malcolm's computer screen showed an architectural drawing of a stately Palladian facade. As his hand made subtle movements with the mouse virtual column drums unstacked themselves and rolled to the side. A nearby CD player emitted a sprightly folk-flavored tune for electric guitar and male voice, ". . . here is where the heart is, beatin' like a drum. . . ." With a few quick dance steps, Amanda retired to her corner and settled down.

She started with Isabel's letters. The first one was dated early 1779, apparently right after the engagement had been announced, and began, "My dear Captain Grant." She was engaged to the man and she addressed him so formally? The odds were that Isabel barely knew him. Back then, Amanda might have found herself engaged to Wayne whether she wanted him or not. But no, she wasn't from his class.

Amanda mouthed the words as she struggled through the light, lacey handwriting. The letter acknowledged Isabel's new relationship with James and expressed respect. Not to mention, Amanda thought, evaluating the subtext, a lot of caution. ". . . I shall miss your presence whilst you are in America, and I pray for your safe return, but I cannot help but feel this separation to be the proper time for reflection . . ."

The next letter was not to James but to another woman—a sister?—identified only as Caroline. Amanda slogged her way through an account of a ball, including minutely detailed descriptions of who had worn what, and at last hit pay dirt. "... I must confess, my dear Caro, that despite the extraordinary pleasure I took in seeing my friends and relations at the engagement ball, I have great doubts as to the wisdom of this match. Capt. Grant is a fine figure of a man, of noble countenance, with a ready wit and a smile that would melt the hardest heart, but I find his manner to be bold in the extreme, such as can hardly surprise me when I am acquainted with his reputation in the South. I am told he has been the ruin of more than one respectable maiden, and is the despair of his family. Whilst his approaches to me are made in good faith and with the approval of our fathers, still I am greatly discomfited. . . ."

Amanda dug down through the stack and found another letter to Caroline, dated just after James left for South Carolina. "... my great and guilty relief at his departure be upon my head, Caro. I know not how to express my distaste for his attentions, which he would have me return to him exclusively, denying me the most ordinary discourse with my friends and family. When he discovered me exchanging the merest pleasantry with his own cousin Lt. Grant of Drumullie, he flew immediately into a rage, accusing me of actions appropriate only to a woman of much lower station. Lt. Grant made his apologies and departed forthwith, whereupon Capt. Grant seized upon me and shook me with such force the flesh of my arms remained red and swollen for three days."

Oh no, don't tell me James was abusive. Isabel was twisting the truth to justify her betrayal. Or was she?

Gritting her teeth, Amanda leafed quickly through the stack and found a letter to Archibald, dated soon after the one to Caroline. "... I wish you a safe journey. Please tender my respects to my betrothed, your cousin." Not one word that would prove a prior understanding between them.

Okay. . . . But all the evidence wasn't in yet, not by a long shot. She suddenly realized that mutter in her ears was Malcolm's voice. "Amanda, wake up! Mum's called us doon to breakfast."

Wordlessly Amanda rose and walked down the stairs beside Malcolm, looking neither at James's portrait nor at the packing crate holding his bones. She had some vague sense of greeting Norah, and of consuming egg, sausage, and tomato, and of making a quick pit stop in her room before going back into the library. But most of her mind was time-traveling.

The top letter in the stack from Donald Grant senior was the one Malcolm had mentioned, bawling James out for womanizing, drinking, fighting, gambling. The implication of one convoluted sentence made Amanda slightly nauseous: James had more than once made money by betting his friends he could seduce some girl of good family.

Like me, she thought.

Like she hadn't known from the get-go he was a charming golden-tongued rake with a line strong enough to hang laundry on? Like she hadn't realized she was going to be just one more notch on the hilt of his sword? She'd thrown herself at him anyway. At his ghost, a different animal entirely from the man even though what he'd wanted from her all along was to reclaim his manhood.

Amanda replaced the letter and shoved the entire stack aside. Acid bubbled into the back of her throat. It was time to get Archibald's side of the story. Maybe the pot hadn't gone too far wrong in calling the kettle black. Whatever, the kettle hadn't rated a shot in the dark.

She pulled the musty manuscript from the folder and glanced at the first few pages. A long-winded genealogy led up to Archibald's birth, which was accomplished with various signs and portents throughout Strathspey. She leafed ahead—thank God the man had dated each chapter—to, "Anno Domini 1781, in the service of His Majesty in North America."

There were some of the initials Malcolm had found so obscure. ". . . and with Earl B—billeted at M—not far removed from the village of W—." Balcarres, Melrose, and Williamsburg, obviously. Amanda skimmed past a long essay on the distribution of the regiment's arms, and an even longer one on the economics of Virginia as compared to that of North Britain—apparently the name "Scotland" wasn't politically correct.

She squinted, the small script writhing before her eyes. ". . . we conversed over astonishingly tolerable port with A——, who despite his ill-advised sympathy for the rebellion is a gentleman of good education and fine mien. . . ." A—— had to be Page Armstrong. And there, halfway down the next page, ". . . the beauteous Miss S.A——, who with her blushes and courtesies charmed the gentlemen of the regiment." James said that Sally set her cap at him. Of course she did. He was kind of like a contagious disease, wasn't he?

This wasn't hard at all, Amanda told herself. Like most codes, all you needed was the key. And unlike the Grants, she had it.

She read on. ". . . letter from I—— which I delivered to C.E. . . ." Oh, Charles Edward, James's code-designation. ". . . as was my duty, distasteful as I found it that such a rogue as he should be promised to a lovely and gentle damsel, to whom I fear he shewed little of the respect due a lady of such good breeding. However I wished the facts of the matter to be otherwise, I could not express such sentiments either to I—— or to J—— but bided my time in silence, flattering myself that whilst I was an honorable man he was not, as was subsequently to be proved to both our great costs. . . ."

What about that "J——?" Archibald blew it there, referring to the man by his first initial, unless he intended to hide how many men he was talking about.

The next page, maddeningly, dived into a discussion of the Marquis de Lafayette's strategy as he closed in on the British forces. Amanda wished she had a machete to cut her way through the undergrowth of verbiage. Somewhere in the distance a set of bagpipes was playing "Bad Moon Rising," which was just weird enough to be refreshing.

She turned the next page, and the next, and found the tangled thread of the narrative. ". . . exhausted my capacity for surprise when I came upon C.E. and S—— in close embrace in the summer house, she pleading for release, he crushing her to his bosom and demanding familiarities to which no gentlewoman, even in Virginia, would willingly accede. My arrival on the scene provided S—— the opportunity to break free and, lifting her skirts, to flee toward the house and A——'s protection, whereupon I upbraided J—— for his presumption. And he, turning upon his heel, told me in tones of the greatest contempt that I had but little knowledge of the fairer sex and that S—— had in truth taken great pleasure in her predicament, which in my audacity I had interrupted to no good purpose."

Whoa, Amanda thought, Archibald wasn't only defending Isabel, he was defending Sally. Or so he said, at least. She turned the page and found a soliloquy on the architecture of M——, which Archibald pronounced a pleasing if uninspired imitation of the model of English elegance. If Archibald had appeared in front of her right then she'd have beaten him about the head and shoulders with her notebook and demanded he hurry up, already.

But there, several pages further on, "... distasteful as it was to air the shortcomings of a family member before a colonial, no matter of what wealth and gentility, I acquainted A. with J——'s reputation for trifling with the affections of the weaker sex, and even went so far as to familiarize him with the discourtesies C.E. had committed upon Miss S——. . . ." Oh, now Isabel was Miss S——, "... and informed A—— of his daughter's peril at the hands of one so unscrupulous. Whereupon A—— and Miss A—— left M—— in great haste, vowing not to return until the armies of His Majesty were dislodged from Virginia's soil, an eventuality I must admit I did not at the time think remotely possible but which subsequent events were to prove all too credible." Archibald segued into another monologue, sneering at the ungentlemanly tactics of the Americans.

Amanda could see it all, Page and Sally bugging out through the darkness, the father indignant, the daughter bewildered—all she'd wanted was a mild flirtation. A little rebellion against Page, even, since James was so obviously unsuitable. James sure wasn't the first guy who'd gone after not only the bait but the hook, the line, and the sinker.

So far the account rang true, even if it wasn't word for word what James had told her. Archibald was just the type to pull on his goody two shoes and play tattletale. To play judge and jury. Amanda flipped ahead, breathing hard, anxious to see how he excused James's death. She leaped on the initial when it appeared again.

"... J——, having spent the evening in drinking and gambling with those of the less moderate among the younger officers, discovered in the course of idle conversation the truth of A——'s sudden departure, the warning I had provided, as seemed to me the least courtesy due our host, be he rebel or no, but C.E. did take my admonition as the vilest sort of insult to his own person, and so up the gracious staircase of the house he flew at me, his sword in his hand cutting great wood splinters from the banister, an act I found barbaric in the extreme. But giving me no opportunity to upbraid him for this latest misconduct, he struck me in the face, calling me a traitor to our family name (for, alas, I must admit we shared that noble appellation) and summoned me to the field of honor, whilst I, having little or no taste for such a deadly contest, plied him with soothing words. But he was well into his cups, his breath loathsome with the scent of strong liquor, and he would not accept my mollifying words but termed me a coward. At this juncture I had no choice but to accept his challenge and name as a second my friend Mac——. . . ."

Good God! Amanda collapsed against back of the settee. The ceiling of the library was white plaster, patterned as intricately as the top of a wedding cake, but she didn't really see it. The shot in the rose-scented dark. A duel. Donald Grant had already reamed his son for dueling.

She dived again into the manuscript, reading faster and faster, her eyes aching from deciphering the faded handwriting. But only a few more words brought the end of the story.

". . . our battle was engaged forthwith, fairly and before witnesses, in the dead of night, for the regiment was to move toward the River at dawn. Poor misbegotten C.E. in his besotted haste to have revenge upon the insult he fancied I had dealt him, fired too soon and wildly, whilst my shot, fired as it was without my heart behind it, even so was by the hand of fate directed truly and so did end his unredeemed life. Like some Roman of old, he had drawn his sword in one last effort to have at me, and so in the end came to fall upon it and his own empty scabbard, which was thereby rendered unfit for use. God have mercy upon his soul and upon mine, for this deed haunts me still. My late wife never knew the truth of the matter, but upon my return bearing C.E.'s undamaged sword greeted me with the most appropriate sorrow graved upon her gentle features, and I pray I consequently pursued her favors with all the delicacy appropriate to such a difficult situation.

"As God is my witness my only sin was in the hasty and unsanctified burial of the body, out of fear that those present would be disciplined for dueling, even though none of us had begun that awful process which concluded in such an untimely death. And so to the skirmish at the crossing of the River, to be detailed below, and then coals of fire upon my head when soon afterward, within the confines of Y——, the Earl B—— gave to me a letter informing the late J—— of his brother's death and so of his accession to the title and the property, which had by the time of the receipt of said letter come to me, by my own hand however unwitting. Oft have I hoped to return to Virginia to provide the poor wretch proper

Christian burial, but my hand was stayed by my reluctance to let my dear wife know the truth, and now that she has gone ahead of me to the Elysian Fields I am too old and infirm to accomplish my purpose, God forgive me."

End of the chapter. Was it ever the end of the chapter.

Swearing beneath her breath, Amanda jammed the manuscript back into the folder. Witnesses, she thought. Archibald had witnesses.

She reached for the bundle of letters labeled "Miscellaneous" and flipped through them. She found a note from a tacksman on the estate, a letter from some minor literary light of the period, and—yes, there were two letters dated 1783, one from Major Alexander MacDonald and one from Major Duncan MacPherson, both of His Majesty's 71st Regiment of Foot.

Amanda's patience with period-speak was fraying fast, and she skimmed quickly through the calligraphy. But it was all there: Congratulations to Archibald, Lord Dundreggan, on his recent marriage to Miss Seaton, and roundabout references to the unfortunate incident at — MacPherson at least spelled it out — Melrose, for which Lord Dundreggan bore no fault, as he was but defending his honor against the rash conduct of another.

Yeah, the "Mac——" who'd been Archibald's second would've wanted to whitewash his role in the episode. But MacDonald and MacPherson were majors, second only to Balcarres himself in the regimental pecking order. Archibald's backer had probably been another lieutenant. How many men in a Highland regiment would be named Mac-something, anyway?

Majors MacDonald and MacPherson would have stopped the duel if they'd known about it, but since James and Archibald had gone at it right away—before James had had time to sober up, let alone come to his senses—the ranking officers probably came on the scene after he was dead. They'd had no choice but to acknowledge that his death was his own damn fault. Whether they'd conspired in his hasty burial and the tale of his honorable death in battle, sparing his family the ugly truth, Amanda had no way of knowing. And, after all these years, it no longer mattered. The words had been exchanged. The shot had been fired. The damage was done.

She could see the scene, lit by lanterns, maybe, or torches, the circle of grim-faced men around James's body, his warm, vital body sprawled on the dark and bloody ground. *God.*

Amanda massaged her temples. She'd found Archibald's confession after all, only—go figure—it wasn't what she'd expected it to be. And it made sense, damn it. It made perfect sense.

Carrie liked to say that researching the original sources always rearranges your preconceptions. Here was a perfect example—James's story, a verbal optical illusion that changed depending on how Amanda looked at it.

A little over two weeks ago she'd proclaimed she had no romantic illusions. Last week she'd admitted to Carrie that she did. Now those nonexistent fantasies were crashing and burning around her. The smoke of the destruction stung her eyes. But then, she'd walked into the fire with them wide open, hadn't she?

Be careful what you ask for, you might get it.

She crammed the papers back into the folder. The truth, at last, was out. And the damage was done.

CHAPTER TWENTY

Amanda looked around as though she'd never seen the room before. A sandwich and a cup of tea sat on a small table beside the settee. She touched the liquid. It was cold. Someone—Norah?—had brought her lunch and she'd never noticed her, let alone thanked her. Not, Amanda thought, that her work was engrossing or anything.

She stood up and shook the kinks out of her limbs. Malcolm wasn't there. Neither was Cerberus, although the two cats were arranged elegantly on the chairs in front of the fireplace. Margaret looked up, scanned Amanda, dismissed her, and went back to sleep.

The images of a *Star Trek* screen saver filled the computer screen. From the speakers of the CD player came several *a cappella* voices: "What force or guile could not subdue, Through many warlike ages, Is wrought now by a coward few, For hireling traitor's wages. The English steel we could disdain, secure in valor's station; But English gold has been our bane, Such a parcel of rogues in a nation!"

Amanda thought of James, eager to identify with everything English, and his family and the Frasers as well, who placed assimilation above. . . . Above what? Honor? Or were they just being practical? Scotland had been bled dry in hopeless quests for independence. Quite a few Scots had fought against Bonnie Prince Charlie in the '45.

Malcolm's accent suggested a nationalistic streak, but his consulting work for English estates confirmed his practicality. She'd have to ask his opinion when he got back.

Except for the electronic equipment and the colorful covers of some of the books, the room probably hadn't changed much since James's day. Any minute now he could walk in the door, smiling that devastating smile, his eyes filled with pain and doubt.

No, the pain and the doubt had come later, in the coherent moments of his second life. Not that he'd been using doubt and pain to play on Amanda's sympathies. It would never have occurred to him that a woman could find a hint of vulnerability attractive.

Everything James told her was true. It was just that he'd told it from his own point of view. He saw himself as Archibald's innocent victim. Now that Amanda knew the truth, the whole truth and nothing but, she also knew that James had no honor to return home with, and no right to revenge of any kind. *Crap,* she thought. *Double crap.* So much for her memories of him staying untarnished.

At least she finally knew why an officer and a gentleman had ended up buried at the foot of Melrose's garden. Because, his birth aside, James had been no gentleman.

James probably would have won the duel if he hadn't been drunk. So drunk he hadn't realized he was dead. And what had he been drinking? Some kind of rotgut, not the aromatic single-malt she'd smelled on his breath. Which proved that James's appearance and manner had been shaped not only by his image of himself, but by what she'd wanted him to be. No, she didn't have ordinary romantic fantasies. She had George Lucas special-effects epic delusions.

If James was no gentleman, Amanda told herself, then she was no lady. But then, only one of them had been playing by the double standard of the eighteenth century. Malcolm was right, there was no shame in appetite. The shame, the remorse, the chagrin, was in satisfying that appetite with a lie. The truth didn't cancel out the intense relationship she alone had shared with James. What it did was take the pathos out of his permanent departure. And that, too, was a shame.

Yes, she was going to tell his tale, even though the tale wasn't what he thought it was. What he wanted it to be.

Amanda's eyes focussed. Malcolm was standing beside her. Judging by the angle of his brows and mouth, part amused, part wary, he'd been there a while. She collected her scattered wits and smiled up at him.

"Hello, lassie," he said. "Welcome back. Where have you been?"

"1781, mostly," she replied. "Having hair-raising adventures in historiography."

"In Archibald's memoirs?"

"Yeah, can you believe it? Let's take a walk outside. I need some air."

"Oh aye, we should be takin' the sunshine whilst we have it."

Malcolm turned off the CD player. Together they walked down the stairs, past the great hall and the portraits, to which Amanda gave a cold shoulder, to the front door and outside.

In the dazzling afternoon light the grass glistened so green Amanda wanted to swim in it. The green of the hills was paler, brushed with the purple of heather. Gray billows of cloud blended with the tender blue of the mountains to the west. "Is it going to rain?" she asked Malcolm.

"You see yon hillside?" he replied, pointing. "When you can see it, it's goin' to rain. When you canna see it, it's rainin'."

Amanda laughed. She took deep breaths of the cool, clean air. Side by side she and Malcolm crunched down the driveway. Cerberus loped across the lawn toward them and for a few minutes they played with him. No wonder people kept dogs around, Amanda thought. They had no pretensions whatsoever.

At last Malcolm stood, his knees damp and grass-stained, his hair once again tousled. "So then, I'm wantin' to hear the amazin' tale. This way."

He led her through the wrought-iron gate into the walled rose garden. Blossoms of every shape and color nodded against the silvery stone walls, filling the air with fragrance. Amanda craned her neck to look four stories up the tower keep, toward the windows of her bedroom and bath. Cerberus followed, checking out every bush with a sniff and pausing to anoint a few select ones.

A stone bench sat in a sunny corner of the wall, framed by dark pink rambler roses. *The garden,* James had said, *where we plighted our troth.* For a little while, maybe, he and Isabel had been happy together, he handing her a flower with a bow, she accepting with a curtsey. Until he found her passing the time of day with Archibald, who bailed out and left James to his jealous tantrum. It would never have occurred to Isabel, Amanda guessed, to be jealous of James not only speaking to other women but bedding them. Isabel would have the wedding ring and the Mrs. in front of her name, and whatever affairs he carried on after the marriage she would have suffered in silent dignity. Or maybe even relief, considering that Dr. Ruth's How-To books were well in the future.

"A penny for your thoughts," Malcolm said.

"I'm just glad I didn't live in the eighteenth century." Amanda sat down on the sun-warmed stone of the bench and patted the space beside her. "Sit down. It's quite a story."

Malcolm sat down. "Fire when ready."

"Oh, I'm ready," she told him. "It all started when Dr. Hewitt dug up some human bones in the gardens behind Melrose Hall. With all the insignia it didn't take long to identify James. Carrie, my friend at the library, and I started looking into his life. The problem we kept having was why he'd been reported killed in the battle, but turned up buried in the garden."

"I've been wonderin' that masel'."

Amanda chose her words carefully, saying nothing that didn't have hard evidence to support it. "So I came up with the bright idea that his cousin Archibald found out about Donald's death, which made James the heir and Archibald himself second in line, and killed James for the inheritance—and maybe even for Isabel. He buried James at Melrose but told everyone James had died in the battle and been buried with the other casualties."

Malcolm's eyes widened. "Oh, that's a guid one. Old dry as dust Archibald, a murderer? But I dinna think you found supportin' evidence the day."

Amanda wondered whether she was that easy to read or whether Malcolm was exceptionally sharp. She might as well cut to the chase. "Yes and no. Archibald did kill James, he says as much in his memoirs."

"Bluidy hell," Malcolm said reverently.

"But it was in a duel. James challenged Archibald when he—Archibald—told the owner of Melrose, Page Armstrong, that James was threatening the virtue of his daughter."

"That's been in that tatty old manuscript all the while?"

"Yes, but I think you'd have to know about the Armstrongs and James's body in the garden and everything in advance, or it wouldn't necessarily make sense. I mean, assuming your grandfather read it all the way through—he must've been a man of rare stamina . . ."

"A proper scholar, he was."

". . . he'd have realized that Archibald killed a fellow officer in a duel. He might even have guessed who it was, because Archibald hints that he and his challenger had the same name, and then says he was horrified when the news of Donald's death arrived after James's death and he realized it was 'by his own hand' he'd inherited the estate."

"But since everyone kent that James died in battle . . ."

". . . your grandfather," concluded Amanda, "might not have made that guess. Even if he did, he must have kept it to himself."

"The thirties bein' a more discreet time than our ain," added Malcolm. "Why, the British papers didna say a word aboot Mrs. Simpson almost until Edward VIII abdicated for her."

He was intrigued, Amanda estimated, but hardly upset. *Good.* That was one weight off her shoulders, at least.

"There're some letters, too," she went on, "which all fit into the picture. I got so absorbed I didn't take a single note. I guess I'd better wade back in tomorrow and make some copies. Maybe you could take some pictures of me at work. Carrie will love it, her—our—article will read like a detective story. From the legend, garbled as it is, to the forensic evidence to the documentation to the sword in your hall, it all fits."

"And posh Mrs. Snotty will love it, too." Malcolm grinned, teeth flashing, his expression for an instant so like James's Amanda felt dizzy. His hand took hers in a firm, warm clasp and she steadied.

She liked the way her hand fit snugly into Malcolm's, and how they both balanced on her denim-clad thigh. . . . *Am I on the rebound or what?*

She asked, "I take it you're not going with anybody, either?"

"No. I'm by way of bein' in the market, though."

"Yeah, me too." *Did I say that?* Amanda had to laugh. Two weeks ago her love life had been dead in the water. Now it was moving at warp speed. "This is all happening a little bit too fast."

"Sorry." With a squeeze he took his hand back. "Noo that I've left university, it's a wee bit difficult meetin' attractive women wi' similar interests. I'm comin' on to you too strong."

"Don't apologize. I'm just preoccupied right now. It's kind of an emotional roller coaster, you know." Well no, he didn't know. "After the funeral," she finished.

"Oh, so he's hauntin' you, is he? I never had a ghost for a rival before."

Amanda opened her mouth and shut it again. He was speaking metaphorically, yes, but what was she supposed to do? Tell him the supernatural and only too literal sequel to the story and have *him* think she was crazy? She didn't think so. She settled for, "Yeah, I've gotten so wrapped up in my work James is almost real to me."

Malcolm nodded soothingly. It was his candid blue-gray gaze that was unsettling. He had James's carved lips and intelligent eyes, but his appreciation of irony was tuned more finely, aimed not at arrogant self-awareness but at perception of everything and everyone around him.

Amanda turned the conversation toward safer areas. "I guess it would be a problem, living out here with just your mother and the Finlays. Of course, if I owned a castle brimming with history, I wouldn't go anywhere else, either."

"Oh aye, it's grand place and no mistake. The problem is I dinna own it. Neither does Mum. It's my brother's. The old law o' primogeniture—the property goes wi' the title, to the eldest child."

"That's right, your mother said something about him not being interested in the property."

"Ah, no, he's too much the Sassenach these days, turnin' his back on his ain history."

"The what?"

"Sassenach. An insultin', if a bit old-fashioned, term for Englishman. Etymologically I'm thinkin' it means 'Saxon.'"

"My name is Saxon," Amanda said.

"But you'd be respectin' an historical property, eh?" Malcolm shook his head. "The title's well and truly Archie's and he's welcome to it. But we're workin' on a way he can sell Dundreggan to Mum and me—for a parcel o' English gold, I reckon. I dinna want to have to kill him for it, another round o' death duties would be the ruin o' us."

Amanda met Malcolm's smile with one of her own. Maybe it was the hand of fate, as the earlier Archibald had put it, which was leading her from the bones in the garden through James's brief embrace to this other garden and to a very alive and substantial Malcolm. Maybe it only a chain of happenstance. Whatever. Tomorrow she'd gladly—if cautiously—dive into the stream and let herself go with the flow.

Shadows stretched across the garden. The roses bobbed up and down coyly. Far overhead glided a hawk or a falcon. Cerberus pulled his head out of a bush and strolled toward the gate, his tail wagging. Norah peered through the doorway. "There you are! How's your work getting on, Amanda?"

Malcolm offered his seat to his mother. With a nod of thanks she sat down.

"It's going really well," Amanda replied. "Thanks."

"Wait 'til you hear the tale," said Malcolm. "Little did we ken all this time that old Archibald had a skeleton in his cupboard. The very skeleton that's dozin' in the hall noo."

"Oh, aye?" Norah prodded.

Amanda repeated what she'd told Malcolm, this time adding more detail.

Norah listened, the rise and fall of her brows annotating the story. At last she whistled. "And here I was thinking Archibald a bit of a prat."

"Like his namesake, my brother," Malcolm said cheerfully.

Norah shot him a warning glance. To Amanda she said, "You'll be wanting to take the proper documentation back to the States with you. Let me know if there's anything I can do to help."

"Thank you. I hope none of this embarrasses you."

"Why should it? I may be my brother's keeper, but I'm certainly not my ancestor's. No one ever thought James a saint. Or Archibald, for that matter. I'll be dining out on this story for months." Norah stood up. "Here, I came to call you for dinner. You must be hungry, Amanda, especially since you had no lunch."

"Did you bring me the sandwich? I'm sorry, I never noticed."

"No worry. The cats made a good job of it."

Amanda laughed. Malcolm grinned. Cerberus bounded through the gate, forging a path toward the kitchen.

The household lingered a long time over raspberry trifle and coffee, discussing the scandalous events of the eighteenth century. If Amanda accidentally let slip one or two items she'd learned not from archaeology or historiography but from the supernatural, the Grants and the Finlays took it in stride, probably thinking it was the usual educated make-believe.

When Amanda walked back through the entrance hall she found a damp wind keening through the front door. The sunny afternoon had turned to an early evening. She glanced outside. Clouds filled the sky and erased the distant mountains. The vibrant green of the grass had faded. It looked like she'd been really lucky to have sunshine her first couple of days in Scotland.

She flicked the light switch at the bottom of the stairwell. The bulbs on each landing left swathes of shadow on the steps themselves. Up she went, and forced herself to stop and look at James's portrait. But his gaze, as usual, was self-absorbed. Now Amanda understood why Isabel had been so skeptical about dashing James. Why she'd defaulted to colorless Archibald.

Dashing might work for a brief affair but for the long haul colorless was the way to.... Well, no, Amanda thought, surely you could split the difference.

She scanned the other portraits as she passed. One was a forbidding Victorian gentleman, mutton chop whiskers and all, who was a dead ringer for Archibald. A grandson, maybe. Hard to believe a personable person like Malcolm was descended from such a line of humorless heavies. *Come on,* she told herself. That's just the way they had their portraits painted is all. In private they probably scratched where it itched just like everyone else.

The dimness in the great hall clotted into deep shadow in the corners. Amanda caught a reflected gleam either from the display case or from the sword inside, but the wooden crate was just a lump on the floor. A lump of clay, which is what James's feet were made of. "Damn it all anyway," she murmured as she turned away, but with more weariness than resentment.

Amanda groped inside the library door for the light switch. She blinked in the sudden burst of light. "Shit!"

The pages of Archibald's memoirs made a trail from the settee to the fireplace. Several were actually inside the grate, wadded like kindling. But, judging by the space heater next to the desk and the polished andirons on the hearth, the fireplace hadn't been used for years.

James was trying to hide the evidence. But it was too late, she'd already read the story—no. His disembodied emotions sensed Archibald's heavy hand and lashed out at it. They sensed Amanda's agitation and tried to eliminate the cause, just like the time. . . .

Oh my God, she thought. Like the time Wayne fell down the staircase, soon after he'd actually laid hands on her. She'd asked him if he'd seen anything. She'd never asked him if he *felt* anything, a push or a trip.

Chilled, Amanda gathered up the pages of Archibald's manuscript and smoothed the crumpled ones. Thank goodness James—James's uncontrolled temper—hadn't found a candle to play with this time. Thank goodness he didn't know he could have turned on the space heater and stuffed the pages inside the bars. They would have burned, then. So would Dundreggan Castle.

By the time Malcolm strolled into the room she was back on the settee, putting the pages into order. He raised a brow at her startled reaction to his entrance, but said nothing.

Malcolm printed out his drawings to the music of the Rolling Stones, every now and then playing accompaniment on air guitar. Amanda kept waiting for thunder and lightning, appropriate special effects for a haunted evening, but except for the occasional gust of wind that echoed Mick Jagger's wail, the evening was silent.

"Will you sit yoursel's doon?" Malcolm demanded.

Amanda looked up. The cats were prowling restlessly around the room, over the desk, and across his drawings. Every now and then one of them would go to the door and peer out. "It's the wind," she stated.

"Oh aye," Malcolm said, but his eye turned speculatively from the cats to Amanda and back again.

From downstairs came a burst of excited barking, quickly shushed by Norah's calm voice. The cats oozed beneath the settee and crouched with their paws tucked tightly beneath their bodies, in the shadows looking like two giant dust-bunnies.

Malcolm was still marking the prints with a red pencil when Amanda gave it up for the night. Tempting as it was to stay here with him, her nerves felt like they'd been stretched on a rack. If she was going to scream, she'd better do it alone.

She tucked all the incriminating papers back into the cabinet and shut the door. "Good night, Malcolm."

He looked up with a smile. "Good night. From ghosties and ghoulies and long-leggity beasties and things that go bump in the night . . ."

"I'd rather have the beasties, thanks." She felt his eyes on her back as she left the room, and was sure she felt other eyes on her back as she walked along the corridors.

Her door had a lock but no key. Not that a lock would keep him out. Amanda turned on the bathroom light. The floor was littered with pink and yellow blossoms. Every flower in the window alcove had been beheaded. The bare stalks stood up like a handful of arrows. *James, don't make it worse!*

Nothing.

Amanda gathered up the scattered petals. She took a hot shower and left the bathroom light on and the door ajar. She pulled the comforter to her chin and gazed into the artificial twilight.

Footsteps walked down the hall, the floor creaking at each stride. It was either Malcolm or Norah. Amanda tried willing herself to sleep. She heard another set of footsteps punctuated by creaks and the sound of a door shutting. Water pipes groaned. The window rattled gently.

Slowly she began to relax. James's childish display of spite had worn him out. He'd gone back to sleep. Tomorrow he'd sleep for eternity, a troubled soul finally at rest.

He'd better rest. She'd done all she could for him.

Through her doze she heard approaching steps. Just steps, no creaks. Instantly she was wide awake, staring through the shadows toward her door. The doorknob turned. But the door never opened. An icy draft billowed through the room. A furtive gleam of scarlet winked in the shadows.

Amanda shut her eyes and slowed her breathing. She didn't want to confront him. She didn't want to tell him no, when just a few days ago she'd so enthusiastically told him yes.

His steps came toward her, the slow, painful steps of a wounded man.

She smelled not whiskey but the repulsive breath of a drinker at the end of a long drunk.

"My own," James said, close beside the bed. "My sweet."

Amanda didn't answer.

"Sweeting."

She felt a tug at the comforter. Fingertips stroked her hair. His reek made her gag. "I'm tired," she murmured drowsily. "The trip over here, you know. . . ."

"Ah yes, the boat a mere cockleshell in Neptune's mighty hand. But we have come at last safely to Dundreggan. It is much changed, I fear."

"Mmmph," she said.

His icy hand grasped her shoulder, his fingers digging into her flesh. She shuddered, and not necessarily from the cold. "Have you changed, Amanda? Here, amid the lying tongues of my relations, Isabel changed."

"James, stop it." She wrenched away and turned toward him.

His scarlet coat and blue and green tartan were translucent against the shadows. His eyes were cool and expressionless. "Amanda," he sighed, his voice only a wisp of sound, "my own, you have cut me to the quick."

And he was gone.

Damn it, he made her feel like it was her fault. Well it was, some of it. But only some.

Downstairs, muffled by walls and corridors, the dog barked and then quieted. Amanda lay back down. She'd done what James asked—she'd found the sword, she'd brought him home, she'd told his story. Except the sword was in a display case. His home was in the hands of Archibald's descendants. The story she'd told hadn't been the one he wanted her to tell.

Funny how she was looking forward to tomorrow's funeral like a kid looking forward to Christmas morning.

CHAPTER TWENTY ONE

Lindley Duncan pitched his voice against the wind, and his usually mild tones took on the resonance appropriate to the ancient words. "Man, that is born of woman, hath but a short time to live, and is full of misery. He cometh up, and is cut down, like a flower; he fleeth as it were a shadow, and never continueth in one stay."

The open grave was a damp, dark gash in the green grass of the churchyard, a miniature of the excavation crater at Melrose. Surely, Amanda thought, it'd been years since James's bones and James's presence emerged from the Virginia mud like a tormented butterfly from its chrysalis. But it hadn't even been three weeks.

"In the midst of life we are in death; of whom may we seek for succor, but of thee, O Lord, who for our sins art justly displeased."

Beyond James's grave sprouted the headstones of several generations of Grants. The older ones tilted wearily to the side, their flowing inscriptions barely legible. The words on the newer ones were cut more sharply, small square letters recording sentiments ranging from sappy to dignified. Just to Amanda's right stood the newest headstone, that of Alexander Grant. Its polished granite surface glowed in the clouded light. Both Norah and Malcolm took more than one solemn peek at it.

"Thou knowest, Lord, the secrets of our hearts; shut not thy merciful ears to our prayer."

Beyond the weather-smoothed stone of the Celtic cross each succeeding fold of land seemed more ethereal, green fading to blue, blue to gray, gray at last blending with the overcast sky. The flush of purple on the nearer hills was a pale reflection of the purple clerical stole fluttering around the neck of Duncan's coat.

The landscape had the soft edges and indirect lighting of a dream. Amanda felt like she'd been in a fever dream—summer in Virginia was pretty feverish, after all—and was only now waking up, numb and bleary-eyed, as the cold wind of sanity slapped her cheeks.

Duncan bent, picked up a clod of earth, and threw it onto the coffin. "Unto Almighty God we commend the soul of our brother departed, and we commit his body to the ground; earth to earth, ashes to ashes, dust to dust."

The air thickened with a fine mist, not quite heavy enough to fall as rain. Amanda hoped the moisture didn't smudge the lenses of the cameras the way her eyes were smudged by a furtive tear or two, so that the greens, blues, and purples smeared and ran. What hurt most of all was that her tears were more relief than sorrow.

Malcolm switched the video camera to his left arm and briefly squeezed Amanda's hand between the flapping tails of their jackets. Norah stared into the grave. The Finlays shifted from side to side. The older John MacRae, serving as sexton, leaned on his shovel and peered into the sky, probably wondering how long he'd have to fill in the grave before the heavens opened up.

"I heard a voice from heaven saying unto me, write, from henceforth blessed are the dead who die in the Lord: even so saith the spirit; for they rest from their labors."

Maybe that was why James had been sent back from the dead, not for revenge but for redemption. He'd done his time in purgatory, paying for his living excesses by revealing the weakness that had driven them. Whether that grudging revelation, soaked in booze and denial, was enough to open the Pearly Gates for him Amanda couldn't say. But she suspected she'd learned more from James's time in purgatory than he had.

"The Lord be with you," said Duncan.

Malcolm and Norah responded, "And with thy spirit."

"Let us pray. Our father who art in heaven. . . ."

Amanda's lips moved silently with the prayer. She hadn't thought of prayer earlier, in the great hall of Dundreggan Castle, when Duncan shifted the bones from their wooden crate to a small coffin and Calum Finlay screwed down its lid. She hadn't felt any sense of loss seeing James's physical remains for the last time. They were only bones, gnawed clean of passion. The words that had come to her mind were those of the song, "When day is over and my life is done, my eyes have closed and my strength is gone . . ."

Malcolm threw dirt onto the coffin. The Finlays did the same. Norah threw down one red rose, not the scarlet of James's coat but crimson, like his blood spilled in an alien land. His blood spilled so uselessly.

Amanda reached down, took an icy clod of soil, and dropped it onto the coffin. It made a hollow thunk, as though the box were empty. In spite of everything, she wished James peace. *Good-bye. It was a heck of an adventure. Thank you.*

"May almighty God, Father, Son, and Holy Spirit, bless you and keep you, for now and evermore." Duncan's voice thinned and was gone. The wind keened a lament through the grass, the stones, and the vacant windows of the ancient chapel. Amanda was cold. She clenched her jaw.

"You may take the photographs now, if you wish," Duncan said.

"Thank you," said Amanda between her teeth. She took pictures of the churchyard and the landscape, but she couldn't bring herself to take any of the pitiful hole in the ground. Then she lowered the still camera and Malcolm taped the entire group re-enacting the Lord's Prayer. The whirs and clicks seemed to cheapen the moment. But then, if Cynthia hadn't set up the photo-op trip, James would never have come home and the truth would never have come out. Trust Cynthia to do the right thing, even if the way she did it drove you up the wall.

By the time Amanda and Malcolm had enough pictures the rain was falling in earnest. The Finlays hurried to their car. "Will you be at the ceilidh tonight?" Duncan asked Norah as he folded his stole into his pocket.

"Yes. I promised to bring scones."

"Lovely. I'll see you there." Duncan, too, drove away.

Malcolm opened the door of his green Land Rover for Amanda, who hung back politely for Norah, who shoved Amanda into the front seat and out of the rain. "What's a—is it a kay-lee?" Amanda asked, fumbling the unfamiliar word.

"It's spelt c-e-i-l-i-d-h," said Malcolm, "just to confuse the outlanders."

"It's a party," Norah answered from the back. "Music and dancing. I'm afraid Saturday night is upon us, funeral or no funeral."

Malcolm slammed his door and started the engine. "It's traditional to be havin' a wake after a funeral, if you'd care to take that point o' view. If you'd care to come along, we'd be pleased to have you."

"Well, James was a party animal," Amanda said. "I'd like to come, thank you."

"It's a date, then." Malcolm put the car in gear and drove jouncing down the narrow track from the chapel.

Amanda glanced back to see MacRae shoveling in the same rhythm as the Land Rover's windshield wipers, brisk and steady. James's parents' and brother's graves were on the other side of the cemetery. But then, so were the graves of Isabel and Archibald. Not that it mattered. It was all over but the documentation.

James's funeral had been like his lovemaking, brief and to the point. But each experience was what she needed at the time—a skyrocket of passion in the depth of her dream and an elegy in cool silence at its end. So much for illusion, sexual, supernatural, or any other kind. Now she was going to do some serious exploration of the brave and very real world that was opening up in front of her.

Past Dundreggan's antique gate was parked an orange-striped police car. "Well, well," said Malcolm with a glance at his mother, "and what does the local polis want wi' us the day?"

"To borrow electric flex for the ceilidh, like as not," said Norah.

They scurried through the rain into the house. Voices came from the kitchen, Calum's and Irene's musical cadences in harmony with slightly flatter masculine voice. "Denny is Newcastle born and bred," Malcolm explained. "But he saw the light and moved house to God's country."

Smiling, Norah led the way into the kitchen. Irene was just putting the kettle on. Calum was reaming and stuffing his pipe. Cerberus, Denis, and Margaret waited expectantly in front of the refrigerator.

Against the cabinet leaned a small, slender man in official navy blue, his cap under his arm. The severe cut of his salt and pepper hair didn't tame the exuberance of his gray moustache. When he smiled his eyes and cheeks etched themselves with fine crinkles.

"Good morning, Denny," Norah said. "Or has it gone noon? You'll take lunch with us, won't you?"

"It's noon, right enough. But as for lunch, no, thank you, I'm needed at the village hall to set up the speakers for the band."

"The extra flex is in the back," Malcolm told him. "I'll fetch it."

"Thank you, Malcolm, but that's not why I'm here. I need to talk to your guest." His dark eyes swept Amanda up and down as though assessing her aptitude for criminality. If she'd had an overdue library book he'd have spotted it.

Amanda braced herself. *Incoming. . . .*

"Denny," said Norah, "this is Amanda Witham. Amanda, this is Police Constable Gibson."

"Nice to meet you," Amanda said politely if not quite truthfully.

"How do you do," returned Gibson. He pulled himself to attention, reached into his pocket, and pulled out what looked like a fax. "You are employed at Melrose Hall by the Colonial Williamsburg Foundation?"

"Yes, I am." So Carrie hadn't managed to cover her tracks. But then, she could only go so far out on Amanda's limb with her.

Norah and Malcolm shared a puzzled glance.

"There's been a theft at Melrose," Gibson said to Amanda.

"I know. My friend Carrie Shaffer called me to tell me. It's upstairs, in the display case with the sword."

"The scabbard?" asked Malcolm.

Amanda didn't know what story Carrie had given the police, but she was willing to bet it didn't include James in its cast of characters. "The scabbard was reported stolen from Melrose. But it wasn't stolen. I brought it here with me, because I decided at the last moment we needed photos of it with the sword, and I'm afraid I didn't make it very clear that that's what I was doing so it was reported stolen." Having come full circle, she stopped and told herself that every truth was in the open but one, wasn't it?

Gibson was looking at her as though she'd started speaking Sanskrit. No way her American accent was that confusing. He unfolded the piece of paper. "An eighteenth century military scabbard, poor condition, brass oval bearing the Grant crest, no sword?"

"It's upstairs in the hall," said Malcolm.

"That item was crossed off the list before I received it," Gibson returned.

"List?" asked Amanda.

"A Paul Revere silver tea service—pot, sugar bowl, creamer, and tray."

"What?"

"A brass inkwell. A Chinese vase, Ming dynasty. Two pewter candlesticks. A pair of shell earrings that once belonged to Pook—Pocahen—Pocahontas."

"Excuse me?"

"Here," said Norah in her best voice of reason. "Denny, I take it that's a list of items stolen from Melrose Hall?"

Silently he reversed the paper, revealing a dozen typewritten lines in the body of a letter. Irene's knife snicked up and down on the cutting board. Calum puffed away like a rotund dragon. The animals, like good extras in a crowd scene, milled around underfoot.

Amanda frowned. "I don't get it. The scabbard was in the box with the bones, but I don't know anything about the other things. They were all at Melrose when I left. Even the earrings, and they're just Victorian fakes."

"The box with the bones," said Gibson. "May I see it?"

"Sure." Amanda headed down the hall toward the spiral staircase, Gibson striding at her elbow, Malcolm and Norah close behind. Nothing like waking up, she thought, and finding herself accused of kleptomania in her sleep. "I take it the charges were filed by Cynthia Chancellor?" she asked. "Mrs. Anthony Chancellor, all-American busybody?"

The gray moustache twitched. "Never heard the name, Miss. Williamsburg P.D. is asking that you help with their inquiries. But no charges have been filed."

"Oh." Up the staircase the procession went, Amanda shooting a sarcastic *thanks a lot* at James's portrait. But why should he take anything besides the scabbard? And how? There wasn't room for anything larger than the scabbard in the box.

The wooden crate stood empty beside the display case, its lid propped against its side, the roll of foam drooping over its edge. Each foam recess was empty now. It could have packed a set of dishes just as well as a human body. Amanda gestured toward it. "Help yourself."

Malcolm helped Gibson remove every bit of foam and each package of silica gel. "And your suitcase, Miss?" the constable asked at last.

"Just clothes, shampoo—you know, my stuff," Amanda said.

"Give over, Denny," said Malcolm. "If she filled her suitcase wi' silver tea services she'd no have anything to wear, would she?"

"When did the items go missing?" Norah asked.

Gibson referred to the letter. "Thursday morning."

"I left Melrose Wednesday," Amanda told him, "which would have been Thursday morning here. But you don't mean here, do you?"

"When it was Thursday morning in Virginia," stated Norah, "it was afternoon here and Amanda was already with us. Speaking to her friend on the telephone about the scabbard."

Gibson nodded, folded the letter and tucked it into his pocket. "Well then, you can't have a better reference than Norah here, Miss. I'd best tell my counterparts in the States to have another go at it. You'll be returning the scabbard?"

"I sure will," Amanda told him. "Thursday."

"Very good then. I'm sorry to have disturbed you." His smile cracked his judicial sobriety. "Norah. Malcolm. Tonight at the ceilidh?"

"Of course, Denny. Let me see you out." Norah walked the policeman out of the hall. Their quiet voices receded into the depths of the house.

Malcolm kicked at the wooden crate. "I'll break this up for firewood, shall I? The foam and the gel can be recycled, I expect."

"I wonder what's going on back at Melrose," said Amanda. "Maybe I should call Carrie again—no, it's Saturday, I'd have to call her at home. I could borrow your computer and try e-mail. But I'm not so sure I really want to know what's going on."

Malcolm was looking at her. He'd make a good policeman himself—his clear, canny eyes saw through layer after layer of falsehood, intentional and otherwise. She ducked his eyes and turned toward the sword and the scabbard, cold artifacts under glass.

"It's a catch-22 situation. Cynthia's worked so hard to publicize Melrose and James and everything now she's got people stealing from the place. With so many visitors, a thief could easily pocket something. I worried about it all the time."

"Even a silver tea service?"

"Several people, then."

"Disna seem likely, does it? And why should Cynthia think you had anything to do wi' the thievery? If she's thinkin' that at all."

"God only knows what's going on in her head. Like this crap about my being engaged to Wayne. He's been after me ever since I got there—I don't mean he's a jerk or anything, just kind of clumsy. Cynthia thought she was doing us a favor sending us over here together. But we had an argument just as we were leaving." Amanda waved her hands like she was shooing away a bee. "No, I told him off. He drove away without me and I came here alone. Maybe she's out to get me because I won't go along with her plans. Maybe she's mad about what I said to Wayne. I didn't think he'd tell her, or that she'd care if he did, but I've called a lot of shots wrong recently."

"You can hardly blame the chap for fancying you," Malcolm observed.

"I don't. He just won't take no for an answer and it's made everything even more complicated than it already was." She turned back around. "I don't want to make an enemy of Cynthia. She can make or break my career. If I ever get a career."

"Nothing was stolen on your watch, was it?"

"No, not—well. . . ." Again she glanced at the scabbard. She was going to have to tell Malcolm eventually. If she wanted to connect with him, that is. And did she ever want to connect with him.

Norah's voice drifted up the stairwell. "Malcolm? Amanda? Lunch!"

Malcolm was still looking at her, his expression indicating deep thought. This man, Amanda told herself, wasn't into delusion, either self- or otherwise. But all he said was, "Shall we go doon?"

"Yes. Suddenly I'm starving."

"You should be fortifyin' yoursel' for the ceilidh." His hand in the small of her back eased her toward the door.

His substantial hand, Amanda thought. *His corporeal hand.* Funny how reality brought along its own set of problems.

She smiled lopsidedly, caught between pleasure and frustration, all the way down the staircase.

CHAPTER TWENTY TWO

The third time Amanda fell asleep over Archibald's manuscript she packed it away and went upstairs for a nap—if she'd slept last night, she couldn't remember it. She made sure her alarm was set and woke up in plenty of time to fix herself up for the evening. Which was a job, she thought with a look at her corrugated face and fright wig hair, right up there with making a silk purse out of a sow's ear.

But by the time she'd washed her hair, applied a light layer of make-up, and dressed in a long skirt and sleek jersey blouse, she felt like a new woman—one who'd learned from her mistakes and was all the better for the lesson.

Amanda walked out the hall just as Malcolm left his room two doors away. *All right!* If Malcolm in a pair of blue jeans was a sight for sore eyes, Malcolm in a kilt could heal the blind.

He saw her expression, grinned, and pirouetted, the red and green tartan swirling above a pair of finely turned knees.

Amanda reeled her tongue back into her mouth before she stepped on it. "I'm impressed. Back in the heathen land where I come from, men dress up in dark suits."

"What a scunner." Malcolm offered her his tweed-jacketed arm. "You're lookin' positively splendid yoursel'."

"Thank you."

Basking in mutual admiration they went downstairs. Norah was rearranging the blossoms in the large vase on the kist. She wore a red jacket and a tartan skirt that revealed legs every bit as well turned as her son's. From somewhere deep in the house came the sound of a sitcom's canned laughter. "The Finlays are stayin' in the night," Malcolm explained as he held Amanda's windbreaker for her.

Except for a few drops scudding down the wind the rain had stopped. Wreaths and swags of cloud spun across the sky, trailing sunbeams which spotlighted first one, then another patch of green hill-side. Norah clambered into the back of the Land Rover, carrying a basket that exuded a warm, floury odor. Amanda tucked herself in beside Malcolm and looked ahead with a smile.

The chapel perched on its headland, a solitary geometrical shape against the curves of the hills. "The headstone should be arriving next month," said Norah. "A small one with his name, dates, and a thistle."

"It's really nice of you to go to all the trouble," Amanda said over her shoulder.

"It's no trouble. He's family, after all."

The chapel dropped behind a shoulder of land. The road headed downward into the river valley. "Glenmoriston," said Malcolm with an inclusive wave of his hand. "Bonnie Prince Charlie hid hereabouts. One o' the local lads put on Charlie's jacket and showed himsel' to the redcoats. They killed him, as you'd expect, but they thought they had their man long enough for the real Charlie to leg it up the glen toward Skye."

"And in the next generation," Amanda pointed out, "James and Archibald were redcoats themselves."

Malcolm nodded. "It's just as well Charlie lost. As usual, the romance plays better than the reality."

"Tell me about it!"

The car emerged onto the main road—or what passed for a main road in this part of the world—and turned toward the village. The village hall was an aluminum barn on the outskirts of town. A procession of people waded through a shoal of playing children toward the door.

Amanda followed her escorts into a brightly-lit vestibule. Lindley Duncan sat next to the cloakroom, collecting a five-pound note from each arrival. "Good evening," he said. "I thought the service went well."

Malcolm produced the admission fee. "He's been laid to rest right and proper."

And not one minute too soon, Amanda added to herself. She said, "Yes, thank you very much for helping out."

Paper streamers and fairy lights hung from the exposed I-beams in the darkened main room, from the corner of her eye looking almost magical. Flames leaped in the mouth of a massive stone fireplace. Norah took plates of scones out of her basket and made room for them on a long table heaped with food. Two men dispensed the liquid sort of refreshment from another table. On a low stage to the left of the fireplace several musicians were warming up. Amanda counted a keyboard, a tin whistle, a fiddle, an accordion, and a set of drums. A piper in full kilt and plaid massaged his pipes behind them.

"What's your pleasure?" Malcolm asked in her ear, above the din of voices and instrumental squeaks.

She smiled, remembering her vision of a cool evening, a handsome man, a fireplace, and a glass of whiskey. Here were all the ingredients, plus music, even. What was the line from Shakespeare? *If music be the food of love, play on.* "Food," she answered generically.

"Oh aye. Food." They grazed down the table, Malcolm initiating Amanda into the secrets of Dundee cake and Forfar bridies. Saving the alcohol for later—no sense in wiping herself out before things even got going—she accepted a glass of what he called lemonade but which turned out to be Seven Up. Again he offered her his arm, and introduced her to half the population of Inverness-shire, none of whose names she remembered. She smiled dazedly and said again and again how much she loved Scotland.

To a chorus of cheers the piper stepped forward and let loose with "Scotland the Brave." The blast parted Amanda's hair and made her ears ring, but the resulting exhilaration was worth it. The party was under way.

Guided by Malcolm's steady hand she danced, stumbling at first and then picking up the steps. Fortunately the band spaced the rough and tumble fast dances with slow ones, letting a little oxygen leak back into the carbon dioxide content of the room.

It was during the slow dances Amanda and Malcolm exchanged life stories. He'd studied historical architecture in Massachusetts, she discovered—"Gey modern buildin's, none older than 1686, but interestin' nonetheless"—and computer science in London. Her life, she told him in return, had ranged from mundane to dull up until this summer—"which is why I got the internship, probably, my profs at Cornell knowing I wasn't going to sell off the artifacts for drugs or hold Satanic rituals in the library."

Even though Malcolm named each song, still the traditional arrangements ran together with the contemporary rock tunes in Amanda's mind until she was dancing to something titled, "The Cape Breton Fiddler's Welcome to the Gay Gordons and Lady Carmichael's Strathspey in the Pride of the Summer O'er the Sea to Skye in the Land of a Thousand Dances."

She was working up a pretty good drunk on the music and on Malcolm's voice. Time for the whiskey.

The whiskey evaporated on her tongue, leaving her mouth filled with the flavor of peat smoke and fire. Yes, it reminded her of James. But that had been far away and long ago. The man had been in his grave two hundred years.

Urged by several good-natured catcalls, Malcolm shed his coat and tie, stepped onto the stage, and set a tin whistle between his lips. His eyes found Amanda's in the crowd and held her spellbound as he played a tune so sweet and clear and pure her skin tingled. Why was it, she asked herself, that every human culture invented both weapons and musical instruments? Maybe grace as well as aggression was hard-wired into the human brain.

Malcolm gave the whistle back to its owner and stepped off the stage. "What was that song?" she asked him.

"A Gaelic piece, I canna even pronounce the title."

"It's beautiful."

"Like you," he said, and swept her into another slow dance.

Funny, when Wayne said things like that they seemed stilted and hollow. When Malcolm said them she melted into his arms.

They didn't bother with dance steps any more, but embraced and turned a slow circle in time to the music. Amanda had never thought an accordion could play sensuous music. Was she ever wrong. The notes vibrated every nerve ending. The drums tapped a soft undercurrent like the beat of her heart. She hung on to Malcolm's shoulders, sensing the warm flesh beneath his shirt, nestling her cheek against his jaw. Through her half-closed eyes she watched the fireplace circle around her, embers glowing.

Malcolm's fingers moved up and down her back just as they'd moved on the tin whistle. His sixth sense must know how she needed to be eased back into reality. She savored every subtlety of the friction between her body and his wonderfully solid flesh—it was soothing and arousing both. He smelled of fresh air, whiskey, and wool, a scent so compelling she was tempted to nibble his ear lobe. But no, not now. Not yet. "What's this song?" she asked.

"The Misty Mountains of Home."

That wasn't appropriate or anything. . . . She recognized the couple dancing, similarly entwined, a few feet away. Norah was a little bit taller than Denny Gibson, but judging by her blissful expression his moustache buried in her neck was more stimulation than annoyance. "Is that relationship what it looks like?"

Malcolm glanced around to see who she was referring to. "Oh aye, Mum and Denny are lovers, right enough."

"Really?" Amanda liked his matter-of-fact attitude. "Denny seemed so correct this afternoon. You know, stiff."

"He'd no be makin' a guid lover otherwise, would he?" Malcolm said with a remorseless grin.

Amanda laughed. She couldn't imagine Cynthia with a lover. Sex tended to be messy, after all.

The evening wound down in a blush of fire and whiskey and just enough sexual tension to make things very, very interesting. Amanda felt relaxed for the first time in weeks, relaxed and paradoxically wide awake.

Duncan stood at the door like at the door of his church, shaking hands and wishing everyone a good night. There were probably more people at the ceilidh than at the church, Amanda reflected. She and Malcolm clung together through the chill of the parking lot. Their breaths made clouds inside the car.

"The evening was great," Amanda said. "Thanks so much."

"The evenin's no over yet," said Malcolm. He cupped her face in his hand, pulling her gently forward.

Oh yeah. She lifted her chin and parted her lips.

The dome light burst through the darkness as Norah opened the back door. "What a lovely evening! Don't you think so?"

"Oh aye," said Malcolm. Laughing, he released Amanda and turned to the steering wheel. "I do think so."

"Denny says to tell you he's sorry about this afternoon, Amanda, and he hopes he didn't upset you."

"I'm not upset. No way." She pulled her jacket closer around her and watched smiling as the night sped away beside the car.

Dusk lingered in the west. In the east stars played tag with wreaths of cloud. Amanda couldn't see a moon. It was like she'd fallen out of time. And yet time was carrying her onward. She'd only met Malcolm two days ago and already she'd fallen hard for him. The strength of her own emotions would've surprised her, except when it came to her emotions she was beyond surprise.

She knew what was going to go wrong now. She herself was booked to disappear into thin air next Thursday. But where there was life there was hope and a second chance. This time she wasn't going to rush anything. This time she was going to get it right.

They turned off the main road. Dundreggan sat on its hilltop, its windows disembodied points of light against the dark. Like a jeweler's display, Amanda thought. Diamonds on velvet.

"Bluidy hell!" Malcolm exclaimed. "Every light in the place is switched on!"

"I hope the fuse box hasn't gone on the blink again," said Norah.

"Calum has it well in hand, I expect." He guided the car up the last hill. The house disappeared behind the trees, then jumped out at them, every window clearly defined, bright arches and rectangles against the black bulk of the walls. The car rolled into its parking place. Without the engine noise, the only thing Amanda could hear was the wind.

"I'll see what they're on about." Norah got out of the car and walked down the driveway to the front door.

Malcolm handed Amanda from the car and looked up at the castle. "It's a sight," he said. "We'll owe a packet to the Hydroboard, but it's a sight."

"So are you," Amanda told him. "Where were we?"

"Just here, I'm thinkin'." He turned to her. She cupped his face in her hand, drew him forward, tilted her lips to his.

From inside the house came the sudden smash of glass. A woman screamed. The sound was harsh and shrill in the silence.

Malcolm and Amanda recoiled from each other, sprinted for the door, and collided in the opening. Norah was just running up the spiral staircase. "Irene!" she called, "Irene, are you all right?"

Amanda's shoes slipped on the flagstones. She glanced down. Rose and iris petals were spread across the floor. Every blossom in the vase on the kist had been shredded.

Something dull and hard thudded into her exhilaration and sent it into a death spiral. *No. No. No.* She followed Malcolm up the staircase and past the three portraits.

Just inside the door of the great hall Calum and Irene stood clutching at each other, Norah beside them. They were staring at the splintered remains of the display case. Shards of glass spattered the floor and the empty wooden crate. The air in the hall was icy cold, sucking the last flush of elation from Amanda's limbs. *Yes.*

"What happened?" Norah asked.

Calum's eyes bulged from his face. "All evenin' there's been noises. Steps clumpin' up and doon the staircase, up and doon. Doors openin' and slammin' shut. The flowers torn to bits. And the animals goin' daft, barkin', whinin', hissin'. We were standin' here at the door, havin' another look, touchin' naethin', and that crate jumps up into the display case, crash, the lot goes tae buggery. Then the sword and the scabbard come flyin' through the air, right at ma heid, oot the door and awa', only the guid Lord kens where."

Amanda took a step forward, glass crunching beneath her feet. The sword and the scabbard were gone. On a rush of air and movement, like the one that had smashed a drinking glass against her kitchen wall. *Damn. Damn. Damn!*

"Well then," said Malcolm, his words reverberating in the frosty silence. "Amanda, it's time you were tellin' us the rest o' the story."

Her thoughts congealed, cold and clear as ice. She wasn't surprised at her own emotions, no. But James's emotions, it seemed, had a totally unwelcome surprise left.

"Yes," she said between her teeth. "It sure is."

CHAPTER TWENTY THREE

Amanda looked into her mug, hoping she could read the future in it. But it was only black tea swirling with milk.

After cleaning up the debris and turning off the lights, Irene and Calum had gone to their rooms in the south wing, too shaken to care how Amanda explained their horror-flick of an evening. She was left facing Norah and Malcolm across the kitchen table, Cerberus a furry bulk huddled on her feet. They'd be lucky, she thought, to see Margaret and Denis before Halloween.

No, James was not going to go quietly into that good night. Or even stay a figment of her and various animals' imaginations. With the evening's special effects he'd given the entire household the finger. Her shoulder blades twitched. But ever since that last spasm of violence the night had been ominously silent.

"Yes, James is haunting me," she told Malcolm. "I know you meant it as a joke or a metaphor or something but . . ."

"No, lass, I was wonderin' even then. Before I heard the footsteps."

Great, Amanda thought. Good thing she'd never wanted to be a politician. Covering up was not her strong point.

"Last night? You heard them, too?" asked Norah.

"Oh aye." Malcolm's uncompromising gaze made Amanda feel like the suspect in an old police drama, cornered and spotlighted. "Steps that didna make the floorboards creak, steps that turned your door knob and then were in your room. But you didna come screamin' oot, did you? We've never had a ghost here, no until you came, you and your box o' bones. James Charles Edward Grant, who was never one for bein' timid."

"I could hardly walk in here and announce, 'I've brought you a ghost,' could I?" Amanda demanded.

"Why the bluidy hell no?"

She met his eyes squarely. He had every right to be mad. So did she, just not at him. "You'd think I was crazy. You'd laugh at me. How was I supposed to know you already believe in ghosts?"

"You weren't," Norah said soothingly. "Look at this way, Amanda. Our traditions of death and the otherworld reach back well into Celtic prehistory. All good Highlanders have a touch of the second sight—my grandmother told me when I was five years old I'd marry a man from Glenmoriston and have two sons. We know families with resident ghosts, if milder-mannered ones than James."

"I thought all that was just tourist stuff. Sorry."

Malcolm offered her a conciliatory if somewhat lopsided smile.

Amanda smiled back. What maddened her more than anything else, she thought, was that she'd come down from the evening's high much too fast. She sipped at the tea. "James said his Highland troops were superstitious. But in his day educated people didn't waste time with ghost stories and stuff. I've thought all along how ironic it was he ended up a ghost himself."

"You were talkin' to him, then?" Malcolm asked.

"Yes. I talked to him. I saw him, I smelled him, I touched him. I knew the bones were his before they were identified. When I asked him what he wanted he told me."

"Aye?"

"He said he wanted his sword, he wanted to come home, and he wanted revenge against Archibald. My theory about Archibald murdering him—I made that fit what he told me."

"Not good scientific practice," said Norah, "but understandable. If his ghost looks anything like his portrait, he must be right dishy."

"Handsome? Oh yeah. Like Malcolm, handsome and charming."

"My dad never ticked me off for gamblin' and drinkin' and fightin'," Malcolm interrupted. "I dinna cut up rough when a lassie gives me the elbow. Tells me good-bye."

He might mean Isabel, but she didn't turn to Archibald until James was dead. He probably meant Amanda herself. *My sweet, my own.* Looked like she was the only one who'd wanted—she had to face the truth—a one-night stand.

Again she ducked Malcolm's perceptive eyes. "I thought James would be able to rest once he saw his sword again. Once he was properly buried at home and I told everyone his story. Not that the story I was going to tell was the real one. Everything he told me was the truth, and yet it was all a lie."

"That's just it. He canna get the revenge he's wantin'. Archibald, alive or dead, owes him nothing." Malcolm tapped his mug on the table. The table, thank goodness, didn't tap back. "Do ghosts have rules, like the laws of physics? Most stories tell of the—the presence—hangin' aboot the person's bones. That's when you first saw him, was it, when his bones were found?"

"Yes. That same night, sitting on the staircase in his scarlet coat and kilt. The next day the archaeologists hauled the bones away to the lab and I didn't see him again until they set up the display in the entrance hall."

"A display of his bones?" Norah asked.

"A few of them. And the miniature portrait, some prints and maps, the snuffbox that was in his sporran, and his scabbard . . ." Amanda stopped dead, her mug halfway to her lips. *That was it!* She put the mug back down with a crash. "It's the scabbard! He was holding it—its ghost—when I first saw him. Even when it was just hanging at his side he kept touching it. That's why he's still here. He shed his bones like a snake sheds its skin. His presence is in the scabbard."

Norah nodded. "He was buried with it, wasn't he? His anger became focussed on it during all those long years beneath the sod, I expect."

"Did you bring the scabbard here?" Malcolm asked Amanda. "Or were you coverin' for James?"

Was it ever a relief to talk to them. No more fudging. No more rationalizing. "He sneaked it into the box with his bones. I didn't know it was there until Carrie called and said it was missing."

"And you didna throw it at my feet, did you?"

"No. It jumped out of my hands. Because you're descended from Archibald, I guess."

"And because I was givin' you a good look, like Archibald tippin' his bonnet to Isabel."

I know, I know, Amanda thought with a squirm, *I should've seen it coming.*

"Now he's carried away both scabbard and sword," said Norah. "Can he actually—discorporate them, do you think?"

"He can move things around," Amanda said. "But as far as I can tell he can only make himself and his uniform disappear."

"Dundreggan has lumber rooms to spare. The sword and the scabbard could be anywhere." Norah drained the teapot into her cup.

"I wonder why ghosts always appear in clothes?" Malcolm asked.

"Some Victorian lady writer," replied Amanda, "once said that if ghosts appeared naked they'd be even more fearsome and horrible."

Malcolm laughed. So did Norah.

Amanda's feet had fallen asleep beneath Cerberus's weight. She tried wiggling her toes. The dog whimpered, but shifted his mass onto Norah.

"Has James ever materialized during the day?" asked Norah.

"No, only at night."

"Then it's just as well we have short nights this time of year."

"But even when he's not material he'll respond to stimulation like a poltergeist." Amanda set her chin. "He'll be back."

"He's never had his revenge," Malcolm said. "But if he intends to skewer Archibald's descendant instead o' Archibald himsel', then he'll no be havin' it."

"He couldn't do that, he's not substantial enough . . . ." And who firmed him up? she asked herself. Who'd made his purgatory a time not of redemption but of renewed strength? "I don't know what he's capable of," she concluded lamely.

Norah smiled in sympathy. "You thought you knew him, didn't you? But he deceived you."

"In a way. But mostly I deceived myself." Amanda stood up. "If you'll excuse me, I think I'll go crawl into a corner. I've caused enough trouble for one night."

"You've no caused any trouble," Malcolm stated. "The fault's on James's head. Come along, I'll walk you to your room."

"Leave your door open," counseled Norah, "and give a shout if you're frightened."

"That's what I hate the most," Amanda said. "I told him once he didn't frighten me, but he does now. Malcolm, watch your back."

"Oh aye, I think I should do. Good night, Mum."

"Good night, Malcolm. Amanda. Try to sleep."

They walked down the hallway and up the staircase, and paused in front of James's portrait. "I bet Archibald was secretly pleased the way things turned out," said Amanda. "Dashing, handsome James, constantly taking center stage—he must have been a real thorn in the side."

"A silver-tongued devil, right enough," said Malcolm, with a narrow sideways glance at Amanda. "The sort that always gets the girl."

She wasn't going to rise to that bait, not now.

Malcolm escorted Amanda to her door and checked over her room. Nothing was messed up or broken. "Well then," he said. His mouth was set in a straight line and his eyes were affectionate but cool, understandably distracted.

"I was going to tell you, really. I'm sorry it happened now, like this."

"I am, too. I feel like a lad rapped across the knuckles for havin' his hand in the box o' sweeties."

"Caught in the cookie jar. Not that I'm a box of sweets . . ."

Malcolm gestured a disclaimer.

". . . but I'll still be here for several more days. Good night."

"Good night," he said with a smile, and turned away.

With a parting look at the kilt, Amanda went into her room and inspected her face in the bathroom mirror. A fine line creased the skin between her brows. She smoothed it with her fingertip. "James, I'm not two-timing you," she said quietly. She'd honored her part of the agreement and now he wasn't honoring his. . . . They hadn't made any agreement. He'd used her, she'd used him, and it was done. "James, please, there's nothing for you here, not any more."

She didn't see any movement behind her reflection, not the least shiver of the fresh flowers in the alcove, nothing. James must be exhausted after his temper tantrum. Or so she hoped.

Propping her door open, Amanda went to bed. But the pale light of dawn was filtering into the room before she fell asleep. She didn't dream about James and his corroded charm but about Malcolm, and woke up filled with determination—*let's just see who's stubborn!*

No one was in the sitting room or the library. In the kitchen a note was propped against the teapot. "Dear Amanda, I thought you might like to have a lie in. Your breakfast is in the oven. Irene, Calum, and I have gone to church. Keep your pecker up. Norah."

Pondering the joys of dialect, Amanda found a plate of eggs and sausage tucked away in the lower warming oven. In the upper, hotter one sat a savory-smelling pot roast obviously intended for Sunday dinner. She made herself a cup of instant coffee. Malcolm must still be around. And James.

She tidied up her dishes, went upstairs and brushed her teeth, and, putting on her windbreaker, went outside. The blue sky was scattered with clouds that sailed like treasure galleons before the wind. The cats sat bundled on the stone bench looking like petulant pincushions. Cerberus was snooping around the corners of the rose garden while Malcolm clipped the withered blooms. Amanda stood in the gateway watching him work.

His movements were precise, contained, without the least bit of swagger. He had James's ease with the language, his penetrating eyes, and his smile, his astounding smile. But he wasn't James. Malcolm had nothing to prove. No way could she resist climbing down the family tree from a hopeless relationship to one with so much possibility. And yet James hadn't exactly dropped off his branch like a dead leaf, which was her own darn fault.

Malcolm spun around. "Oh, it's you, is it? I kent someone watchin' me and thought it might be himsel'."

Amanda glanced up at the windows overlooking the garden. They shone in the sun, empty. "Has anyone found the sword and the scabbard?"

"No."

"So now what happens? In most haunted house stories the living inhabitants simply move out, but I don't think that's an option here."

"No a bit of it. We'll see if he makes an appearance tonight. Maybe pinchin' the sword will settle him."

"Yeah, right," Amanda said. "Can we get out of earshot for a while?"

"I was goin' to suggest just that." Malcolm set down the clippers and rinsed his hands at a nearby faucet. When he took Amanda's hand his was ice-cold, but it warmed up fast. It wasn't only the scent of the flowers and his closeness that made her giddy. She felt like she was standing on top of a cliff, peering over the edge before taking the plunge. *This is it. The last bit of truth, take it or leave it.*

Silently they strolled out of the garden toward the stone gateway, Cerberus at point. He frisked on down the drive in the cool shadow of the trees. The vault of green leaves made a mosaic of the sky. Bits of sunlight spattered Malcolm's hair with bronze. "Did you sleep well?" he asked.

"When I finally got to sleep, yes, I did, oddly enough."

"I decided it was no use barricadin' my door. He can probably walk through it."

"I've never seen him do that. He just materializes inside."

"Oh. Right."

So far Malcolm had been pretty darned empathic, Amanda told herself. Surely he could handle the rest of it. If not. . . . If not, he couldn't, that was all. And that would be all, which was just the problem.

"I think that at first," she said, "James was animated—activated, whatever—by being at Melrose, where he died. But now he has me as an animating force. He's like an incubus."

"An incubus?" One of Malcolm's eyebrows arched upward. "You ken the proper connotation o' that, I expect."

"You do, don't you?" Amanda kicked a pebble clattering down the crumbled asphalt of the drive. Cerberus made a right-angle turn and nudged it with his nose. "Yeah, I had sex with him. Big surprise, right?"

"No." Malcolm's grasp of her hand didn't falter. Neither did his steps. Both his brows were askew. "How? James may be able to carry things aboot, but still, he disna have real substance, does he?"

"He had plenty of substance then. For a couple of minutes anyway."

"Just a couple of minutes, was it?"

She wasn't going to fudge that, either. "It was good. Really intense. I wasn't as if I started from a standstill, I'd been turned on all week. It was what I wanted. Then."

"Then?"

"Yeah, now it's all looking like a really bad choice."

"Well then," he said, just about as noncommittal a statement as she'd ever heard. His brows settled down into their usual intelligent arcs, like diacritical marks over his eyes.

They left the shelter of the trees and walked out onto the hillside. Glenmoriston stretched westward at their feet, the river and its tree-lined banks fading into the hazy blue horizon. Cerberus slipped through a fence into a field and in some glimmering of instinct raced toward a group of sheep. They braced themselves for orders, and then, as the dog scampered aimlessly around, shrugged and went back to grazing.

"So," Amanda went on, stepping over the edge. "Are you okay with that? That I had sex with him? I mean, my bad choice wouldn't necessarily be any of your business, except that this guy's trashing your house and threatening people. Which makes it your business."

"You're makin' the assumption, lass, that I'm wantin' you for masel'."

Oh. She'd thought they connected last night. But James had broken that, too. . . . She saw the twinkle in Malcolm's eyes. "You rat! Like I really need to be teased right now!"

Laughing, he released her hand and tucked his arm securely around her waist. She hung on for dear life. They walked on down the lane and turned onto a twin-rutted track that climbed up the hill. In the distance a herd of deer picked their way among the gray stones that emerged from the mottled green of heather, gorse, and fern.

"Mind you," Malcolm said. "My ain record's no so tidy. I've sown my share o' wild oats. Canna say I've ever had to pray for a crop failure, though."

"Which is what I'm doing right now," Amanda said with a rueful laugh.

"Maybe I've been careful. Maybe I've been lucky. But I've seen my mates usin' the lassies for games o' power and ego—like James, I reckon—and I've no stomach for it. Call me unmanly, if you like." He shot her a sharp look.

"Unmanly? No way. It takes a real man to admit he's not the helpless victim of raging hormones. Not," she added, "that women don't play games of power and ego, too."

"But you've no stomach for them?"

"God, I hope I don't play games."

"You're no playin' wi' me." His arm tightened around her waist.

She felt his heart thrumming in his chest, and the muscles in his flank contracting and relaxing. "Trust me, Miss Mundane and Dull, to fall for a silver-tongued devil. If it were just my problem that'd be one thing. But I've dumped him on you. He's going to be out to get you not only because of Archibald but because of me." Amanda pulled Malcolm to a stop, untangled herself from his arm, and looked into his face. "We're past flirting, aren't we?"

"That we are, lassie. Well past." He frowned slightly, choosing his words. "You did the right thing bringin' James hame. Dinna worry yoursel' aboot it. Or aboot me. James'll be after me, aye. But I'm as much a Grant as he was. Is. It's 'Stand Fast' for me too."

"And?" Amanda prompted.

"And he'll no be comin' between us. We'll be standin' too tight together. If that's what you're wantin' to know."

"It's what I'm wanting to know," Amanda replied, and she eased slowly to earth. "What's beyond ironic is that if it wasn't for James we'd never have met."

"It's himsel' who brought us together, right enough." Malcolm grinned. He'd gone over the edge, too, not sure what she felt, not sure what she'd tell him, but his landing, too, was soft.

He gestured toward the castle on its crag, green leaves lapping its foundation, flag waving bravely from its highest tower. A cloud covered the sun, casting the hillside and the rutted track into shadow, but the castle stayed glowing in the sunlight. "That's right magic."

"Magic," Amanda repeated. "Is it ever."

"Are you sure we only met a few days ago? Have we no been together for years?"

"In your dreams," she told him with a grin of her own. "And in mine."

Malcolm turned back to her, taking her shoulders in his strong hands. "Noo then. Is there anything else needs tellin'?"

"Not unless you're interested in my grandmother's maiden name or the grades I made in elementary school."

Sunlight swept over them, but it didn't shine as brightly as his eyes. "You'd better stop smilin' then, so we can make a proper kiss o' it."

She stopped smiling. Gently she pressed her lips against his, testing for warmth and texture. A shiver ran down her back. *Yeah.*

She wrapped her arms around his chest and angled her head the other way. This time her mouth melted against his and his tongue greeted hers so delicately her nipples prickled. *Oh yeah.*

Another repositioning, for maximum effect, and they came together again, lips and tongues moving in a slow dance of heat and tension and taste until Amanda's knees wobbled and sparks twirled behind her eyes. *Oh yeah, oh yeah.* Maybe it was love, maybe it was oxygen deprivation. She didn't care. It worked.

They stood molded together from thigh to throat, panting in the same rhythm. Malcolm's lips teased her ear. The moisture on her lips turned tingling cold in the wind. She felt light, almost transparent, like she could surf on the wind. In fact, she could hear the wind rushing past her ears, making an odd rumbling sound.

She was hearing an engine. She turned her head against Malcolm's as he peered around hers. A car climbed the lane toward Dundreggan and disappeared into the trees. "Church must be out," she wheezed.

"No," he wheezed back. "That's a taxi. We're havin' a visitor, it seems. We'd better go and see."

But not before several more kisses. At last they parted, clasped hands, and started down the track. Cerberus bounded out of the field and sniffed at them, probably assessing the reek of hormones.

The taxi was just emerging from the stone gateway. Its door was stenciled ABERTARFF MOTORS, INVERNESS. Malcolm exchanged a wave with the driver. "Good job gettin' a taxi on a Sunday, especially one to come all the way oot here. Our visitor has more siller ¾ more silver, money ¾ than sense."

"Oh no." Amanda's glow popped like a soap bubble. "That describes Cynthia to a tee."

But it was Wayne's beefy shape slumped on the stone bench, two suitcases at his feet. Margaret and Denis sat a few meters away, eyeing him as suspiciously as he was eyeing them. *Great,* Amanda thought, *Cynthia sent her stooge to do her dirty work.*

"Wayne!" she called. "What the hell are you doing here?"

Wayne looked up to see Cerberus's black-and-white shape bearing down on him. He leaped to his feet and stood stiffly while the dog circled around him, giving him the smell of approval.

Amanda couldn't swear Wayne was wearing the same clothes he'd had on last Wednesday, but his suit looked like he'd slept in it every night since then. His cheeks were stubbled and his eyes were puffy and streaked with red. "I saw you up there on the hill," he said accusingly. "Who is this guy, anyway?"

Malcolm extended his hand. "Malcolm Grant. Welcome to Dundreggan Castle."

Wayne lifted his paw and let Malcolm shake it. "I thought you were some old geezer."

"No," Malcolm told him, and took a wary step backward.

"Wayne," said Amanda. "To repeat, what the hell are you doing here? Did your mother send you to check up on me?"

"Oh." Wayne looked down at his feet, his belligerence deflating. "No. She doesn't know I'm here. I kind of ran away from home."

Malcolm turned and started checking over the herbaceous border. Cerberus ran playfully at the cats. They responded with humorless glints of claw and tooth. Amanda said, "Excuse me?"

"What you said about me being a mama's boy and all that."

"Yeah, well, I was way out of line. . . ."

"No you weren't," said Wayne. "You were right on target. I'm sorry I drove away without you. That was a cheap shot. I'm glad you came without me."

Not half as glad as I am, Amanda told herself.

"I had the limo guy drive me around until after dark. Then I went home, meaning to tell Mother off, but she wasn't there. So I went out to the Benedetto's house and spent the night with them. She didn't call there looking for me or anything."

"She thought you were here," Amanda said.

"There were police cars all over the Hall. Vernon said the scabbard was missing, but I called Carrie the next morning and she said you had it with you, to make pictures with the sword. That was so cool, the way you took it without asking. I figured if you did it, I could too."

Malcolm turned back around. Amanda felt panic welling up in her throat. "Do what, Wayne?"

His smile was smug. "I went over to Melrose Thursday morning and just filled up my suitcase. The tea service. The inkwell. I have a right to be there, I work there, after all. And all that stuff is mine. Well, more or less."

"It belongs to CW," Amanda said faintly. "Your mother gave it to them, remember?"

Wayne waved his hand dismissively. "She'll settle up with them. That's what she gets for keeping me on a stupid allowance and not letting me have my fair share. I mean, I had to have money if I was going to break off with her and make my own way. And she could trace my credit card."

"You still had your plane ticket."

"Yeah. I took the stuff to London. Got there Friday morning and went to the National Gallery and 'Phantom of the Opera' that afternoon—that was sweet!—and Saturday I went into Sotheby's and tried to sell the Chinese vase, because it was the thing most likely to break." His smug smile wobbled into the queasy expression of a vegetarian confronting a rare steak. "Only one problem."

Malcolm stopped pretending to ignore the conversation. "Sotheby's had an inventory o' the items. Listed as stolen goods."

"Yeah. So I played dumb and as soon as the guy's back was turned I ran. He didn't chase me very far."

Amanda visualized Wayne running down a London sidewalk chased by a frock-coated functionary. The image would be funny if it wasn't so pathetic.

"I rushed back to the hotel and checked out before they could send out an APB," Wayne concluded. "I still had my plane ticket on to Inverness, and I knew you were here. So I spent the night on a bench at the airport and came up here this morning. I used the rest of my cash to pay the taxi driver. Everything you hear about the Scotch being stingy is right, he wanted a fortune to drive me here."

Malcolm favored Wayne with a tight smile. "That's 'Scots,' Sunshine.

We'd be pleased if you'd accept a meal, a bed, and a bath here wi' us. The door's no locked, you could've gone inside and helped yoursel' to everything we own."

"Oh," Wayne said.

"Come on," said Amanda, feeling like she was sitting a particularly ungainly baby. "You'll feel better once you get cleaned up."

"And we're needin' to . . ." Malcolm began, but was distracted by the car that drove in through the gateway. Denny Gibson's police car, with Gibson behind the wheel and Norah installed comfortably on the passenger side.

Wayne emitted a small yelp.

"P.C. Gibson's a friend of the family," Amanda told him. "He'll give you a fair hearing."

Malcolm stepped forward and opened Norah's door. "Mum, Denny. The plot's thickenin'."

Gibson got out of the car and put on his cap. "Is it, then?"

"Then we'd best have a spot of lunch," said Norah. "Mr. Chancellor, I presume? I'm Norah Grant. Shall we go inside?"

Wayne mumbled something polite and let himself be herded into Dundreggan Castle, Malcolm and Amanda trading incredulous looks behind his back.

CHAPTER TWENTY FOUR

Norah announced they'd eat lunch in the dining room, although Amanda wasn't sure whether the occasion was Wayne or Sunday. As she set the table she sent more than one wary glance up to the arch of the barrel-vaulted ceiling. The stones seemed to be securely in place, which was more than she could say for her feelings. One part of her danced arabesques of joy, one part slammed the dishes around in angry frustration, one part listened for the sound of footsteps.

Wayne lurked in the downstairs lavatory until Norah called him to the table. He found himself seated next to Gibson, and kept shooting glances at the policeman like those Amanda was making at the ceiling. From the head of the table Norah doled out roast beef, potatoes, carrots, Brussels sprouts, and small popovers she called puddings. Appetite overcoming a guilty conscience, Wayne slathered everything with gravy and started forking it into his mouth.

Amanda dismembered a sprout. Of all the idiotic half-baked schemes he could have come up with! She hadn't taken the scabbard at all, let along taken it without permission. Cynthia was sure as hell on the warpath now—she'd probably think Amanda had led him on or set him a bad example or something. Malcolm's foot nudged hers companionably beneath the table and she decided that the moment had its compensations.

"Whilst I was driving to church with the Finlays this morning," said Norah, and, parenthetically to Wayne, "The Finlays do for us here at

Dundreggan, but they've gone on to their daughter's in Kyle of Lochalsh the day . . ."

Wayne acknowledged her words with a vague nod.

". . . Irene was telling me about her aunt, who lived in a house in Culloden, close to the battlefield. It was a new house, mind you, but her aunt would sometimes see soldiers marching through the walls on their way to battle. And more than once she heard the wailing of the clanswomen searching for their husbands and sons amongst the bodies."

"So you explained last night's stramach?" Malcolm asked, and amended, "commotion," for the benefit of the outlanders.

"Yes. They had some idea of what was going on, of course."

Gibson calmly mashed potatoes and carrots onto his fork. Norah had probably told him all about it on the way back from church. A ghost. No big deal. Amanda shook her head. Their acceptance was like lugging a heavy suitcase up six flights of stairs and then finding an elevator.

"You see," Norah said to Wayne, "ghosts happen in the best of families."

His expression hung between dazed and dubious.

That was Amanda's cue. "Wayne, you've got the wrong idea. I didn't take the scabbard without asking permission. I didn't take it, period. It wasn't until I got here I realized I had it with me. The ghost of James Grant took it and put it in the box with his bones. His consciousness is in it."

Wayne put a forkful of meat and pudding into his mouth without taking his eyes from Amanda's face.

He thinks we're messing with his mind. "I never believed in ghosts until I met this one. He exists. Really. Last night he smashed the display case and took both the scabbard and sword that goes with it."

"I bet it was my mother and her stupid seance, wasn't it?" he said, and swallowed. "She stirred something up. Something you're calling a ghost."

"This is one thing your mother has no control over," Amanda told him.

Wayne shook his head, rejecting either the ghost or any doubt in Cynthia's omnipotence.

Gibson turned to Wayne. "I understand you have several items from Melrose with you."

"I guess that looks pretty bad, like they were stolen or something."

"I'm afraid that in the legal definition they have been stolen."

Wayne's chin wobbled. "Are you going to call my mother?"

"I'll take a statement," Gibson told him. "And I'll contact the police in Williamsburg. How you deal with your mother is your own affair."

Norah stood up and started stacking the empty plates. "After you and Denny finish the statement, Wayne, you'll phone her."

"Yes, ma'am." Wayne handed over his plate, no doubt thinking, *moms always stick together.*

Amanda and Malcolm helped Norah carry the plates to the kitchen. They went back to the dining room with chocolate mousse cake and a pot of coffee. The odor of the coffee was almost as bracing as actually drinking the caffeine, Amanda thought. And the way the flavors of coffee and chocolate combined in the mouth was sure one of Mother Nature's best botanical feats.

Norah asked Wayne about Cynthia and listened to his confused account of life with mother. "She must have a great deal of trouble seeing you as an adult," Norah said at last.

"No kidding," said Wayne.

"It might help if you were to start acting as an adult."

"Like not going off half-cocked and taking stuff from Melrose?"

"That would make a good start," Norah told him.

Gibson folded his napkin onto the tablecloth and took a notebook from his pocket. "Let's be getting on with the statement, I'm booked to guide a fishing party this afternoon."

"But you're a policeman," said Wayne.

"Yes, but there's not much of a living in it."

Wayne scraped the last smear of icing from his plate. "Anything you say," he said, sounding like Alice at the Mad Hatter's tea party.

In the kitchen Amanda and Malcolm washed the dishes, sneaked bits of meat to the animals, and listened to the voices in the dining room. Gibson got Wayne's story out of him as calmly as a dentist extracting a tooth. Every now and then Norah interjected a comment or question. Finally all three went into the entrance hall to get the artifacts out of Wayne's suitcases.

"They're handling him beautifully," Amanda said. "The poor guy has to be stressed out."

Malcolm cut a thin slice from the remaining cake. "I dinna have to be jealous o' him, do I?"

"Good lord, no. It's been a comedy of errors right from the beginning."

"Guid." He set a morsel of cake in Amanda's mouth and followed her smiling lick of her lips with a kiss.

She could get used to this, chocolate and kisses and Scotland. . . . A crash made them spin around. In a scramble of paws Cerberus dived for one doorway, the cats for the other. A wine bottle lay broken at the foot of the rack, its shards sparkling islands in an expanding pool of red.

Norah ran in the door. "That wasn't my Staffordshire platter, was it?"

"No," Malcolm said tightly. "That was James playin' up again."

Amanda scowled. It was like James was deliberately trying to kill the last traces of her feelings for him—and pity was about all she had left—even though his motives, if he had coherent motives, were just the opposite.

Norah eyed the blood-red pool for a long moment. Then she sighed and started picking up the larger pieces of glass. "Amanda, Denny would like for you to identify the items from Melrose."

"Yes, ma'am." Feeling obscurely guilty over both the wine bottle and the stolen items, Amanda went into the entrance hall.

Wayne's two suitcases lay open against the wall, exposing a collection of dirty underwear. Amanda averted her eyes to the objects lined up on the kist and a couple of chairs. The tea service, the inkwell, the candlesticks. Even the bogus earrings were there, still in their Lucite box. Amanda thought of Wayne sneaking through the house one jump ahead of a tour group, filling his suitcase and priding himself on his initiative, and cringed.

"Yes," she said. "The last time I saw all these things they were at Melrose. I'd check them over every night."

Gibson handed her his notebook. "Would you be signing that, please?"

She signed.

Wayne sat on the bottom step of the stairwell, initiative drained to lethargy. "I'll take them all back. I'll face the music."

"Whatever music you'll be facing," Gibson told him, "depends on whether charges are filed against you. Bringing the items back will help to mitigate, I imagine, although your being an employee of the Foundation might make it a wee bit dicey. If I were you I'd obtain legal advice."

"My mum has a lawyer," Wayne said. "But he'll be working for her."

"When I get back to my office I'll ring Williamsburg and tell them matters are in hand. Norah?" Gibson tucked his notebook into his pocket and walked back toward the kitchen. "I'll be leaving now."

Norah emerged drying her hands. "Thank you for taking care of matters. I didn't intend for you to work for your lunch."

"No problem. You'll walk me to the car, then?" Retrieving his cap from the coat rack, he and Norah strolled out the front door. A gust of damp, chilly wind whistled down the hallway.

Amanda gave Wayne a comradely pat on the shoulder. "You need to call your mother and let her know you're all right."

"And the things are all right."

"Yes, them too. I'll find the phone for you."

The phone was on its stand in the kitchen, where Malcolm was just squeezing pink water from the mop. There was nothing left of James's show of spite but a wet mark on the floor. "I'm sorry," Amanda said.

"No apologizin'. Let him answer for himsel'"

"He stopped answering for himself two hundred years ago."

"That's just the problem."

She could only worry about one thing at a time. Amanda took the phone to Wayne and dialed the international area code for him. "It's Sunday morning there," she told him, and retreated down the hall to the door.

It was growing dark outside. The clouds had congealed into a pewter lid. A few raindrops plunked down at her feet. They already had a ghost, why not the sinister Gothic atmosphere to go with him?

The rain thickened, obscuring the already soft shapes of the hills. Norah and Denny were a double outline behind the fogged windows of the police car, closing to a single one as Amanda watched. Smiling, she turned around and went back into the entrance hall.

"Yes, Mother," Wayne was saying. "I'm just fine. Yes, I know you were worried. I'm sorry. I was upset, I didn't think. No, I never think, do I. Yes, everything's okay, even the vase." He stopped, staring down at his feet.

Amanda heard a thin buzz emanating from the phone, Cynthia's electronically amplified voice.

"Yes, Amanda's here. No, she wasn't upset, she didn't know what I was up to. . . . Oh. The engagement."

Amanda shot Wayne a look like a cattle prod.

He sat bolt upright. "Mother, there never was any engagement. Yes, I like her an awful lot, but she never led me on, not once. I guess I thought if I went along with all that engagement stuff she'd soften up. But she didn't. She hasn't. I don't blame her for going off without me." He paused, then started in again, taking it from the top, pausing every now and then to let the insect-like buzz rise to a crescendo and fall again.

Amanda gave Wayne a smile and an A-OK sign. Malcolm emerged from the kitchen, raised a brow at her, and turned to inspect the booty laid out on the kist and the chairs.

"Yes. She's standing right here." Wayne thrust the phone so abruptly at Amanda she almost fumbled it.

"Oh, ah, hello, Mrs. Chancellor."

Cynthia's voice poured into Amanda's ear like honey over biscuits. "Amanda dear, I can't apologize to you enough. How embarrassed you must have been. You have the most exquisite manners, of course you hesitated to explain things to me, but you really should have told me. You always have my ear."

"Erk." Cynthia's words weren't quite registering, they were so different from the ones Amanda had been expecting.

"I hope the police officer there didn't give you too hard a time over the missing artifacts. I knew you hadn't taken them, just the scabbard. To make photos with the sword—wasn't that my clever girl! A shame everyone's wires got crossed the day you left, but then, I wasn't there."

"No problem," Amanda said brightly.

"Now I want you to do me a very big favor. Can you look out for Wayne? He's such a—well, just between us, dear—he doesn't always act his age. I'm sure you'll take good care of him."

"No problem," Amanda said again, her voice rising even higher. She sat down on an empty chair. Trust Cynthia to pull the rug out from beneath her yet again, simply by cutting her about ten miles of slack.

"How is your work going?" Cynthia went on. "Are you finding lots of good documentation for our film and our book?"

"Lots."

"Good. Good. James Grant must have cut such a dashing figure, I can hardly wait to hear more about him."

She couldn't wait to hear what she wanted to hear. Selective deafness seemed to be going around. "Thanks. Here's Wayne." Amanda handed the phone back across the hall and rolled her eyes at Malcolm. He propped himself on the back of her chair.

"Hello, Mother. It's me. Yes, yes, I'll pack everything up and bring it back. Yes, the policeman here's going to call the police there. All a misunderstanding, that's right. Thank you, Mother. I'm really sorry. I'll come back with Amanda on Thursday. Yes, I know an old castle's very romantic and everything." Wayne glanced at Malcolm and his face suffused the color of the spilled wine. "No, she's not going to change her mind."

Amanda realized she and Malcolm were posed like the husband and wife in an old tintype. She bounced to her feet. He straightened.

"Yes, Mother. Yes, the Grants are very nice. Yes, I'm sure they'd appreciate your sending them a thank-you gift. I'm not sure they'd enjoy a book about the Yorktown campaign, the British lost . . . No, I won't ever pull something like this again. Good-bye." Wayne turned off the phone and went so limp Amanda thought he was going to slide off the step and puddle on the floor. When he rubbed his face it stretched like a rubber mask. "It's all right. She's going to clear everything up with the police. No charges or anything."

"Good," Amanda told him.

"You said something about a bath, Mr. Grant. Malcolm."

"By all means. Collect your luggage and I'll show you to a room."

Norah came back inside, cheeks pink, just as they were starting up the stairs. "Did you sort it with Mrs. Chancellor, then?"

"Oh, yeah," Amanda told her. "Everything's okay."

"Good." Norah nodded at the row of artifacts. "I'll find packing material for this lot."

"Thanks." She owed Norah. Did she ever owe Norah.

Wayne and Malcolm had gotten ahead of her. Amanda caught up with them in front of the row of portraits on the landing. "There's the original o' your mum's miniature," Malcolm was saying.

"So that's the rest of James," Wayne returned. "He looks better with his skin on. What was all that about his ghost?"

"His ghost was at Melrose," explained Amanda. "Now it's here."

"Okay," Wayne said indulgently, with a glance at Malcolm that seemed to say, *you work fast, don't you?*

And she'd thought Wayne would be the only person who'd believe her, Amanda told herself. Her batting average was going from bad to worse.

"That's James's cousin Archibald," Malcolm went on, "who inherited the estate when he died. And Archibald's wife Isabel."

Wayne considered the other two portraits. "Archibald looks like Page, doesn't he? A nice solid citizen."

He trudged on up the staircase, Malcolm herding him from behind. Of course, Amanda told herself, a home run with Malcolm would skew the stats to her side, no doubt about it.

She frowned up at Archibald's portrait. No, he didn't look like Page. He looked like Wayne, with the broad forehead, the heavy jaw, and the general air of constipation—which in Archibald came across as complacency but in Wayne as anxiety. She'd been trying so hard the last few days not to think about Wayne she hadn't noticed that he looked just about as much like Archibald as Malcolm looked like James. *Weird.* But then, there were only so many faces and body types to go around.

The men disappeared around the curve of the steps. Amanda went into the library. She turned on all the lights and the electric fire, but still shadows crammed the corners. Cerberus came ambling forward, whining and wagging his tail hopefully. "I know, I know," she told him, "you were minding your own business and this crazy American dumps a ghost on you."

The wagging tail changed rhythm. Good. Like Malcolm, he was okay with the issues. Not that the issues were in the least okay. She sat down with her references, gripping her pencil like a sword.

CHAPTER TWENTY FIVE

The library windows might have been those of a submarine, streaked with damp, gray and sullen. The sound of the rain ebbed and flooded like the tide. When Malcolm showed up he peered resignedly outside, gave Amanda a quick kiss, and sat down at his computer. Cerberus stretched out before the electric fire, his chin resting between his paws.

Amanda tried to focus on her work, choosing which pages of Archibald's memoirs to actually copy and which to summarize, but she felt twitchy. The walls really did have eyes. Somewhere in the house doors opened and shut. The telephone rang. Maybe Wayne had drowned in the bathtub—he didn't reappear.

For a time the room was quiet, the only sound the occasional chirp of Malcolm's computer. Then the notes of the tin whistle floated through the air, snatches of melody mixed with contemplative trills. Yes, Amanda thought, Malcolm had a versatile tongue. She gave up any hope of concentrating and put the papers back in the cabinet. "How about a walk?"

"It's teemin' doon ootside," he returned. "But we can have a dander roond the house."

Cerberus leaped to his feet, ready to go. Malcolm and Amanda secured the electrical gear and headed out, up the flights of steps, past the blocked-off doors, and down the dead-end hallways that testified to each generation's bright ideas in home improvement. Along the way they rooted through drawers and cupboards, turning up everything from rusted agricultural equipment to crumbling butterfly collections. They didn't really expect to find the sword and the scabbard. Even in the cellar, a damp and dark but thoroughly clean stone box, there was no trace of James. Still, as afternoon darkened into night, Amanda was sure she was sensing his presence. *My sweet, my own.*

She and Malcolm strolled into the great hall. Amanda inspected the tapestry, wondering if she could duplicate such an intricate pattern in 14-count needlepoint. She looked up at the pikes, halberds, and muskets fanned out on the walls and remembered what Carrie had said about her own tours of Great Britain: *All those old houses have enough weaponry stuck on the walls to supply a good-sized army.*

But the sword and its scabbard weren't hidden in plain sight. "I keep expecting James to jump out and say 'gotcha.' Or, 'unhand that damsel, you knave.' Whatever."

"So do I," Malcolm returned. "But you're no callin' him any more, are you?"

"No way." She heard a mocking echo of her own voice, *with me you're strong.* "Maybe when I leave he'll leave ¾ no, he has the sword back, doesn't he? He may not need me any more. And I sure don't want to go away and leave you with a freaked-out ghost." *I don't want to leave you.* But she didn't have to say that.

"What matters noo," Malcolm said, "is findin' a way to turf him oot."

"To get rid of him? Or to help him rest?"

"However you're wantin' to say it."

Maybe she still felt some furtive sympathy for James, the little kid camouflaging his weaknesses with bravado. . . . Like she hadn't had a damn good chance to notice he was a grown man? "He needs to go away. Absolutely. Got any ideas?"

"Oh aye, that I do," Malcolm said with a nod. "I agree James's energy's in his scabbard noo, but I'm wonderin', even so—if it was you made him strong, then it could be his fate's in your hands."

"In my . . . You think that just by telling him to go I can send him away?"

"I dinna ken, lass, but it'd make a gey interestin' exercise in positive thinkin', eh?"

"Yeah, I guess so," Amanda said. But she wasn't putting much trust in her thinking skills. She'd made a habit recently of forcing illusionary square pegs into the round holes of reality. She'd been wrong about James, the Grants, even Wayne. And she still couldn't get a handle on Cynthia, the fairy godmother from hell.

That image made her smile. So did Cerberus, sitting on the floor between them and watching their conversation like he was watching a tennis match. "My emotions aren't jet-lagged or anything," she admitted.

"Mine too, and I've no even gone travelin'." Malcolm angled his forehead so that it touched Amanda's. "Which disna mean I'd no consider a spot o' travelin'—a bit o' research into historic property management."

The regimental flags ranked high overhead waved in a breeze. A cold breeze, that trailed icy fingers through the roots of Amanda's hair. The tapestry billowed from the wall and settled back again. Cerberus cringed.

"Stuff that for a game of soldiers," stated Malcolm. "Come along, let's see what Mum did wi' Wayne's ill-gotten gains."

Yeah, right, James. Like I'm really going to get off on a supernatural stalker. Her lips crimped, Amanda walked beside Malcolm and almost on top of the dog down to the dining room. Tidy cardboard and tissue paper packages were arranged along the sideboard. Norah was like Cynthia in one way, Amanda thought. She did things up right.

Amanda followed Malcolm into the kitchen, where they built sandwiches, fried chips, and brewed tea. Each with a tray, they went back up the stairs to the sitting room.

Norah was seated with Denis on her lap, Margaret tucked in beside her, and Wayne ensconced in an easy chair nearby. The television was tuned to a cricket match. "Lovely, very good of you," Norah said when she saw the food, and added, "Irene rang. They'll be spending the night with Marie."

"There's no need for them to be drivin' in the rain and dark," Malcolm agreed, and made room on the coffee table for the trays.

Cerberus trotted over to Wayne and fixed him with an adoring expression. Wayne's expression was a lot less depressed than Amanda would have thought, considering. Norah probably had been doing some counseling. If she could raise a fully integrated male like Malcolm, she could rein in some of Wayne's galloping insecurities.

The four humans and three animals were barely finished with their supper before the footsteps began, steady steps that marched across the floor of the great hall below like those of a sentry guarding his post.

Cerberus hurled himself onto Malcolm's feet. The cats did their vanishing act. Norah, Malcolm, and Amanda shared a glance that was part cautious, part exasperated. Wayne muttered, "Yeah, we used to hear funny noises at Melrose when I was a kid, tree branches and stuff like that."

His equivalent of Morag. Once again Amanda tried some consciousness-raising. "It's the ghost of James Grant, Wayne, like we told you earlier. He's not a happy camper."

"After camping out at Melrose for two hundred years, I'd guess not." Wayne chuckled at his joke. The others managed to contain their amusement. "Malcolm, Lady Norah, I really appreciate the hospitality, but I'm bushed. A plastic couch at the airport isn't nearly as nice a bed as the one you've given me upstairs. Do you mind if I go ahead and climb into it?"

Norah made a gracious gesture toward the doorway. "Good night," everyone chorused.

Wayne's plodding steps receded down the hall and disappeared. The crisp steps below stopped. A door opened and shut. Amanda held her breath, waiting for Wayne to come racing back babbling about scarlet coats and swords, but no, he'd passed unscathed. Something about fools rushing in, probably.

"Well then," said Norah, "I think we should leave the dishes 'til the morn. I'm taking a book to my room. Good night." She left with a smile.

If she'd seen Norah and Denny at the ceilidh, Amanda told herself, Norah had seen her and Malcolm. Not that now was the time or the place to get closer. Malcolm sat at the far end of the couch, tense as a twelve-year-old at his first boy-girl party. The electronic laughter of a televised game show couldn't penetrate the hush of the house. After a while Amanda realized she was holding her breath. "This is ridiculous."

"Oh aye," Malcolm agreed.

Footsteps rang on the staircase, not growing louder and louder but starting suddenly out of nothing. A tearing, ripping sound followed by a crash reverberated through the corridor.

Sharing a dubious look, Amanda and Malcolm crept down the steps to the landing outside the great hall. Where they found Archibald's portrait lying across the angle of floor and wall, its gilt frame twisted. A vicious slash had turned his prim expression into a scream and eviscerated his ample chest. The edges of the canvas waved faintly in a cold draft that seemed to blow less from the ground floor than from the grave.

"Bugger it," said Malcolm.

Amanda scowled up at James's portrait, at his self-satisfied smile, at his hand resting on the hilt of his sword. "Are you happy now?" she asked.

"I'd no make book on it." Malcolm propped up the painting, trying to straighten its twisted frame. "Another job for the restorer in Edinburgh, right enough. The man's a bull in a china shop."

He meant James, not the restorer. "Maybe he's finished his search and destroy mission for the day."

"One way or the other, we'll be layin' doon some plans the morn." Defiantly Malcolm put his arm around Amanda's shoulders and walked her to her room. "Would you like me to sleep on the floor, to keep you company?"

"He'd love that."

"Like wavin' a red flag afore his nose? All right, then, but give a shout if he comes courtin'. He needs a lesson in manners." They indulged in one kiss, a wary look up and down the corridor, and then another. "Good night."

"Watch your back," Amanda told him, and went into her room. There was another evening gone of the precious few remaining, damn it all anyway.

Her cosmetics lay scattered across the dressing table, eye shadow crumbled over the starched linen mat, lipstick a gory gash across the mirror. In the bathroom the flowers were not only beheaded but crushed into the tile floor. *Oh shit.*

A cold gust of wind chilled her to the bone. She spun around.

"Amanda, Sweeting," James said. "Were your words of love but lies?"

She'd never seen him like this, dream distorted into nightmare. His eyes were hard and cold as marble. His mouth was set in so determined a line she suspected he was trying to keep it from quivering, either with rage or hurt or some explosive combination of the two.

His hand rested on the hilt of the sword. The genuine sword, its brass hilt catching and shading the light as his hand, as his entire body, did not. Of course the real sword fit the undamaged memory of the scabbard, and yet. . . . She squinted. Yes, the twisted and time-abraded scabbard hung partly over and partly under its smooth twin, making a weird double image.

"My sweet, would you betray me?"

"No," Amanda returned. "You weren't exactly honest with me, were you?"

"Fie, madam! How dare you judge my account of such weighty matters as my very death!" He stepped toward her. The light bled from the not quite solid scarlet of his coat.

She stood her ground. If only his eyes weren't so hurt. He made her feel she'd done him wrong. He made her feel sorry for him.

"I had thought you different from the others of your sex. I had thought you not fickle but faithful. But no. You are but a strumpet, a trollop, spreading your legs for any man with the words to woo and the coin to pay."

"Oh, for the love of . . . Come off it, James. I never lied to you. Yes, I told you I loved you. I got carried away. I'm sorry. But you took my feelings for you and stomped on them. If that's not betrayal, what is?"

His pain seared into anger. His lip curled. "You speak of love, do you? So did Clytemnestra love Agamemnon. So did Medea love her sons by Jason. Love, in a woman's voice, is nothing but an infernal lie."

"It is? Is that why I did what you asked me to? I brought you home. I gave you back your sword. I warned you back in Virginia you couldn't get revenge against Archibald, but I promised to tell your story. And I did, damn it, I did."

"Archibald and his wicked lies!"

"Archibald was telling the truth," Amanda said, "and you know it."

One stride and James was in her face. His breath reeked. He reeked, like he hadn't had a bath in two hundred years. She edged away and found her back pressed against the doorframe. "You would betray me, Madame? No, I think not." He caressed her cheek.

His hand felt like the clod of mud she'd thrown on his coffin. She shuddered, rejecting him, rejecting any sympathy she could still find for him. "It's over, James. It's finished. It's time for you to go."

His eyes glinted. His caressing hand tightened into a fist pressing into the softness of her cheek.

She jerked away. "Stop it! Leave me alone!"

"Oh my sweet," he whispered. "Such hideous words to fall from your delicious lips, like ripe fruit become ashes. It is the greatest shame that if you will not have me, if I cannot have you, then no one will."

With a sleek rasp of metal he drew his sword. The blade passed so close beneath her chin she felt its cold steel kiss. "Hey!"

She twisted, ducking beneath his arm and stumbling to the side. Scarlet and tartan swirled. James seized her hair, jerking her forward so she landed hard on her knees. He knotted his fingers in her hair like he'd done while they were having sex. Making love. At least, she'd been making love. But James probably didn't see the contrast between then and now.

"James, stop it!" She wrenched away, by the sharp pain leaving several strands of hair in his hand. "Ow!"

Amanda leaped to her feet, but a weight, not as much as a man's body, perhaps, but a substantial force, hit her from behind. Falling against the window seat, she scrambled onto it and turned at bay. She kicked at him, but her feet struck uselessly against no more resistance than draped fabric.

James stood over her, sword upraised. The hand wielding the sword might be incorporeal, but the blade itself was thirty-two inches of fine Stirling steel. Amanda shrank back. This was beyond nightmare. This was real. She was gasping like a fish, unable to breathe, unable to cry out.

He smiled. Her terror was probably turning him on, damn him. A flick of his wrist and the sword tip snicked the catch on the window. A thrust, the ping of metal against glass, and the window flew open. The cold wet air that gushed inside raised goose bumps on her skin.

The sword gleamed, drawing arcs in the shadows, more vivid than James's hand or face or body. Tenderly its cold, hard length slipped past Amanda's cheek, first one side, then the other. She edged backward. Her hands scrabbled at the window frame. Behind her yawned empty air. Her shoulders cramped as she tried desperately to keep her balance.

In an outburst of fear and denial mixed, Amanda screamed. "Malcolm!" The name seemed to swell and echo until the wind itself repeated the cry, whisking it away into nothingness.

James's lips parted. His voice was gentle as velvet. "Ah, my sweet, the poet Marvell said that no one embraces in the privacy of the grave. Shall we determine the truth of his words?"

She tried to inhale enough air to scream again. But his eyes fixed hers, drowning her in lust and rage and fear, and she choked. The lace at his wrist shivered. The tip of the sword touched the placket of her blouse between her breasts. With the briefest hesitation the blade cut the cloth. When it pricked her skin it stung like cold fire. The heavens gaped at her back, and for a moment she wondered if they'd bury her, too, in the old churchyard.

From miles away came Wayne's voice. "Holy shit. That's James Grant."

Malcolm's voice was louder, like a clang of sword against sword. "You filthy sod. Where's your honor then, murderin' a defenseless woman?"

The bright streak of the blade vanished. Amanda blinked. *Oh.* She forced one burning inhalation into her lungs, then another.

In front of her she saw James's back, the red coat tails and the pleats of his kilt. Beyond him stood Malcolm, just inside the door of the room. No wonder he hadn't heard their voices. His hair was wet and he was wearing only a pair of jeans. He'd been in the shower, probably seeing the murder scene from *Psycho* with himself as the victim.

But no, Amanda managed to think. James was after her. He had to take her out first. He had something to prove to her.

Two pale ovals in the doorway, ripped with the black holes of eyes and mouths, were Wayne and Norah. Somewhere Cerberus was barking hysterically. He'd been barking for several minutes now.

Like a hunting cat's tail the sword flicked back and forth. *He knows how to use it,* Amanda thought, easing herself off the window seat and along the wall. She suspected Malcolm knew that. "Give over, James," he said. "You're finished here."

"So then, it's you, the insolent dog," James said. Their voices were uncannily similar. "How dare you walk about my father's house as though you were its master? How dare you lay your hands upon my woman? By my troth, I'll sup upon your giblets before this night is done."

"He's not Archibald," Amanda croaked from the other side of the dressing table.

James snickered. "Of course he's not Archibald, do you take me for a fool, woman?"

She took him for a lot of things, but a fool was not one of them.

"It's no your father's house," said Malcolm. "No any more. And she's no your woman. She can choose who she wants, and she's no wantin' you."

Amanda groped frantically for her lines. "Go away, James. I don't want you any more. You're here because of me, but now I want you gone."

He half-turned toward her, brows drawn down. "Sweeting, your words lay such a heavy burden upon my heart that in just a moment I shall be obliged to stop them, but first, if I may beg your indulgence, I have this dog to spit."

In one smooth motion James spun and lunged at Malcolm. The sword flashed. A woman cried out. It could've been Norah. It could've been Amanda herself. She didn't know.

Malcolm grabbed the chair from beside the door and jerked it upward. With a solid thunk of metal against wood it knocked the sword away. He yanked the chair to the side. The sword, imbedded in the chair's leg, almost came out of James's hand.

Almost. But James's battle-honed instincts went with the sword's momentum, so his hand never left the hilt. A wrench, and he retrieved it. He raised it again. "A fine attempt, dog, but it will not save your life."

"Go to hell," Malcolm told him, "where you belong." He dodged, swinging the chair in a circle in front of him. With a clang it met the scabbard at James's side and then continued on through James's insubstantial body. Streaks of scarlet spun away through the shadows.

With an unintelligible cry James seized the scabbard. His form wavered and thinned around the twisted length of metal and its straighter but immaterial phantom.

His body winked out. The sword and the scabbard hung in mid-air for a long moment and then faded, swallowed by darkness, and were gone. A rush of wind toward the door, invisible movement, sent Malcolm diving to one side and Wayne and Norah retreating down the hall. Cerberus stopped barking and started whining. Somewhere in the distance a cat yowled.

Amanda slid bonelessly down the wall and sat hard on the floor. Geological ages passed as she breathed, in and out, in and out. One by one her thoughts came creeping back into her mind. Melrose. Dundreggan.

Malcolm. He was kneeling beside her. "Are you all right, lassie? You're bleedin'." He unbuttoned her blouse, reached into the bathroom, and pressed a towel against her chest.

Malcolm was touching her breasts. It wasn't happening at all the way it should be, but she couldn't remember just what she'd had in mind.

"Holy shit," said Wayne's voice. "That was James Grant."

Something large and furry appeared in Amanda's peripheral vision. It was either Cerberus or Norah in a plush robe. "Amanda, are you all right?"

It was talking. It must be Norah.

"He tried to kill me," Amanda croaked.

"That he did."

"How could he do that?"

"There's much too fine a line between love and hate," said Norah. "Malcolm, you hair needs drying, you'll catch your death of cold."

"I almost caught my death o' cold steel, Mum, and you're worryin' yoursel' aboot my hair?"

"I'm a mother," she returned, voice quavering. "Mothers default to the mundane in moments of terror."

"Terror," Malcolm repeated with a slightly crazed laugh. "Oh aye."

Amanda focussed on his face. His brows were clenched, his lips were parted, damp strands of his hair hung across his pale forehead. His chest was rising and falling as though he'd run a marathon. "You saved my life," she told him. "My hero and—and everything."

"James Grant," said Wayne. "It was really him. Geez."

A fierce wave of nausea swept over her. She swept Malcolm aside, scrambled to her feet, and staggered into the bathroom.

CHAPTER TWENTY SIX

"So much for positive thinking," Amanda said. "James has taken on a life of his own. He doesn't need me any more." She eased herself down onto the sitting room couch next to Malcolm and accepted a sloppy glass of whiskey from Wayne's shaking hand.

Norah took her own glass and drank deeply. "The only reason he still wants you, I expect, is on principal. His principal."

She'd shooed Wayne downstairs to get a bottle of whiskey and Malcolm to his room while she helped Amanda rinse out her mouth, bandage her cut, and wrap herself up in the warmest garments she owned, her flannel nightgown and robe. Now Amanda snuggled shamelessly into Malcolm's sweater-covered side, right there in front of Wayne, Norah, and God. The tang of the whiskey blessed her cold limbs and scoured the nasty taste from her mouth.

So she'd thrown up in front of him. This business of falling hard for a guy, falling into what might be a really positive relationship, allowed for awkward moments like that. Unlike infatuation, which winked out the moment the going got tough.

Better to throw up than make mulch for the roses below her window. She shivered.

Malcolm's arm tightened around her waist. "I'm sorry. I told you to confront him, I was wrong."

"It was worth a try," Amanda told him firmly. "It's okay."

He'd looked great wearing only his jeans, she thought. Not that she'd exactly noticed at the time. Now he was pale, close to shivering himself. His hair was a shining auburn mane, his blue-gray eyes seething with thought and emotion intertwined. No way his eyes looked like James's, with their self-absorbed rage.

Beside the couch Cerberus sighed dolefully. The cats huddled in front of the electric fire, every now and then shooting a resentful glance toward the humans. Wayne frowned like he was working his way through a crossword puzzle. "What did he say? 'I'll sup upon your giblets?'"

"He has a right flair for the language," said Norah.

"Most educated people did, two hundred years ago," Amanda pointed out.

"What did he call you?" Wayne went on. "Sweeting?"

"Yeah. Better than 'hey you broad', I guess."

Norah's brows listed to the side. If she realized the full significance of the endearment, she was too polite to blurt it out.

Wayne was either too naive or too slow. "I've never seen anyone waving a sword around like that. Not in real life. You know what I think? I think it's a kind of—whatchamacallit—a folic symbol."

"Phallic symbol," Amanda corrected, adding silently, *No kidding.*

Malcolm snorted, "I've no seen the theory o' over-compensatin' for inadequacy demonstrated quite so effectively."

Norah grinned. Wayne did too, after working it through.

Good shot. While Amanda didn't think James had plotted ever since that first moment on the staircase to use her to re-animate himself—the seduction was simply his own default mechanism—still she felt betrayed. *Would you betray me, Madame?* You bet, she thought, if that's what it takes to make you go away.

She wasn't going to waste sympathy on him any more. He'd taken her—love, infatuation, lust, whatever—and turned it to bitterness. He'd raped her. Not with his body, which she'd welcomed, but with his sword and his spite. As Norah said, there was much too fine a line between love and hate. And Amanda had just crossed it.

Malcolm's unshaven cheek prickled against her temple. "You'd best be tellin' Wayne the story."

Edited for general audiences. "I first saw James the same day Bill

Hewitt dug up his bones," Amanda began. "I knew who he was before Hewitt and Carrie identified him. . . ."

As the story wound down to the present Wayne's bewilderment gelled into stunned comprehension. "So he knows he's dead, he can't accept it, and he's bummed out."

"Sorry?" Norah asked,

"Angry," translated Amanda.

"And he's got a crush on you—like everybody else, I guess." To his credit, Wayne wasn't getting either hurt or huffy with the spectacle Malcolm and Amanda were making of themselves. "At least I never went around. . . . Good God! That's what happened! I thought I was nuts."

"What?"

"You remember the afternoon I fell down the stairs, Amanda? Just as I stuck my foot out for the top step, I felt a real hard push right between my shoulder blades. But no one was there. So I decided I'd tripped or stumbled or something and was imagining the push."

"Do I remember?" Amanda retorted. "I thought maybe you'd caught a glimpse of James and been so startled you fell. But when I asked you if you'd seen anything you seemed totally baffled."

"That was just it—I didn't *see* a thing."

"It didn't hit me until just a couple of days ago that James might have pushed you. Trying to keep me away from another man. I wish you'd told me."

Norah asked, "Would you have believed him?"

"Well, no, but not for the obvious reason. I believed in James's ghost one hundred per cent by that time. I just wouldn't have believed he could do something so malicious. I'm sorry, Wayne. I'm an idiot."

"That's okay, and no, you're not." He reached for the whiskey bottle and refilled his glass.

"You know," Amanda went on, "I did wonder at the time if James shut Lafayette in the kitchen cabinet."

"Who?" Malcolm asked.

"Melrose's cat. One night I found him shut in the kitchen cabinet. At first I thought he'd just wandered in there, you know how curious cats are, and then I thought maybe James had closed the door on him, since

Lafayette was always hissing at him. Even so, I figured he was just being nervous around cats. Some people are."

Margaret flicked her ears—*Lafayette had more perception than you did.*

She wasn't going to debate that one. "I can't believe this is happening. It's like when Page dragged Sally off into the night. All she'd wanted was to flirt with James—his flattery must have been pretty stimulating, he being the enemy and everything—but it got away from her. I wonder if she felt a twinge when she heard he was dead."

"Never realizin'," said Malcolm, "how she hersel' was the indirect cause."

"And his body lay moldering beneath her feet as she took tea in the summerhouse," Wayne intoned. "When I was a kid, I used to think the place was really creepy. Of course it was all overgrown and rickety by then."

"There's never been a woman yet who wasn't beguiled by a handsome face and a clever tongue at least once," Norah said, with a crinkle that made Amanda wonder just what she was remembering. "You behaved honorably, Amanda. So did Sally, for that matter. James did not."

"Thanks," Amanda said, not at all sarcastically. She tucked her hand into Malcolm's and squeezed. Cerberus shifted his weight on her feet. Between the dog, the whiskey, and Malcolm, she was finally starting to warm up. But the night wasn't over.

"I wish I'd seen him when he was in a good mood," Wayne said with a sigh. "Wow. A real ghost."

"I don't know," said Norah, "whether to ring Lindley and ask for an exorcism, or to ring Denny and ask for a SWAT team."

"I'm no so sure either'd turn the trick," returned Malcolm. "But we're no goin' on like this, I'm tellin' you that."

Somewhere in the back of her mind, Amanda heard Carrie saying, *Climb onto the bank and walk.*

"Tomorrow," Norah said, "we'll be having a council of war."

For a long moment the room was so silent the tic-tic of the electric fire sounded like footsteps. Everyone looked a different direction. But the cats were licking themselves clean of occult influences, and, judging by his dead weight, Cerberus was asleep.

"It's gone midnight," Malcolm said at last. "I vote for spendin' the rest o' the night in here, all together."

"Yeah," said Wayne. "Better uncomfortable than dead. I bet he'd zap any of us he could catch."

"Zap? He's no muckin' aboot wi' a laser gun."

Wayne drained his whiskey, smacked his lips, and stood up. "Just a figure of speech. Zap. Exterminate. Obliterate."

"Oh aye," Malcolm said faintly.

"Come along, Wayne," said Norah. "Let's collect some blankets and pillows."

As soon as they left the room Malcolm asked quietly, "Are you sure you're all right?"

"Maybe not all right, but a lot better than I was," Amanda replied. "The worst part, beyond being scared, was feeling so helpless. Your line about 'defenseless woman',wasn't just a gimmick to distract him."

"You're no Xena, Warrior Princess, are you noo? The sod had you cornered."

She set her palms flat on Malcolm's chest, letting the beat of his heart flow throw her fingertips and into her own body. "Oddly enough, I like having you protect me. You're not taking something away from me, you're giving me something. Like my life. Thank you."

"Thank you for havin' a life I could save."

Things were just about to get sappy when Norah reappeared, followed by Wayne, who looked like a pile of bed linen with feet. "Here we are. Pillow, Amanda? And the duvet from your bed, it's nice and thick."

Reluctantly Amanda released Malcolm and let him make himself a bed on the floor between Wayne and Cerberus. Norah chose a reclining chair.

They left a small desk lamp on, and one bar of the electric fire. Amanda stretched out on the couch cocooned in her comforter. She stared into the feeble glow, at the rounded shapes of people and animals, at the two closed doors.

From Norah's shallow breathing Amanda figured she wasn't asleep either. Wayne snored lustily. Malcolm's breath was deep and even. Like his soldier ancestors, he must've learned how to sleep in the midst of battle. Amanda twisted and turned and dug up one positive thought: from now on she'd identify the flavor of whiskey not with James but with Malcolm.

At last she dozed, only to be haunted by re-enactments—swords, heights, darkness. By the time night thinned she was aching for action, notebooks at twenty paces, anything that would give James an attitude adjustment and send him to his long-overdue reward.

Cerberus went to the door and whined. The cats hiked over the supine male bodies and meowed their breakfast orders. Yawning and bedraggled, Wayne sat up and loudly complained he hadn't slept a wink.

Amanda staggered to her room, dressed, and joined the others in a quick inspection of the house. Except for Archibald's portrait, nothing outside Amanda's room was damaged. Norah shook her head over the ripped canvas, but all she said was, "Breakfast in the hotel, I should think. Shall we?"

Just to be on the safe side Wayne and Amanda packed the artifacts from Melrose in the back of the Land Rover. The morning was fresh, clear, and cool, the rain clouds only a dark smudge low on the horizon. The thin crescent of a waxing moon pierced the blue arc of the sky. As they drove past the chapel the sun topped the clouds and poured light over the landscape. Every green leaf and gray stone sparkled, washed clean, and the Moriston burbled like club soda in its rocky bed. The white-painted hotel was just opening for business.

If its owner was startled to see the bleary-looking crew appear at his reception desk he was nice enough not to say so. "Lachlan," said Norah, "these are our guests from America. Can you lay on breakfast for us?"

"Of course, Norah, only the best for you and yours." Lachlan disappeared into the kitchen.

Norah led the way to a table in a window alcove of the deserted dining room. "Well then. I'll ring the Finlays and tell them to stay away until we have it sorted. No sense in giving James a go at them, too. Wayne, Lachlan can find you a room here."

"No ma'am," said Wayne with a firm nod. "This is my fight, too. Melrose, you know."

Norah may not have followed his reasoning, but Amanda did. He'd found a chance to re-invent himself. To grow up, already. *Go for it.* "Me, too," she said. "If I'd just dumped off his bones and left, he might never have bothered you. I don't know. But now my leaving wouldn't help. Wayne's right, James will be after anyone he can catch."

Malcolm's lips thinned, but he didn't say anything.

Lachlan appeared with a teapot and cups. The first sip of hot, sweet tea was the best thing Amanda had ever tasted. Unless it was the bowl of oatmeal which followed. Or the eggs and bacon and tomato which followed that. The sun was shining and Malcolm was sitting next to her. It was good to be alive. Very good.

She was nibbling on her third piece of toast with marmalade when Malcolm opened the meeting. "All right then. James Grant."

"We could try shooting him with a silver bullet," Wayne proposed.

"He's been shot," Amanda told him. "Through the heart."

"Oh. Yeah."

"The sword and scabbard need findin'," said Malcolm.

"The only way we're going to find them," Amanda said, "is to get James to bring them back."

Norah nodded firmly. "Good job the scabbard's crooked—he fell on it, did he? If he could actually sheathe the sword in it he might be even stronger. Does he realize how much time has passed since the duel, Amanda?"

"I don't think so. He always just ignored my computer and the kitchen appliances and stuff at Melrose, I guess because he didn't want to admit he didn't know what they were. As for my clothes and the way I talk—well, he put his own interpretation on those. He never appeared while I was playing Sally. I don't know how he'd take that."

"I don't guess we can lure him into an airport and really confuse him," said Wayne.

"He seems to be tied to familiar surroundings like Melrose or Dundreggan," Amanda told him. "Although he can be confused." Not so much an idea as the tiny glimmering of an idea circled the back of her mind like a firefly. *Sally. Sally caused, however indirectly, his death.*

"What else?" Malcolm asked.

"He can only appear after dark, but he can move things around any time. Although I'm not so sure he realizes what he's doing when he moves things—he's more like a poltergeist then, unfocussed energy. Like when he pushed Wayne. I asked him about playing with the candles at Cynthia's seance and he didn't know what I was talking about."

"But he came when she called him?" Wayne asked.

"Something of him did, yeah. I think. . . ." Amanda frowned. "Maybe he's like the two-year-old I used to baby-sit. I don't mean just in the uncontrolled emotions. You could say all sorts of stuff in front of the kid, but he wouldn't understand unless you pitched it to his level. James is—aware, conscious—only when he's visible and interacting with someone who's alive."

"Since we're talking in Freudian terms anyway," said Norah, "we could speak of his ego and his id. What was that old science fiction film? *Forbidden Planet.* Monsters from the id. And from the ego as well."

"Carryin' the sword and scabbard aboot, and becomin' visible and conscious all at once, must be hard work for him." Malcolm's brows did a slow wave, registering deliberation.

Lachlan was hovering with a fresh pot of tea. Everyone complimented him on the food and waited while a teenage girl with a punk hairdo carried away the plates. A few other guests were in the room now, but no one close enough to overhear.

"James may have been halfway round the bend when he was alive," Malcolm went on, "but he's right off his head noo. We have to use that against him. Amanda, he told you he wanted three things."

"To go home, to get his sword back—he died with it in his hand—and to avenge himself on Archibald. Not necessarily for killing him, because at first he didn't realize he was dead. For making trouble for him and Isabel and then adding insult to injury by winning the duel."

"He's home," said Norah. "And he has his sword."

Amanda nodded. No, she wasn't going to think about the chill steel kiss of the blade.

"But he canna get revenge," Malcolm said. "Cuttin' Archibald's portrait is no enough for him. I thought at first James was thinkin' I'm Archibald, or kent I'm Archibald's descendant. But after last nicht I'm thinkin' he disna realize who I am at all, just the chap wi' the house and wi' Amanda."

"And a dab hand with a chair," added Norah, her voice flat.

"I never thought that course o' karate lessons would prove so helpful, especially the series wi' a bo, a staff." He shook his head. "Ah well, then, whoever James thinks I am, he's after doing me noo. I suppose I'd make a fine decoy to lure him oot o'—wherever he is."

"And what then?" Amanda asked.

"Destroy the scabbard. It's been his—crutch, I suppose?—all this time. You saw how protective he was o' it last night."

Amanda blinked. "But the scabbard's property of the Colonial Williamsburg Foundation. It's a historical artifact. It's—it's . . ." She knew what it was.

"You can always blame me," said Wayne. "I'll tell my mother I lost it or sat on it or something. Everybody expects me to be a klutz anyway."

"We don't," Norah told him, and he smiled. "If necessary," she went on, "Malcolm and I could argue that the scabbard is our property, no matter where it's been the last two centuries."

"We're no talkin' aboot the legal details," Malcolm stated. He leaned forward, placing his elbows on the table. A ray of sunlight made his unshaven whiskers shine reddish-gold. "We're talkin' aboot gettin' the scabbard. What if we kept James busy 'til he's fair puggled oot, wi'oot lettin' him disappear."

"Well," suggested Wayne, "you could get fresh with Amanda—not that she wouldn't want you to, but you know what I mean." His jowls drooped and then firmed up again. "Anyway, when he starts flailing away at you with the sword I could rush up and grab the scabbard."

Malcolm covered his eyes with his hand. "Wayne, you'll excuse me for no wantin' to put my life in your hands."

The firefly in the back of Amanda's mind glowed and faded and glowed again. *If it was you made him strong. . . .* She leaned forward as well, closer to Malcolm, drawing Wayne and Norah into a tight circle. "James's weakness is that he's afraid to look weak."

"So we have to be throwing him off his guard by making him appear weak?" Norah asked. "By confusing him?"

"By confusing him, yes, but we've got to confuse him by making him think he's strong." She grimaced, the firefly just getting away from her.

It was Wayne who picked up the dim bulb of her thought and

increased its wattage. "He can't accept he'll never get revenge. So what if we make him think he can?"

"Oh aye?" Norah asked cautiously.

Wayne went on, "Archibald looked like Page Armstrong. I play Page all the time. I'm pretty good at it, too, if I do say so myself."

"You're very good at it," Amanda stated. "But it isn't that Archibald looked like Page, but that you look like Archibald."

"Really? Cool! I'll make James appear by playing Archibald. I'll get him to re-enact the duel, except this time I'll let him win."

The clash of cutlery and crockery swelled and faded in the background. "They dueled wi' pistols," Malcolm hissed. "James's shot went wide. He drew his sword and charged and Archibald's shot did for him. Assumin' we had a set o' pistols—and we dinna have a one—you're no intendin' to stand there and either let the man shoot you or run you through!"

"Oh no, no. I mean, recreate the circumstances of the duel, make him challenge Archibald, but then have Archibald—me—grovel and apologize and act too scared to fight. All I need to do is distract him for a few minutes, Malcolm, and you can grab the scabbard. Simple." Wayne opened his hands like a magician who'd just produced a rabbit out of a hat. Funny how much the gesture reminded Amanda of Cynthia. "I owe you something, Amanda," he went on, "for making such a pest out of myself at Melrose."

"Yeah right," she returned. "If you hadn't been a pest I wouldn't have gotten to come here, would I? You don't owe me your life, Wayne."

"Which you're puttin' in my hands?" demanded Malcolm.

"That—that's very generous of you, Wayne," Norah stammered, "but it's much too dangerous."

"Not if we do it right," said Wayne, cool, composed, in control.

Malcolm's eyes brightened, polished by the reflected glow of the scheme. "It might work at that. We've wardrobes o' old clothes, we could find Wayne a proper uniform."

"A kilt? Uh-uh. I'll wear knee breeches, but not a skirt."

Geez, Wayne, Amanda thought. *Way to insult the natives!*

Malcolm dismissed the heresy with a roll of his eyes. "What if James disna challenge you? I'm no so sure he's in a mood for talkin'."

"That's where I come in." Amanda set her chin. Like getting a flu shot, it was painful but necessary. "To do it up right we'll need a Sally. That's me. Maybe I'd remind James of Isabel, too—there's a description of the dress she wore to their engagement party in one of her letters. Sally may have been the direct cause of the duel, but Isabel was sure an issue. Even if he realizes it's me, finally wearing what he thinks are normal clothes, it doesn't matter. Just as long as he's confused, or tired, or at least lets down his guard long enough for Malcolm to get the scabbard—and maybe even the sword—away from him."

Norah gulped, probably swallowing her maternal instincts. "I don't like this. Not one bit. But I like even less having Malcolm killed, or Amanda killed, or being turfed out of my home by a malevolant ghost. You're right, the plan might work. But I'm going to be there, too. The more hands the better. And you'll be needing someone with a clear head as well."

"But Lady Norah," protested Wayne, probably knowing what would happen if *his* mother got her dainty little hands into the plan—she'd be arranging dance-studio-style footprints on the floor.

"Ah, Mum, you're a right Jenny Cameron. The Amazon o' the '45," Malcolm explained to the uninitiated, and sat back in his chair. His brilliant blue-gray eyes moved from face to face, compelling as a blood oath. He didn't have to say the words: *Either we work together or we lose.*

Wayne threw his napkin down with a flourish. "Let's do it."

Amanda was impressed. If only Wayne survived long enough to show off his new persona back home. They could all play their parts, yeah, but James had to play his, too. Not that everyone wasn't thoroughly aware of that.

In a tight group they left the hotel, piled into the car, and started back toward Dundreggan.

CHAPTER TWENTY SEVEN

Amanda twirled in front of Norah's full-length mirror, flounces rustling. Her bodice was framed with pink and white muslin ruffles, like the ruffles that cascaded over a green satin underskirt. Her three-quarter length sleeves ended with linen frills. Sally would have sold her soul for this dress.

And it was just about Sally's size. The hemline hit well above Amanda's ankles, which Norah camouflaged with a long ruffled petticoat. And the waist was impossibly small, even after Amanda squeezed her rib cage into a Victorian-era corset. *Great.* If she hyperventilated and fainted somebody, possibly herself, might die. Maybe it was just as well the dress stank of mothballs. She was carrying smelling salts around with her.

Amanda poked at her tiny ribboned cap. It didn't quite hide her short hair, but the sausage-like fake curls hanging from it confused the issue. Which was the point of this drill anyway.

"What do you think?" Norah shoved one last pin into the frayed edge of a ruffle and sat back on her heels.

Amanda flicked open her fan and fluttered it back and forth. Its carved ivory had yellowed with age, but its bindings seemed sturdy enough for the evening's masquerade. "Fie, sir, would you have me credit such flatteries? Venus herself would blush to be so addressed." She snapped the fan shut and tapped it flirtatiously against her reflection.

"Well done," said Norah with a laugh. "That's similar to the dress Isabel described. But you know men, they don't remember that sort of detail. Especially after two hundred years." She started piling pins and spools of thread back into her sewing basket. "Alex and I used to hold costume parties. That's why we still have the old clothes. I simply can't bring myself to throw them out." She closed the basket and stood up. Her expression balanced on a razor's edge between fear and resolve.

Amanda gave her a hug. "It'll be all right."

"So it will," Norah replied, and hugged her back.

Footsteps came down the hall. Margaret and Denis looked up from their nests on Norah's canopied bed, ears moving front to back to front again like furry radar dishes. "Mum? Amanda? Are you decent?" Malcolm peered around the door.

As one, Norah and Amanda exhaled.

"Lassie, you look a treat," Malcolm said. "Pretty enough to raise the dead."

She curtsied. "Thank you, kind sir. But I must ask you to guard your tongue, as those japeries you might find amusing could well serve to dismay some members of our party."

"Don't worry yourself," said Norah. "He'd make jokes on his way to . . ."

The gallows? Amanda finished for her. *Thanks.*

Norah grimaced. "You go on ahead, I'll catch you up."

"May I?" Malcolm offered Amanda his arm. She tucked her hand beneath the reassuring warmth of his sweater. Together they walked out into the lengthening shadows of the corridor. "It's getting on for sunset at last," he said.

"I've never had a day last this long," Amanda returned.

"Oh aye. I was expectin' to hear doom crackin' any moment." He crushed her arm against his side. "I found the song you were quotin' me on a CD. I thought I recognized it."

"Really? Is it sung in Gaelic?"

"That it is. A woman's voice, a cross between a siren and a banshee."

"Just the right sound effect, then." *This is going to work. It is.*

"Wayne's in the hall," Malcolm went on. "He's a sight."

Whoa, Amanda thought. It was deja vu all over again. Here she was walking through an old house with her waist encased in a cage, fabric floating at her ankles, hoping she wouldn't say something dumb. But instead of an elegant Georgian staircase she stepped carefully down a muscular medieval spiral stair. Instead of a wood-paneled parlor with spindly furniture she walked into a stone-walled great hall, its furnishings larger than life.

Darkness disguised the beams of the ceiling. The flags hung limp and lifeless. The lights made delicate glowing circles across the floor but left the corners dim. A fire burned in the fireplace, looking as puny as a match on the vast hearth. Shadows licked up the chimney and across the floor. An odor of smoke and mildew and mothballs hung on the air.

An apparition in a scarlet coat rose from behind the massive sideboard and its display of pewter. Amanda guffawed. "Wayne, that's enough to make George Washington spin in his grave."

Wayne struck a pose imitating the father of his country crossing the Delaware, although his scarlet coat, gold trim, white breeches, and black boots suited British commander Cornwallis, not the upstart Washington. As Amanda got closer she saw that the gold trim was tarnished brass, the boots were a spray-painted brown, and the scarlet coat was threadbare. But with a curled white wig around his ruddy face, Wayne did look vaguely like Archibald must have looked that fateful evening at Melrose. Well, without the kilt, but even if Wayne had agreed to wear one he probably would've gotten tangled up in it or it would've fallen off at a critical moment.

"It was like the ceremonial clothin' o' the matador," Malcolm told Amanda.

"But a bull would have two sharp points instead of just one," Wayne said. "The CD player's plugged in and set to the right track."

"Super. Where's the dog?"

"Oh. He needed to go outside. I left the front door open."

With a pat Malcolm released Amanda's hand and stepped to the door. "Cerberus! Here boy!" A distant woof replied. "Half a tick," Malcolm said, and hurried off down the stairs.

Wayne and Amanda looked gravely at each other. "We've done this before," she told him.

"Well, sort of. Did you see anything flying around today?"

"No. He's keeping a low profile."

"Probably hoarding his strength."

"Great."

Cerberus bounded into the room, Malcolm on his tail. Norah walked in carrying an indignant cat under each arm. She set them down on the floor. Malcolm beckoned her toward the sideboard and explained about switching on the CD player. She nodded. Not that you needed to explain anything to Norah. No wonder Malcolm was so bright.

The dog ambled sociably from person to person. The cats sat down, their expressions set in world-weary boredom. The humans paced back and forth, shifted and sighed.

The windows faded from gray to black. Dundreggan Castle was so silent Amanda wondered if she'd gone deaf. When the fire cracked, a log fell, and sparks flew, everyone jumped. Malcolm hefted another log behind the andirons, and with bellows and poker from the nearby rack teased it into flame.

"Come on, come on," said Wayne under his breath.

The fire gleaming in his eyes, Malcolm climbed on a chair and detached a Lochaber axe from one of the displays. He propped the six-foot long pole with its wide, curved head, part axe, part spear, against the corner of the fireplace and melted into the shadows beside the mantel.

Amanda breathed out, breathed in, breathed out. Her ribs hurt. She felt like her forehead was bulging. *Contents under pressure.*

"Let's get this over with," Wayne muttered.

Amanda breathed in. "James," she whispered into the silence, "when you're with me you're strong."

The words of the mantra hovered invisibly in the air. One heartbeat, two, and the glow of the lights dimmed, so slightly Amanda thought she'd imagined it except Wayne, too, looked up.

A cold draft sent smoke swirling through the air. The flags rippled. Denis and Margaret sat up, ears alert, whiskers flared. Cerberus barked, short and sharp.

Wayne straightened his shoulders and set his chin. Except this time his expression wasn't childishly stubborn but firm, tenacious, mature. So what if sweat was breaking out on his forehead. He sure got points for style.

In the shadows by the hearth Malcolm was standing very straight, hands on hips, jaw tight, in a bestriding-the-globe stance. In the shadows next to the sideboard, Norah folded her arms. Her blue eyes were a determined glitter.

A glitter like the one forming in the center of the room. Denis and Margaret hissed, clawed, yowled, and made tracks for the doorway. Barking furiously, Cerberus backed from the room. His barks echoed from the stairwell, faded to a distant whine, then stilled.

The lights dimmed further, shading to an odd tint of blue. "Ladies and gentlemen," whispered Wayne, "start your engines."

The glitter solidified into the brass hilt of a sword. A sheathed sword, Amanda noted with relief. A sword sheathed in two scabbards, one transparent perfection, the other warped and corroded, like James's image of himself shadowed by the reality.

The shoulder belt with its silver fittings appeared out of nothingness. The draped kilt. The scarlet jacket. And finally James's face, looking suspiciously around him. *He knows we're up to something,* Amanda thought. Not that he was going to come rushing in, not after last night.

His eyes fell on Amanda and Wayne standing side by side. His brows tightened and his lips thinned. His hand grasped the hilt of the sword. But he showed no more uncertainty than that.

Let's do it. Amanda curtsied and flipped open her fan. "Good evening, Captain Grant. Your cousin Lieutenant Grant has been acquainting me with your exploits upon the field of battle."

Wayne bowed. "James, my good man, you will be pleased to know I have omitted certain of those exploits from my account, those that would be unfit for the ear of a lady of good breeding."

James returned the bow, curtly. But his eyes were gleaming slits, like those of a cat in reflected light. "So, Archibald, that, too, was a lie. You are not gone. The words that fall from a woman's lips are like dew, quickly dried." He frowned at Amanda. But he wasn't sure who she was—Sally? Isabel? Amanda herself?

She raised the fan coyly, hiding her mouth and chin. "Lieutenant Grant, your cousin's every aspect is one of courage and fortitude. I confess myself amazed by the glow of his appearance, like Phoebus overturned by Apollo's chariot. It is too much, I shall swoon, I place my trust in your hands." She swayed, just enough to lean against Wayne's side, just enough so he had to put his arm around her to steady her.

"Now James," said Wayne, with the perfect priggish inflection, "respecting the ladies you must take care, upon my word, weak as they are they cannot tolerate such advances as you make, but are obliged to find them improper. Allow me to acquaint you with the proper means of dealing with the fairer sex."

Scowling, James stepped forward, his steps ringing on the floor, metal clanking at his waist. "And what foolishness is this, that mewling and puking Archibald should know the whys and wherefores of womanhood? Unhand the lady, you dog, and stand away."

Over Wayne's shoulder Amanda saw Malcolm edging forward, the axe in his hand. Briskly she fanned her face, the fan creaking almost like the creaking of the floor beneath Malcolm's—well, he was wearing sneakers, wasn't he? "Captain Grant, I am undone by your potency, I beg you, be gentle with me." She stepped away from Wayne and extended her hand limply toward James.

Shit! He kept his left hand fixed on the sword, ready to boost its hilt into his right. He caught her fingers and pressed them, his grasp tenuous and yet so cold a shudder ran up her arm. Between her corset and the reek of decay Amanda's head spun. She batted her lashes, ordering herself to stay alert.

"So, then, Madame," James said, "you show unwonted wisdom for a woman. But you must wait upon my return. I have unfinished business with this man, with whom I am so unfortunate as to share a name." He edged her to the side—saving dessert for later—released her hand and took another step toward Wayne.

Amanda didn't dare look toward Malcolm. She opened and shut the fan so fast part of its binding broke and one slat dangled loose.

Wayne shriveled, shoulders curling, head hanging. "My most humble apologies, cousin, if I have offended you. You are, as in all other respects, quite correct in your estimation of my abilities. I know nothing of womanhood—nay, I insult the very presence of a lady with my clumsiness." Either the strange bluish light or his own fear made his jowls look green.

James smiled. Amanda flinched—she'd seen that smile the night before, up close and personal. "James," she cooed, "my dearest, I yearn for the strength of your arms. Please, he is not worth your troubling yourself, return to me."

James ignored her. The sword hissed from the scabbard—it couldn't fit in the real one, and yet the undamaged scabbard wasn't real, so how could it hiss. . . . That didn't matter now.

Light flowed down the blade as James moved it back and forth in front of Wayne's bulging eyes, a hypnotist waving a gold watch in front of his victim's face. "Shall we have it out, then, cousin? Shall we carry it to the grave, and then beyond? It is too late for the apology. Much too late."

He spat the last words. His eyes blazed. He lunged.

Amanda leaped forward. The seams of her dress ripped open. Wayne dived to the side and fell down hard. His wig went flying.

Malcolm stopped tiptoeing and ran.

James raised the sword over Wayne's cowering form. Wayne yelped and scrabbled backwards like an upended turtle. A pewter goblet came flying from the shadows behind the sideboard, skimmed so close to James's face he jerked back, then clanged against the wall and onto the floor.

"Sorry," Malcolm said, and shoved Amanda so hard she went sprawling. A dull iron gleam darted horizontally above her head. The concave side of the axe head connected with the scabbard at James's side and knocked it clattering away. As the blade passed through his insubstantial body, James himself shredded into streamers of scarlet and tartan, then formed again. Wayne scrambled to his feet.

James glanced around at Malcolm, his handsome face contorting into something less recognizable as human than his skull, and turned back to Wayne. "So, Archibald, this is a trick! Such as I would expect of you, not man enough to fight face to face, honorably, but enlisting this scurvy dog to do your work!" The sword flashed.

But Wayne was already scuttling toward the door, gasping, "I beg of you, the quality of mercy is not strained, to be or not to be, a name by any other rose. . . ."

James leaped after him, then stopped dead and spun around.

Too late. Grasping the shaft of the axe in his right hand, Malcolm scooped up the scabbard with his left. He sprinted for the fireplace and with an echoing clank he threw the scabbard onto the stone hearth. "Here it is, James! Come and get it!"

"No!" James shouted.

Malcolm raised the axe and with the sharp crack of metal on stone brought it down on the scabbard. Amanda thought of James's great-grandfather Simon Fraser meeting his maker on Tower Hill, going to his reward on the blade of an axe.

The scabbard was in two pieces. Malcolm hit it again. Three.

Strong hands—Norah's—heaved Amanda to her feet. Black spots swam before her eyes and another set of seams gave way. *The bellows!* She shook Norah away and raced toward the hearth. "Throw it in the fire, Malcolm!"

Malcolm threw the pieces of the scabbard into the depths of the flames.

"No!" James shouted again, on a higher, more desperate note. He ran toward the fireplace, sword raised.

Malcolm spun around, parrying James's blow with the long handle of the axe.

Amanda seized the bellows and started pumping for all she was worth, her wheezing lungs filling with smoke, her eyes running, her face burning hot. The flames leaped, chasing shadows up the stone walls. The acrid smell of hot metal filled the air. In the scarlet heart of the fire the pieces of the scabbard darkened, blacker and blacker, until they took on a color deeper than red—scarlet, crimson, dried blood.

James shrieked in mortal pain, the cry he'd never had a chance to make at the moment of his death. Amanda glanced over her shoulder. The sword licked up and down, slower now, like it was getting heavier or James's hand weaker. . . . Their plan was working.

Malcolm danced aside, the axe handle horizontal between his hands, just far enough to deflect the blows, not far enough to leave Amanda's back unprotected.

Wayne slipped along the mantelpiece behind Malcolm. Picking up the poker, he smashed it again and again onto the chunks of metal that had been the scabbard, sending up clouds of sparks and soot. The dull thuds reverberated from the high ceiling.

Levering herself on his shoulder, Amanda stood up. She squinted dizzily through the dim blue-tinted light of the room. James's form thinned and swayed. Through his transparent chest and the silver thistle of the 71st regiment the door made a rectangular shape like a coffin. Still he held the sword upright, but his thrusts at Malcolm were slow and weak.

The thuds of the poker stopped. Amanda's breath rasped. James, gasping for his own ephemeral breath, backed off and lowered the sword. His scowl faded, leaving his face blank with exhaustion, lips parted, eyes half-closed. He raised his free hand. His voice was a wisp of sound. "Madame, whoever you may be, do not cast me out!"

Since when had it been up to her? Amanda bit her lip, hard. She saw him sitting wearily on the staircase. She saw him peeling off layer after layer of his uniform beside her bed. She saw him smiling at her, his sword at her breast, while she cowered on the windowsill.

Pulling away her cap and curls and dumping them on the floor, she dredged her memory—"Thou knowest, Lord, the secrets of our hearts; shut not thy merciful ears to our prayers."

From the far corner of the room rose a woman's voice, singing, "An ciaradh m'fheasgair mo bheath' air claoidh, mo rosg air dunadh's a' bhas gun chli . . ." The words swelled up and out, twining about the beams of the ceiling, making the flags and the tapestries shiver. *O westwards take me, and quietly lay me, in Aignish graveyard above the sea.*

Malcolm grounded the butt of the axe. "Sorry, cousin, but Dundreggan graveyard above the Moriston will have to do."

"Amanda," said James, his face twisting in agony, "Amanda, my sweet, I am confounded. . . ." In the scarlet mist that was his body only his eyes were distinct, his eyes and the length of the sword. Slowly, with terrible effort, he extended the sword, hilt first, toward her.

She stepped forward, shaking off first Wayne's, then Malcolm's hands. She took the icy hilt of the sword just as James's hand thinned into nothingness. For a long moment she held his eyes, two anguished blue gleams against the blue-tinted shadows. Then they, too, faded away. A long moan, part groan, part sigh, filled the room and then slowly, achingly, ebbed into nothingness.

He was gone. "Rest in peace," Amanda whispered.

From the corner Norah said, "Amen."

The lights shone out so brightly she winced. The song stopped. After a pause another began, a soft instrumental piece filled with the sounds of dusk and rain.

The sword was heavy. Her knees were trembling. The room was spinning. Amanda sat down hard, fabric billowing. The sword thumped onto the floor beside her. She mopped at her sooty eyes but they got even wetter, until the tears spilled over and ran in cool rivulets down her scorched cheeks.

"He's gone now," Norah said, kneeling at Amanda's side. "He can rest."

I sure hope so, her mind hiccuped.

Malcolm's arms closed around her and drew her into his chest, safe. "My heroine," he said into her ear.

She got hold of herself with a gulp. "Sorry."

"Dinna worry yoursel'. We've had the blood and the sweat, we're needin' a few tears as well."

Norah pressed a handkerchief into her hand and stood. "That was good acting, Wayne. Thank you."

"I wasn't acting. I was scared." He cleared his throat. "Thank you for throwing that mug. Great arm. You ought to try out for the Orioles."

"I captained a cricket side at school, but it's been donkey's years since I bowled a game. Nothing like sheer terror to concentrate one's faculties."

"Oh aye," said Malcolm.

Tell me about it, Amanda thought.

Wayne picked up the sword and balanced it in his hand. "It worked. I don't believe it. But I guess the man had to be tired after two hundred years of holding a grudge."

"Yes, I should expect so," Norah said.

It's over. . . . No it's not. James is over is all. Amanda leaned against Malcolm's chest and mopped her face. The rest of her brain was logging back on. Coherent thought, what a concept. Feeling, ditto.

Two nights in a row she'd sat there hanging out of her bodice right in front of Malcolm's face—not that his face was exactly turned away in disgust or apathy or anything, but it wasn't the way these things were supposed to go.

So how were you supposed to fall in love? she asked herself, and answered, by any means that worked. And this whole—comedy, tragedy, historical pageant—had definitely worked.

Wayne brandished the sword, thrust his fist into the air, and shouted, "Yes!" Then he looked around, startled, like it was someone else who'd shouted. He tiptoed to the sideboard and laid the sword down.

Far, far away a telephone started ringing. It was, after all, the twenty-first century. It was a Monday night at the end of July. So maybe Irene and Calum were calling to see if it was safe to come home. Or Lindley Duncan, making his rounds. Or Denny Gibson, checking in with people who mattered to him. Each of them would have his or her own take on James's story. Fine. The important part was that each of them would believe it.

Smiling, Norah went off to answer the phone. A black and white face peered quizzically through the doorway. Wayne called the dog and bent over him, scratching his ears. "Scared you, huh? Well that makes two of us."

Malcolm settled himself more comfortably on the floor, keeping firm hold of Amanda. "So you'll be goin' back to Virginia the Thursday?"

She blew her nose. "Yeah. I have my job, and my thesis, and the book about—about James—and maybe I should call or e-mail or something and let Carrie know I'm still alive."

"She'll no be wonderin' one way or the other, will she?"

"No."

"But you could be askin' her for course information and internships and the lot. You'll no be here long enough for a proper lesson in—ah, historic property management—I suppose I'll just have to be goin' to Virginia masel', doin' a bit o' hands-on research, eh?"

"You'd better," she said into the slightly smoky odor of his throat. "Just promise me one thing."

"Anything."

"Don't ever call me 'sweet.'"

Malcolm laughed.

Amanda felt a similar laugh welling up. The whole thing had been so stupid, and so ridiculous, and so right. She gave in to the laugh, and drifted easily away with the flow.

CHAPTER TWENTY EIGHT

Amanda snugged her robe around her naked body and peered out the window. Beyond Melrose's lawns a shimmering curtain of mist hung over the river. A few remaining yellow and orange leaves looked like confetti pasted to the black limbs of the trees. Pumpkins and Indian corn decorated the walkways.

The tile of the bathroom floor was icy beneath her feet. Funny—when she'd moved in last June she hadn't checked out Melrose's heating system, an old-fashioned furnace that gave up the ghost on a cold morning.

The word "ghost" wasn't ever going to sound the same again. And yet if she'd never met James she'd never have met Malcolm. Fate, she guessed. Or whatever it was she'd said to Wayne that time, about Mr. Right sneaking up on you when you weren't looking.

A gleam of sun sliced through the mist, laying a bright path across the lawn and into the window. Amanda raised her left hand to it. The diamond in her ring flashed and sparked. *Wow,* she thought with something between a grimace and a grin.

The ring was an antique, appropriately enough, its Celtic interlace design worn smooth, its tiny stone scratched. Malcolm had sent her a photo of it a month ago—maybe she didn't want his grandmother's ring, maybe she'd rather have a new one—maybe she'd rather not have one at all. But Amanda had no problem with the traditional public announcement: *Hey, we're serious about this!*

The evening before she left Dundreggan, in the middle of yet another clinch, Malcolm had whispered in her ear, "You're expectin' me to come to your room the night?"

Oh yeah, she thought. They needed to lose the clothes, no doubt about it. . . . *Oh. Wayne.* Getting it on right across the hall from his room just didn't cut it. And she wasn't sure she'd worked it all out about James yet. More than the clothes, what they needed to lose were the issues.

"It's too soon, is it?" Malcolm asked with a smile.

"Wayne's been so cool with everything, it just wouldn't be fair to get into his face. And James only—left—a couple of days ago. So yeah, it's too soon." She moved her hands from the back pockets of his jeans to the front pockets of his shirt, neutral territory. "But I'll be expecting you in my bedroom at Melrose. Soon."

"I'll be there," he'd told her, actually taking *not yet* for an answer.

She'd wondered every now and then as summer segued into fall if she'd been stupid to pass up the chance. But no, her eyes were wide open this time around. This guy was there for the backstretch.

And the wait had been worth it. So what if her thighs were so sore this morning she could hardly walk?

Dumping her robe, Amanda tiptoed out of the bathroom into the shadowed bedroom. On the nightstand sat two glasses and a bottle of Glenmoriston single malt. She hadn't needed Malcolm's joking quote about drink provoking the desire but taking away the performance to keep her from downing more than a symbolic sip or two last night. Not that anything less than anesthesia would've taken away either their desire or their performance, not when everything—means, motive, opportunity—had come together at last.

Malcolm's auburn hair lay tousled on the pillow. She lifted the blankets and slipped into the whiskey-scented warmth beside him. With her fingertips she traced the line of his flank. He blinked, then focussed. "You're playin' wi' fire, lass."

"I hope so," she replied. "I'm freezing."

"Well then." He scooped her into his arms, pressing against her, legs tangled, lips locked. Funny how fast his smooth, warm naked body wiped out her chill. Malcolm was real. This was real.

He pulled away just far enough to stroke the white scar between her breasts. She answered the question in his eyes. "It's all right. Really."

"Oh aye, that it is." Malcolm smiled, and bent his head to kiss the scar, and moved on from there, his lips and tongue plying the peaks and hollows of her body—ears, breasts, navel—so deftly she wondered if he'd been practicing with the tin whistle.

But she'd found out last night he was a fast learner. "Oh yeah. There, like that . . ." Her voice caught in her throat.

She could get used to this. She had every intention of getting used to it, of connecting with him physically just like they'd connected emotionally and intellectually during three months of e-mails and paper letters and long phone calls that'd just about busted her budget. But that was the only way she could hear his voice.

"Oh aye," he sighed. "Just that." The bronze hair on his chest curled between her fingers. His skin was sweet salt on her lips. When she pushed him onto his back he pulled her over with him and propped his shoulders against the headboard. He was comfortable in his own skin, she thought, returning his smile. He was, for that matter, totally comfortable in hers.

Slowly, savoring every exquisite millimeter, she settled onto him. Like a glove, like a sheath even—no problem. . . . *All right!* She wrapped him tightly, one of her hands lodged in his hair, and gauged the flow of expression across his face—*that, there, oh yeah.* Like the night they'd danced together his hands moved up and down her spine, and then across her ribs and over her breasts, playing her as she played him.

They rolled over and tried another rhythm, and laughed and fitted themselves at a different angle, until at last their breaths made little wisps of steam in the cold room. *Yes, yes!* The flash points were like lanterns lit in the dusk, welcoming the weary traveler home. *Home,* Amanda thought fuzzily, *is where the heart is.*

And she'd told herself there was no magic and mystery in sex any more. *Yeah, right.* She'd only needed the right spells and the right clues. She'd only needed the right guy.

They were still exchanging sweaty nothings when the alarm rang. Malcolm's jump of surprise repeated Amanda's. She reached out and smacked the clock, which shut it up. From the doorway came a demanding, "Meow!"

Malcolm levered himself onto one elbow. "It's a workin' day, is it? My debut as an interpreter?"

"At least the house opens later on Sunday. Okay, Lafayette, hold your paws, I'm coming."

The tabby watched the disentanglement process with his head cocked to the side and his tail making Js on the rag rug, as though to say, *they could be eating breakfast right now, but no.*

Amanda shrugged on her robe, limped off toward the kitchen, fed the cat and made a pot of tea. By the time she got back to the bedroom Malcolm was bathed, shampooed, and shaved, gleaming like he'd been polished. A white shirt reached to his thighs and red and white checkered socks rose to his knees. He was bending over the bed pleating several yards of tartan wool, providing Amanda with a very nice flash of bare buttocks. Yep, she thought with a grin, a guy in a kilt was so gorgeous he had to be ready for action at any moment.

She clasped her hands behind her back to keep from grabbing for him. "You sure you can get that on to where it'll actually stay on? I mean, your modern kilt has straps and buckles and sewn-down pleats but that one's more of a do-it-yourself job. There're some sights I'd like to keep for myself, you know."

He winked at her. "I've worn one a time or two. It's no so awkward.... There." He belted the fabric around his waist, attached the sporran, and reached for the white waistcoat. That properly buttoned, he turned to the mirror and tied the neck cloth around his throat.

Amanda took the scarlet coat from its hanger and held it while he slipped his arms into the sleeves. The shoulder belt with its silver fittings went on next. Malcolm stepped into his shoes and, at last, picked up the sword.

He'd brought the sword with him, along with its new scabbard—Calum Finlay had really strutted his stuff with that. Yesterday afternoon Amanda had burnished the basket hilt of the sword until it gleamed like gold, and wiped the shining steel of the blade clean of memory. It really was a thing of beauty, if you looked at it right. And yet, at the end of the day, that's just what it was, a thing. Malcolm didn't need it or anything else to prove his manhood.

She hung the sword from his belt and stepped back to admire the effect—was he ever a thing of beauty himself! "Are you going to wear the wig?"

"Should I?" He picked up the white curled and pony tailed wig and held it over his head like a halo.

"No. Your own hair's much too nice, even if the cut is contemporary."

"Very well then." The wig went back on its block. "I'll say one thing for Cynthia, Mrs. Snotty, she does things up proper."

"Which just makes her even more annoying," Amanda admitted. "You'd think someone with an ego that big could at least be incompetent."

"Did she actually credit Wayne's story aboot breakin' the scabbard?"

"She did when I backed him up."

"Own up to it, lassie, you're her pet."

"Like she's not fixing a collar for you?"

Malcolm tugged at his neck cloth and gagged.

"You're going to knock the eyes out of every woman in the place," Amanda went on. "I'll be jealous."

"No need. I'm no givin' any o' them my granny's ring, am I?" He took her in his arms. The hem of the kilt was a fuzzy tickle against her thigh. The buttons of his waistcoat pressed into her breast. The belt and sword clanked as she hugged him back.

"I love you," she said. There was an entire sentence that had taken on a new meaning.

"I love you," he said.

Amanda wouldn't have minded a few more seriously sappy minutes, but she could see the clock from the corner of her eye. Reluctantly she let him go. "I'd better hit the shower before I find myself signed up to interpret Medusa."

"No a bit o' it," Malcolm said gallantly, and added, "You look like you've been havin' yoursel' a fine roll in the hay is all."

Shoving playfully at him, Amanda headed for the bathroom. She washed and blew dry and hurried into her own costume, a much easier job with Malcolm tugging on the strings of the stays. Breakfast was less of an occasion than she'd planned—she had to throw toast and marmalade onto the table instead of baking scones. But womankind didn't even begin to live by bread alone.

At the apartment door they exchanged a formal bow and curtsey. Malcolm captured her left hand and kissed it, his lips warm, his clear, bright blue-gray eyes looking up at her over her knuckles and the point of the ring. *Wow,* she thought again. *Way to go.*

Off they went through the house, making sure all the empty glasses and crumpled napkins had been cleared away after last night's welcome party. Engagement party. Announcement of intentions party. Whatever.

Amanda turned on the lights over the display in the entrance hall. Malcolm tipped a quick, rueful salute to James's reconstructed head. The miniature stood in its Lucite box, the small painted face gazing into eternity. Where, Amanda assumed, his troubled soul was at rest. Better late than never. *Poor James.* But, at the end of the day, pity was all she had left for him.

The artifacts Wayne had borrowed last summer were all accounted for. Amanda opened the front door and turned the sign around just as Roy crunched up the gravel walk, trailing the banner of his breath behind him. "Whoa, Malcolm," he called. "That's a hell of a get-up. I can't believe your ancestor wore it all for real, in the summer yet. I bet Hewitt's got it wrong, he really died from heat stroke."

"I expect the heat didna improve their tempers," Malcolm returned.

"There's coffee in the kitchen," Amanda said, and Roy headed inside.

Carrie rounded the corner at a fast trot. "Nippy, isn't it? Wasn't the mist this morning pretty? I bet it reminded you of Scotland, Malcolm."

"In a way."

"Scotland's all hazy green and blue and purple," explained Amanda. "Here, now. . . ." She waved at the lawn, the trees, and the river. The crisp orange and yellow hues sparkled beneath a crystalline blue sky.

"The red uniform blends right in," Carrie finished. "Malcolm, I hope my kids didn't bug you too much about the kilt last night."

"They're fine lads, Carrie. I didna mind answerin' their questions."

Carrie stage-whispered, "This guy's a keeper, Amanda."

"You think?" Amanda waggled the fingers of her left hand.

Wayne came strolling down the walk, every powdered hair in place, tapping his cane rhythmically. "View halloo!" he called.

"It's a grand mornin', Mr. Chancellor," replied Malcolm.

Wayne mounted the steps, every corpuscle radiating dignity. "A most excellent example of military garb, Captain Grant, but we shall have no need of swordplay today."

"Indeed," Malcolm returned. "It was with the greatest satisfaction I heard of the recent cessation of hostilities."

"Your appearance is even lovelier than usual, Miss Witham," Wayne went on. "One might think that your bright eyes and rosy cheeks signified . . ." He suddenly realized what they signified and went as red as Malcolm's coat.

Amanda snapped open her fan and hid her face behind it. Malcolm cleared his throat and, bless him, looked more embarrassed than smug.

"Gotta get to work." Wayne hurried inside. Carrie, with a sentimental sigh, followed.

The first group of tourists tramped around the corner and the day settled into its familiar routine, spiced by Malcolm's presence. His haircut might be wrong, Amanda thought, but his style was all right.

The boys and men among the sightseers stared at the kilt, not sure whether to be offended or impressed—especially when the women flocked around Malcolm like bees around a flower. Amanda and Malcolm posed for photo after photo, he bowing over her hand, she curtseying, although Sally slapping James silly would've been more to the historical point. The tourists left clutching Cynthia's new, revised brochure, incorporating the material from Dundreggan but putting her own spin on it.

"Is that really his sword?" a teenaged boy asked. "Will you run up the staircase for my camcorder?" asked a girl. "A duel," sighed one middle-aged lady. "He died for her in a duel. How romantic."

Malcolm drew the sword and posed by the staircase, back straight, chin up, only the angle of his brows giving away his sense of humor. He politely but firmly refused any action shots.

Over lunch Amanda, Malcolm, and Carrie shook their heads. "Even when the book comes out," Amanda said, "we're never going to drive a stake through the heart of the Sally-and-James-as-tragic-lovers story. People have to have their illusions."

"Like believin' their ancestors were romantic heroes," said Malcolm, "no ordinary folks like themsel's."

Carrie shook her head. She was the only person who knew the full story, not just the truth about James, but the truth about his ghost. "The book will make your reputation as a scholar, Amanda."

"You're doing the hard part," Amanda told her.

"No, you and Malcolm did the hard part, you lived to tell the tale."

Malcolm lowered his voice conspiratorially. "If you wrote aboot the ghost you'd spoil your academic reputation but make a pile o' brass."

"Yeah, like I'm going to go on the tabloid talk shows with the sordid details," Amanda retorted.

"For God's sakes don't tell Cynthia about the ghost," added Carrie, "or she'll make that film of hers even mushier than it already is. James Grant, dead for love."

"Love had very little to do wi' it," Malcolm stated.

Speak of the devil. . . . Cynthia's melodic voice drifted into the kitchen, playing counterpoint to Bill Hewitt's staccato sentences. ". . . enough material, Bill? Good, good, the reconstruction is going beautifully, we'll start serving tea in the summerhouse this spring. Wayne, you naughty boy, there you are."

"Good afternoon, Mother," said Wayne's courteous voice.

"How's the new apartment? Are you hanging up your clothes? Honestly, Bill, I know children have to have their little rebellious moments, but it's just so hard on the parents."

Hewitt's mutter was unintelligible, not that Cynthia was listening to him anyway.

"Wasn't Amanda pretty as a picture last night? So sweet. If you children would just communicate properly, be up front, like I am, we'd never have had that little misunderstanding over an engagement."

Cynthia and her entourage, Hewitt and Wayne, swept into the kitchen. "And here the little lovebirds are!" she trilled, air-kissing in Malcolm and Amanda's direction. "I'm so glad I was able to play a part, however small, in bringing you two together."

"Very kind o' you." Malcolm bowed. "Most obliged."

"I'll be at the summerhouse," Hewitt said. "No need for you to come, Cynthia. It's very muddy." He fled through the back door, slamming it emphatically behind him.

"How considerate," said Cynthia, glancing down at her black patent pumps. The rest of her outfit consisted of red stockings, a starched white blouse, and a wool jacket and skirt in what must have been the tartan of Clan Las Vegas. "Wayne, call that Ms. Brown and tell her I'll be much too busy to receive her this afternoon." She turned to the others. "Another one of these so-called psychics, she says she's doing a story for the Washington Post but I suspect it's more like the National Enquirer. Honestly, where do these people come from? The real story of Sally and James is interesting enough without dragging in supernatural claptrap."

You think? Amanda forced herself to keep a straight face. Carrie said something about the next tour group and made a break for it. Wayne turned on his heel and followed, almost making it out the door before he laughed.

"Well then," said Cynthia, beaming so broadly at Malcolm and Amanda they shared a cautious glance, "a winter wedding, how lovely, we'll decorate the church with Christmas lilies and poinsettias and evergreen boughs. I insist we hold the reception at my home. And I've had another of my inspirations! We can have a period wedding! I'm sure we can re-create an eighteenth-century bridal gown, and that uniform, Malcolm, defines glamorous."

"I'd really like to keep the role-playing compartmentalized," Amanda told her. "And December is too soon."

Cynthia waved her hand airily—easy come, easy go. "Lady Norah is planning to attend, Malcolm? And Lord Dundreggan?"

"When we've set a date, I expect so, aye."

"My family couldn't care less," said Amanda.

Cynthia sailed on. "Good, good. How about the middle of January? It's sort of a dull spot, a wedding would get everyone's interest."

"My internship's up in December," Amanda reminded her, setting up a future discussion on references. "And I have to go back to Ithaca to defend my thesis in January."

"As though anyone would be attackin' it." Malcolm had read her completed thesis while she polished the sword and given it his seal of approval. Not that he was going to disparage her work, but she hoped he'd have told her if he found anything off base.

"I'll have to reserve the florist," Cynthia went on, "and the caterer, and I know a baker who makes a perfectly scrumptious groom's cake, but he's always booked well in advance."

"We may not even be here when the time comes," Amanda said. "I have to find a job somewhere. And Malcolm has his business to run—I mean, thank goodness for computers and everything, he can do it from here for now, but . . ."

Malcolm concluded, "It's gey early to makin' weddin' plans."

"Absolutely," said Amanda, and added, "Right now we're basically in it for the sex."

Cynthia's face went blank. Her cheeks took on a rosy color deeper than the delicate pink of their cosmetic coating. "Oh, ah—oh, well. . . ." She turned and hurried from the room.

"Well played," Malcolm said with a grin.

"Yeah, I've thought all along she must've found Wayne under a cabbage leaf. Not that we are only in it for the sex, there's a lot more going on here than the biomechanics."

"Oh aye? And here I was thinkin' you were usin' me for my . . ."

"Amanda? Malcolm?" Lucy Benedetto stepped through the back door, carrying a towel-covered bundle scented with cinnamon.

"Oh, hello, Lucy." Malcolm offered her a smile as gracious as the one he'd used on Cynthia, just without the edge.

"I thought you'd like a pie," said Lucy. "American as apple pie, you know."

Amanda took the warm plate from her hand. "Thank you very much. This is really above and beyond, Lucy."

"Oh no, no, we so enjoyed the party last night. It was really nice of you to invite us." Lucy backpedaled toward the door and disappeared.

"Thank you kindly," Malcolm called after her.

"I'll put this away. We can have it tonight." Amanda took the pie to her kitchen, and was turning back toward the front of the house when the outside door opened.

"Amanda! Hi!" Helen Medina burst into the hallway, her cameras clinking like Malcolm's belt. "I'm on my way down to the summer-house, but I wanted to bring you the proofs of the pictures for the book. You got some nice shots at the castle last summer."

"Malcolm and Wayne got the nice shots. Most of mine are off-center or blurred." Amanda accepted a big brown envelope. "How's the film going?"

Helen made a face. "Right now it's a tug-of-war between a documentary and a soap opera. I'm thinking of doing two, one for the academic and tourist circuits and one for Cynthia to show her garden club buddies."

"Hang in there, Helen," Amanda said with a laugh.

Helen turned to go, then glanced back. "Oh, you remember those pictures you took with my camera right before you left last summer? The ones of your apartment?"

Oh. Those. "Yeah. . . ."

"They're in the envelope. Kind of dark, you should've used the flash."

"Thanks," Amanda told her, adding, "I think" under her breath after the door shut.

She opened the envelope. Between the slick contact sheets were two snapshots. There was her living room again, looking in the photos just as it did now, except that the colors were murky. She saw the bedroom door. She saw the furniture. What she didn't see was a man wearing a scarlet coat and a tartan kilt, his hand resting firmly on an empty scabbard.

Go figure, Amanda told herself. But she didn't need to prove he'd been there. Not any more.

Leaving the envelope on the counter next to the warm apple pie, she walked briskly back toward the main house, opened the door into the entrance hall, and stepped through.

The front door stood ajar, framing a block of color and sunshine. Malcolm sat on the staircase, sword resting against a tread, kilt draped gracefully, petting Lafayette as he rubbed against the checkered socks. The cat's purr rumbled like a tiny engine in the momentary silence of the house.

Leaning on the banister, Amanda asked, "Do you think history moves in cycles, with each turn a little bit different from the one before?"

"Oh aye, it does that. The trick is to recycle the parts that bear repeatin' and move on beyond the rest." Malcolm smiled, a broad, brilliant smile that had nothing in it of devastation.

Amanda caught his smile and repeated it. Beneath her hands the banister stretched smoothly upwards, its scars healed at last.